Ful

Katie Flynn has lived for many years in the north-west. A compulsive writer, she started with short stories and articles and many of her early stories were broadcast on Radio Merseyside. She decided to write her Liverpool series after hearing the reminiscences of family members about life in the city in the early years of the twentieth century. She also writes as Judith Saxton. For the past few years, she has had to cope with ME but has continued to write.

KATIE FLYNN

Writing as JUDITH SAXTON

Full Circle

arrow books

1 3 5 7 9 10 8 6 4 2

Arrow Books
20 Vauxhall Bridge Road
London SW1V 2SA

Arrow Books is part of the Penguin Random House group of companies
whose addresses can be found at global.penguinrandomhouse.com.

Penguin
Random House
UK

First published in Great Britain by Century 1985
First published in paperback by Arrow Books in 1989
This edition reissued by Arrow Books in 2018

www.penguin.co.uk

A CIP catalogue record for this book is available from the British Library.

ISBN 9781787460867

Printed and bound in Great Britain by Clays Ltd, St Ives Plc

For Brian, who spends hours in libraries,
roots around in antiquarian bookshops,
tramps city streets and talks to museum curators
in the interests of my research.
And who, into the bargain,
puts up with me!

Author's Acknowledgements

I should like to thank Steven Pattinson, who lent me his collection of aircraft books, and John Pattinson, who read the finished manuscript of this particular volume and corrected my misapprehensions over the flying of Second World War aircraft. My thanks also to Maureen Jardine, for her collection of 1939–45 newspapers – invaluable in finding out what the British people thought was happening, against what really was going on. And thanks to Derrick Edwards, for unravelling the mysteries of Burma, the campaign there, and the monsoon season. As always, I am deeply indebted to the staff of the International Library, Liverpool, for their help and interest, and also to Marina Thomas and the rest of the staff of Wrexham Branch Library, who leave no stone unturned (and no book unopened) to find me the information I am seeking.

Dear Reader,

Once again I sit down to tell you what's been happening in the Flynn household, which was enlivened recently by a big party to celebrate our Diamond Wedding Anniversary.

I was surprised, and also delighted, looking down both sides of the lunch table at the hotel where we held the party, to see two Silver Weddings, a Golden one and lots of other couples, who were using this occasion to hold hands unobtrusively and exchange thoughts of their own celebrations. Lovely to think, though we might be alone in reaching sixty years of marriage, that there were plenty of others galloping up behind.

We had chosen a local hotel for our party and a great many people stayed overnight, so that our celebrations began at eleven in the morning and did not stop till eleven the next morning, but in between, many things happened!

The setting was delightful, the food was excellent, and we eventually cut the cake, which was a delicious confection made by a local baker from the firm 'Dot to Dot', finishing off with coffee and mints.

All was very satisfactory and much enjoyed but personally, and I knew Brian felt the same, we were mostly looking forward to the chat we planned to have later, particularly with those old friends who had come a great distance and whom we seldom saw.

It was at this point that things began to go pear-shaped. A member of staff showed us a suite on the top floor which he thought we might like to use for our stay, leaving us to decide for ourselves as to whether it was suitable. After only a cursory glance, we thought it unsuitable and so went to follow him, only to discover that we were locked in!

We were stuck inside, our guests assuming, we later discovered, that we had gone for a nap. After a couple of hours our eldest son, Tim, realising that something was amiss, finally discovered where we were and enlisted the help of two members of staff to release us. Gosh, we certainly live dangerously!

Unfortunately, on returning to Reception, we were told that the room we had originally booked had been allocated to someone else, and as no other room was available we had no option but to go home that evening. It was a terrible night, pouring with rain and with a howling wind. Just to make everything perfect, the heater in the car had packed up so it was a chilly ride back home. However, we were buoyed up by the thought that some of the guests would still be there the next day, when we could have a get-together.

And as it happened, everything turned out all right in the end; we joined our friends the following morning for the catch-up we had wanted and were able to laugh over our accidental incarceration, albeit ruefully.

With all best wishes,
Katie Flynn

THE NEYLER AND ROSE FAMILIES

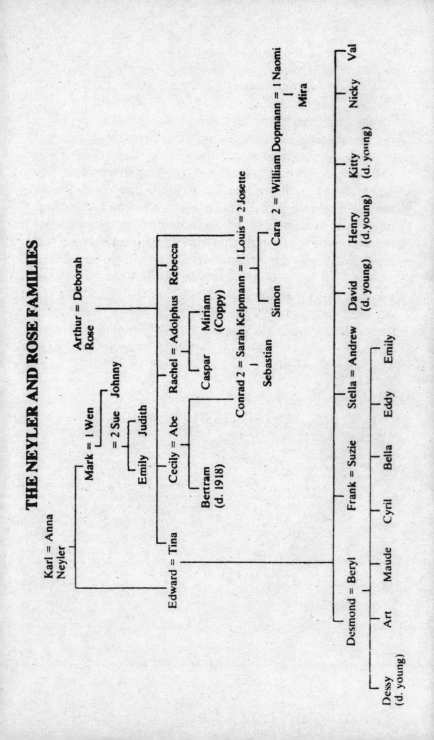

Chapter One

MAY 1940

'The safest place in a raid are the cellars; the boys say so.' Tina glanced round her with some satisfaction. 'It's cosy now, don't you think? I had it done out when there was a scare before, way back in 'thirty-eight . . . at least, I had the walls whitewashed and the new stairs put in. I've done the rest since, bit by bit, whenever I had the time.'

'It's very nice,' Jenny said, looking round at the white-washed brickwork, the stout wooden stairs and the narrow seats along the walls which would convert into bunks if it became necessary. 'Why the oil lamp, though? You've got electricity in all the cellars now, haven't you?'

'Oh, yes. But it might fail, so I brought down the lamp and had it filled and primed. I've done my best to think of everything, though I don't suppose they'll bomb Norwich, surely? I mean, we haven't got a lot of big industry, have we? And anyway, The Pride is a good way from the city. But just in case . . . see?'

She flung open a cupboard door, revealing that the impedimenta of gardening it had once contained had been banished. Instead, the shelves, covered with clean oil-cloth, now held quantities of tinned and packeted food. 'What about that, eh? We could survive for *weeks* on the food in there, I believe.' She surveyed her store with satisfaction for a moment, then swung round to face her favourite nephew's wife. 'What have you and Val done at the flat in London? I hope you wouldn't go hungry if something dreadful happened?'

'There is a cellar,' Jenny said vaguely. 'Simon and Nick went down before they left and thought it would be safe enough. There are metal rafters or something which were put in when they did the conversion. But we've neither of us thought much about raids, I suppose.'

Tina clicked her tongue disapprovingly. She was extremely glad that Jenny had come down with the baby this weekend, if only so that she might receive a good talking-to. It was foolish not to prepare for any eventuality, though the war – rudely referred to as the Bore War by her lively grandchildren – had not brought the immediate and terrible air raids that she most feared. Or not yet. She glanced back at her store cupboard, registered the fact that someone had taken a tin of condensed milk, and then closed the door firmly and turned to the stairs.

'Jenny, my dear, you and Val must think! I'll have a word with Val, too, when she comes in. Just you have a good look round, and you'll have a better idea how to make your cellar homely.' She waited whilst Jenny obediently inspected the first of the large cellars. 'Well?'

'It's very nice. Much better than the Anderson,' Jenny said, hoping that this praise did not sound as half-hearted as it felt. The fact was that no matter how Auntie Tina might pretty them up with chintz cushions and fancy lampshades, these were still the cellars she had dreaded as a child, playing here with Simon, who was now her husband, and his cousin Val, now her flat-mate and dearest friend. She and Val had both hated the cellars, associating them with big spiders, weird shadows thrown by the candles the boys brought down here, and the smell of earth and decay.

Tina was only small, but she drew herself up to her full height and gave poor Jenny an affronted stare. It was plainly not the thing to say about her beloved cellars.

'Better than the Anderson? I should hope so! I'm sure I

2

don't know why it is, because we haven't had rain, but that shelter is always damp. And it has a most peculiar smell.' She lowered her voice. 'If I didn't know better, I'd think people were using the Anderson as a public convenience! But of course it can't be that.'

Following the older woman back up the stairs, Jenny thought that there were none so blind as those who wouldn't see. Val had already told Jenny all about the Anderson.

'Mother doesn't know, and I'd rather not tell her, but the kids play in it and the little ones – maybe the larger ones, too – wee up in the corner rather than waste time going back to the house. And Mrs Elrich, the woman who comes in to help with the housework, says soldiers take their girls down there – only at nights, mind – so no wonder it niffs a bit! I'm just thankful that Mother had the cellars to play around with or heaven knows what might have happened.'

But now, going ahead of Jenny up the steps, Tina was talking busily, no longer allowing the thought of the odd smell in the Anderson to annoy her.

'The inner cellar is just bunks and curtains and things, so that we can pop the children in there when there's a raid on and they can sleep through it. We can play cards or knit and so on in the outer cellar until we're ready to make up the bunks in there.' She opened the heavy fire door at the head of the stairs and held it back for Jenny, then closed and locked it carefully behind her. 'Someone's been at that store cupboard again, so I'll just pop the key up on the lintel. I'm afraid the children regard it as a source of quick snacks. I'll have to keep it locked in future. Unless it's Mrs Elrich, though I can't believe she'd take anything that wasn't her own.'

'And you think the children would? Fie on you, Auntie Tina!'

Tina laughed and patted Jenny's cheek.

'Now that they're living here most of the time, the children regard the whole place and everything in it as theirs. But perhaps I'm wronging them. I could have used the milk myself and forgotten to replace it. I'm not always as careful as I should be.'

'Ouch! Watch it, Eddy!' Miriam Siegal, known to one and all as Coppy, sat back on her heels, nursing a bruised thumb. She narrowed her eyes at her cousin. 'That hurt like hell, you beast!'

'Sorry, but you know it was an accident. Let Emily hold it, since you're wounded. She won't mind if I hit her, will you, Em?'

'Coppy'll do it,' Eddy's sister said diplomatically. She was only nine and knew that twelve-year-old Coppy would scorn to draw back just because of a sore thumb. 'Why didn't you open it in the house, when you were in the kitchen getting the buns?'

The children were in the Anderson. Despised by Tina it might be, but they thought it an excellent place, shunned by adults. Today it was lit by a candle, and most of the gang was there, waiting eagerly for the tin of condensed milk to give way beneath repeated blows from the large flint Eddy had found.

Mira Dopmann watched the others. At five, she was honoured to be allowed to share their games, and she thought they were all wonderful – the Neylers, fair-haired Eddy and Emily; their cousins Coppy Siegal and Sebastian Solstein, both dark and intense. Mira was only a cousin by marriage, since she was Aunt Cara's stepdaughter, but she was completely accepted by them.

'I nicked the milk, so I could scarcely ask for the tin-opener, could I?' Eddy explained practically. He raised his flint and brought it crashing down on the tin, then gave a

4

crow of triumph. 'She's gone! Hold out your bread, everyone!'

Mira held out her bread with the rest, then took a sticky and luxurious bite. Odd, that grown-ups could not appreciate the charms of food like this, but had to spoil it by adding water or trickling it over tinned fruit! She smiled at Sebastian, who was her favourite. He was so beautiful, so clever, so popular – and so different from herself, though he was only three years older. Mira knew very well that she was plain, but even if she had not known it her stepmother would have pointed it out. Cara, so beautiful herself, had little time for a plain stepdaughter. She pushed Mira aside and ignored her, particularly now that Daddy was away fighting in France; but at least, now they were living at The Pride instead of in the flat, she had the comfort and consolation of her cousins!

And Sebastian loved her. He had always paid her more attention than anyone else, dragging her around after him, introducing her to cricket, tree-climbing and fishing for tiddlers. He bullied her, but he would never allow anyone else to do so; and besides, being bossed about by Sebastian was Mira's idea of heaven. What was more, she basked in his glow, for his parents and all the aunts adored him, school-teachers softened beneath his charm, and even bus-conductors, notoriously difficult persons to please, seemed to mind him less than they minded other small and impertinent boys.

Sitting next to Mira now, Sebastian finished off his own slice and took hers without anything but a grin. He bit into it, then handed it back. Mira beamed. It was a singular honour to have Sebastian take a bite out of her humble bread and milk!

'Do you want it all? You can, if you like. I'll be full up with my bun.'

But he only grinned again and rumpled her hair with a

5

hard and probably very dirty hand. Mira sighed, totally content. Life was lovely when Sebastian was near and Cara far. It would be quite perfect if only Daddy were home!

Cara, in fact, was nearer than her small daughter thought. She had taken Jenny's baby, Marianne, for a walk, and was now pushing the pram back up the steepest incline of the drive before turning it thankfully on to the flat sweep before the front door, coming from the shade of the beech trees into the full glare of the sun.

It had been a successful walk, because Marianne had slept in the park while Cara enjoyed a pleasant flirtation with two charming young RAF officers, but had woken just as they entered the drive in time to wave a chubby paw at her aunt's new friends and to coo and gurgle charmingly, making Cara feel useful and loved.

The Dopmanns had moved out of their flat in the city centre because of the difficulties of obtaining fuel the previous winter. The coldest temperatures for forty years had been recorded, and the government had advised people to move in together and warm one room instead of several.

Auntie Tina had promptly swept up her son Desmond, his wife Beryl and their large family; and then, when Cara's mother had moved to London to be with her husband, she had taken on Cara's young half-brother, Sebastian. With Sebastian in residence, it had been the natural thing, Cara supposed, for Auntie Tina to suggest that Cara and little Mira might like to move in as well, particularly when the porter in charge of the flats began to refuse to light fires for her, and actually dared to turn the central heating off for hours at a time because he had run out of the coke that the big boiler, it seemed, had needed.

So now, as she wrote to William in France, they were

just one big family, and Auntie Tina seemed to get a good deal of pleasure from catering and buying for the entire bunch. Ruthie, who had been Auntie Tina's cook for simply ages, did most of the actual work, Cara suspected, but Auntie Tina organised, saw that things ran smoothly, and bossed everyone about.

Cara had never done much work. In the flat there had been a succession of maids, a nurse for Mira and the devoted William to do her bidding. When William had left, there had still been a nurse and a succession of maids. But then the nurse had gone, saying that Mira was quite old enough for Cara to manage on her own, and the maids found that they could earn more money in the factories or on the land. Cara, just at the moment when she might have had to start doing her own work, had seized on Tina's offer and moved into The Pride.

At first, she had missed William. Not just because he managed everything for her but because of his loving. The tenderness that she had not recognised while he was with her could not, it seemed, be supplied by anyone else. But lately she had discovered that she could find something very like it in other men. Oh, she had no desire for affairs; such behaviour was unthinkable. But she enjoyed admiration, flirtations and a discreet cuddle from time to time. William was a lot older than she; now she discovered what it was like to have a young and extremely passionate man clutch her hands, kiss any part of her face he could reach, and vow undying love. It was delicious! A heady excitement coursed through her, and sometimes she even returned the kisses. The young men, of course, wanted more, but since she did not that was no problem. She had always got her own way, and saw no reason why this should not continue.

So now she pushed the pram as far as the three steps, then turned and pulled it, bump, bump, bump, up backwards and into the hall. She was going to the cinema tonight with one of those young men – she could not immediately recall which, but that did not matter since only one of them would pick her up, at the end of the drive, at seven o'clock.

Humming a little tune, Cara parked the pram and went into the kitchen to tell Jenny that her daughter, duly exercised, was home. She would have a lovely time tonight. She would let the young officer kiss her, and hold her hand during the film. And then she would let him take her out somewhere nice for supper, and then they would come by taxi to the bottom of the drive and he might, if he was really very nice and charming, be allowed to walk her as far as the front door. That, she knew, implied goodnight kisses, cuddles, and perhaps a further date.

It never occurred to Cara that she was playing with fire. Married to a man of thirty-five when she was seventeen, she had managed to remain sublimely ignorant about the male sex. Cousin Val, or Jenny, her sister-in-law, could have warned her, but some sixth sense made Cara keep her new men friends strictly to herself. Though she was carelessly fond of her brother Simon, she thought his wife was dull and terribly hidebound. If she had suspected that Jenny was seeing other men she would have been outraged, but it was, she told herself, 'different' for her. William, surely, would not mind her seeking a little companionship from others, when he was in no position to be with her himself?

She walked into the kitchen, patting the curls which clung to her head and framed her delicate, heart-shaped face. Jenny was there, peeling potatoes.

'I'm back, Jen. We had a lovely walk. Marianne's woken up, but she's still in her straps, so I've left her in the pram for you to deal with.'

'Oh, thanks, Cara.' Jenny, flushed from the stove's

heat, smiled at her lovely sister-in-law. 'Did you meet anyone we know?'

'Not a soul, darling.' Cara yawned and patted her mouth with one small, ring-laden hand. 'What time's luncheon? I'm starved. As soon as we've eaten I'll simply have to lie down for half an hour or so. My dear, sunshine and brisk exercise are *exhausting*!'

The two girls laughed together.

The shrilling of the telephone bell made Tina purse her lips. Who could be so thoughtless as to ring now, just when, having despatched Jenny, Cara and the children to Earlham Park, where they would catch tiddlers with flour bags on garden canes until teatime, she was seizing the opportunity to bake? She waited, floury hands poised over a tea-towel. Usually, the phone had only to ring once for a descent to be made upon it by a wife longing to hear from her husband, or a child hoping it would be a best friend, or Maude and Bella briskly pushing and shoving, expecting the call to be for them.

But the bell continued to ring. Tina grabbed the tea-towel and trotted briskly out of the kitchen, up the passage, through the green baize door and across the hall, to pick up the receiver through a muffling handful of material as though it had some contagious disease. She spoke into it a trifle impatiently and then, recognising her caller, allowed her voice to thaw into real pleasure.

'Frank! What a nice surprise to hear your voice, dear. Are you in the city?'

Her son's voice, sounding a little faster than usual, came clearly across the thirty or so miles that separated Norwich from his cottage at Oulton Broad.

'I'm still at the yard, but I shan't be much longer. Mama, could you possibly do me a favour?'

'Of course, if I can. What is it, dear?'

9

Frank rarely asked favours. Partly, Tina thought, because he was very independent, but also because he so much enjoyed his life, designing boats, building them, testing them and, in peacetime, selling them. Now she supposed vaguely that the government must pay Frank for all those ugly craft he built for it, though such transactions could scarcely be termed buying and selling. But it would be nice to do something for her second son, instead of asking him to do something for her.

'It's Lenny. If I put him on a train, could you meet him at the station and keep him with you for a few days? Just until I get back from . . . until I get back?'

The alteration in the last sentence was not lost on Tina. Her ears metaphorically pricked.

'Until you get back from where, dear?'

Frank laughed. 'From where I'm going, of course, Mama! Are you sure it won't be too much of an imposition? He can be quite naughty, I suppose, though he never bothers me.'

Lenny was Frank's evacuee, a small boy of eight or nine who managed to fit in very well with his casual and unorthodox host. Tina suspected that the pair of them ate when they were hungry, washed when the dirt was just too much, and went to bed when they were exhausted. She also thought that though one could scarcely blame Lenny for such behaviour Frank, at nearly forty, ought to be more sensible. But it would not do to say so; or, at least, it would be pointless to do so. Frank would laugh indulgently, send her a box of chocolates, and continue to live as he liked.

'Lenny won't be a bit of trouble,' Tina said now. 'He'll be happy with the other children, and he and Sebastian have always got on well. What train shall I meet? There's no one here but me, so I'll have to catch a bus . . .' The front door opened and Tina turned to see Maude tiptoeing across the marble tiles. 'No, wait, Frank, Maudie's just come in. She'll run me down to the station, won't you, dear?' Maude, realising she was being addressed, nodded vigorously. 'Right, then we'll be at the station in half an hour. Oh, by the way, where are you going? Last week shipbuilding was so important that you wouldn't even leave the yard for an hour to come to your aunt's birthday party.'

Tina had been aggrieved at the time, and now she wondered what could have got into Frank. The birthday party had been on a Sunday, yet this was a weekday and still whatever it was had Frank eager to go. But Frank, it seemed, intended to go on keeping his own counsel.

'Look, I'll tell you all about it when I get back. I'll have to fetch Lenny, so I'll see you then. All right?'

'Yes, but . . .'

'Goodbye, Mama. Thank you!'

Tina replaced the receiver with a crispness which indicated her disapproval and turned to Maude, who was fanning herself with a copy of the *Evening News*.

'What's the matter, Gran? You look rather cross!'

'No, dear, not cross exactly, just a little impatient with your Uncle Frank. He's going off somewhere and he won't say where, but he wants me to have Lenny for a few days. Really, some people are so thoughtless. All I wanted to know was where he was going so I wouldn't worry needlessly.'

'Oh, he'll be going to France,' Maude said carelessly, following Tina through the green baize door and back to the warm, sweet-smelling kitchen. 'Belgium's chucked in the sponge, hasn't it? He'll be buzzing off over there.'

'France?' Tina turned to stare at her granddaughter, then snorted. 'Nonsense. He'll be off up to the Admiralty or something. And I'm just in the middle of making teacakes, too, and the oven's nice and hot . . . Maudie, you know Lenny quite well. Do you suppose . . .'

The back door opening cut short her request, as Val, her youngest daughter, lounged into the kitchen, red curls tucked under a white straw hat, a tennis racquet under one arm.

'Hello, Mother. Something smells good. Hi, Maudie!'

'Ah, Val, darling, I'm glad you're home. Frank just rang and I've got to go down to the station to fetch Lenny. Your brother's off somewhere for a few days, and he wants me to have the child for the time he's away.'

'Oh, he'll be going to France,' Val said, slinging her racquet on to the dresser with a clatter. 'I popped into the Centre on my way back and they're full of it down there. They've been appealing to all small boat owners to go over and help to fetch the BEF off. Us east-coasters are to make our way round to the channel ports and they'll give us charts or whatever to take us across. Good old Frank. He'll have a stronger reason than most for going over, of course.'

'You and Maudie are as bad as one another,' Tina grumbled, rolling out her mixture with one eye on the kitchen clock. 'Why on earth should they want small boats? They got them over without using small boats!'

'Gran, this is a retreat! They took them over in their own good time, but they'll be bringing them back in a hell of a hurry!' Maude picked the car keys up from the dresser and threw them to Val. 'Going to drive, Val? If so, I'd better stay here and finish Gran's teacakes whilst the oven's hot.'

'You're a good girl,' Tina said, handing over the rolling pin with alacrity and rinsing her hands beneath the cold tap. 'Don't let the teacakes burn if you can possibly help it. I used two people's fat ration in them, to say nothing of over a pound of dried fruit.'

'I'll be careful. Tell Lenny he can have a hot teacake when he gets back, and perhaps he'll feel a bit happier,' Maude said, busily cutting out the large circular cakes.

Tina, hurrying across to the back door, looked surprised.

'Why should he be unhappy? He'll be with us!'

Maude and Val exchanged glances but neither said anything. Val hurried her mother out to the garage and into the grey Talbot which stood waiting. Only when they were making their way down the drive, the engine purring smoothly, did Val revert to the topic on both their minds.

'Lenny's had some upheavals in his little life. I expect Maudie guessed he wouldn't relish another. As for Frank, he must be hoping against hope that Mabel will get out.'

'Mabel Walters that was, you mean? I know he was fond of her once, but it's years since they met . . . do they write? Hmm, I daresay they do. Frank isn't the sort to give up a friendship. But surely, Mabel's French now, and the French haven't given up yet. They're a strong country, not small and easily overrun like Holland. And Luxembourg. And Norway, and now Belguim. Surely France will fight on?'

Val shrugged.

'I don't know, but I do know that Mabel's husband is a sensible man and will want to get his wife out of it. His son too, if he can, though I doubt whether he can dictate to André, who must be in his twenties. But I think Matthieu will try to persuade Mabel to leave.'

Tina sighed but vouchsafed no reply, leaving Val free to follow her own thoughts. She had met Mabel only twice in her life, Matthieu only once, but she liked and respected them both. The summer before the war Frank and she had gone over to France, ostensibly on holiday but really to see Mabel. That Frank still loved her could not be in doubt once you had seen them together; nor, oddly enough, that Matthieu de Recourte loved his wife. Yet, though Val thought the de Recourtes were fond of one another, she acknowledged that it was not the sort of love which would bind Mabel to Matthieu if she had a chance of being with Frank.

Until now she must have felt that in time of war one's loyalty was to one's husband and child and adopted country. But surely now she would come home? As an Englishwoman, indeed, she might be in great danger if France did capitulate. Reasoning thus, Val assumed that Mabel would be coming home at last.

Beside her in the car, Tina's thoughts followed a similar pattern. She supposed that her silly son did still love that Mabel, for all she was a respectable married woman with a son. But what was the use? If Mabel came home Frank would not be able to marry her, so it would be no better than if she were abroad. Anyway, why should Frank go over there and risk his life for a woman who had married someone else? Suppose Mabel did come back, suppose Frank saw nothing wrong in inviting her to live at the cottage with him? Tina's scalp prickled. It *was* wrong, even if they did nothing, because people would think bad things about them, and . . . and . . .

'Just in nice time! I'll park here, Mother, and we'll be on the platform just as the train gets in. Did Frank say if he'd packed Lenny up some clothes and so on?'

'Oh! No, he didn't say and I forgot to remind him. Never mind. Madge won't let him come with nothing.' Madge was Frank's housekeeper, and a friend of long standing. 'That must be the train. Let's hurry.'

The train drew in and Lenny climbed down, his wild and spiky hair subdued with Brylcreem, his expression anxious and resentful. He had an old cricketing bag of Frank's, and hefted it sturdily as soon as he saw them, but Val, who had a kind heart, saw that he was miserably unsure and took the bag from him, putting an arm round his skinny shoulders. Lenny, no womaniser, evidently, shook it off and scowled warningly. Liberties, it seemed, were not to be taken.

'Hello, Lenny. Nice to have you visit us for a few days. The other kids are all out, or we'd have brought them down to meet you, but they'll be back in time for tea so you can see them then. Did Uncle Frank say how long he'd be away?'

Tina sighed. That this cockney waif should refer to her son as Uncle had taken some swallowing, but she had swallowed it at last, though it made her wonder what the world was coming to. She saw Lenny wrest his bag back from Val with approval, though. Evidently Frank was teaching the lad some manners.

'Naw,' Lenny said in answer to Val's question, listing heavily to port with the weight of his bag but sternly clinging to the handle. 'Went off wi' Ben and Donnie in a boat they'd jist repaired. I could've gone an' all. I can swim near's dammit from the staithe to Fletchers, but 'e said no. Too young, 'e said.' Lenny's voice was laden with bitterness.

'Well, if he's taken Ben and Donnie the boat must be quite full,' Val said consolingly. Ben was Frank's right-hand man at the yard and Donnie, Ben's son, was simple, so he had to go wherever Ben went. Val knew that Ben would unhesitatingly take Donnie into danger rather than leave him behind. Countrymen, Val reflected, were seldom sentimental. Ben reckoned that Donnie would be better off dead than cast rudderless on a sea of life which did not contain his father.

They reached the car and Lenny climbed into the back. His cricketing bag, it seemed, contained a pair of pyjamas, his washing things, and a clean shirt. He informed Val aggressively that since he would not be staying long there was little point in bringing more and Val, seeing that he derived comfort from the frugality of his luggage, agreed that this was a sure sign of a short stay and drove out of the station yard. Tina, less sensitive to the mysteries of male logic, nearly spoiled everything by assuring Lenny that Sebastian would lend him anything he needed, but then the car turned into Newmarket Road and Lenny began to look a bit perkier and announced, with seeming casualness, that it must be 'rahnd abaht teatime'.

'That's right. We'll probably get back to the house before the kids, so you can settle in and then walk down to meet them. You can tell them there are hot teacakes – Maudie's been baking them – and a chocolate sandwich, and we've made some strawberry flans, too.'

'I like chocolate,' Lenny admitted. He bounced once on the springs of the back seat. 'Think Seb'll be pleased to see me?'

'Not half,' Val said truthfully. 'He's been complaining for ages that he's sick of feminine rule. In the gang, I understand, boys are outnumbered heavily by girls.'

'Yeh, I reckon,' Lenny said, having digested this remark. 'Where'm I sleepin'?'

The car swished round the gravel sweep in front of the house and came to rest somewhat showily with a spurt of loose stones right at the front of the steps. Val got out, helped her mother to alight, and then turned to Lenny, hopping out by himself and already mounting the front steps and giving an appreciative glance to the cannons which flanked the front door. She hastily revised her mother's plan to put Lenny in the little room over the study.

'Oh, we thought with Seb and Eddy, if you wouldn't find it too crowded. You can have a room of your own if you're set on it, but . . .'

'Nah! It'll be fine wi' the others,' Lenny assured her rather grandly. 'Don't go to no bovver. Boys ain't like girls.'

'Right, we'll bear it in mind,' Val said, as the three of them crossed the hall. Tina looked resigned. Val knew her mother could not bring herself to accept that Lenny was a suitable stable-companion for her adored grandson and great-nephew. But Val could see that she was mentally shrugging, reminding herself that there was a war on.

Lenny threw his bag down on the dressing-table in the bedroom which he was to share, viewed the camp-bed he would occupy with every sign of approval, and then accompanied Val and her mother down to the kitchen, where he evaded Maude's attempt at a kiss, grabbed the largest teacake off the wire cooling tray, and settled himself on the draining-board from where, he informed his audience, he could just get a glimpse of the drive, if he craned a bit. Val, taking pity on him, advised him to hop off and see if the others were in sight yet and he did so with alacrity, presently returning with Seb and Eddy to descend like locusts on the tea and play horribly rowdy games until bedtime.

It was only then, while Val was supervising baths, that Lenny descended a little from his lofty perch of masculine cynicism.

'I'm missin' ole Frank,' he said as he scrubbed his teeth and spat with furious energy at the plughole. 'I wonder where 'e is now? Cor, I wish 'e'd teken me too, I does!'

'Oh, Frank will be fine,' Val said with an airiness she was far from feeling. 'He and Ben are the best sailors I know. They'll be OK.'

Lenny rinsed, spat again, and then turned a chilly eye on Val.

"Course they're good sailors. I ain't worried about *that* side o' fings,' he said scornfully. 'I just wonder where 'e *is*, that's all. There ain't no 'arm in wonderin'!'

Chapter Two

'I wonder what tha' boy Lenny's doing now?'

Ben's murmur was so low that only Frank could possibly have caught it, yet he glanced round sharply in the darkness, wanting to tell Ben to be careful, to remind him that they must not be heard, though he knew it would be ridiculous. They were at sea, and the nearest craft was well out of earshot.

They were making their way, as Val and Maude had guessed they would, to France – to Dunkirk, to be precise. They had been told, briefly, to stay with the convoy of small vessels, and when they reached the beaches to ferry the men out into deeper water where the big ships would lie. They had been warned that the enemy occupied at least a part of Calais and were shelling everything within range, and that during daylight the beaches and the sea were constantly strafed and bombed by enemy aircraft. There had been a good deal of talk about which routes should be used. The shortest route could only be used at night, since enemy planes were patrolling it; the longest route, though safe, was a good deal too long for some of the smaller craft, and the middle route was not yet possible since it was still thickly sown with mines.

They knew that the short route – a mere thirty-nine miles of unlit, heaving seaway – would be closed quite soon, but their convoy had used it safely enough so far. There had been bad moments, of course. Two of the convoy had rammed one another and someone, leaping to conclusions from the freaks of wind and sea, had alerted everyone to the presence of a U-boat, which had caused a good deal of veering and tacking. It had proved to be a school of dolphin, blazing a trail of phosphorescence through the water, their backs gleaming liquid silver, but though it had been a false alarm it had made them all that bit more uneasy.

'What should Lenny be doing, Ben? I sincerely trust he's sleeping soundly. But I do wonder what Miss Tuckett and Miss Sears would say if they could see their boat now!'

Ben grinned, a flash of teeth in the dark.

'Aye, that's a point. She's misnamed for this job, eh, Mr Frank?'

Frank grinned too. However misnamed *Gay Times* might be she was doing all that was expected of her, keeping up with the fleet and behaving as though she had been made for the channel crossing, instead of cruises on Oulton Broad while her two spinster owners searched for butterflies, entered notes in their books concerning the nesting habits of grebe, and indulged in flasked tea and gentleman's relish sandwiches.

'You could say that. But she isn't the only odd one!'

This was true, as one could see at a glance. There were small yachts, tugs, a lifeboat, and a couple of craft which looked remarkably like cockleboats. A motley crew, perhaps, but everyone who had heard the appeal on the lunchtime news for owners of small boats to assemble in Margate, Ramsgate and Dover must surely be eager to help. No seaman worth his salt would have hesitated, no matter how small the craft at his disposal at that particular moment. Frank, who built motor torpedo boats and patrol boats for the navy, was caught with nothing ready to go to sea, since he had just despatched the most recently completed vessel. But Miss Sears had brought *Gay Times* in for a new propeller and it had been the work of a moment to fit it, test it briefly, and then borrow the small sailing and motor cruiser. A moment to take Lenny to the station, another to rush round to Madge and ask her to take care of the place, and then he, Ben and Donnie had put a few necessities aboard in the small, cosy cabin and set off.

Now, looking round, he appreciated the beauties of the night. Clear, with a light wind, the stars already seemed paler. Presently, straining to see ahead, he thought he could make out a line of land which resolved itself, as time passed, into pale beaches. And there was a rumbling, which he guessed must be shellfire, perhaps even vehicles driving down to the port. His heart began to beat faster. They were getting nearer to the work they had come so far to do; they would soon be bringing the boys back! It did not do to think too much of your own particular people; just think of those others, brothers, husbands, sons, who would be waiting even now at the top of those pale beaches, where the humps of the dunes could be faintly seen in the first dawn light.

'How many've you got over there, Mr Frank? My cousin Bert's lad, he's in the Royal Norfolks. Somewhere over there.'

Mabel. I've got Mabel over there, Frank's mind groaned. Of course no one knew she was still his Mabel – would always be his Mabel if he lived to be a hundred or died tomorrow – though she was another man's wife. So when he answered, he left out the name that was nearest to his heart because he had no right to say it. Mabel had married Matthieu, and until she chose to leave him that act flung Frank's rights straight into the fiery furnace. She was his only for two weeks each year, when, in September, they went secretly away to the wild north of Scotland together. Only then. Fourteen days out of the three hundred and fifty or whatever it was.

'Let me see. There's baby brother Nick, of course.

Always in trouble, baby brothers, if there's trouble to be found. And William Dopmann, you've met him, that nice chap who married my cousin Cara. And there's young Paul Butcher. I don't know if you've met him, but he's in the army. James, the elder one who's been over to the yard a couple of times, is in the air force, like my nephew Art, and Cyril, my younger nephew, is in the navy, so he could be in one of those ships out there, I suppose.'

'Aye. I remember seeing him in them bell-bottoms at the back end o' last year. And Mr Simon's flying, of course. Him and James Butcher are good friends and rare alike, I always think. Wonder if they'll be up there shootin' down Jerry tomorrow?'

Last time, Frank remembered, he had thought, 'I wonder if that's Uncle Lou up there?' every time a plane flew over the trenches. He hated to think about the first war, but it was that more than anything, he supposed, which had brought him here, in his absurd craft with his odd companions, to do what he could to help. Terrible, confused memories of mud, crippling fear, deafening noise and unbearable pain: that was last time. And how grateful the young Frank would have been to anyone who could have got him out of there! His best friend had died in the trenches, and he himself had been severely gassed. He knew that the smell of the gas was on him still, that he would probably always smell of it. If the night were so cold that he had to sleep with his bedroom window closed, then the smell would be thick in the air by morning: acrid, metallic. His stomach would heave at the recollection.

'Probably. Uncle Lou was always in the thick of it, and Simon's just like his father in some ways.' Frank jerked his head towards the cabin. 'Want to wake the lad? It won't be long now.'

'No, we'll let him have his sleep out. Can you see what's happenin' ahead now, Mr Frank?'

For the pale beaches were darkening with men as the soldiers came out of the dunes and began to form great queues, stretching into the sea as far as they could wade so that they could be picked up more easily. Presently a signal was flashed round the fleet and the small boats began to pick out their mother ships – the ship to which each would carry its cargo of men.

Frank grinned across at Ben as the older man came up from the cabin with Donnie, who was knuckling his eyes. It was starting! He steered *Gay Times* over to the cross-channel ferry which would receive his men, then headed for the beaches. The long queues beckoned. Quiet, ravenous, drugged with weariness, the troops waited. The only thing they had in common was the hope on their grey faces.

Home. They all wanted to go home. Frank brought his boat alongside the nearest queue and glanced back towards his mother ship. She would hold hundreds of men. He looked towards the beaches again and revised his opinion. Thousands. Dawn was close, and the men were thronging into the water. Every ship capable of it would have to carry thousands.

The men began to scramble aboard. Frank helped them, lugging the smaller, weaker men bodily out of the sea and over the gunwale. At first he could not help scanning the faces in the hope that one of them might be Nicky, but presently he just worked on, grimly. They were all young, dirty, worn out. Somewhere, someone like him might be hauling Nicky on to a small craft, so it scarcely mattered who it was. Just let's get them off, he prayed, as, with a full boat and scarcely an inch of freeboard, they set off as fast as they could back to the cross-channel ferry. Let them all get away, all these exhausted, brave, dirty young men!

Nicky was heading for the coast, but he was still a long

way from the beaches and he had lost most of his company. Once the heavy strafing began it had been next to impossible to stay together on the busy roads. Thronged with men, horses, artillery, loud with the noise of different languages, choked with all the paraphernalia of an army in retreat and a civilian population fleeing before the enemy, main roads had been all but impassable for a group of men.

'Split up and meet again a mile the other side of this village,' Nicky had told them, but he, Sergeant Manvers and Smiffy, still a private but undoubtedly destined for greater things, had been the only ones who had managed to rendezvous there. Smiffy could have been a lieutenant, as Nick was, except that he had not believed there would be a war. He had even played with the idea of being a flier, until his medical had let him down. So now he was just Smithers, John Edmund, 30891541, until someone, somewhere, had time to see how cool, intelligent and unperturbed he was, whether under fire, underfed, or misunderstood. He and Nick both spoke reasonable French, but they could do little with Belgian, or with some of the other languages which had been shot at them today. Nick and Sergeant Manvers got hot under the collar at first, but not Smiffy. Smiffy just used sign language, grins, and a natural quickness at mimicry to get them all through.

This morning, at dawn, there had been three of them, but now they had gained two more: Irish and Tartan, as they called each other, had emerged from a wood and simply tagged on. They had been involved in heavy fighting, had lost their battalions and now just wanted to reach the coast so that they could get home, re-form, and teach 'dem jerries not to go grabbin' other people's property', as Irish put it. Nick gathered that this was less altruistic than it might seem after Tartan told him, when they stopped at a stream for a drink, that Irish had been forced to evacuate a farmhouse he had been holding so rapidly that he had left a full flask of whiskey behind.

'It wasnae even decent stuff,' the Scot had said, grinning. 'Only Irish plonk; but he was fair grieved by the loss.'

It was strange, Nick thought now as they trudged on through the light drizzle, that they had so suddenly escaped from the brawl of the roads into these deserted country lanes. He suspected that the enemy was probably now all round them and Smiffy, consulted, agreed.

'But if we go slowly and quietly round corners, and skulk a bit, we should be all right,' he said optimistically. 'Or we could leave the lanes, if you'd rather, and stick to the meadows.'

'Well, so long as we continue to head for the coast,' Nick said rather dubiously. 'I feel we ought to make for main roads, except that it was the devil's own work getting along. At least this way we stand a chance of reaching Dunkirk before the navy pulls out.'

Because of the risk of meeting the German army, or a part of it, face to face, therefore, they did keep, whenever they could, to the fields and woods bordering the quiet lanes. At last they reached a track so deep and so secret, the hedges almost meeting overhead, that they decided they would do best, in this instance, to remain in the lane where they were well hidden, and to proceed as quietly as possible.

Puddles had formed on the carriageway and the foliage overhead was dripping constantly. Water channelled down Nick's neck into his battledress, and although his feet were dry his legs from just above the knee were saturated. It was chilly, too, and difficult to remember that only a day earlier there had been hot sunshine, flies buzzing, birds singing on every side. Now, it seemed as though the whole world had been depressed into silence by the rain.

The voices took them by surprise. They slowed their pace and glanced uneasily at each other. What language was that, for God's sake? And where did it come from? Above their heads, hidden by the hedge's thick tangle, men were speaking. A rumble of talk. There were a lot of men up there, a whole company or more . . .

Nick grabbed Sergeant Manvers by the elbow and jerked his head at the others. German! He had distinctly heard a few words in that language! It was coming from the meadow to the right of the sunken lane, but without climbing the bank and looking he could not tell what was happening. It could be that some English soldiers had taken prisoners – he would have to see what was going on.

Slowly and with infinite caution he scrambled up the soggy, grassy bank. At the top of it there was a mass of wild flowers and weeds and then the thickness of the hedge. He forced his way into the thinnest part of it, so that he could, he hoped, see without being seen. Beside him, he could hear Smiffy following suit and, further up, Manvers, Irish and Tartan did the same. He felt a moment's sharp annoyance, until it occurred to him that they were only doing what he should have told them to do – it was madness just to stand about in the sunken lane, waiting for someone to come along and see them. Better, by far, to hide up here, where no one would think of looking, until they could see whether the coast was clear.

Nicky forced himself a little further into the hedge. A wild rose, creamy white with a gold centre, hung down before his eyes. It was rain-spangled and very beautiful and he knew a strange reluctance, almost a foreknowledge, when his hand moved it aside.

He peered, then turned to Smiffy, a remark very nearly on his lips. It was the Royal Norfolks. He would know them anywhere, having so many friends in the battalion. And then, looking closer, he saw that they were herded together in the middle of the meadow, the grass, wet and sweet, at knee-height, and were surrounded by Germans. His heart plummeted. They had evidently been taken prisoner, and presumably their captors were about to take names, ranks and numbers. That was why the men had been formed into lines.

The Norfolks looked tired out. But in a way they must have been relieved that their forced march was over. One or two of them were exchanging quiet remarks, a hand went into a pocket, someone asked a question in halting, schoolboy German.

When the firing broke out Nick did not realise where it came from nor what was happening. It was horrendous, the noise ear-shattering, the suddenness of it terrifying to men lying hidden. It was, Nick thought afterwards, several seconds before he took in the fact that not one of the battalion was left standing. The bodies lay as if hit by blast, untidily, some still twitching as reflexes jumped, breath whistling from a mutilated chest.

Nick was curled up, gripping Smiffy's arm. Smiffy's hand was over Nick's mouth, but there were tears on his cheeks, white amongst the dirt.

Behind the hedge, a German soldier was being sick. Vomiting into the meadowsweet, staining his battledress. Nick saw the insignia on the man's shoulder, but was scarcely conscious of seeing it. The world was mad, the hand over his mouth stifling . . . he must get in there, and shoot and shoot and shoot . . .

He was in command of himself again quite quickly, really. Smiffy seemed to know when the moment came, and released him. They continued to crouch by the hedge as the Germans were shouted at, formed into columns and marched away.

Stillness and silence settled on that dreadful meadow. A bird cheeped somewhere. After a long time, they heard a cow lowing to be milked, a long way away.

Stiffly, Nick stood up. He said nothing, but they all followed suit. They found their way through the hedge and went over to the mound of bodies. Irish was crying, openly, as a child cries. The others were tight-lipped, bright-eyed.

'We'd best check, sir,' Sergeant Manvers said awkwardly. 'Then we'd best move on.'

'Right. Irish, could you keep an eye on the lane? Keep out of sight. Someone may come; they can't just leave . . .' The words stuck in his throat and he turned away as he saw Irish move obediently back to the highest point of the meadow.

Crouching, Nick and Manvers and Smiffy began to check the bodies. A young, red-haired man, dead. Another. Another. Methodically they worked as best they could, but were not halfway through before Irish called them.

'Boys dere's someone comin'! Best leave by the far gate.'

Nick took a last look at the next body. Just a boy with his head turned away, but there was something about the curve of his cheek, the way his hair grew . . .

Nick dropped on his knees and touched the cold fingers of Paul Butcher, twenty-one years old. Blood of my blood, Nick thought. Bone of my bone, flesh of my flesh. And a great rage flowered in him.

'Got time for a bite?'

Frank smiled at the naval rating who was handing out big mugs of hot tea and cheese sandwiches. He took his share thankfully, desperately hungry and thirsty. He and Ben and Donnie had been ferrying men off the beaches now for almost thirty-six hours. They were not as tired as they might have been, though, because catnaps were possible when, because of the bombing and strafing from the enemy aircraft overhead, the little boats were told to stop ferrying so that the men would return to hide in the dunes. Then, of course, the big ships would leave with their laden decks to face the hell of the channel, where they were under constant attack from the air and from U-boats. Several had gone down no more than half a mile from the shore, and Frank's heart had been wrung for those men who had thought themselves safe and had still died, dreadful, frightening deaths, while the watchers could do so pitifully little.

Now, he bit into his sandwich, chewed, swallowed, and then drank his tea. He spoke to the naval rating, who was waiting for the mugs before climbing, monkey-like, back up the rope ladder and on to the big ship.

'What was your last voyage over like? The *Queen of the Channel* bought it, I'm told.'

'Aye. Bombed and then sank. Coming through the Zuydecoote Pass you can see the masts showing in the shallows, where they've sunk. You've got to watch for hazards like that now, as well as all the others – shipping without lights, shoal water, wrecks – you name it, we're faced with it.'

'You came by the long route, then? The one they're calling Route Y?'

'That's right. The minesweepers are working all out to get the middle route clear, though – Route X. It'll be a deal quicker and probably safer when we can use that way.' The rating took Frank's mug and held out a hand for Ben's, then gave them a casual salute and swarmed up the ladder. He would be climbing up and down for a while yet, taking tea and bread and cheese round to the small boats.

Ben walked across the deck and peered down into the cabin where Donnie, worn out, had crept as soon as they told him they were taking a break. Now, Ben turned back and grinned at Frank.

'Sleepin' like a baby still. Give 'im half an hour, and we'll be movin' again. Don't sound too good, do it – all them wrecks? Sounds as if gettin' 'em off int the only difficult job.'

'No, I'm afraid it's just the start of their troubles. But at least getting them off is a better start than letting them stay there to be killed or captured.' Frank watched one of the big cross-channel ferries steaming out to sea, its decks crowded with so many men that it was definitely standing room only. Poor devils, he thought, as some of the men waved and called out, they think it's all over bar the shouting. Well, so it might be, if their rescuer could manage to avoid all the dangers which lay ahead.

He was feeling cheerful despite the tiredness and the constant noise from the German aircraft which recommenced as soon as there was light in the sky. He had heard that some nurses had been taken off, from the Mole in the town's harbour. Mabel, he knew, had been working as a nursing auxiliary since the start of the war. That was how she would come, then, in her capacity as a nurse. He had not seen any women himself, but just to know that she could get back was a comfort.

The ferry was just a dot on the horizon now, and another big ship was nosing into the anchorage she had vacated. Frank braced himself and saw Ben follow suit.

'I'll wake the lad,' Ben said gruffly. 'Then we'll go in for the next lot.'

In the lorry, Mabel sat hunched up on the floor, pressed close to a dozen other women. Her hospital had been closed down after a near miss had shattered every window and made it patently unsafe, and the word had gone out that the English nurses were to be sent back to the coast for evacuation to England. She had been uncertain what she should do, but Matthieu, looking incredibly handsome and distinguished in his officer's uniform, had had no doubt.

'My wife is English and would be in danger if the Germans captured her,' he said crisply to the matron of the hospital. 'Please take her with you when you leave. Her parents are alive, so she can go to them and help with the war effort from there.'

She had said nothing then, not with matron so obviously agreeing, but when she was seeing Matthieu off she returned to the subject.

'Do you really think I should go, Matthieu, with you and André here? Surely the Germans will be pushed back, and then you'll wish I'd stayed.'

It was odd, how one reacted. She did not want to stay. She had intended to leave him the previous autumn, only war had broken out. Then, it had seemed cruel and disloyal to leave the man and the country who had sheltered her for twenty years, taking her in when she had been lost, lonely, desperately unhappy. But now? Surely France would be safe? The Maginot line, the sheer numbers of French troops she had seen . . . surely they would manage, somehow, to keep the Germans out?

But Matthieu knew things that other people did not. A good two years before the war she had heard him saying that the Maginot line would not keep anyone out of France because it was twenty years out of date. It could not reach up into the sky and pluck the German planes down; it could not stand for long against modern weapons such as tanks and bombs. If he insisted that she leave, it was because he did not think France would be able to resist the horrors that were about to descend on her. So when he nodded, patting her shoulder in an unusually overt gesture of affection, she sighed, nodded too, and kissed him.

Usually Matthieu hated being kissed. Despite the fact that they had been married for more than twenty years and, in his way, he loved her more than anyone except André, nothing could make physical contact other than embarrassing for him. He had not fathered André, though no one save for herself and Matthieu knew that. He was not homosexual; neither was he strictly speaking heterosexual. He was just . . . Matthieu, rather a cold fish, perhaps, who had been kinder to her than she had any right to expect, who had treated her illegitimate son as though he were his own flesh and blood and who, she knew, would strain every nerve in his body to save her from the holocaust he believed was to come.

This time, when her arms went round him, he held her too, and kissed her. Tenderly, on the side of her mouth. And there was so much painful farewell in that rare kiss that she very nearly defied him, very nearly told him that she would not be ordered away, that she would stay and fight beside him.

But not quite. She told herself that there was no point in staying here, an embarrassment to Matthieu if France were forced to capitulate. And André, brought up as a Frenchman, speaking English only as a second language, would also be better off without her. He was in the French air force; perhaps he would come to England too, if the worst happened. And anyway, she owed something to herself, and to Frank. His love had never faltered and he had waited patiently for the moment when she would feel her debt to Matthieu had been paid. Twenty years was quite long enough. She and Frank deserved a little time together. Sitting in the chilly and bumpy lorry she visualised living in the little cottage close by the Broad, taking care of Frank, cooking his meals, darning his socks, and loving him. Frank was the least selfish person she knew, the most straightforward and honourable. He had never seen André, believed the boy to be Matthieu's son, and she intended him to continue believing it. But when she got home she would explain, somehow, that Matthieu would not blame her for turning to him.

'Where you going back to then, eh?'

The girl sitting on the dusty floor of the lorry with her navy blue cloak cuddled round her smiled encouragingly at Mabel.

'Who, me? I'm from Norfolk. What about you?'

'Suffolk, actually. Small world, isn't it? I'm from Bury St Edmunds.'

'Oh, Bury; I know it well. It's a lovely place. Especially in autumn, when the trees round the abbey are turning.'

Sitting in the ancient lorry as it creaked and groaned across the rutted and congested lanes of France, the two women forgot their surroundings and the discomforts and the smell. They dreamed of home, of peaceful gardens, the scent of summer, the quiet contentment of the English countryside.

The planes were overhead again. Wave after wave of them, unidentifiable save that they were enemies, swooping low over the beaches, their gunfire chattering, the smell of the fuel they used in the air.

William Dopmann dug himself a little lower into his sandhole beneath the dune and tried not to think about the rain, the crump of bombs landing and the vicious clatter of the guns. Instead, he fixed his mind on thoughts of home, and Cara. What would his beautiful child-wife be doing now? William knew perfectly well that Cara, though pretty as a picture and a charmer as well, was also selfish and shallow, but he hoped that these defects would pass as she grew older, given his loving but firm treatment. He hated it when she let herself down with some display of thoughtlessness or selfishness, but he told himself that such displays were getting fewer and fewer, that Cara was growing a nature to fit that lovely face.

Even thinking about her made him feel happier. He was a lucky blighter! Though she could be difficult, could sulk or grab like a spoilt five-year-old or throw a tantrum with the best, that was only when they were alone. She had charming manners and had learned in the course of their four years of marriage to be an excellent hostess, the envy of a good many of his friends.

'A baby, he married,' one of his friends had said a few weeks before war broke out. 'Yet how well she is maturing! She's a good hostess, a marvellous mother for little Mira, and she dances divinely!'

William, gazing at the sodden slope of the sand dune only inches from his nose, nodded vehemently to himself. Yes, she was a wonderful girl. So why, then, should he feel such unease at the thought of leaving Mira in her sole care, should he himself be killed? Mira was a darling, and the image of his first wife. Naomi had been a good woman, and he had loved her truly, though quite differently from the way he loved Cara. Naomi had been plain, but intelligence and humour had lit her thin, dark face, making you forget the large, rather hooky nose and the sallow complexion. She had died of an infection shortly after Cara's birth, and when she had known how gravely ill she was she had all but ordered him to remarry. He had not wanted to, he remembered. Not until he met Cara.

As soon as he set eyes on Cara he had known that it must be she or no one. He had not found it difficult to sweep her off her feet despite being nearly twenty years older than she, and once he had her on his side he had known he would win.

Sarah, his mother-in-law, had allowed the marriage to go ahead principally, he suspected, because she could not stand the thought of Cara's sulks and tantrums if her will

33

were to be crossed. He had to admit that Cara did sulk, though he had all but cured her of that. People probably thought he was besotted; they just did not understand. Much as Cara loved him, she also needed him. It was just rather a pity that Cara gave all her love and devotion to William, so that it seemed she had none to spare for her stepdaughter.

Mira needed love. He had tried to impress this fact on Cara, but she would only say, impatiently, that of course she loved Mira. Just because she loved her, however, did not mean she wanted to spend her every waking moment at the child's beck and call.

He found it impossible to explain to Cara that her whole attitude to his daughter was wrong. She treated her like a puppy or a kitten, or had done so when Mira was a baby and even a toddler. But now that Mira was five it was not hard to see that Cara had no patience with her, little time for her. Knowing how Mira adored him, knowing that he must leave her, William's conscience had stepped in. He had cast his pride aside and gone to Sarah and Con Solstein. They were good people and they probably knew Cara better than most, though Con, her stepfather, had only married Sarah in the early 1930s. They had not asked him why he should seek help for his small daughter when he had a wife who would be with her; they had simply promised to do their best for her. And when Con's appointment to the War Office made it clear that they would probably be in London for most of the time, they had enlisted the aid of Tina Neyler.

William's thoughts were interrupted by Sergeant Craig, who appeared, genie-like, around the corner of the dune.

'Awright, sir? We're to move forward now, as it's duskish. The new wave of boats is coming ashore.'

'Oh, good.' William got to his knees. 'When?'

'Right now, I should think. Some of the men have already gone.'

They waited until there seemed a temporary lull overhead, for the dusk was, as yet, merely wishful thinking – though the low cloud and heavy gusts of rain made it safer on the beach than clear skies would have done – and then, crouching, they made for the sea. As they waded into the water, William's dry throat almost groaned. God, he was thirsty. He would have given a small fortune for a nice cup of tea, or a beer! At least his lips were moist from the rain. Yesterday he had collected rainwater in his helmet and that had been a help, but today he had been too full of his own thoughts to be practical. Stupid, that, but soon, surely, they would be on their way home!

There was a queue in front of him. Directly before him was a young man in khaki trousers and a scarlet shirt. After thirty minutes had passed, William tapped him on the shoulder.

'I say, old chap, couldn't you put something on over that red shirt? It makes you look like a target, and you're right in front of me,' he said only half jokingly. The young man turned round.

'Comment?'

I should have guessed the young idiot was French, William thought rather unfairly. He rephrased his remark in that language, and the young Frenchman, in his turn, began to explain in very bad English indeed how he came to be wearing such an unsoldierly garment. They talked of the retreat, now in French, now in English. They discussed what the French on the beaches would do when they reached Britain, how the rest would react to the news of the evacuation, and what was the best sort of wine to keep the cold out. It helped, William discovered, to talk in another language, because that way you could concentrate on what you were saying and forget – more or less – the constant menace of the planes overhead.

The queue moved forward, the water crept from

William's knees to his chest. He and his oddly garbed companion chatted on.

'It's the worst day yet.'

Frank had to roar to make himself heard above the racket. Today the Luftwaffe had done more damage than ever before. The town of Dunkirk itself seemed to be in flames and the thick pall of smoke which hung over it had made even the men out on the beaches cough and tie handkerchiefs over their mouths to try to combat the bitter taste of the air. The evacuation continued steadily, but the Luftwaffe had managed to get through the screen of British fighter aircraft striving to protect the embarking men, and they had bombed the ships waiting to be loaded, the men queuing to be taken aboard, and the Mole itself. There had been heavy losses, both in shipping and in lives. Frank and Ben had watched, helpless, as ship after ship started to flame, then keeled over and went down.

They had seen the big ship HMS *Crested Eagle* hit and catch fire, had watched, helpless, as the burning wreck came aground just off the beach. They did the best they could, the little boats, crowding round to take off any survivors who managed to escape from the flames, but it was agony picking the burnt and screaming men out of the surf knowing that there was little that anyone could do for them.

'They bombed the hospital ships, despite the Red Cross signs,' someone said, and Frank's heart, which had been high all day despite the carnage, fell into his boots. But only temporarily. It was as if he knew that Mabel would survive all this.

But now the evening had arrived at last and the planes overhead gradually gave up and returned to their bases. The *Gay Times*, a hardened warrior now, chugged in to the beaches to pick up another load of men and take them out to a destroyer waiting in deep water. A plane droned overhead, perhaps hoping to get in to the actual harbour once more and give the East Mole another pasting. It was ignored. Getting the troops off was all people thought about.

The boat was heading for a particular queue when there was a mighty explosion, water fountained up into the air and smoke drifted, thick and white, over the surface of the sea. When it cleared, there was no queue. No one, it appeared, had survived the impact of that bomb. The *Gay Times* continued to chug, but she was filling with water far too rapidly for Frank's liking and he glanced across at Ben.

'Splinter, I reckon,' Ben said in answer to Frank's unspoken question. 'Get the hole bunged up, be back picking up in an hour. We'd have been dead mutton if that thing had been a bit closer.'

'Yes, all right. We'd best take her ashore where there aren't any troops waiting, though.'

Ben agreed. They had experienced the panic which can hit men under fire – particularly, it seemed, Frenchmen. The British would stand stolidly under the most fearsome conditions, waiting to be told what to do, but the French were a very different kettle of fish. The moment the *Gay Times* was near enough they would simply jump aboard and refuse to move, even when the boat had come rather too far inshore and grounded under their weight. So if they were to drag her up the beach while they made a temporary repair, it had better be well clear of troops.

They got her on to the sand, shouting to a few men who came hopefully towards them that she was holed but would return to the water as soon as they had plugged the leak. They were working on it when Ben made another remark.

'Odd, Mr Frank, what ideas you'll get into your head, time like this. I was lookin' at that queue, the one that got wiped out, and I was thinkin' to myself, I bet that chap in the red shirt's a Frenchie; he looks like the bull in the middle of the dart board, standin' in the water in that there red shirt. And my heart alive, didn't that bomb land right on top of the poor blighter?'

'Yes, it must've. Poor devil, I don't suppose he could be seen at all from above, but that didn't save him.' Frank straightened. 'That seems all right to me. You hop aboard, Donnie, and Dad and I will get her afloat.'

Chapter Three

William came round to find himself in total darkness, lying on his face with something smooth and hard against his cheek. There were voices round him and hands touched, pulled at him.

'You're right, 'e's still breaving,' someone announced hoarsely. 'Well done, Perkie-boy, you were blooming well right! Nah, whadder we do wiv 'im?'

'Git 'im to the boats, I say,' another voice put in. 'Can you stand, mate?'

No one answered and William realised he had been addressed. He tried to move, but something held him where he was, as in a vice. He jerked, and felt his face shift; then he answered, though his throat was so sore that even the few words he spoke were agony.

'Dunno. I'll try.'

There were helping hands in plenty, and they got him more or less upright, but try as he would his legs seemed unable to bear his own weight. Life was made more difficult by the inexplicable heaviness of his left arm. The only thing that seemed light, in fact, was his head, and that really felt as though it were detached from the rest of him and floating a foot above the scene.

'There's something wrong with my legs,' he croaked at last. 'And my arm.' He could turn his head easily enough and did so, but though his arm really did look rather odd – the thought crossed his mind that it had been put on backwards by some careless person – his legs just looked

39

black and useless, the feet oddly angled perhaps, but otherwise just a pair of legs in soaked khaki trousers.

'Legs 'urt, do they, mate?' The young men supporting him held him more firmly and a third chap, a little bow-legged cockney with hair that looked as though his blind old mother had cut it for him, wrinkled his brow in simian concentration. 'Let's 'ave a butcher's.'

He could not feel the hands on his legs, he realised suddenly. He would never have known that his trouser leg was being rolled up had he not seen it. But before he had a chance to wonder overmuch the little man had rolled the trouser leg down and was standing once more, eyeing him uneasily.

'I fink you're worse'n what we fought,' he said apologetically. 'You copped a near enough direct hit, see. We saw you fly through the air like the feller on the flying trapeze and 'it the water and we thought you was a gonner, only Perks 'ere clawed you outer the drink and there we are. I reckon we'd better git you to a quack.'

The journey back up the beach was a nightmare, though William only half suffered it, since consciousness advanced and retreated in waves, so that at times the black of the night, the shuffling of his new friends, the soft tug of the night wind against his flesh, were lost in sickening decents into the pit of oblivion. But he always came out of it again, weak, giddy, feeling increasingly ill, until the moment when he felt himself lifted and laid down on something which yielded a little to his weight.

'Awright, feller? Don't even know your name, does we?'

It was an effort to raise his lids but he did it, and tried to concentrate on the face of the little cockney above him. He smiled.

'Dopmann, William.'

The cockney smiled too, bracingly.

'Sorry to tell you, Bill, they're leavin' the wounded. But you'll be fine and dandy – they're leavin' all the prettiest nurses and the best doctors, too. Got anything you'd like to send back to the wife, if you're married?' He glanced self-consciously down at William, then at someone standing beside him. 'Your watch, perhaps? This feller thinks mebbe you won't be needin' it for a bit.'

Despite the faintness caused by loss of blood, William realised that he might well be dying. He tried to lift his left arm and could not, and that made him look at it. It was hanging from the elbow, at an impossible, incredible angle. Someone at some time had removed his battledress, and now he could see, through the torn and bloodied shirt, that his arm was dangling, useless, all but in two. He could see, now, why the doctor had advised the little cockney to take his watch back to Cara.

'Can you take it off for me, mate?' His voice was smaller, thinner somehow, than he remembered it. 'Give it to Cara Dopmann . . . Norwich . . . with my dear love. Tell her I'm all right, tell her . . .'

But someone was shouting and the little cockney was undoing the strap of the heavy gold wristwatch, patting his shoulder, assuring him that the watch would be taken straight to Cara if he, Albert Gibson, had the good luck to get back alive. And then he was saying , 'Yessir, yessir, just comin', sir,' and stepping back from the stretcher.

Moments later, William was alone in the makeshift little shelter at the top of the beach, save for his pain, his fear, and the whirling, giddying nightmares.

'The arm will have to come off, old chap, and possibly a leg as well. You've lost a lot of blood.'

William had been moved, a nightmare journey in an ambulance this time, with a dear little girl no older than Cara holding his good hand and telling him that he would soon be in a proper hospital. Arriving at the 'proper hospital' he found it to be full of French nuns in weird headdresses and long wards full of wounded men. He gathered, from listening to the conversations around him, that the convent had only been a hospital for a fortnight and would go back to being a convent again as soon as the patients could be taken elsewhere. But then the doctor was at his bedside, telling him that he would have to lose an arm and possibly a leg too, and looking at him with sympathy but not with pity, and William had been given a drink of boiled water with honey dissolved in it and was almost able to face whatever was to come.

It did not come then and there, of course. He had a whole day and a night and then the beginning of another day to face first, while they fed him more sweetened drinks and gruel and tried to get him fit, he supposed, to face the operating table.

They put him on another stretcher at last and two orderlies carried him through to the room they had chosen to use for operations – one could scarcely call it an operating theatre. It had an altar at one end and some rather good Stations of the Cross round the walls, yet it did not look quite like a church or chapel. Halfway to the table, which was of white scrubbed wood raised on hefty wooden blocks, William realised that the orderlies were speaking German, which was a bit of a shock. Then for some reason he began to think about the Crimea, and Waterloo, and to remember more than he wished about battlefield operations conducted at such times, and he had to grip the edge of his stretcher very hard with his good hand and tell himself how lucky he was to be alive, or he might have fainted, or worse.

He was still nerving himself up for butcher-shop surgery when he felt the ether-soaked pad come down firmly over his nose and mouth and he was so grateful for the prospect of oblivion that he breathed in deeply without being asked, and did not struggle at all as the concentric circles began to buzz into his vision, advancing and retreating, carrying him far from the makeshift operating theatre, far from the French convent, far from the war.

He knew nothing more until he woke, many hours or days later, with a dreadful thirst, a fearful headache, and a cradle over the leg that was no longer there.

His left arm ended halfway between wrist and elbow, his right leg just about at the knee. He rapidly became feverish, seeing things that were not there, crying out, lashing around in the bed, hurting himself.

Two days passed in a torment of illness and wild imaginings, and then on the third he woke up, ravenously hungry, tormentingly thirsty, but with a clear head, a bright eye, and an awareness of his surroundings.

The nurses were wonderful, and the nuns, though not trained nurses, were fat, comfortable women with very little English who were doing all they could for the patients. Food was scarce, but William was a favourite because of the way he had fought back after his ordeal, and because of his unfailing good temper and sense of humour. People brought food parcels and one of the orderlies, a German chap with the nature of a friendly puppy, was always turning up with little 'treats'. Chocolate one day, a tin of sauerkraut the next, a delicious, strong-smelling smoked sausage the next.

William remembered now what he had been trying to forget on the beaches. He had killed. He had been responsible for the deaths of young men like the one who brought him chocolate, and though no doubt the German doctor who had told him 'For you, the war is over' was right, he still had boundless faith in Britain, and in the channel. The Frenchman in the next bed, crossgrained and bitter, a hater of all things English, kept insisting that

William need not worry about his wife and family, for he would be home soon enough to see them for himself.

'England will be overrun, as France has been. Why should the English not suffer? They ran away and left us to face the music, and now they can try to dance to the Huns' piping,' he said. 'It won't be long before you see your white cliffs with the Swastika flying over them.'

But William did not believe it. He remembered the retreat, the part he had played in it, and his belief in the people of England surged up, stronger and surer than ever. He let his mind go back to those days in the middle of May, when they first began to withdraw towards the coast.

It had been a brilliant afternoon, and William's platoon had been told to hold a bridge. The British, French and Belgian troops were to be seen safely across and then, when it was clear that the majority of the armies was over, the bridge was to be blown. A detachment of sappers had placed the charges but William's company was to be the rearguard and would give the signal when the bridge was no longer an asset. William was anxious, rather ill-at-ease, but at least it was comforting to know exactly what one was expected to do and to know very well how to do it. It was just a question of waiting and of choosing the right moment to make the bridge impassable.

They were also providing tea and hunks of bread and cheese for anyone who wanted it, which was most of the troops who passed along the road. William chatted to the men, absorbing any information they could give about the enemy's positions and strength. They were tired out and some of them had little enough idea of what was happening to them, let alone to the enemy, but it was a job that had to be done, and William was almost enjoying himself.

Then another Tommy came towards him. He had a flesh

wound on the neck, grimily bandaged; his boots were cracked and opening in front like hungry mouths, and his short, bristly, hay-coloured hair was full of fragments of earth and dried leaves. His face was grey with tiredness, the lines etched deep so that William guessed him to be fifty at first glance and, shockingly, no more than twenty or so when he came closer. But when he stopped beside the jugs of tea he grinned at William, a wide and somehow carefree grin despite the fact that he had lost a front tooth recently enough for the gap still to be bloody.

'Right road for 'ome, sir?' he said hopefully. 'Far, izzit?'

William was beginning to reply when there was a commotion inside the man's dusty battledress and a head appeared in the gap where a button should have been.

A puppy. Not a small one, either, but a good-sized creature probably four or five months old. And no light-weight, William guessed. Heavy for a five-foot cockney reared on chips and bread and marg at the best of times, but now, when they were in retreat? Why had he done it? The roads were jammed with guns, horses, men of several different nationalities all wanting to escape from the menace at the rear but otherwise with very different ambitions. Yet this small, square, wounded private had burdened himself with what looked like a leggy, rather unattractive puppy.

'You'll find it seems shorter without the dog,' William said. He knew it was true but he hated saying it. 'They won't let it go aboard a ship, you know. Better put a bullet through it, old man; save it a lot of misery.'

The man's hand descended on the puppy's head, pushing it back into the shelter of his battledress. His grin was wry, the grin of one who has spent a lifetime ignoring good advice and avoiding the consequences of rash actions.

'Nah, we'll manage, sir, 'im and me. Reckon 'e copped a

packet an' all.' He undid another button and displayed the puppy's front legs. One ended above the foot in a bloody, ill-bandaged stump. 'Can't walk proper, see? Mebbe I'll find someone to give 'im an 'ome. Until then, he's company.'

William knew he should insist on the puppy's being left; the man had quite enough to do to get himself down to the coast. But what the hell? He looked into the ugly, battered face and saw, detachedly, that the bright little eyes shone with trust as clear and in a way as endearing as the light in the puppy's eyes. He patted the fellow's shoulder and handed him a mug of tea. He knew, of course, what would happen. The soldier knelt, poured the tea into the tin plate which was part of the baggage strapped to his kitbag, and offered it to the dog, which drank thirstily and with relish. William, without being asked, refilled the mug. Then he watched as the small, square figure made its way once more into the jostling throng crowding down towards the coast. Not pushing or shoving, not asking for a lift or leaning on a friendly shoulder; just getting on with it, one foot in front of the other. Going home. Me and my dog.

It had been an odd experience, holding that bridge as the weary armies streamed over it. On other roads there would be other bridges, with other men, just like him perhaps, holding them. His company was searching farm vehicles, interrogating anyone who looked as though he might be a German spy, and checking on the passing equipment. The stream, by now, was becoming a trickle. Presently, at dusk, the trickle too ceased, and William decided it was time to blow the bridge. The river was in a natural dip in the ground, so it would not be an easy place to defend, particularly by night. The sappers were told to go ahead, everyone withdrew to a safe distance, and presently, with a muffled bang far less impressive than William had expected, the ancient and beautiful bridge had a gaping hole in it and the river was clogged with masonry for a moment before the water bore it further downstream.

He sent a messenger back to the small château which had been chosen as their headquarters to ask if they should now retreat, but to his surprise they were ordered to dig themselves in on the ridge. They were to remain out of sight and ambush any Germans who tried to cross there.

They were lucky with the terrain, as it happened, and were able to make themselves comfortable in a thicket halfway up the gentle slope. There was a cottage just behind the ridge which they could fall back on if the enemy managed to get across the river despite their fire from above. William hoped, however, that they would not be driven to such lengths. The cottage was deserted, but a few chickens still scratched about in the yard and by the kennel a dog lay, dead, stiff-legged. William remembered the private with the puppy and swallowed. This dog was full-grown and not particularly prepossessing, big and rather mangy with its lips still pulled back in a snarl over yellowing teeth. Yet it seemed a terrible thing that it should have been shot still chained, unable to run, only doing its duty in menacing anyone who walked into its owner's yard and tried to approach its owner's home.

If I feel like that about a dog, William caught himself wondering, what shall I feel like if I see a dead German? Or a dead anyone, come to that. It occurred to him then that he might find himself, despite all the training, unable when it came to the point to kill. He pictured a man in his twenties with a cowlick of blond hair falling over his forehead and a smile on his lips as he thought about a sweetheart at home, or the meal he was about to enjoy, or his child. Could he cry 'stop' to all that? The patter of heartbeat, the tick of the pulse, the quiet surge of the bloodstream? To say nothing of the dreams, the thoughts and fancies, of another intelligent human being?

He could not answer his own question. He could only wait and hope that he would not be put to the test.

The night wore on, moonlit, quiet, and then they heard a scuffling, as of feet approaching quietly along the sunken summer lane which led to the round-backed, double-arched bridge.

William, lying next to Sergeant Petter, stiffened, and knew that they had all seen, in the moonlight, four men coming up the lane. Tired, dusty, their uniforms tattered and almost unidentifiable in the silver and black of the light and shadow, they made their way slowly to the bridge, not at first realising that it had been destroyed. One of them, a shorter man, was heavily bandaged about the head and was walking with the assistance of two of the others and with a couple of sticks. He looked deathly tired. Wounded men, being slower on their feet than the other soldiers, were bound to find themselves unfairly penalised by obstructions such as blown bridges intended to foil the enemy.

The four men conferred, then lumbered down to the water's edge. The water swirled, oily and treacherous, narrowing to rush even faster between the massive piles which supported what was left of the bridge. Yet it was probably the best place to cross, if only they could somehow get their wounded companion over.

One of the four men raised his head. His voice came to them, softly, above the splashing of the river.

'Hi, anyone over there? Any chance of giving us a hand? My mate's injured and he can't swim.'

The sergeant was on his feet and out of the thicket before William had done more than get up on his elbow. Petter must have realised that the four would need assistance. Private Allyn, a cheerful, chatty fellow whose main interest in life was football, was right on Petter's heels. William stayed where he was. Two of them should be quite enough. If they could not get the chaps over they could call for assistance. He and the rest of the company would stay here just in case someone else came down the lane.

The two men, with Petter in the lead, were right on the margin of the river when the night-silence was shattered. A roar, a whistling shriek, a guttural cry choked off short, and Petter lay on the ground in a pool of black, his head half blown away. Young Allyn came galloping back, snorting with fear as a horse snorts, one arm hanging useless and blood dappling his fingers and the ground beneath him as he fled.

William, on his knees, was still wondering what the hell was happening when he saw that the injured soldier was running back up the road quite as fast as his three companions, bandages and sticks forgotten. Almost before he knew what he was doing he had cuddled the rifle against his cheek, had fanned the barrel as coldly and calculatingly as ever he had done on the ranges back home, and was watching the Germans drop. One spun, the smile still fixed on his face, and fell heavily on to the moon-bright dust. Another fell across him. The third lasted perhaps three paces more before he, too, fell. In the silence, a limb twitched. Then, nothing. The fourth man seemed to have disappeared.

One of the men turned to him, his face white and shocked in the pale light.

'You got 'em, sir,' he whispered. 'Cunning buggers, ain't they?'

There was reluctant admiration on his face; William did not know whether it was for his shooting or for the cunning of the buggers. But he nodded and went carefully over to see what could be done for Allyn.

They stayed by their ambush until they were recalled to the château, and it was there, as he was sitting in the kitchen having breakfast and drinking coffee with three fellow officers, that it struck William for the first time that the challenge had arisen and been faced. He had killed. Not three rifle-range shapes, though they had been somewhat unreal in the moonlight, but three flesh and blood human beings. They had tried to lure out anyone in hiding by a despicable trick, to clear the ground so that their own platoon could cross the river. They had been brave men, and one of them at least had spoken English as well as William himself. And had it been such a despicable trick? Not really. More fools they, to have fallen for it. Poor Petter had died because his officer had not realised that it was a trick – if he felt any guilt, it should be over Petter. Petter was the best sort of sergeant for someone like William, because he was an old soldier who understood in fact what William only knew about in theory. Soldiering, to Petter, was real, earnest, a way of life. And, now, a way of death.

William stared at his plate. The eggs, astonishingly, still looked appetising, the fried tomatoes did not make him think of blood or wounds but of fried tomatoes, which he had always enjoyed. He ate stolidly on, finishing up with toast and butter and two big mugs of coffee.

He thought about Petter, of course, but he knew that the older man would not have blamed him. He could almost hear Petter's self-disgust: 'Fooled by a bunch of Krauts,' he would have said. 'Blimey, what a mug! That'll larn me!'

It comforted William all through the trek down to the coast, herding his company through crowds of panic-stricken French soldiers throwing down their arms and tearing off their uniforms, anxious only to get back to their homes and pretend they had never taken up arms against the Germans. They jeered at the English, told them they were fools who would soon be beaten, but the Tommies, for the most part, took it well. Besides, there were other French troops deeply ashamed of what their comrades were doing and saying. They were struggling to the coast as well, anxious to re-form their regiments in Britain and start fighting once more.

Until they reached the long beaches at Dunkirk, William managed to keep his company together. But once in the dunes, desperately tired, thirsty, very hungry, it was inevitable that to a certain extent it should become every man for himself. All you could do was remain hidden while the bombing and shelling were heaviest, and then make for the sea, join the shortest queue you could see, or the nearest, or the one that seemed to be getting picked up the fastest, and then wait. And pray.

'I swear I've never seen anything like it!' Simon's face was shadowed with weariness and the strain of long hours of flying. His hair stood on end where he had raked his fingers through it, but his eyes gleamed with remembered excitement. 'The sky over Dunkirk is black with Jerry, black with 'em! We did our best, but eight of us . . . well, we did our best. But those poor devils down there, on the ships, on the beaches . . . I don't see how the hell we're going to get 'em all off.'

'We? You proposin' to fly *that* low, Simon?'

There was a burst of laughter from the pilots lounging in the mess, exhausted though they were. One of them, Sawyer, who had flown with Simon that day, stood up and stretched.

'Don't answer that, fella! I'm going to get some shut-eye, and you'd better do the same if you want to be able to see a Hun at five paces tomorrow. As for it being impossible to get 'em all off, they weren't doing so badly today. The ships were loaded down to the plimsoll line, and of course some of 'em were being sunk, but others were getting through. What's the date? I've lost track.'

'First of June,' someone said. 'Why? Don't say you forgot to wish!'

More laughter, though the heart was going out of it.

'I just wondered when the evacuation will finish, that's all. I thought someone forecast they'd all be off by June.'

'Well, they aren't,' Simon said positively, heading for the door. 'I've cousins and uncles down there, so I want to see the very last one picked up. But I am tired.'

'If Roses are at risk, I suppose we ought to fly double shifts,' a ginger-haired youth said languidly. 'I know what you mean by the skies being black with 'em, though. I read about the Blitzkrieg on Spain back in the 'thirties, and then on Poland and Belgium, but I never thought it would be as fearful as it is. Just wave after wave of planes, the bombers dropping their eggs and the fighters strafing everything that moves. You can't help dreading what would happen if they turned it on England – on somewhere like London.'

'Oh, they won't,' Simon said easily, still lounging in the doorway. 'Too far, for a start. Anyway, think what a bad press it would give them to fire on London, capital of Europe! The Yanks wouldn't like that at all at all!'

'Well, we'll see,' Sawyer said. 'Come on, Rose. I could sleep for a week, but a few hours will have to do.'

Simon followed Sawyer out and went to his own small room, where he drew the curtains across the darkening sky and fell heavily into bed. As soon as his head touched the pillow, however, the tiredness that had so overwhelmed him seemed to lift and he knew the familiar dread of a sleepless night, in the course of which he would fight every air battle of the day over and over again. He had a small bottle of aspirin by the bed and wondered whether he should take a couple to help him to sleep. The trouble was, he was afraid they might combine with his very real exhaustion to do their job too well, so that he would not have woken up properly when the time came to take off the next morning. It would be a nightmare to find oneself up in the air and not one hundred per cent effective and efficient. Yet if he just lay here he might end up thinking about Nick. Nick was his cousin and best friend, his partner in the pre-war world in a car and bus hire firm; and now he was soldiering somewhere in France. Perhaps on one of those bloody beaches, looking up and cursing when he saw the weary, hopelessly outnumbered aircraft turning for England once more. Or he might be at sea, dodging U-boats, wrecks, enemy shipping. Or . . .

He tried to banish the thoughts, but they persisted. He had never been cursed with a too-vivid imagination – he left that to Nick – but now, as if real terrors were not sufficient, imaginary ones reared up their ugly heads to haunt him as well. Frank, too, was out there in some horrible little pleasure cruiser he had borrowed. He'd be in the thick of it, would Frank. He'd rung home at the weekend and been told that Frank had gone and not returned, but that meant nothing; small boats didn't go back and forth, they stayed to ferry troops from the shore to the deeper water where the big ships lay. Frank would be all right.

And now that he thought about it, Cyril would probably be hovering off Dunkirk, too. Cyril was in the navy, on a destroyer. Several destroyers had gone. Suppose . . . He grabbed his imagination and tried to put it on a stricter rein. This was ridiculous. Cyril would be all right; of course he would! But it was impossible to sponge from the memory the sight of Dunkirk harbour as he had seen it that morning from the air. A graveyard for ships, that was what it had looked like. Masts sticking up in shoal water; the great grey bulk of big vessels lying beneath the surface of the waves clearly visible to Simon from on high. He could not count the forest of masts, the funnels, the heaps of debris which piled up on the beach at each low tide and lay there until high water floated it off again.

Could they get them off? Was it possible that, after this, there would be sufficient men to defend Britain, sufficient ships to keep the channel safe, to fend off invasion attempts? Simon's hand reached out for the aspirin bottle, and he shook two tablets into his hand. Even if he did wake up a bit muzzy, anything was better than lying here worrying!

He swallowed the tablets and almost immediately sank into sleep.

'Fancy seeing you, Uncle Frank!' Cyril stared in unconcealed astonishment at the grimy, weary man in the faded and filthy boiler suit who stood before him on the deck of his ship. 'I didn't know you'd joined the senior service!'

They were going home. It was the third of June and the beaches were bare, waiting for the gulls to return, and the other sea-birds. The skies were empty, though, as if the gulls had abandoned them to those other, larger birds which had roared and screamed and strafed for days and days.

In vain. Did they know it, yet? Did they know the marvellous fact that most of the BEF had been evacuated, that the ones who were left, floating or drowned deep, had not died without reason? The BEF was almost all home, the remnants were going over now, and Britain would live to fight another day. But here, on the deck of the destroyer *Viper*, Frank wiped his hand across his eyes and tried to focus on the tall, cotton-topped figure in front of him.

'I'm sorry . . . is that you, Cyril?'

'Just about. You're worn out, Uncle Frank. You ought to rest. But what in hell are you doing here? You're in a reserved occupation. You should be at home building boats for us.'

'I've been bringing 'em off, same as you. I had a cruiser, but she went hours ago – or was it days? Since then we've been aboard anything where we could give a hand – me and Ben, that is.'

Cyril turned and recognised Ben Coates, despite the grime and the odd assortment of garments. He shook the older man's hand.

'Hello, Mr Coates! Where's Donnie?'

It was a natural enough question, for the two had been inseparable, but he wished he had not asked it as he saw Ben's face change and become cold and secret.

'Went down with the cruiser, Mr Cyril. Is there any chance of a cuppa? We're dying for one.'

'I'll take you down to the mess,' Cyril said quickly. 'I'm terribly sorry about Donnie, Mr Coates. He was a good son to you.'

He had never felt worse, never wished more passionately that he was the sort of person who could be easily overlooked, but a lanky blond of six foot two inches becomes used to standing out in a crowd. But Uncle Frank understood. He took over the burden of conversation, tired though he must have been, telling Cyril that they had raised the *Gay Times* once but had had to abandon her when she sank for the second time.

Escaping from them, Cyril went back to his duties, but the thought of Donnie's death lay heavy on him. Donnie was an innocent soul who had hurt no one. He was not fighting in this wretched war – he knew nothing about such things – he was saving lives, and in so doing, he had lost his own.

He knew, too, why Ben's face had closed at the mention of Donnie. Ben must know that some people would say the boy's death was a mercy. They would reason that in the normal course of things Ben could not have expected to outlive his son, and what would have become of Donnie, alone? Young though he was, Cyril saw that such an argument could only hurt Ben. The pain of his loss was now, and the sharing of that loss was the only way to ease it. There could be no comfort in attributing Donnie's death to the hand of Providence.

Chapter Four

Val drove the ambulance carefully along the narrow suburban road. She was tired, and when one was tired it was as well to be careful. The woman sitting beside her, who was the wrong side of fifty, must be even more tired, but she was bearing up very well. Now, she glanced across at Val.

'If you take the next left-hand turn, my dear, I live in the third house along. Then, if you continue, the road curves back on to the main road we've just left.'

It was a decidedly 'county' voice, but Val had worked with Mrs Fletcher for a whole week, and knew that this was the sort of woman the ambulance service needed. She had come forward with an offer of help because she 'knew first-aid', but in the event she had been far more useful than a mere first-aider. Full of commonsense, brisk, cheerful, with an inborn knowledge of how to get what she wanted, she had helped Val to bring her ambulance to just where it was most needed, been wonderful to the men they had taken to various hospitals, and then, when the lines of weary troops had gradually dwindled, had insisted that she and Val were put up in a house in Dover so that they could get a good night's sleep before tackling the return drive to London.

Now, as her new friend climbed down from the ambulance, Val leaned forward, a hand held out.

'Goodbye, Mrs Fletcher, and thank you. I can't think of a living soul I'd rather have with me in an emergency than you! You're wasted on your nice husband and your teenage sons, so if you ever decide you want to help on the ambulances, just get in touch with my boss.'

Mrs Fletcher, greying hair determinedly permed, fresh complexion going rosier with pleasure, shook Val's hand vigorously.

'I'm determined to do more than I manage at present. It's rather shameful to admit it, but I've enjoyed this past week more than you could imagine! Doing a real job, being really useful . . . well, you can't waste time worrying when there are so many real problems confronting you!'

'True. You've got my phone number, so if you do want work you can always get in touch. Lucky that we live so close.'

She watched Mrs Fletcher arrive at her front door, fumble with the key and then disappear inside before starting up the engine and driving off down the road. She sighed, settled herself in her seat, and allowed her mind to dwell on her own imminent arrival home. A huge pot of tea, from which she would take many cups; a large meal – she would not weep if she never saw another sandwich – and a hot bath. In what order she wanted these things she did not know, only that she wanted them. And would get them, no doubt. Jenny was a very good cook and ran their little flat beautifully. She worked hard, too, at being a good mother to Marianne, at housekeeping, and at running the car and bus hire firm which Nick, Val's twin, and Simon had started before the war. It was different now, of course, since it was often a borough or some government department which hired the buses, and Jenny combined looking after the firm with a good deal of telephone answering and unofficial liaison with the ambulance service. Two ambulances, the one Val was driving and another, were now kept in the big garage beneath the flats. Richie, who was chief mechanic to the firm of Neyler & Rose, drove the ambulance on a shift system, and when Val had volunteered he had taken her in hand, teaching her London patiently, night after night, allowing her to go with him when he was driving for a hire, until she began to know the streets almost as well as he did.

But until the Dunkirk evacuation there had been very little work for her, other than routine and standard trips. She had taken old people and children to day-clinics, delivered one or two emergencies with her blue light flashing, and picked up folk who had been treated but were not yet up to struggling with public transport. It had been fun – there were several intelligent and amusing young women who for one reason or another were tied to London and so had volunteered to drive ambulances – and she did not regret her decision since it meant that she was at the flat a good deal with Jenny. But sometimes, in the night, she woke to find herself fighting a dreadful trapped feeling. Why me, she wanted to shout. Why me? Before the war she had been forced by circumstance to stay in Norwich with her mother, because Tina could not face living alone at The Pride after her husband died. In those days Val's dearest wish had been to live in London with Jenny, Simon and Nick, and to help with their business. But now that she was doing it she still felt dissatisfied. She would have preferred to join one of the women's services, be posted abroad, perhaps, do something really useful for the war effort, instead of helping Jenny to run the business and driving tamely around London for the ambulance service.

However, it was silly to be discontented. Perhaps one day ambulance-driving in London would not be so tame, and she would feel she was doing something every bit as useful as plotting aircraft, like Maude, or ferrying fat generals from one barracks to another, or being a typist or a telephonist, albeit snugly fitted up in uniform.

She drove into Granville Gardens and tooted once, glancing up at the end flat above the garages. A hand waved briefly and she waved back, then drew her ambulance to a halt beside the other one, got out, slammed the door, and made for the stairs.

The bottom door could be shut and locked but rarely was, except at night. Now it stood open and she shambled through it and up the stairs, suddenly aware of how very tired she was. She was even grateful that she did not have to get out her doorkey at the top – such a physical challenge, to turn a key in a lock! – but could simply walk through it, as Jenny, smiling broadly, held it open for her.

'Val, you must be utterly worn out! But I understand from the newspapers and the wireless that you've done it. The boys are home, and I keep thinking of all *our* boys, and being so very grateful.'

She ushered Val into the kitchen and Val flopped into the shabby old wing chair near the stove.

'Thanks, Jen. Is the kettle on? Oh, you *wonderful* girl, that tea is just what I've been dreaming of for the past hour!' Val drank the tea, hot though it was, in large, thirsty gulps, then held out her cup for refilling. 'Crumbs, that was good! Yes, we've done it. They're home – jolly nearly all of 'em, I should think, from the number we saw. Now, get me up to date on *our* boys!'

'Ah, well, Frank came back, and Ben Coates. Donnie was drowned – wasn't that horrible, Val? – when the cruiser went down the first time. It was worse because some French soldiers got on board although Frank and Ben told them not to, and it just sank. Ben didn't realise that Donnie had gone down to the cabin to get some sleep. He thought he was on the deck of the mother ship, or that's how I heard it. When they got the cruiser up again they found him.'

'That's awful,' Val murmured, drinking tea. 'I'm glad

Frank's back; as brothers go, he's one of the best. I suppose you haven't heard from Nick?'

'Well, no, not in person. But Frank said he did meet someone who knew Nick, and the chap told him he'd seen Nick taken off, though he couldn't say which boat. So that sounds hopeful, doesn't it?'

Val murmured something noncommittal. No one who had watched the troops disembarking and listened to their stories could have considered that particularly hopeful, but she could scarcely say so to Jenny. One batch of men told her that they had been bombed out of their first craft, the second one had been in a collision and had sunk, and the third had been so badly strafed that it had only just made harbour. They could give her little idea how many men had been lost, but knew that it had been a heavy tally.

'Were the men relieved to be back? I bet they're longing to get at the enemy again, show them we don't scare that easily,' Jenny said. She handed Val a thick round of toast and butter. 'Cheer up, love. It says in the papers that the men are cheerful, but I suppose you saw the worst side of it.'

Again, Val murmured noncommittally, then changed her mind. She bit into the toast and spoke, rather thickly, through her first mouthful.

'Cheerful? The press must be mad, or keen propagandists, to say that! As for tackling the Hun, I think the fellows would rather get their hands round the throats of whoever sent them over there and whoever brought them back in such disarray! Oh, I don't deny it's wonderful that we *did* get so many back, but if the planning had been better, if the top brass had known more about the German strength and the way wars are fought now, the men need never have gone! You should have heard them, Jenny! Old-fashioned equipment and not enough of it, and just about all of that left behind for the enemy to use!

Contradictory orders, a shambles . . . They're not thrilled with the way things have been handled. They're bitter, fed-up, browned-off.'

'Yes, but . . . you must have got the men who'd had it hardest,' Jenny said, unwilling to forgo her picture of brave and bright-eyed Tommies swearing vengeance on Jerry. 'Surely there were others who realised that we'd done our best? Perhaps more intelligent ones . . . men who can see more clearly that we had to *try*, just to show them . . .'

Her voice trailed off uncertainly. Val finished her toast, laughed, and got to her feet. She gave Jenny a quick hug.

'Poor old Jen, illusions shattered! I had one chap – he came up front, actually, to guide me to the hospital – who said it was a good sign. In all the wars Britain has fought and won, he said, we've always started with a retreat. Very heartening if you're a historian, I suppose, but for the ordinary Tommy, seeing his mates slaughtered . . . well, it's a lot more difficult to take a detached view. Mind if I go and get myself bathed? Oh, by the way, what's smelling so good in the oven? And where's my best girl?'

Jenny laughed and returned the hug.

'To take your questions in order of importance, Mari is in bed and asleep, there's a beef stew with jacket potatoes in the oven, and you can have a bath with pleasure! Only don't take too long over it, because I don't want the food getting dried up and it'll be absolutely perfect in about fifteen minutes.'

'Don't worry, I'll be quick.'

Val ran the bath deep and hot, cast down her dirty clothing, and jumped into the water. She was in the middle of rinsing off the soap and telling herself how good it was to be clean when the doorbell rang. She listened, and heard a familiar voice. Richie! He, too, had been helping to get the men home, though he had been driving the big blue bus. She crashed out of the bath, wrapped a towel round herself and charged through into the kitchen. Richie, drinking tea, raised startled eyes at her entrance, then grinned.

'Hello, Val. You got back first, then? Well done, my woman. I popped back in here 'fore going in to Minnie because I thought you'd like to know I seen Mr Nick. He weren't on my bus – he was with the Norfolks, I reckon – but he said he was fit an' well, though tired, like they all were.'

Val heaved an enormous sigh and pressed her hands to her cheeks. She grinned at Richie, though tears filled her eyes and overflowed on to her fingers.

'Thank God! Bless you, Richie, for putting me out of my misery! If you and Minnie will come round, later, we'll have a drink to celebrate.'

'We'd be glad to.' Richie headed for the kitchen door, then turned back, lively curiosity shining from his seamed brown face. 'Say, Val, didn't you know, like, that Mr Nick was safe? Like they say twins know about each other?'

'I don't think Nick and I are that sort of twins. We tried, when he was away at school, to pass messages, sort of, but it never really worked. I did wonder if . . . but I suppose you can't tell until it happens. Nick broke his arm once, ice-skating, and I never felt a thing, didn't have any sort of premonition that all wasn't well with him. No, I think we're probably closer than an ordinary brother and sister, but we've missed out on that special sort of closeness you read about. I needed to know he was all right; I couldn't sense it.'

She saw Richie out, and then, passing the small room where Marianne slept, was halted in her tracks by a brisk hail.

'Vally, Vally, I hear you! I'm awake, I am!'

'Oh, Mari darling, you should have been sound asleep

63

and dreaming,' Val said, crossing the bedroom in a couple of swift strides and picking up the sleeping-suited Marianne. 'What will Mummy say?' She cuddled the baby's warm little body close and kissed her all over her face while Marianne giggled and snuggled. 'Shall we go into the kitchen and see?'

'Ess, ess, ess,' Marianne remarked, bouncing, as they crossed the corridor. 'Mummy mum mummy mum!'

As she re-entered the kitchen the telephone shrilled and Jenny, passing them in the doorway, gave her erring child a quick kiss before going to answer it.

'Who's a pest?' she remarked over her shoulder. 'Marianne Elizabeth Rose is a pest! I suppose you'll want some supper?'

Marianne stopped bouncing for a moment, apparently to consider the question seriously. Val held her over the high chair and raised her brows.

'Well, miss? Do you want some supper or don't you?'

'Ess, ess, ess,' Marianne decided. She was obviously in high good humour, for she made no demur at being slipped into the chair and strapped in as well. Val, with nightmare memories of the time she had walked into the kitchen and found Jenny at the sink, Simon hunkered down trying to unscrew the S-bend to clear an obstruction and Marianne, then a mere eight months old, standing, swaying precariously, about to climb over the side of her high chair, never forgot her straps.

Val, having dealt with the baby, dropped the towel and picked up her silk dressing-gown, sliding into it just as Jenny returned from the hall.

'That was Simon,' she announced; not that Val needed telling. One look at her friend's shining eyes and the smile that curved her lips had told her the identity of the caller. 'He's coming home for a couple of days, since he's been on pretty constant call. Isn't that nice?'

'Mm hmm, lovely. Can I get the casserole out?'

'Yes, sure.' Jenny added her daughter's little pottery plate to the two already on the table. 'Perhaps it's a good thing Mari woke, in fact, since she just played around at teatime and she's probably quite hungry.'

'Like me,' Val said. She sat down in her place as Jenny began to dish out. 'Shall I mash the babe's helping? I'm rather good at that. I forgot to ask, is Simon bringing Laddy?'

Laddy was a tall, skinny, rather serious young Polish fighter pilot to whom Simon had taken a liking. Laddy was always happy to come to the young Roses' home for leaves, since he had few friends in England, and the last few times he had visited them he had taken Val out; to the cinema, to a concert, to the zoo. Now they exchanged letters and the odd telephone call. Jenny approved, Val knew, so she did not tell her friend that much as she liked Laddy her feeling for him stopped there. She had no desire for a greater degree of involvement; might never have encouraged his friendship had it not been for his obvious loneliness and for the fact that she knew Simon and Jenny felt rather guilty in their own happiness when she was playing gooseberry at home.

But now Jenny stopped, her spoon poised.

'Oh, damn. I was so pleased at the thought of seeing Simon that I didn't ask! But it must be no, or he'd have said. Simon's thoughtful about things like that. Laddy's quite all right,' she added hastily. 'Simon told me no one else had bought it since he last phoned, and Laddy was fine then.'

'It's all right. I don't mind Laddy not coming. In fact, it will be quite a relief. I'm dog-tired and don't feel very entertaining,' Val said quickly. 'Is this cool enough for Mari, do you think?'

After that, the three of them concentrated on their food

65

for a time, Jenny and Val taking it in turns to assist Marianne's wobbling spoon while that young lady kept up the fairly constant babble that so surprised strangers, who did not expect a child of sixteen months to talk at all. But by the time they reached the pudding stage, and Jenny was dishing out delicious syrup roll, Marianne's chatter was becoming slower and slower, like a gramophone winding down, and she began to rub her eyes and show a tendency to suck a curly thumb instead of her spoon.

'I think bed is called for,' Jenny remarked, as Marianne's head leaned for a moment against the back of the chair and showed no disposition to move again. 'Shan't be a tick.'

She whisked her child out of the chair and carried her from the kitchen, advising Val, over her shoulder, to 'dig in'. Val, doing so, did not hear the front door open, but she heard Jenny's squeak of delight, then a deep, teasing voice she knew well; so she was not surprised when, presently, the door opened and husband and wife entered the kitchen, arms round each other, faces bright.

'Guess who's here, Val? He came sneaking up the stairs so quietly that I didn't hear a thing until his key turned in the lock.' Jenny detached herself from Simon's embrace and hurried over to the table. 'You must be starving, pet. There's plenty of stew – I kept it hot – and there are your favourite potatoes, and we won't eat every bit of the pudding, so you can even have some of that!'

Simon returned Val's greeting, then leaned over and kissed her, rumpling her hair, still wet from the bath and curling tightly.

'Hello, little coz! Sorry Laddy couldn't come, but he's on call today. When he comes off I'm due back, so I don't suppose you'll see him for a fortnight or so.'

'Oh, well, as I was saying to Jen, I'm pretty tired myself,' Val was beginning, when a thought struck her. 'I say, Simon, how long are you off for?'

'Ages. Well, four days. Why?'

'Because I'm off, and Nick will be, and probably there are lots of chaps home in Norwich now. I wondered . . . I've still got some petrol. I thought I might take myself back to The Pride for a bit. I'd love to see Nick and hear how he got on.'

'Good idea,' Simon said. His glance was approving, but something more. Knowing? Did Simon, on whom she had once had such a huge crush, understand how hard it was, sometimes, for her to be here with him and Jenny? When she had no one of her own she could clutch and cry over? She thought that perhaps Simon did have an inkling – though of course it was possible that he was more concerned over the fact that he and Jenny could not behave quite as uninhibitedly as they might otherwise do while she was in the flat.

'I could go down first thing tomorrow, or I could even go tonight,' Val was saying, when Simon glanced at his watch and leaned over to turn the wireless on. 'Oh, sorry, it's newstime. Is Mr Churchull going to say something tonight?'

Simon, twiddling the dial, nodded.

'That's right, only Jenny's had the set on some wretched music station, haven't you, love? Ah . . .'

A voice which the nation was beginning to know and to love more than any other spoke over the crackling air.

'. . . we shall defend our Island, whatever the cost may be. We shall fight on the beaches, we shall fight on the landing-grounds, we shall fight in the fields and in the streets, we shall fight on the hills; we shall never surrender.'

After the speech, there was a short silence; then Val leaned forward and clicked the wireless off. Her eyes shone with unshed tears and she suspected that she was not the only person in the room so moved.

'Well!' she said softly into the silence. 'That's telling 'em!'

'Who was it on the phone, Mother?'

Beryl's permanently pallid, worried face turned anxiously as Tina came back into the study. Tina crossed the room and picked up her knitting again. She smiled at her daughter-in-law, trying not to show the irritation she felt. Why did the woman always sound as though she expected the worst, for goodness sake? But there. It was a part of her nature, and, contrary to what people so frequently supposed, it was not always possible to change one's nature.

'It was Val, dear, asking whether we'd had any news from Mabel. When she was down here there was still quite a lot of hope, but now . . . oh well, I keep telling myself that Mabel may yet surprise us all. The door might open and she might walk in, large as life. We must all keep cheerful, that's what I tell poor Ada.'

'That's what you kept saying about Cara's William,' Beryl reminded her mother-in-law with considerable lack of tact. 'It isn't always sensible to be too optimistic, that's what I always say. If you face the worst . . .'

Tina let her continue because, over William, she had been so resoundingly proved wrong. That very morning she had been busy telling Cara not to make a fuss, that William would walk in at the door presently and laugh at his wife's long face, when the doorbell had sounded.

A boy, it was, no more than fifteen or sixteen, who asked for Cara. When he was ushered into the living-room, where they were all assembled, he had handed her a small package wrapped in newspaper which Cara undid with trembling fingers, to reveal William's heavy gold wristwatch.

'It's awright,' the boy had assured her. 'Me dad come back from France three days ago. Someone 'ad give it 'im, asked 'im to pass it on to you with love. 'E was all right, the feller wot give it 'im.'

'Then why did he give away his watch?' Cara wailed, her big brown eyes filling with easy tears. 'Oh, Auntie Tina, what does it mean?'

Tina turned to the boy.

'Come along, there must have been some message! Why did Mr Dopmann not come home himself? Was he wounded?'

'I dunno,' the boy said uneasily, sounding sulky when driven into a corner. 'It weren't the feller that owned the watch wot give it to me dad. It was anuvver feller wot 'ad 'ad it off of someone else.'

Tina, realising that they would get nothing more out of the boy since he knew nothing himself, took him off into the kitchen for a meal. Des, who was off duty for once, then ran him back to Thorpe Station. He went clutching a five-pound note, for Des, at least, was fully alive to the service the boy had rendered them by coming all the way down from Poplar, wherever that might be, to Norwich to hand over the watch in person.

Going down to the station in the car, Desmond had asked a few more casual questions and managed to piece together a little more of the story.

'You women frightened him, pouncing on him like that,' he told them reproachfully on his return. 'From what he told me, I think William was wounded. Not seriously, Cara, so don't start wailing. He was obviously in control of himself since he gave the fellow not only the watch but also your name and this address, which he wouldn't have remembered if he'd been gravely ill. The trouble was the chap he gave the watch to was killed, only fortunately he had told someone else of his trust, and that chap took the watch off him, wrapped in a bit of paper with Cara's name and address on it, and gave it to this lad's father. When he got home he persuaded his son to bring it straight down to us, which was pretty good, I thought.'

'But why? Why didn't William keep the watch?' Cara said shrilly. 'I don't understand it at all!'

'If he was wounded he would have been put into hospital over there. The boy said they weren't even trying to get the wounded off because the Huns were bombing the hospital ships. And hospitals aren't always the most honest of places, not when you've got a mixture of different nationalities in 'em.'

'Oh. Will the Germans send him back, then? I mean, what good will he be to them?'

'They might,' Desmond said rather guardedly. 'Or they might put him in a prisoner of war camp. But he'll be all right, you mark my words.'

Later, however, when Cara had gone to see a film with some friend or other, he and Tina were able to discuss other theories.

'That watch was valuable, all right, but it was something else, too. It was dangerous,' Desmond reminded his mother. 'It was the one his father gave him for his Bar Mitzvah. So he wouldn't want to be picked up by the Huns with that on his wrist, all engraved.'

Tina's face had blanched, for she had helped Jewish refugees from Germany before the war, and knew more than most what sufferings Hitler had inflicted even on German Jews.

'Could *that* be why . . . oh, Desmond, I really rather hope you're right, because I'd thought of something far worse. I thought that perhaps William had been so badly wounded that they had had to take his arm off and he had no further use for the watch.'

Desmond shook his head at her and then gave her an indulgent hug.

'Mama, your imagination always runs riot, given the slightest opportunity! Losing an arm, indeed! You mark

70

my words, it was the engraving on the back which persuaded William to part with it.'

'Well, I shall be very glad to be proved wrong on this occasion,' Tina said. 'When shall we get real news of William, though, Des? Surely they'll let us know what has happened to him?' She had grown very fond of Cara's husband, admiring the way he handled her spoilt little niece.

'I'll ask some questions tomorrow,' Desmond promised her. 'I'll ring Con this evening, for a start. I bet he can find something out for us at the War Office. Oh, by the way, Auntie Ray rang earlier. She's bringing a cold roast chicken and coming round for supper. She wants to see the conquering hero, which I take it means Nick.'

So now, knitting in the study while Beryl struggled to make a khaki balaclava helmet, Tina decided that they had been very lucky. Nick was back safe, and Frank, and her favourite sister was coming to supper. It was very sad that Mabel was still in France, but she was as good as French, after all, and her homecoming, Tina could not help thinking, might have proved rather complicated. William, on the other hand, was a great loss, but at least he was all right!

'I think,' she said presently, 'that after dinner we might play a little bridge. Those of us who are interested. I daresay Nick will want to go chasing off somewhere.'

'That would be very nice,' Beryl said dutifully. She was not a bridge player. 'What about dinner, Mother? Shouldn't we be in the kitchen starting the cooking?'

Tina stared a little indignantly at the younger woman over the top of her glasses. As if she would be sitting here, calmly knitting, were not preparations for dinner well in hand! Oh, dear, would Beryl never learn to use her head?

'Mrs Walters is there now, with Ruthie, preparing salads to go with the cold chicken – ours, as well as Ray's.

I've managed to make a very acceptable shrimp and crab meat pâté to start the meal, and we're having strawberries and cream for pudding. We've got enough strawberries to feed an army, thanks to Mr Walters's netting, but sugar might be a problem. However, I've been hoarding icing sugar ever since the phoney war in 'thirty-eight, so if ordinary sugar fails we can always fall back on that. Even so, I'll have enough icing sugar to ice cakes for the whole family for a decade or so.'

'I thought it was wrong to hoard,' Beryl said faintly. 'I thought Mr Morrison said . . .'

'Did you, dear? Well, it may be wrong now, but when I did it it was sensible.' Tina spoke with unrepentant satisfaction; it was so nice to see one's foresight pay off! 'So we shall have an excellent dinner, dear, without you having to put yourself out at all.'

Briskly, Tina cast off. She was knitting – at popular request, she told herself ruefully – the sort of gloves that the government seemed to think the soldiery would be most comfortable in, though God knew why: the sort that got called mittens though they were certainly no such thing, but had only half-fingers and a half-thumb on each hand. Just enough, she thought perplexedly, to ensure that the wearers were never really cosy; but if that was what the army wanted . . .

Tina began to cast on a second glove.

'Mum? Come on, my old darling, I can't bear to see you like this! Look, you're upsetting me, and you'll upset Dad, and, to be blunt, Paul would be furious to see you making yourself ill in this way, you know he would.'

Say Butcher could see herself in the little round mirror above the fireplace. She was old. Yesterday she had been middle-aged, but today, with the knowledge that the telegram had brought her, she was old. Yesterday she had

had a loving husband, two good sons, and lots of friends. Today, they had told her that her boy was dead. Paul. Her baby. Some soldiers had seen him shot by the Germans. Dead. Paul, who was so good and cheerful, such a comfort as a son, who had a nice little girlfriend waiting for him. She would have to tell Anna. Dead. Paul. Her baby.

'Mum?' James's voice was deeply concerned, full of love and understanding. He and Paul had always been close. She clung to his blue uniform coat, wetting the front of it with her tears, trying to tell herself, as James was telling her, that it could have been a mistake, that Paul might not be dead, might just be hurt. In a few days perhaps they would write again and tell her that Paul was a prisoner and would be home again, some time.

The telegram, you see, she found herself telling Paul, just said 'Missing, presumed dead', but someone had given evidence at some court or other that someone else had claimed to have seen Paul's body in a field near a little village with a pretty name . . . Le Paradis, that was it . . . and that was supposed to convince her.

'Come on, you come over here and sit down,' James said. He settled her in a chair and she heard him begin to make tea. Even through her tears and grief, she could not help smiling a little. How the boys had teased her for her belief in the curative powers of tea! Anything that happened – a hiding from an older boy, the loss of some beloved object, a friend's betrayal – all had been powerless, according to their mother, to withstand the panacea of a cup of tea.

But with the cup in her hand, all Say could do was stare down into the swirling brown depths of the tea. She would have to tell her husband, and Winkie adored Paul. He loved James too, but there had never been any question of Winkie's being James's father. James was her son by her sometime lover, Louis Rose. And Paul? We-ell, Paul had been born in wedlock but conceived out of it, and she had never known, from his conception to this day, whose son he was. But Winkie certainly thought he had fathered Paul. And Louis? It didn't matter much what Louis thought, because he lived in Australia with a young wife and two small daughters. He still wrote, sometimes, but the letters were detached and impersonal. Louis would be conventionally shocked to hear of Paul's death, but he scarcely knew the boy, had probably never spared him a thought these past dozen years.

'Drink it, Mum,' James was urging, and with a rush of affection Say made her first real effort to stem the tears and began to sip the tea. He was a good boy, James. Tall, dark-haired, handsome, with his father's good looks yet totally devoid of that wicked appeal which had made Louis so irresistible. James was responsible, steady, all the things that Louis had not been. Nor I, she thought now, with some wonder, nor I. So how on earth had she produced James? But she loved him, her serious changeling, and for his sake and for Winkie's she would pull herself together now. There would be time enough for weeping.

She had finished the tea and repaired the ravages the tears had wrought by the time the shop door opened and she heard Winkie's heavy footsteps crossing the floor. He came across and into their living-room, pausing for a moment to close the communicating door behind him. He looked old.

Say stood up, forcing herself to smile, determined that she would be good, would help Winkie by being strong. Because he knew. He had gone out that morning looking just as he always did: tanned, cheerful, sure of himself. Broad in the shoulder, upright in carriage. And now he was crumpled and shrunk by the news. He put a hand up to his face, wearily, and she saw that she was not the only one who had shed tears. Then she ran into his arms and knew, in a moment, that he needed her to cry, needed her to give way, so that, in comforting her, he could assuage his own awful, helpless emptiness.

Leaning against him, she began to weep.

Chapter Five

It was very early in the morning, so early that the sun was not yet up, though at thirty thousand feet it was shining on the wings and fuselage of Otto von Eckner's Junkers 88. Below him, Britain lay stretched out like a map, the fields still grey, the rivers pewter, though presently both would spring into vivid life as the sun brought out their colours.

Otto's glance strayed automatically over the fuel gauge, the air speed indicator and the altimeter. He would go higher for a while, then lose height when he was returning to the coast, for this was a photo-reconnaissance flight and he had no wish to be spotted by the fighters on the airfields he had been despatched to record.

I wish I'd visited Britain before the war, Otto thought, as he flew high above the coloured counties. If I had listened to Val, visited her in her home . . . but it was no use wishing. He was German, Val was English, and he had taken his decision. He hated Hitler, but he loved his country. He wanted the war to end, but not to see Germany on her knees because of it. He did not mind reconnaissance flights, though he was practical enough to realise that their purpose might be every bit as deadly as a bombing raid. Anyway, he had his crew to think of. Uri and Hans were his friends, as unimpressed by the Fuehrer as himself, but still fighting for Germany.

The time to worry over the rights and wrongs of it was over; the time had come to fight and to hope that, if Germany conquered, the people in power would put down the madman and bring the country to its senses. I am a tiny cog in a huge wheel, and the wheel is grinding my chance of personal happiness smaller and smaller, he said to himself. Last night he had danced with a beautiful German girl, yellow-haired, blue-eyed, as sweet and wholesome as a freshly baked sponge cake – and just about as intelligent. But she had been cuddly and comfortable in his arms and he knew she would willingly have helped him to pass the night. So why, dammit, could he think of nothing but an English girl, red-haired, green-eyed, with a great many freckles and a mouth the size of a pillar box? Loving her made the war more difficult, divided his loyalties; made it impossible to accept second best in the form of the blonde sponge cake, and it was so thankless!

Loving someone who lived many miles away was hard, but how much worse to love someone separated from you by a war! No day-to-day news, no painfully brief meetings, not even a crackly, oft-interrupted telephone conversation. Only a faded snapshot, a pile of flimsy, out-of-date letters, and the memory of her. Though that was fresh enough. No one who met Val could forget her, Otto thought, and found himself grinning. She was an odd girl, his love, the sort of person who makes an indelible impression either for better or worse. He had heartily disliked her at first, he remembered with astonishment. The English friend of his sister Minna, how gaudy, self-confident, loud she had seemed beside the girl he had thought himself in love with! But his love for Salka, he knew now, had been in a way a sort of rebellion, because it was forbidden to love a Jewish girl; and it had been pity, because he knew what she risked in loving him. And admiration, for her courage in meeting him when she could.

It had not lasted and his great relief had been that she

broke off their understanding and not he. She had written from America, once she was safely there, telling him quite bluntly that she knew they were not suited and that she was engaged to a Jew living in the next apartment block in New York. She wished him well.

Otto had often wondered idly whether Salka had spotted the truth before any of them – certainly before he and Val had realised it. He thought that she probably had. She was shrewd, and, if Val had let her read the letters he sent her, then she might even then have had an inkling. He had noticed himself that his letters to Val were easier, more informal, than his letters to the girl he was secretly engaged to marry.

Ahead of him, he could see the sprawl of the airfield and knew that he must turn and lose height for the photographic work, though the camera was powerful and he must not drop below thirty thousand feet. He eased the stick forward. It was a marvellously clear day. The air seemed to shimmer, and the huts in which the aircrew would be sleeping, the buildings which housed offices, operations rooms and canteens, the vehicles parked outside, the hangars, were all clear as clear, like tiny models neatly placed at the end of the long concrete runways.

He began, methodically, to take his pictures. He had Hans in the rear gunnery position, though they had no desire to fire at anyone but merely to get home safely with their information. Which would be used for what purpose? He shrugged the thought away and Uri, seeing that he had finished, told him which airfield to head for next and how to recognise it.

Below him, as he swung away, he saw some dots moving around by the huts. Suppose one of those dots was Val? Suppose, as a result of his photographs, this airfield were to be bombed in a week or ten days, and Val really *was* down there?

He eased the stick back to gain height and banished Val from his mind. This was work. He thanked God, nevertheless, that he flew fighters and not bombers, for, though he could with a clear conscience take part in the one-to-one battle against another fighter, he knew that he could never have brought himself to bomb Britain. Bombing had to be done in cold blood, whereas in a dog fight the blood was hot. The battle was not so much to kill your opponent as to avoid being killed, and excitement and pleasure in your skill kept you on your toes as long as the action lasted. Only afterwards, going home, with the red warning light glowing before you reached the airfield, telling you that you had only twenty minutes' fuel left, fifteen . . . ten . . .

The red light came on as they crossed the channel, but it did not matter; experience told him he would be down before the engine began to cough. He felt peaceful, almost happy, with the quiet confidence of one who has awoken in bed, alive and well, after a serious operation. The photographs were taken, no one had so much as noticed him, far less challenged, and the Jumo engines sounded as sweetly as though they had only just taken off. His companions were happy too; he could sense it because they were a good team, had confidence in each other, wanted to continue to work together.

'A good day's work, eh? And all before breakfast!'

He shouted the words above the engines' roar, and received joking replies. Yes, Hans and Uri were well content. Such peaceful happiness could not last, but it was nice while it did. Once they got back – to France, of course; one did not fly sorties from Germany now that France had been conquered – they would have the rest of the day to relax before the tension began to build up once more.

For there was always another mission. Accompanying bombers perhaps, or more reconnaissance, or an attack on the British fighters, if they could be persuaded to leave their hangars. And when you knew another mission was coming up it was impossible not to have that tightening of the stomach muscles, the miserable tension, the fear, even, of being afraid. It came hours, usually, before you were due to take off, and lasted until the moment of combat. Then, for a brief, wonderful spell, instinct took over. You fought, and flew, as if possessed by divine inspiration, and then you disengaged and flew home, always with that same peaceful glow of happiness.

Until the next time. Until you met the Spitfire with your name on its roundels, or you missed noticing the control tower until you met it head on, or . . .

Below them, the airfield loomed. Otto brought the aircraft down with faultless precision, went through the landing routine and handed the Junkers over to his mechanic. As they walked back across the short grass to their quarters he could feel exhaustion hovering like a dark cloud on the edge of his consciousness, waiting to grab him. He ought to go and boast a little about the ease with which the flight had been accomplished, the way his beloved aeroplane had behaved; but all he really wanted to do was to fall into his bed and sleep and sleep and sleep. And dream of Val.

Ruthie, standing in the hall, swung the stick with vigour, crashing it against the gong. Wallop! The noise reverberated around the hall and up the stairs, and the second blow was, in consequence, a little less violent. She was very excited and longing for everyone to come down for breakfast, but it was forbidden to hoot horns, ring bells or blow whistles, so for all she knew it might be equally bad to wallop gongs; better keep it down a bit.

'Nicely done, my dear.' Tina stood in the kitchen doorway, swathed in an apron of Ruthie's which, since

Ruthie was a large woman and Tina barely five foot two, nearly reached the floor. 'I feel a little guilty about waking Maude,' she continued as they crossed the kitchen to the stove, 'but in the circumstances . . .'

'Good news is worth waking for,' Ruthie concluded for her. She flourished a wicked-looking kitchen knife. 'Time to slice the cold spuds, is it?'

Tina shook her head and continued to stir porridge. She remembered rather wistfully the days that had gone, when one made a massive breakfast regardless of who was around to eat it. If it got left, it got left. Now the only pre-cooking she and Ruthie allowed themselves was the porridge; even toasting bread was left until the would-be toast eaters had actually arrived at table. But today, since they were celebrating – and since the hens were laying well – they would have porridge, then fried eggs, potatoes and tomatoes, and finally toast and marmalade. If only the family would appear!

'If them kids don't hurry, I'll go and roust 'em myself,' Ruthie remarked, gathering ingredients for breakfast and adding, after judicious thought, a pot of raspberry jam for those who did not care for marmalade. 'What are the children up to today? That's a lovely sunny one.'

'They're collecting aluminium to make a Spitfire; that's what the schools are doing over the holiday,' Tina told her. 'They'll be getting themselves up now. You know how they all hate lying in bed.'

'Aluminium? They aren't having my milk pan,' Ruthie declared, showing the whites of her eyes. 'Things are hard enough without me boiling milk in an old baked bean tin, or whatever they've thought up this time. Just you don't let them children touch my pans.'

'No, it's all right. I told Sebby quite forcefully that you'd not be pleased, and he's promised only to take pans with holes in. It's a good thing we're such awful hoarders.

When I turned out the cellar I found dozens and dozens of tins and pans and kettles and bits and bobs, so I put them all in the old potting shed, and that's where the kids will root around this morning.'

'Hmm. Well, so long as you told 'em. They aren't bad, just thoughtless. And if they're out all day, I'll make 'em a picnic lunch,' Ruthie was saying magnanimously as the kitchen door burst open. 'Ah, here they are at last!'

Sebastian and Mira shot in, crashed on to chairs, and turned angelic eyes in the direction of the porridge. Extreme hunger was evident in their expressions – and extreme impatience. Ruthie, clucking, began to spoon porridge into two bowls, then added another as the door opened again and Maude appeared, moving zombie-like towards the table with her eyes half closed and a dressing-gown dragged on anyhow over her blue cotton pyjamas.

'Maude, darling, perhaps it was mean to wake you,' Tina said guiltily, guiding her eldest granddaughter into a chair. 'But it's a beautiful day and we've had some good news . . .'

'Hitler's dead! Lord Haw Haw went berserk and shot him right between his mean little eyes! Or he fell out of one of his stinking old Heinkels and got splattered all over Yarmouth beach! Or Mussolini's been strangled with a plateful of his own spaghetti! Oh, yes, or . . .'

'Sebby, be quiet and get on with your porridge,' Tina said regretfully. The pictures conjured up by Sebastian's wild talk were rather fetching! 'It's a personal thing and I shan't tell you until we're all here.'

'My brother Simon's killed Hitler? That would be pretty personal,' Sebastian suggested hopefully. 'Or Nick could have done it – that would be personal too. Or . . .'

Maude woke out of her trance, slitted a malevolent eye at her cousin, and grabbed a handful of his hair.

'Shut up, sprat, and let Granny get me a cup of tea

before I die of thirst. Why can't you be like Mira, and simply eat your porridge?'

'I'll finish before her anyway. I can't help it, I'm a phenomenally quick eater,' Sebastian said complacently, eating porridge at a terrific rate of knots. 'I say, do I see fried potatoes? And tomatoes? Gee whizz, we're having cooked brekker – that's nearly as good as seeing Hitler's insides squelched all over Yarmouth beach!'

Cara, trailing into the room with a hand pressed to her brow and her mouth twisted into an expression of suffering, took Sebastian's mind off Hitler's fate and probably saved him from Ruthie's wrath.

'Good morning, everyone. What on earth was that awful noise?' she said plaintively. 'I really don't see any necessity to crash a gong at breakfast-time, when some people are still trying to sleep.' Slight animation crossed her face as her eyes alighted on Maude. 'Hello, Maudie. I didn't know you were back. Is there a cup of tea going for me?'

'There's fried eggs and potatoes and porridge and all sorts of things to eat,' Mira volunteered, suspending her frantic spooning for a moment. But Cara merely gave her stepdaughter a pained glance.

'Your wits will be addled by tea-drinking by the time you're thirty, Auntie Cara,' Sebastian said darkly. 'Anyway, why won't you have some porridge?'

'For once, I agree with Sebby,' Tina observed, handing Cara a cup of tea. 'An army marches on its stomach, you know.'

'It doesn't march on Mummy's, though,' Mira said, and was surprised when Maude, who had appeared to be drinking tea in her sleep, gave a muffled giggle. 'Where's Auntie Beryl?'

'She and Uncle Des are having a nice little break with the children,' Tina told the small girl. 'That's why Maude is having her breakfast here and not at home.'

'Except that Mummy's usually living here anyway,' Maude put in. 'Here, I'm waking up! Can I have some porridge, Gran? And what's this about good news?'

'Hitler's dead! Shot between . . .'

'Sebby, if you want some breakfast, just you keep quiet a minute,' Ruthie advised in a voice of dangerous calm. 'In fact, if you ever want to eat again, just let someone else talk for once.'

'I'll tell you when we've all got food on our plates and bottoms on our chairs,' Tina said. 'That means Ruthie as well. Now, who wants more porridge?'

It transpired that both children did, then Maude had hers, and Cara, with assumed reluctance, added her own plaintive request for 'just a spot', and so it was another five minutes before they were all seated, and looking expectantly at Tina over filled plates.

'Well? Go on, Gran!'

'It's Paul Butcher. Do you remember hearing he'd been killed at Dunkirk? Well, his mother rang me last night – yesterday at around teatime he just walked in! Alive and well, with another fellow who'd been reported missing, a Sergeant Jimmy something or other. I can't remember his name.'

'Alive? Paul?' Maude's pale face flushed rosily. 'Oh, Gran, that's absolutely wonderful! He's such a good fellow. Everyone likes him.'

'Yes, he's a dear. His brother's over the moon, but nothing can describe how dear Say Butcher felt. She said she kept going into the living-room from the shop, just to take a peep to convince herself she wasn't dreaming. Apparently he was wounded, but managed to hide up in a farmhouse until he was better. Then he and this Jimmy got themselves down to the coast and they made a raft and came across on a very dark night, with only a small torch between them. Talk about invasion fleets – what a strange sight they must have been!'

'Crumbs!' Sebastian was starry-eyed, his mouth at half-cock. 'He's a hero, Auntie Tina, and he's almost a member of this family!' He lowered his voice. 'Wait until I tell the chaps. Almost my cousin – in fact almost a brother!'

Tina, uneasily conscious of the relationships which her brother Louis had scattered around the county before departing for Australia, hastily interrupted.

'Yes, well, don't keep butting in, Sebby. Don't you want to know the details?'

A chorus of affirmation from everyone at the table was gratifying and Tina took a deep breath. All the Neylers and the Roses were natural story-tellers and enjoyed exercising their art; what she did not know she could always imagine, after all!

'Well, Paul had been shot and left for dead, but he'd only been winged – I think that's the word – in the shoulder. He and Jimmy managed to escape somehow, and got to this farm . . .'

She had their complete attention until she got to the part where the two men, after a crossing rendered hideous, in her version, by fear of sharks and of enemy aircraft, reached land. Then the first doubt was raised, and by Cara, of all people.

'But Auntie Tina, don't say the British defences just let them walk ashore? If they did I don't understand it! We've been told we mustn't go down to the beaches and they say they've dug mines in under the sand . . . how on earth did they manage it?'

'In a secluded creek, I daresay,' Tina said vaguely. 'Or perhaps they were challenged and able to prove their identity. I don't know exactly, but I do know that it was a miracle, and we should all thank God for Paul's escape, and add a little extra bit to our prayers each night to make sure no one suffers for helping our two brave English boys.'

Mira, already weighed down by the responsibilities of prayer, looked thoughtful. God was already blessing Mummy, Daddy in the prisoner of war camp, Uncle Nick, Uncle Simon, Auntie Val, Auntie Jenny, Art in the air force, Cyril in the navy, Mrs Walters's Mabel in France, and her grandparents – extended to six by her father's second marriage – as well as all her cousins. She was a very fair-minded child, too, and realised that if she was to pray for Paul and Jimmy and their French friends, she could not possibly leave out Paul's elder brother James, nor his younger sister Primrose. Where would it end?

'Smashing,' Sebastian announced, ending the slightly uncomfortable silence which the mention of prayers had brought. 'Any more toast? Oh, Ruthie, your raspberry jam – and only the other day you said it wasn't to be started until the winter was here!'

He reached for the jar, had his hand smacked, and sat waiting as Ruthie spread the jam far more thinly than a chap could possibly appreciate over his slice of buttered toast.

Maude had enjoyed Auntie Tina's spirited rendering of Paul's escape, and she was truly delighted that Paul was safe. He was very good-looking, she thought judiciously. Not quite as handsome as James, but then James was so very sensible and steady that it took away most of the glamour his good looks might otherwise have conferred. James was also courting, though having seen his young lady, as he called her, Maude felt, without undue conceit, that she could easily have wooed him from his Janette, had she so wished.

However, once Auntie Tina had got her story off her chest the conversation became general, and Maude was able to sink into a reverie which went down very well with her third cup of tea. She was not, however, thinking about

86

her latest victim, a handsome and sought after young flight lieutenant, nor about Laurence Olivier, whose profile and lovely dark brown voice were great aids to Maude's fantasy life. She remembered, instead, the bolshie rear gunner who had been so rude to her.

Maude, with her ash-blonde hair and strikingly vivid blue eyes, was not used to young men being rude. Usually they were quite the opposite. Working in the operations room at Kennet RAF station she knew plenty of young men, some of them the very pilots she talked to over her headset when she was plotting fighters across the board. She was never short of partners at the local hops, and seldom had to buy her own drinks at the village pub. In short, Maude was in demand, and knew it.

On this occasion she and her friend Sandy had gone into the public bar of the Grapes, straight from duty and eager for relaxation. They had been hailed by a group of young men perched on stools up against the bar.

'Hello, girls. What'll you have?'

Sandy's hair was long, shiny, and genuinely black, so she and Maude made a striking pair. It helped, they sometimes remarked to each other, to go about together. Men didn't forget two girls with such definite colouring. Now, they smiled and joined the young men.

With a pint of mild each, the girls were happy to flirt and be flirted with. It was innocent, enjoyable fun. No one was taking anything very seriously, but Maude could not help noticing that one of the men was taking more than a casual interest in her. His name, she learned, was Alan, and he had lovely goldy-brown eyes. He sat very close to her and, though he did not talk a lot, he listened well, smiling often. He had nice even white teeth.

It was some moments before she realised that Alan was not the only man present who was watching her. But the other watcher made no attempt to come nearer or to talk to her. He fixed her with steady, somehow critical eyes, a slight, sarcastic smile on his face. At first it put her on her mettle, made her sparkle a little more, laugh perhaps rather too defiantly, and then it began to annoy her. Damn it, why should he stare like that when he was a member of the group she was with? He had only to say something and the tension she could feel between them would ease. But he said nothing, and presently she decided that he despised her as a giggly little blonde. She stared straight back angrily, hot-eyed, before letting her eyes go out of focus so that his face blurred into nothing. Which was what he was to her – nothing!

She did not know him, though she felt that she had seen him before. Probably around the station; or perhaps he had come down to the ops room to watch the board to see how a friend was getting on. The men did come in sometimes when they were not on duty themselves.

The watcher was square-chinned, with dark bristly hair cut very short. Not handsome and certainly not well dressed. He was wearing a loud sports jacket and flannels which were the wrong shade for it. He was well built, though, with broad shoulders, and she guessed that he was tall, then knew she was right as he stood up and leaned, hands in pockets, against the bar. He looked angry as well as critical and she saw that he stood a little apart from the others as though, even while with them, he was not *of* them. Only afterwards, when she got to know him better, did she realise how shrewd that judgement had been.

Maude, suddenly realising that her own scrutiny could not have been totally casual, began to talk quickly, anxious that he should not realise she cared who was staring at her so rudely. She began to tell the story of how her father, faced with his first air raid, had rushed into a sweet shop which had received a direct hit and had skated right across it on the loose aniseed balls and bullseyes scattered over the floor, becoming a casualty himself with badly cut knees and a wrenched ankle.

After the roar of laughter had subsided, Maude remarked: 'Daddy felt the most awful fool at the first-aid post when they asked him how he'd been injured.'

More laughter, which a voice cut across contemptuously. It came from the sarcastic young man with the bristly hair.

'I daresay Daddy often feels a fool, doesn't he?'

Maude had not realised she had an accent until that moment. But his rendering of a high little upper-class voice was unmistakable, and somehow shocking. Maude felt her cheeks burn and found herself speechless for a moment.

Roger Casey, a round-faced, sweet-natured young man who often sat and chatted to Maude, broke the uncomfortable silence. He leaned across and tapped Maude's knee, saying, 'Is your father LDV then, old girl? So's mine, and some of the stories he tells damn near beat *my* tales of derring-do.' He then turned to face Maude's foe and added casually, 'D'you have to be so bloody offensive, Bill?' He had turned back before the other had a chance to reply. And then, almost imperceptibly, the circle around the bar stools closed, shutting Bill out.

He did not seem to mind, though, Maude noticed, once the conversation became general again. What a horrid young man he was! He finished his drink, stood the glass down on the bar and walked over to another group, joining them without any shyness or self-consciousness. Presently, she noticed he had a hand on the waist of another WAAF. So he really likes fluffy little floosies and probably dislikes me because I'm not one, Maude thought with uncharacteristic viciousness. Barbara Phelps had a reputation for being even sillier than she pretended. The only sensible thing about her, someone had remarked earlier in the evening, was the way she managed to sleep with every aircraftman who asked her without getting pregnant.

When closing time came, Sandy was escorted home by Roger Casey and Maude and invited to take the front passenger seat in Alan's Morris convertible. Agreeing, Maude told herself that Alan was a decent fellow and would make a pleasant companion, but underneath she knew she was going with him out of curiosity. She wanted, very badly, to know who 'Bill' was and what he did.

'Trained as a rear gunner on bombers, but did a bit of flying in peacetime and wants to fly fighters,' her escort said briefly, in reply to her casual question. 'Bolshie devil, he is. Goes on about privilege and how the underdogs will rise up and crush the oppressors, which is anyone with tuppence more than he has, if you ask me. I expect you know the type.'

Maude, who did not, murmured that of course she did, but added a rider.

'Only . . . all that was before the war. Surely, now, it's different? I mean, we're all in it together. There's no privilege in the air force.'

Alan smiled rather sweetly at her in the moonlight and drove, if anything, even more slowly.

'Good thing Bill didn't hear you say that! According to him the RAF's a hotbed of privilege, and in a way I know what he means. When you look at the officers, all the ones I know went to decent schools and not the board sort, and if their people don't have money they do have the right accent; that sort of thing. I think you've got to be like that to be able to lead effectively; men will follow someone they respect, not someone who's got the brains of Einstein and the manners of a coal-heaver.'

'Does he want to be an officer, then? Well, why shouldn't he? If he's going to be a fighter pilot . . .'

'It doesn't follow. There are perfectly splendid chaps flying fighters with the rank of sergeant.' Alan drew up in a gateway and put an arm round her shoulders. 'Now how about forgetting boring Bill and remembering me!'

Maude was a polite girl, and Alan had bought her drinks and was giving her a ride home in his car. Besides, she liked him, so she obediently turned her fair little face up to his and was soundly kissed, and liked it. But it did not stop her thinking about Bill.

In a way she was sorry for him. It must be rather difficult being the only person in his set who was not an officer. But she had done nothing to him, so why had he so spitefully imitated her words and her accent, made fun – or tried to – of her father? He did not know her, far less Desmond, so he was simply assuming, because of her accent, that her father was a member of the ruling classes. Which, she supposed, gently detaching herself from Alan's ardent embrace when she felt it had lasted quite long enough, was not far off the mark. But even so . . .

As is the way of life, that first encounter was speedily followed by another. She was having lunch in the canteen with Sandy and another friend, Penelope Travers, when Bill came over to their table. He hooked out a chair with one foot and raised a brow at her.

'All right if I join you?'

With her mouth full and her mind in a turmoil, Maude nodded uncertainly. What on earth did he want to sit with them for? The better to despise her, perhaps? The better to imitate her, next time he got the chance? She knew she would not dare open her mouth while he was sitting there waiting to be horrible. She shot a quick look at him, but he was hungrily wolfing shepherd's pie. She glanced across at Sandy, who was as puzzled as herself, then at Penelope.

Pen, she suddenly realised, had a drawly, rather plummy voice, which would be a gift to Bill if he chose to try to take them all down a peg. She had thought herself unable to say a word, but now she burst into rapid, nervous speech. She would never forgive him if he picked on Penelope.

'Girls, someone was saying that there is a beach open, if we really want to bathe! We c-could go this afternoon, if you don't mind the bus journey. We're all off duty, so we could have tea out – I think there's a café open too – and we could . . .' Bill was staring at her, and so were Sandy and Penelope. Her voice stuttered into silence. She cleared her throat and turned to him. 'We're on the graveyard shift, but I don't see why we couldn't take a nap on the beach, do you?'

'What's the graveyard shift?'

'Nights.' That was Sandy, courteous but brief. 'We really ought to get some sleep, Maude, but if you want to try the beach . . .'

Before she could speak again, Bill interrupted. His voice, rather to her surprise, was deep and pleasant, with a trace of an accent which was familiar to her. He's from Suffolk, or perhaps even Norfolk, she thought triumphantly, and nearly dared to smile at him.

'I live by the seaside. Not round here, of course.'

'Are you from East Anglia?'

Poor Maude, who had meant it in the nicest possible way, immediately realised, perhaps even before Bill did, that she had shown he spoke with an accent. But it seemed he had decided not to take offence. He grinned at her.

'That's it. Lowestoft. My dad works the trawlers.'

'I don't envy him,' Sandy said. 'Why didn't you join the navy, if you've been brought up to shipping?'

'Wanted to fly. I had to take aircrew at first, but now I'm flying.'

'My brother's learning to fly as well – Wellingtons,'

Maude said, and then hoped that bombers were not a sign of privilege. In case he should think she only had one brother she added hastily. 'That's Art. He's the eldest. Cyril's on destroyers. He loves it.'

To her dismay, the dark face opposite her own had that Look again. Black brows rose.

'Really? I daresay he's a Jimmy the One already. You know, a first lieutenant.'

Maude tilted her chin and gave him her frostiest look. All right, then, if he wanted war!

'Yes, of course he is; we think he's done very well considering he's only just sixteen. We expect him to be made Admiral of the Fleet in the next twelve months. And my younger brother, Eddy, is very keen on the army, so I daresay he'll be starting as a brigadier any time now. He's eleven, after all.'

'And you?' He was really grinning now, the bitter, sarcastic look quite gone. His eyes were so dark that they looked black, but they were twinkling. He looked completely different, younger and much more attractive. 'And you? What about you?'

'Oh, me? I'm the next Queen of England – can't you tell?'

They were all laughing, though probably Maude and Bill were the only ones who knew exactly why, when a girl's voice was raised above the hubbub.

'Hey, Bill, what are you doing, leaving me for other women?'

Maude, sure of her own attractions, reared in a society where a man does not just desert the woman he's talking to, glanced impatiently over at the speaker. A small, sprout-faced object was her first conclusion, with a lot of spots and frizzy, bleached hair. When she turned back, Bill was on his feet, his half-empty dinner plate abandoned. He looked down at Maude and the sardonic look was curling his lip again, hardening those too-dark eyes.

'Sorry, girls,' he said, but the words were meant for Maude alone, and she knew it. 'I must be off – there's a real woman calling me.'

And off he went, to let the sprout-faced one hang on his arm, upbraid him shrilly for not waiting for her, and then lead him off to a corner table where she plied him with coffee and cigarettes.

'Just what did he mean by that?' Penelope drawled, rather offended, as she was no doubt meant to be. 'Aren't we real women, then? If he means real tarts, then he should say so.'

'He's a red-hot socialist,' Maude explained. 'Alan told me, the night he brought me home from the Grapes. That chap – Bill's his name – has got a chip on his shoulder and for some reason he's taken a dislike to me. That's why he was so rude.'

'To you, Maudie? Rubbish. All men go for deceptively frail blondes who look as though a wind would blow them over but drink pints and can outmarch any man,' Sandy said. But she looked thoughtfully across the table at her friend. 'I've come across men like that before, actually, and, though it sounds a funny thing to say, I think they can only get close to a woman by picking a fight and pretending to despise her. So watch out, because he isn't for you, my girl.'

'You think he's just trying to scrape acquaintance by being rude?' Maude said. She could cope with that. 'Well, if so, he's wasting his time. He isn't at all good-looking and he doesn't have an ounce of charm, and if I want rudeness I've got three brothers who are only too willing to oblige!'

Yet, on and off, she continued to think about Bill, and to wonder about him.

Chapter Six

'This is the life!'

Val shouted the words above the roar of the engine, for her car had its roof down, the better for the occupants to enjoy the sunshine and breeze of a perfect August day. It was the start of a break for them, a weekend of peace and quiet down in the Surrey countryside. It was the nearest they seemed likely to get to a holiday, since going back to Norwich, which had already suffered several air raids, could scarcely be termed relaxation. But Val, determined to see that both she and Jenny got a break from work and from London, had booked a double room at a pub she had known quite well before the war – the Swan – and she, Jenny and Marianne were driving down there now, very early so that they would have two whole days of peace.

'You're right; I'm glad we decided to come.'

Jenny's voice sounded as elated as she felt, and once again Val was glad she had forced the issue when Jenny had dithered. She knew that the strain Jenny was under was almost unbearable, for what the newspapers were calling the Battle of Britain was being fought above the home counties, and Simon was flying almost non-stop. Leave had been cancelled and reports of what was happening, who was safe, were slow to come through, though Simon rang whenever he could. Life at the flat was nerve-racking because one was either working or waiting, so Val had got in touch with Simon and enlisted his help.

Simon, always generous, had backed her up, so here

they were, the three of them, driving through the quiet lanes to the village she remembered so well, with its green, the tall elms and beeches lining the village street, the shop which sold everything and the cottage which did teas. And it was not too far from the sea, so they might even get a paddle!

Bouncing up and down on Jenny's lap Marianne, infected by the happiness all around her, began to sing. Loudly and somewhat tunelessly, she praised the sky, the sunshine, and the purring engine of Val's car, known to Marianne, for some obscure reason, as Lillypooh.

'I'll tell you one thing Mari won't be when she's grown up, and that's a singer,' Val remarked, slowing to take a sharp bend. 'Mind you, I shouldn't criticise since I do recognise the tune, vaguely. Isn't it "My Little Nut-Tree"?'

'No, surely it's "Georgie-porgie",' Jenny said, listening, and Marianne broke off long enough to add her penny-worth and thoroughly confuse the issue.

'Owl and Pussycat,' she shouted. 'Is Owl and Pussycat!'

Baffled, the adults laughed and began to sing themselves. Marianne, leaning against Jenny's chest, returned to her own tune. She was totally happy.

They had a lovely day exploring the countryside and the small town where they stopped for lunch. They arrived at the Swan just in time to get Marianne a high tea and pop her into bed, and then they went down to the bar and chatted to the locals before going to bed themselves and sleeping deeply and dreamlessly until morning. Then, to be sure, they were woken as dawn broke by cockerels announcing the new day, but although Jenny did remark in a sleep-drugged voice that she would like to strangle the birds she was asleep again before Val had time to answer.

Breakfast was delicious – all the more so because it had been cooked by someone else – and as soon as it was over the girls decided to take a stroll down the village street and see what amusements were available on a quiet Sunday morning.

It was another glorious day, though there was a heat-haze in the distance so that the sky was a milky, opalescent blue. They strolled beneath the trees, a little stream separating them from the cottages on the right of the dusty road. There was a church not far from the green and a service was in progress. Faintly, they could hear the sound of an organ being played. Presently the stream wound round so that the road had to cross it by means of a small, hump-backed bridge. Armed with twigs, they settled themselves on one side of this and instructed Marianne in the art of playing Poohsticks, hurling the twigs of their choice into the water and then rushing across to the other side to see whose twig would appear first. With only a little manipulation it was possible to see that Marianne won three times out of four, which thrilled her enormously.

When this innocent diversion began to pall – though Marianne would have played on all day, given the chance – the three of them went further up the street, bought some sweets and a paper at the local shop and learned that further up the road there was a pig-farm with sties quite close to the road.

'The Harmers won't mind if you want to go into the yard and show the little gal the pigs,' the lady in the shop assured them. 'That'll be nice for 'er.'

In fact, the farm proved to be further than they had thought; not that it mattered on such a day. Slowly, they wandered up the road, with Marianne running along the grass verge picking big, moon-faced daisies and cow parsley and ladies' bedstraw. Whenever her small, hot little hand became uncomfortably full she would pass on her bouquet to Val and Jenny so that they, too, were flower-laden by the time they saw – and smelt – the pig-farm.

They had heard aircraft overhead but had taken little notice since the planes were hidden by the heat-haze, but just as they drew level with the farm the air battle which must have been warming up began right above them.

Jenny glanced up and Val swooped on Marianne and carried her over to the pig-sties, whose gleaming and rotund occupants showed not the smallest interest in their sudden audience.

'We're surrounded by airfields here,' Val said. 'Maudie's station can't be more than five miles away. We'll just keep under this roof until the fight moves on.'

The noise was considerable, but both young women felt themselves safe beneath the partially sheltering roof, until, all at once, the heat-haze lifted. It was as though it had muffled the noise as well as the sight of the aeroplanes, for suddenly it seemed as though all hell had been let loose above them. Staring up, fascinated, they saw literally hundreds of Heinkels, Dorniers, Junkers and Messerschmitts above them, and higher yet the little planes with the familiar roundels on their wings – Spitfires and Hurricanes.

Marianne was pointing, eyes round, cheeks pink with excitement.

'Daddy's up there! Daddy's up there!'

She had no thought of danger; she was just repeating what Jenny had told her when they saw Spitfires overhead. She tried to wriggle out of Val's arms, and was restrained. Somehow, although she supposed that the airmen were far too busy fighting each other to think about the ground, Val did not want to see her darling baby cousin out in the open, with spent shells no doubt about to rain to earth.

And then there was an appalling roar and out of nowhere, it seemed, a flight of huge aeroplanes came roaring towards them. They looked huge because they were so low, skimming the rooftops, almost touching the trees, so close that the black crosses on their underwings looked as if they could touch them, so low that the pilots' faces were clearly visible for one astonished, terrified second.

The three females suddenly discovered the advantages of a whole roof above them and dived simultaneously amongst the pigs. Jenny landed on all fours and Val landed on a pig but at the time no one cared. They made for the far side of the sty with such determination that not even an evil-faced and belligerent sow tried to stop them.

Cowering, they heard the staccato crack of bullets and saw, across the yard, a double line of tiny dust-storms as the ammunition hit the ground. They heard the shriek of a descending fighter, the roar of its engines as it pulled out of its dive, and then the noise gradually faded into the distance.

Trembling and feeling thoroughly silly, Jenny and Val climbed out of the pig-sty and helped a chuckling Marianne out too. Jenny, vainly trying to brush sloshy pig manure off her skirt, did not, for a moment, glance skywards, and Val, trying to scrape it off a new pair of suede shoes, was equally preoccupied. Marianne, however, indifferent to appearances and having rather enjoyed paddling in pig-muck, drew their attention to what was going on overhead.

'Look, Mummy! Daddy's up there, Daddy's up there!'

They looked, and could not move. It was a ballet, but, as they well knew, a dance of death, between a Spitfire and a Messerschmitt. Both pilots knew what they were doing. Both circled, jinked, dived and then soared, and from both the gleam of tracer kept appearing without, it seemed, scoring a hit. And then, suddenly, it was over. The German plane was circling, but differently. Every spiral carried it closer and closer to the earth below, and white smoke was issuing from its tail. Lower and lower it came, louder and louder shrieked the engine, and Val found herself screaming 'Bale out, you bloody fool, bale out!' whilst Jenny clutched her baby and watched, white-faced, with an expression that was almost vindictive satisfaction as the machine disappeared behind a belt of trees to the south.

It landed with a sound like a bomb, and they saw flames and a column of black and oily smoke. Then, once more, the silence was back. Behind them the pigs grunted softly and chickens clucked and scratched.

Jenny released Marianne and turned to her cousin, to find Val bent over the ditch, weeping and vomiting. Jenny ran to her, held her head, comforted her. Or thought she did.

'It's all right, we won. The Jerry bought it,' she was saying, holding Val's curls away from her face. 'He's dead, poor devil, but at least our chap's alive and probably hurrying off to snatch another one out of the sky.'

And Val, dizzy and empty, could not tell her that she was crying for the German, because it might so easily have been Otto. You could not say, to a girl married to an English fighter pilot, that you were in love with a fellow who flew in the Luftwaffe. Val could not admit that every time she read the heartening stories in the papers of German losses, German deaths, she could not find it in her heart to rejoice, because one of those dead might be her love.

Presently, Jenny supported her friend up to the farm-house, where they begged a cup of tea from Mrs Harmer, who was happy to make them one and to chat. Val, like most red-haired people, always looked ghastly when she had been crying, and no one remarked on her unusual quietness as they drank the tea. Even when Mrs Harmer told them that the big cloud of smoke to the right of the trees probably came from the Kennet airfield, where Maude worked, Val could not express her feelings. Instead, she agreed with Jenny's suggestion that they should make their way quietly back to the Swan, and telephone from there to see what they could find out.

All the way back to the village, Val fought with herself. She wanted to confide in Jenny – after all, Jenny was the nearest thing she had to a sister since Stella had run away to Australia – but would it be fair? Jenny had been her best friend for years . . . would she understand, sympathise?

She did not tell Jenny.

Maude had been to the canteen for her lunch and had returned to her position at the table in the ops room. She had barely settled herself, barely adjusted her headset, when the attack began. Observer posts in the area were reporting huge numbers of enemy aircraft and two flights seemed to be heading straight for Kennet. One was flying high, but the other was roof-hopping, coming in very fast, obviously hoping by this method to escape both detection and attacks by fighter aircraft which, for obvious reasons, always tried to get above the enemy.

Rake poised, blocks which would represent the fighters of her squadron once they got into the air ready, Maude stood tense, listening to the subdued mutterings on either side of her. Sandy was to the right. Penelope to the left; all three were used to working together and had evolved sufficient understanding of each other's needs and methods to be amongst the best plotters on the station. When they were working on the table, the situations map was as near correct as it was possible to make it.

The low-flying enemy aircraft were on the table simultaneously, it seemed, with the stupendous roar as they swept overhead. At the same moment, everyone heard the whine and crashing thunder of the bombs being hurled earthwards and the staccato burst of machine-gun fire. Maude, pushing her rake neatly between the bombers, managed to get her fighters in position just as the duty flight controller raised his voice in an unnecessary bellow.

'Bandits overhead!'

Someone muttered 'You don't say!' and then all Maude was conscious of were the voices coming over her headset, the vital necessity to get everything right so that the controller and his assistants, with their godlike view of the map on the plotting table, could advise the pilots how to act. She could still hear the droning throb of the engines as the enemy attacked, and the crashes and thunder of the bombs, but it was all background noise, something to be ignored as you strove to hear the voices coming through your headset. Sometimes one glanced continually at the weather board and the tote, which showed a composite picture of which aircraft were airborne, which available and which on standby, but today there was simply not time. Maude's rake was constantly pulling in, moving, pushing out. Beside her, Sandy and Penelope were similarly occupied. The din was appalling and she had to force herself to speak quietly so that she did not add to it and make the task of those around her more difficult. When a bomb fell near enough to bring the tote board crashing down from the wall, narrowly missing the officer who was plotting on it, she scarcely lifted her eyes from the table, though she heard, above the clatter, the officer's voice rise for a moment, the swear words seeming oddly frivolous and out of place in this dedicated atmosphere.

When silence came suddenly it was more frightening, even, than the noise. Maude put her hands to her earphones, thinking that she had gone deaf, and saw by their faces that others had leapt to the same conclusion. Above them, on the dais, the officers, too, showed their confusion. But only momentarily. The controller raised his voice.

'Right, that's it, they've got the telephones. We can't do any more here. Get to the shelters, girls, and make it snappy!'

The operations room at Kennet was only four steps below ground level, so all the plotters and their officers had to do was to walk through the door and out round the blast wall. It was then that they saw what had happened to their airfield during the raid. Maude stopped short, her hand going to her throat. At first glance all she could see were smoking ruins – buildings, planes, a jeep, broken in two like a toy. There were planes on the ground, too; the ones which had not been scrambled quickly enough, evidently. They were shattered, at odd angles, with wheels torn off, and wings chopped in two.

Nearby, a hangar was burning; she could feel the heat of it. Unexploded bombs protruded from craters. There was one, nose down, tail up, in the middle of Sergeant Collins's salad patch. His lettuces, tomatoes and radishes were his pride and joy – or had been. The bomb had done for most of them.

'Get moving!'

Someone gave her a sharp shove in the back and, turning to grab Sandy's hand, she moved away from the hut, suddenly uncertain. Where should they go? Everywhere seemed to have been blown up!

'Into the nearest shelter, muggins,' someone said and Maude, round-eyed but obedient, followed her friends down a flight of concrete steps and into the small, oblong room with the wooden benches round the walls. There were already a lot of WAAFs in the shelter, knitting, playing cards, even singing. They asked the plotters what it was like outside and were told 'noisy', 'a bit of a mess', 'not too good'. No one wanted to be accused of spreading alarm and despondency.

They were in the shelter a long time. Sandy, clutching Maude's arm, muttered that she didn't care what anyone said, she'd got to have a wee, and if they weren't allowed out soon there would be a puddle on the floor, so there. Maude, who had not even thought about it, promptly began to want to go as well. Penelope, confided in, immediately began to shift uneasily and to cross and uncross her legs.

They were, happily, released before the worst happened, but as they emerged from the shelter, blinking in the sudden brilliance of the afternoon, Maude made a startling discovery.

'Girls, all the bogs have gone!'

For a moment, they all stared at the scene of smoking devastation around them. Then, with one accord, they made for the blast wall of the operations room, which was still standing. Crouched in its shelter, they looked at each other for the first time since they had emerged, and began to giggle. What else was there to do – and the relief of that moment!

It was amazing, really, how quickly everyone got back to work. The damage was bad, but nor irremediable. Three hours after they had used the blast wall of the operations room for such an unusual purpose, Maude and her friends were again at the table, bringing things back to order. There would be a lot of work to do – the hospital wing had been hit for a start, so the occupants had been moved along to the WAAFs' huts; heaven knew where they would sleep tonight.

They were packed off to the canteen for hot tea and a cold meal once dark had fallen. They were all but asleep on their feet, but Maude was still conscious of a stab of pleasure every time she saw a fighter pilot she knew. Another one alive and well . . . and Scotty was in hospital, Fletcher had landed at Croydon, Alan was here, and most of her friends were reassuring about other friends.

She left the canteen at last and went to the room – and the bed – she was to share with Sandy. They divided the bedding between them and she was actually wrapped up in her share, naked beneath the sheet because her clothing was covered with filth and her pyjamas had been borrowed for the hospital patients, when someone tapped on her door. She groaned, dug Sandy in the ribs, and then staggered blearily out of bed and across the dusty lino to the door. She had some difficulty in finding the key and more difficulty in turning it, but she got it open at last.

A man stood there. She was dimly conscious that if this had been an ordinary day that man would undoubtedly have been shot at dawn for being in the WAAFs' hut, and then she managed to blink her eyes open a bit more and unstick her eyelashes from each other, and she saw that it was Bill.

Afterwards, she could only sigh over her peculiar behaviour, but at the time she saw nothing strange in it whatsoever. She gave a strangled squeak and fell into his arms. She clutched his shoulders, bulky beneath his flying jacket, pushed her body as close to his as she could and returned the kisses that he was raining down on her face, hair, neck and shoulders with enthusiasm.

She did not speak a word, and neither did he. She had come to the door with the sheet wrapped, sarong-like, around her body just above her breasts, and with a blanket draped across her shoulders. The blanket fell, disregarded, to the floor and the sheet was in danger of following it before the fierce, possessive behaviour of his hands and his body.

She had somehow got herself back into the room, and

was against the wall with cold plaster across her shoulders and a very hot Bill against her front. She was not resisting, she was encouraging, when they heard footsteps in the corridor.

It brought Maude to her senses. She pushed him away, opened her mouth to warn him that she was sure an officer was checking the building over, and realised she was speaking to thin air. Bill, obviously used to such goings-on, had crossed the small room in a couple of strides, cocked his leg over the windowsill, and disappeared into the darkness.

Out in the corridor, someone stopped outside the door, and Maude moved almost as quickly as her visitor had done. She was in – or on – the bed and curled up with her back to the door before it had opened more than a crack. She lay, death-still, until the door closed as gently as it had opened, and then she listened for a moment, got off the bed, ran and locked the door, and returned to her former position.

To her astonishment, Sandy continued to slumber deeply. How could she, when that awful man had been into the room, had kissed and cuddled Sandy's best friend, and had gone out again through the window? I'm sure I shall never dare to sleep again, Maude thought righteously, and then fell to wondering why she had let him kiss and cuddle her if he really was such an awful man.

I must still be in a state of shock, she told herself at last, as sleep began to make her thoughts slide and slur. If I'd been in full command of myself I would never have behaved like that.

Or of course I could be in love, her mind remarked conversationally to her intelligence, just before she succumbed to sleep. But you didn't love people you didn't know, people who had only spoken to you twice, and had been rude on both occasions. Yes, it was shock. If it had been Alan, that would have been different.

More ordinary, not so exciting, her mind said. Maude, shocked, told it to shut up and not to pester a girl suffering from shock. And slept.

At five to two that afternoon, Simon had been in readiness, which meant that he could be airborne in five minutes. At four minutes to two, when the call to scramble came over the loudspeakers, he was actually moving, running across the grass. He reached his aeroplane, grabbed his parachute from the mechanic, scrambled into it with the mechanic's frenzied help in fastening straps, and leapt into the pilot's seat, doing up the seat-straps the moment he was in. Once that was done he crammed the helmet down over his head, plugged in the R/T lead, and began engine checks. Everything seemed to be behaving itself, so he gestured to Sid, his mechanic, to pull away the chocks, opened the throttle and moved across the grass to his take-off position. The whole procedure had taken rather less than two minutes.

As soon as the flight was airborne control told the pilots to climb to twenty thousand feet, so Simon got into formation and pulled back the stick. As they gained altitude he checked his position and his instruments, and then looked around him for the enemy.

They were already in sight. A group of five Stuka dive bombers and three attendant fighters, then another group and another, until the sky was so full of aircraft that it seemed impossible they could avoid collision. But Simon knew that once the fighting started he would develop not only eyes in the back of his head but a sort of second sight, combined with a pair of hands and feet which very often did the right thing at the right moment, seconds before his brain had got round to ordering them to do it.

Manoeuvring for just the right position to attack, he watched a Stuka go into the crabbing side-slip which meant that its attacker would overshoot. Then he moved in quickly, catching the dive bomber with his tracer before the pilot knew he was there. He was moving up and away, going after another, before the crippled plane could have realised where it had been hit, but now he had a Me 109 coming down on him. He jinked, saw it loop and swerve after another fighter, and had time to glance down at his kill and see the white mushrooms which were parachutes billow into the air as the crew baled out. He had time for a small feeling of satisfaction, because both pilot and navigator had got well clear before the machine screamed to earth. But then another Me 109 was coming down on him, coming fast, and he was back in the thick of it, jinking, turning, losing and gaining height, making himself as difficult a target as he knew how whilst automatically loosing off at anything which crossed his sights.

When he felt the plane shudder and knew he had been hit, he also knew that the tracer had been fired before he reached the point of impact, and had been intended for another plane; he could not tell whether the tracer was British or Hun, not that it mattered. What mattered was the result. He turned in his seat and was surprised to find the cockpit apparently intact, and was turning back again when something clouted him, hard, across the shoulder. A moment, perhaps a second, later he knew that the cockpit had been breached because something was blown across his goggles. He drew his glove across them because he could not afford to be temporarily blinded by oil or whatever, and found that it was blood. He glanced at the dials, but everything seemed to be all right, and though he had been hit it could only be a glancing blow. His arm felt numb and rather cold, but not really painful.

He turned back into the thick of the fight once more,

108

fired a rapid burst as the underbelly of a Dornier bomber crossed his sights, then nearly let go the stick as a shudder shook the aircraft. Collision? That could mean going down a bloody sight too fast and too far!

But it was not another aeroplane. Sickeningly, he realised he'd hit a bloke who had just jumped, whose parachute was beginning to open. He pushed the feeling off because it was the way to get killed yourself, to start thinking instead of reacting, and fired another burst, which came to nothing halfway through. No more ammunition. Damn. Better get out of this, then. He would be nothing more than a passenger without ammo.

He curved away from the fight and thought he heard a slight stutter in the engine. Immediately all his attention centred on that. The petrol warning light was all right, it had been blood on his glove and not oil . . . he did not even realise that he had a Messerschmitt on his tail until he felt the impact of its tracer whack the Spitfire into an involuntary half-turn. He went into a dive, wanting to shake off the enemy, wanting the other pilot to assume he was a gonner and return to the fight, but he was by no means out of control, though something must have given as the tracer struck. Control wires to the rudder or elevator? Wheels shot away? He wiggled the stick cautiously. No, the control wires were all right at the moment, and he was low, now, too low for baling out. It would have to be an emergency landing then, unless he could nurse the machine along for a few more miles and find an airfield? But the odd noise in the engine had not been imagination. There it was again, a snuffly, irritable cough, the sort of sound a tiger makes when it wants to warn you it's going to spring.

He was low enough, now, to have a good look at the surrounding terrain. It was obviously a fairly urgent matter to get down. Better try for a soft spot. But the farmers and landowners round here were a careful lot, all their heads filled with fears that enemy invasion forces might use their fields, their pastures. He saw some soft ploughland, but . . . Break my back and the machine's, he thought grimly, continuing to nurse the Spitfire along. Better find somewhere soon. The engine coughed again. It sounded worse, or was that merely because he could not see a clear piece of pasture?

And then he saw it. A stretch of grass surrounded by trees, but he could cope with them. He wiped his glove across his face again and this time it came away covered in blood. Hmm. Flesh wound? He glanced down at his shoulder, and discovered that the blood was coming from a gash of some description, and not from his face at all. He tried to see what had caused it, but could not do so while flying the aeroplane, so he decided to concentrate on one thing at a time and lowered his flaps, which seemed stiff, but came down, slowing his approach. Good, good, everything was going well so far. He touched, bounced, touched again . . . and then she slewed right round until she was facing the way he had come, her nose burying itself in the soft ground like a bird digging for worms. Simon, thanking God that he was alive, thought that a tyre must have been badly damaged by something, to bring her round like that.

The moment the plane juddered to a halt, he began to unbuckle his safety straps so that he could climb out; more pilots were killed when their aircraft burst into flames than was comfortable to contemplate. The thought made him feverishly anxious, but for some reason the fingers on his right hand refused to obey him. And undoing the straps with the left hand alone was a fumbling, stupid sort of business.

But he did it. He climbed out of the cockpit and discovered that his nose was bleeding, which seemed pretty damned amateurish – fancy getting a nosebleed just from a bit of junketing around the sky! His right arm, alarmingly, was beginning to ache horribly and as he swung himself on to the ground he saw the grass beneath his feet tilt and the trees and the little hedges dance a slow jig. Faintness and nausea fought for top priority in his mind even as he, in his turn, fought to dismiss them both. He steadied himself against the plane and glanced down at the wheel, feeling a degree of satisfaction to find his diagnosis was correct and the tyre was in ribbons. Then, since the giddiness seemed to have receded, he began to make his way across the pasture to the gate which led, he thought, to a country lane. It was not easy walking, but he had to make it. He could not just lie down here in this field and tamely bleed to death.

He had nearly reached the gate when someone swung it open. An ancient farm worker, cloth capped, a dog at his heel. And, to Simon's alarm, an ancient blunderbuss which looked at though it was last used in the Wars of the Roses pointing at him.

'I gotta gun on you, you Nazi bastard,' the old man croaked, waving his weapon in a most alarming manner. 'I don't believe in taking prisoners. Shoot your bloody head off soon's look at you, I would! You come over 'ere, bombing innocent folk, shooting at us what was 'aving a quiet pint . . .'

Simon began to protest, aware that he was in some considerable danger. To make a landing and then to be found by a madman who recognised neither the roundels on a Spitfire's wings nor a genuine English accent was hard luck of no common order! But before he had got more than a few words out the cold and numbness which had afflicted his arm spread remorselessly throughout his body. His captor, toothless mouth dropping open, looked very anxious indeed as Simon slumped to his knees and then on to his side, as if he suspected yet another Nazi trick. But Simon, plunging into unconsciousness, knew nothing of this.

If he had been able to see his captor thirty seconds later, kneeling beside him, supporting his head, trying to get cold tea from a beer bottle between his clenched teeth, he might have been quite touched, for old Mr Clarke still thought he'd caught a German bomber pilot. But even a German bomber pilot could not be left, wounded and bleeding, in the middle of the five-acre. Mr Clarke called his dog, told Jess to guard, and left her sitting by Simon, watching him with some puzzlement, while he himself tottered off to get help.

Simon came round once, saw her sincere, doggy face, and felt vaguely comforted. But then he lost consciousness once more.

Jenny and Val, on their way home, saw the Spitfire come down from afar and Jenny, with Simon always on her mind, wanted to see if the pilot was all right. They drove, accordingly, through the narrow country lanes, peering through gateways and having no luck whatsoever, until at last they found it. Tilted up like a bird grubbing for worms, it stood in the field, deserted. Not even a little boy searched for souvenirs, not a cow rubbed against it.

'Well, there you are,' Val said, stopping by the gate. 'Whoever was in it must have got out by now, I should think.'

'Yes, sure to.' But Jenny was out of the car, nervous energy sending her through the gateway and across the grass before Val had done more than pluck Marianne from the back seat. Calling back over her shoulder, she added, 'No one inside, I don't think. I'll just . . . Oh!'

Val catching up with her, grabbed her arm as she swayed.

'What is it? Jenny? What is it?'

'It's Simon's. Look!'

Val looked, and saw, written along the side of the

cockpit, one word: Lillypooh. She felt the blood drain from her cheeks, remembering Simon telling them that he had named his aircraft after her little car because they were both small, game vehicles.

'Yes, I see . . . but the pilot must have been all right. There's no one here. He must have got away under his own steam . . .'

Her voice petered out as Jenny pointed. The wing nearest them was smeared with something horrible. And, lavishly, with blood.

Jenny whipped round and made for the car at a trot. Val, following her, felt sick with fear and misery and knew how much worse Jenny must be feeling.

'We'll find him, love, and I'm sure he's all right. That blood must be someone else's,' she said wildly, pushing Jenny into the passenger seat and plonking Marianne down on her lap. 'Come on, we'll stop at the very first cottage.'

The first cottage door was opened by an ancient farmhand, still in his cap. He gazed at them, then shouted, 'Down, Jess,' to the spotted sheepdog which was eagerly exploring Val's sheepskin jacket.

'Yis, ladies?'

'We've just seen a plane in a field,' Val explained, seeing that Jenny was still in shock. 'We recognised it. It's my friend's husband's Spitfire, and we wondered if you knew where the pilot had gone.'

A cunning look crossed the seamed face.

'Your 'usband, lady? No, no, 'e couldn't have been your 'usband. 'E was a Hun.'

'In a Spitfire? Scarcely! Where is he?' Val stared past the old man into the dim interior of his cottage. 'Did you bring him back here? Can we see him please?'

'Me an' the wife fetched 'im back,' the old fellow agreed. 'He's still asleep. The wife's gorn to fetch a policeman or two. They'll likely bring an ambulance. He's bleeding from 'is arm.'

Jenny pushed past him and into the dark, low-ceilinged living-room. A man lay on the sofa, his head turned away from them. She went towards him, but someone beat her to it. Marianne, who had stood between the two women staring into the cottage, rushed past them all and cast herself joyfully on the man's chest.

'Daddy! It's Daddy!' she announced joyfully. 'Hello, Daddy. Don't sleep, please, Marianne's come to see you!'

At the sound of the shrill, much-loved little voice, Simon opened his eyes and saw, bending over him, the face he most wanted to see. Curly, sun-kissed brown hair, clear skin, the most loving, giving pair of eyes he knew. Jenny. He shut his eyes again, quickly. Hallucinating now. The last time he had opened his eyes he had thought he saw a dog!

'Simon? Darling, are you badly hurt?'

It certainly sounded like Jenny. And a hand, with a touch just like hers, was stroking his brow. He opened his eyes again and the face was still there. She looked worried.

Quickly, Simon pulled himself together. He grinned at her. And then he said something which, afterwards, he was at a loss to account for, though at the time it seemed perfectly reasonable.

'I'm all right. It wasn't my blood, I hit some poor devil on a parachute on my way down. I've just gashed my arm open on something.'

'I'm sorry, love, if you hurt someone, but I'm terribly glad you're all right yourself. Val's gone off in the car with the old chap who owns this place, to find you a doctor.'

'Good. Though I'll be OK now you're here.' Simon smiled drowsily and took her hand. 'Don't mind admitting I've been worried – do you know the old boy thought I was a Hun, Spitfire and all?'

'Yes, he said something of the sort. It just shows, you know, that all this invasion fever's not a very good thing. People get so scared they'll believe anything.'

'You're right.' There was a short silence, a comfortable, loving sort of silence, and then Simon remembered something. 'I say, Jen, just before I was hit I knocked a Stuka out of the sky! Good, eh?'

Marianne, who must have been quiet for a good five minutes, probably an all-time record, leaned forward and patted Simon's arm.

'Yes, Daddy, *bloody* good,' she said solemnly.

'It's been quite a weekend,' Val remarked very late that night, as she garaged the car between the two ambulances. 'Not quite the peaceful break we'd planned, but an experience I'm glad we didn't miss.'

'And me.' Jenny spoke softly over Marianne's sleeping head. 'Do you know, it's wonderful knowing that Simon's safely tucked up in a hospital bed, getting a lovely blood transfusion? The uncertainty of these past few weeks has been killing, though I've done my best to hide it.'

'And so you have; hidden it, I mean,' Val said, letting them both into the flat. She waited until the baby had been laid down in her cot and cuddled beneath the covers and then went into the kitchen. 'I'm parched – shall we have a hot drink?'

'Yes, that would be lovely. Cocoa and biscuits, I think. Do you realise, Val, that what with finding Simon and getting him into hospital and so on, we never got round to having dinner? But I'd rather miss a dozen dinners than one meeting with Simon, so I shan't allow my tummy rumblings to bother me.'

'Fool!' Val rummaged around in the pantry, dug out a loaf and some butter and began to make large sandwiches with the aid of a jar of jam and the bread-knife. 'I say,

Jenny, wasn't it odd, Simon knowing that you'd seen the blood on the wing of the plane and thought it was his?'

'It was.' Jenny hesitated, then turned to her friend. 'There's something even odder, though, Val. Simon never saw the blood.'

Val raised her eyebrows.

'Don't be daft. He must have! How could he have known that we had if he hadn't?'

Jenny shrugged.

'I'm not saying I understand it, I'm just telling you what he told me. He knew he'd hit someone, guessed it must be a parachutist, and then never gave it another thought. When he landed he was feeling pretty grim with losing so much blood – he had a nosebleed, too; Simon's always been prone to them if he hurls the plane around the sky too much – and he just sort of lurched out with his eyes half shut and didn't notice anything except that the tyre had been torn to bits by shellfire. But he said that when he saw me he could see what I was seeing, and it was blood and stuff on the wing.'

'Weird. Horrid, really.' Val shook herself. 'Was he very upset about Lillypooh – his, I mean, not mine?'

'Oh yes, but not terribly. He said it was Lillypooh Mark 1 and the next would be Lillypooh Mark 2. But you know Simon.'

Val smiled and agreed that she did, but, as she made her way to her room when the sandwiches were finished and the cups of cocoa drunk, she decided that this was far from the truth. Simon was not the sort of person to let a mere cousin know him; it took a loving wife to do that.

Chapter Seven

'Hop in, Maudie! Now, tell me where you'd like to go!'

Maude, settling herself in the passenger seat of Art's wheezing, noisy little car, considered the question, or pretended to do so. Really, she was enjoying the sensation of getting away from the station for a bit, and of being with Art once more.

Her elder by a year, he had always been her favourite brother even though there had been times, in their youth, when they had fought bitterly, hated vigorously, and treated each other with contemptuous scorn. But she had always known that Art was her other half, really, as Nick was Val's. She and Art were not twins, but they had always been close, held together when they were small by the constant friction between their parents and then, after Dessy, the eldest, had died of scarlet fever so that his loss brought their parents to a better understanding, by the fact that they had so many younger brothers and sisters to boss and be plagued by.

'We-ell . . . I've never visited Bath, I'd like to go there. Or we could go to Windsor, where the King and Queen live when they aren't at Buckingham Palace, or Brighton . . . there are lots of places really. The south of England may not be home, but it's not bad.'

'Or we could just doodle around,' Art suggested. 'If you've nowhere definite in mind, that is.'

Maude gave him an indulgent glance. He looked very different, with his white-blond hair cut short and bristly

117

and his shoulders suddenly broad, filling his tunic, but he was just the same. He had come a long way to see her, he was probably fairly short on petrol coupons and he was always short on money, but would he admit it? Not he!

'Doodling around would be lovely,' she said equably. 'Could we doodle down that road, there . . . to the right? There's a village green, and a river where you can hire boats, and a lovely thatched pub.'

'Oh? Yes, that might be a bit of fun, to row down the river and then have a jar or two. And you, little sister, can tell me about your war.'

'Thanks, big brother. You can tell me about yours, if you won't shoot too many lines to try and impress me. After the way we were bashed by Jerry a couple of weeks ago we've got our own lines to shoot.' The car turned off down a leafy lane and Maude leaned back and sighed. 'I've been under fire, and I didn't do any of the things I was afraid I might . . . well, I did get taken short and had to squat down very unladyishly behind the ops room, but other than that I was very good.'

'Thought you would be. I remember one of the aunts saying once, when she didn't know I was listening, that Desmond's children had to be tough because our whole lives were one long fight for survival. I thought at the time it was an odd thing to say, but now I do see her point. And we are tough, all of us, despite appearances.' Art shot her an approving glance. 'Though you look very sweet in your uniform, my child. I expect all the AC plonks tell you how it matches your eyes.'

'Some do,' Maude admitted. 'Others compare me to a summer's day! Seriously though, I did wonder what I'd do when people were bombing me and firing guns at me. And I was very calm and collected. I didn't scream, or faint, or run amok or anything like that.'

'Nor did anyone else, I daresay,' Art commented. 'I say,

I like that little pink house with the old-fashioned garden.'

'Yes, it's pretty, isn't it? Some of them did scream, though, and afterwards several of them cried. One girl cried because she had a nightdress case her mother had made, and it got torn to shreds by blast. I had a *nightdress* torn to shreds, to say nothing of some rather pretty summer dresses, and not a tear did I shed.'

'Hard as nails; I always suspected it,' Art told her. 'It must have been nasty, though, seeing the place in flames and so on. They started operating again pretty damn quick, though, didn't they?'

'Yes, very quickly. Oh, look at the ducks!'

'Want to stop? We'll buy some buns and feed 'em, if you like,' Art said, drawing the car to a halt. 'Got a boyfriend yet?'

'There's someone called Alan,' Maude said rather guardedly as they entered the village shop. 'And one called Roger – he's quite keen on me, I think. And another bloke, only I don't like him at all really, and he doesn't like me. But he hangs around.'

That was Bill, of course. Maude had wondered, after his unexpected night-time visit, how they would face each other when they next met, what he would say, what she would do. She need not have worried. They met next day, at lunchtime in the canteen, and Bill not only ignored her completely but managed to give her the impression, when their eyes did meet, that he did not remember her at all, had certainly never been friendly, and did not wish to be.

So convincing was he that Maude was no longer certain that the thing had happened at all. She remembered the feel of his hands, hot on her body through the cotton sheet, but that could easily be wishful thinking, a very vivid dream. And yet why should she have dreamed their abrupt parting, Bill climbing through the window, the officer entering the room, checking that all was quiet, leaving? It seemed such a very odd, complete sort of thing to dream!

She had wondered, at first, whether to ask Sandy what she thought, but had fairly easily decided not to do so. It would be so horrible if Sandy assumed that she, Maude, was keen on the man, chasing him in her dreams! Maude now felt, having been rudely ignored for days and days, that the last thing she wanted was any attention from Bill. No, he was exactly what Alan had once called him, in a fit of annoyance. A boor with a taste for a different poppet every night.

There was no doubt that he was attractive to women – some women, she reminded herself quickly, not decent women of taste! There was something about him . . . even Penelope, who had a very high opinion of her own worth, admitted to a certain attraction when he had danced with her one night in the village hall.

He had never asked Maude to dance. If he did, I would refuse, she reminded herself now. Damned wretch, daring to come to her room and virtually haul her out of bed . . . if he had come to her room, of course. If she had not dreamed it, conjured him up, because she secretly wanted him to make love to her.

But this would never do, standing by Art in the bright sunlight, feeding the ducks and taking surreptitious bites out of the big soft currant buns every now and then, and thinking about a man who didn't give a tinker's cuss for her. She wrenched her mind back to the present.

'And you, Art? Have you got a girlfriend?'

He shook his fair head, his face suddenly closing, becoming secretive.

'No. It's a funny job, you know, flying bombers. I suppose you could call it antisocial, to say the least. It's risky, too – if you go down it's usually over the sea or over occupied territory. Anyway, I haven't time for girls; not yet.'

'Hmm.' Maude threw her last piece of bun to the clamouring ducks and turned back to the car. 'Been home lately?'

'What a question, with leave cancelled! But actually, I did rush back for a forty-eight. There are three of us on the station from Norwich, so we pooled petrol and went together. Mummy's better, you know, living at The Pride. Gran does all her worrying for her, or at least Mummy doesn't worry when she's got Gran there. And Daddy's having a whale of a time. He told me the cinemas are doing unbelievably good business, and he enjoys the LDV activities – gives him a sense of importance, a feeling of being useful, I suppose. Good for him.' He and Maude contemplated their father's usefulness in silence for a moment. 'Old people need to feel they're doing something for the war effort,' Art concluded, ruthlessly condemning his father, all of forty-one years old, to decrepitude.

'I love going back,' Maude admitted, as they climbed into the car once more. 'Although I sometimes wish I wasn't, I'm a very *family* person. Not just your own special bit of the family either, but the whole lot. Cousins, aunts, uncles, the odd ones and the mad ones and the naughty ones – I really like them all, and I'm proud of them in an odd sort of way, too. Cara's a bitch, but you couldn't have a prettier one, could you? And Val couldn't be called pretty, but she's so fascinating and lively that no one ever notices. And think of Gran – she's a holy terror, bossy and dictatorial and a helluva snob and as narrow-minded as anything over some things, but I wouldn't change a hair of her head.'

'Me neither,' Art agreed, driving off. 'Even you, old cotton-top, have your good points.'

'Mm. And the sibs are a nice lot. Growing nicer as they age, of course.'

Art chuckled. 'The sibs! Remember the first time Gran heard you calling them that? She nearly had a heart attack! Heaven knows what she thought it was short for, but she calmed down a lot when you explained about siblings.'

Maude yawned and stretched.

'Turn right down here, you owl, or we shan't get our boating! I do miss the Broads, and Uncle Frank's place. Tell you what, when we next get leave, can't we somehow manage it at the same time? I could come over to your airfield by train – well, near it – and then you could run us both home in your little car.'

Art pulled a face.

'Next to impossible, but you never know. I got this leave, I might add, because my commanding officer heard me telling someone that my sister had been in the raid on the Kennet operations room. He came over and asked if I'd like to pop round and make sure you were all right, so of course I said yes, and bob's your uncle.' He gestured ahead of him, to where a broad stretch of grass ran down to a placid river. 'Is that it? Shall I park here?'

'Have some more potatoes, Reg.' Jenny pushed the tureen towards him, then smiled round at her guests. It was a Saturday and since the old team, as she called them, were all off duty for the evening she and Val were giving them dinner, with young Reg as the guest of honour, for it was the first time they had seen him since he started his Fire Service training. He had kept the other four – Jenny, Val, Minnie and Richie – amused with his anecdotes ever since they sat down.

'I don't mind if I do,' Reg said, ladling them out on to his already full plate. 'Hard work, running out them heavy hoses.'

As a mechanic he had been wiry and strong, but already, Jenny thought, she could see extra muscles appearing. And considering what might be required of him, this was just as well.

The sixth member of the party, sitting in her high chair, glanced meaningly at the almost empty tureen and waved her spoon commandingly.

'I don't mind if I do,' she said, in a strong cockney accent. 'Jammy pudding next!'

'She's a one, she is,' Minnie said. 'Want another potato, love? Do you know, there's nothing she doesn't notice? Fancy her watching you cooking, Jenny, close enough so's she knows what you've made.'

'She probably heard me cursing every wretched ingredient,' Jenny said ruefully, taking her place and drawing her own plate towards her again. 'We were in that beastly shelter for hours and hours. It completely wrecked our picnic in the park, though we did have jam sandwiches and apples on those horrid wooden benches. When the All Clear went we rushed home to get started on the meal, didn't we, Val?'

'Where were you, Richie?' Val said, having nodded briefly to Jenny's observations. 'I don't suppose you know any more than we do what got hit.'

'Where was I, on the first Saturday I've had off for weeks? Football, of course.'

'Of course. Which shelter did you use when the sirens sounded, then?'

Richie took a huge mouthful of stew and spoke rather thickly through it.

'None. Got on a bus first thing, see, and followed my team, because they were playing away. Missed the excitement, though they said on the bus coming home that the East Enders had got it, poor sods.'

'Oh? We thought it was the oil installations at Thames

Haven and Purfleet again,' Val said. 'Crumbs, if they've hit the docks . . . those poor blighters, they didn't have much to start with. Those little houses weren't built to last.'

'It'll be nine o'clock in a few minutes,' Reg said. 'We'll likely hear it on the news.' He finished the food on his plate and glanced around. 'Shall I help you to clear, miss?'

'Oh, thanks, Reg. The pudding should be well and truly cooked by now.'

'Jammy pudding,' Marianne reminded them, banging her spoon on the edge of her dish. 'Jammy pudding!'

'That's right. Don't bang with your spoon, darling,' Jenny said, as gravy droplets showered those nearest the small offender. 'It isn't polite.'

Marianne promptly raised her spoon and brought it down once more on her dish, just as there was a tremendous explosion from outside. With one accord, the adults left the table to rush to the window while Marianne, blinking, stared from her spoon to her dish, almost overcome by the volume of noise she had managed to produce.

Over at the window, a cacophony of talk had broken out.

'What the hell was that?'

'A bomb! That was a near one!'

'Where? Where?'

'You won't be able to see it, idiot, it could have been a mile away.'

'A mile away? To make a noise like that?'

Their voices faded as they saw a glow in the sky where no glow had been before. Reg jerked his head at it, then made for the table, where jammy pudding had not yet been served out. He spooned off a chunk, shoved it straight into his mouth, then began to cut off another piece which he wrapped in his handkerchief.

'You don't mind, miss? It's me favourite, but I'll have to go. Mind if I use . . .'

The telephone bell, ringing shrilly, cut his words off short.

'I'll go!'

Jenny rushed and Reg, already struggling into his mackintosh, headed for the door, talking over his shoulder.

'If it's for me, tell 'em I'm on my way. 'Bye, all, and fanks for the dinner.'

Jenny waved, but her attention was on the telephone. She scribbled busily on a piece of paper.

'Yes, they're here. Yes, both ambulances, too. Where?'

The voice on the other end snapped something and they all heard the ting of his receiver going down just before Jenny, too, replaced hers.

'Here, they want you two to take an ambulance down there,' she said, handing Richie her paper. 'They say they'll send another driver and conductor to take the second vehicle as soon as someone calls in.'

'Hmm, that's Silvertown,' Richie remarked as he and Val headed for the door. 'Down by the docks, it is . . . Nasty spot if there's trouble.' He turned in the doorway, struggling into his coat. 'Sorry to bust up the party, Jenny, but when you've gotta go . . .'

'It's all right, off with you.' Jenny watched them clatter down the stairs, then turned ruefully to Minnie, who was standing just behind her. 'Could you possibly give the babe her pudding, Minnie, whilst I ring the hospital? I ought to see if they need me – you can babysit for me, I suppose?' Jenny had volunteered as a nursing auxiliary.

'Love to,' Minnie declared. 'I'll kip down in the spare bed in Mari's room unless the warning goes off again and if it does I'll take her down to the basement with a couple of blankets round her. The pair of us will be all right down there.'

Even as she spoke, they heard the long drawn out wail of the air-raid siren. Heaving a sigh, Minnie removed Marianne from the high chair and ran with her into her bedroom, dragging blankets off the cot as soon as she entered and taking one off the spare bed, too.

'They want me to go round straight away,' Jenny said, appearing in the doorway struggling into her coat. 'Can you cope, my dear? Bless you! I hope she won't be too much trouble.'

As Jenny ran ahead of them down the stairs she could not help smiling to herself.

Behind her, a desperate wail rent the air.

'Oh, oh, oh! Jammy pu-udding!'

'This is my idea of hell,' Val shouted as the ambulance, with Richie driving, drew nearer to the stricken East End. They were forbidden to use headlights, or even sidelights, which usually made driving extremely hazardous, but tonight they did not even notice their lack, for on every side fires blazed and the roads were lit by the inferno.

Which was as well, Val reflected, because of the bomb craters. Everywhere huge holes pitted the roads and if it wasn't craters it was rubble, for scarcely a house seemed to be standing. Judging by the thick and choking dust which rose on all sides, most of them had been hit fairly recently, what was more. The smell, as they penetrated further into the dock area, was extraordinary, pungent and frightening, and Val guessed that a paintshop or a chemical works had also been hit.

'Bad bit here!'

Richie had to shout, because the noise was unbelievable. The throb of the aircraft overhead was scarcely heard against the sound of the bombs as they shrieked earthwards; then there was the louder sound as they exploded, and the worst noise yet as the buildings tottered and fell.

And fire, of course, is one of the noisiest of the elements, roaring as it devours. Even the traffic was noisy, since it was nearly all ambulances and fire engines.

'Where are we heading?'

Val had completely lost all sense of direction. She had never grown as familiar with this area as Richie had, for she had mainly gone with him when he was taking vehicles for hire. When he drove buses into the East End he did so to take trips out, so Val had never accompanied him. But Richie, it was plain, knew it like the back of his hand. Presently he drew up beside some firefighters where the road ahead was clogged with a long queue of traffic. Ambulances, fire engines and tenders were waiting to cross what appeared to be a bridge ahead, yet it was blazing already and the water-jets seemed thin and powerless against the strength of the flames.

'What's the 'old-up, mate?' Richie bawled, and a smoke-blackened fireman gestured forward.

'It ain't the bridge, though it looks like it; it's a warehouse. Fell across the road. Going to take a bit of time to clear it, and of course we've got to keep the water spraying on the bridge. You'll 'ave to wait, if you asks me.'

Richie wound his window up again, swore pungently, fought his way into a tight turn, and then began to drive as fast as he could back the way they had come.

'Is there another way through?' Val gasped, hanging on to her seat as the vehicle bucked and bounded over piles of rubble and round craters. 'Don't wreck the old girl, Richie, or we shan't be much help to anyone!'

'I know what I'm doing.' Richie continued to drive onwards, lurching across ground which Val would have sworn had never been a road even before the bombing. 'I know the area well enough if I can just take a right turn here . . .' he wrenched the ambulance round between two wobbly and burning dwellings '. . . and another at the end of this wharf . . .'

They had reached what surely must be the heart of the conflagration, with the hellish roar of burning now out-shouting the bombs. The firemen, holding hoses with a dribble of water emerging, must have felt pretty helpless, Val thought, but at Richie's command she jumped down and ran over to the nearest, enquiring where an ambulance was needed. The man, smoke-blackened and hoarse after hours of fighting the fires, could not help.

'All dead here,' he croaked. 'You'll have to go further in.'

They continued on their mad journey. They passed down roads where not one house had a roof, as if a gigantic hand had lifted them all off, uniformly, for some sort of joke. They went down mean little streets where every house was ablaze, along others where warehouses lined the roadway and through the glassless windows you could see the fires which raged within. Every now and then one of these warehouses must have contained something extra-inflammable, for it would go up like a rocket, with a tremendous whoosh of noise and a column of sparks and fire like a volcano.

'This must be it,' Richie bawled at last. He drew his vehicle to a halt beside a group of LDV workers, who hailed him eagerly. One of them spoke to Val as she lowered her window.

'Glad you're here. There are injured in the shelter. You won't get the vehicle through, but we'll give you a hand to get them out to it. Got any stretchers?'

'Two.' Val hurled herself out of the cab and round the back, seized the stretchers, and set off at a trot after the man, Richie on her heels. She had supposed the warden referred to a deep shelter, similar to the one she and Jenny had occupied earlier in the day, but when they reached it it was a poor thing, only partly below ground and badly built, so that it shook with every blast, offering an extremely doubtful refuge.

The warden began marshalling people towards the ambulance, leaving Val and Richie with the wounded, while other workers took over the second stretcher. Val went to a woman who lay on the floor, white-faced and silent. Her legs were bathed in scarlet and one of them, though towel-wrapped, was plainly broken. She and Richie helped the woman on to the stretcher and carried her to the ambulance and all the while she never said a word or made a sound but only watched, big-eyed, as they passed the blazing buildings. Later, Val was to realise that it was shock which kept people silent after the most dreadful wounds and ordeals, but now she thought the woman extraordinarily stoical as they hurried her back to the relative comfort of the ambulance.

When they left, the vehicle was packed. They took as many as they could because it was clear there was no safety here, though the LDV workers stayed on. They would go to another part of their patch and try to help people stranded there.

Richie drove carefully now, not very fast, though he confided to Val after they had unloaded their passengers at the nearest hospital that he had been terribly worried on that return drive.

'Silvertown's like an island, see,' he told her. 'Couple of swing bridges, all those docks, and if one of the big warehouses had fallen wrong we could have been trapped, along with all them other poor buggers.'

But they had not been trapped that time, and nor were they trapped the other times, for they continued, throughout the dreadful night, to drive through impossible conditions in order to bring what succour they could to the people of the East End. They found their way by ask and by guess, using a sense of direction which Val would have sworn neither of them possessed in such abundance. The bombing continued unabated until about three in the morning and even then, at first, because of the noise of the fires and the rumble of collapsing buildings, they did not realise that the enemy had, for the moment, finished with them. When it finally occurred to them they could scarcely take it in because they were, by then, so physically and mentally exhausted.

Richie drove them home at six in the morning and they went straight to their flats with no more than a tired grin as farewell. Ascending the stairs, Val turned her key in the lock as quietly as she could and made for her bedroom. She just wanted to sleep and sleep . . . but as she took her clothes off she realised, for the first time, that she was black as any fireman with her skin, her hair, and even the insides of her ears and nostrils, thick with soot and dust. She would have to bathe before getting between those nice clean sheets.

She fell asleep twice in the bath, frightening herself, and was climbing out and wrapping herself in a towel when she heard someone on the stairs. Could it be Simon? He was due out of hospital any day, and would come home for a while before starting work once more. She dried herself quickly, pulled on her nightdress and a dressing-gown and hurried to the door. It must be Simon! For some reason her tired and confused brain was certain that her cousin had managed to get away earlier than planned and was waiting to be let in. She heard a key in the lock and was disproportionately astonished when Jenny, looking quite grey with exhaustion, dragged herself into the hall. She had imagined her friend asleep in bed for hours!

'What a night!' Jenny was still in uniform, which she began to drag off as they stood there, dropping her clothing straight on to the floor. 'Lawks, we've had a time of it! A lot of the senior staff went off to deal with casualties direct – a school full of people was hit – and that meant that there weren't enough of us to go round, so I've been doing whatever I was told to do and finding out how to do it afterwards! Have you run out your bath water?'

'Oh, sorry, no . . .' Val began, but Jenny merely smiled and pushed open the bathroom door.

'Good. I'll get straight into it, then. I'll just have a quick one because I'm awfully tired; we'll talk in the morning.'

'It is morning,' Val pointed out, swaying on her feet. She watched Jenny drop into the filthy water in the tub, then picked up her friend's clothes. The white cuffs of the dress and the full white apron were speckled red. It was clear that she was not the only one who had been baptised with fire that night.

A week later, Jenny was in the flat making an early tea when the doorbell rang. She hurred to answer it, hoping against hope that it might be Simon, for he was out of hospital and, though he had resolutely refused to take the leave due to him, he had promised her that as soon as he felt he could he would come home. But it was not. Reg stood on the doorstep, with a number of paper carrier bags in his arms.

'Sorry to descend on you, Miz Rose, but Richie told me to come.'

'Come in, Reg. D'you mind the kitchen? I'm getting tea so that we can have it before the raids start.' Reg followed her and she cut him a slice of bread and butter before continuing to dip pieces of cod in batter. 'Now, can I help you?'

'We've been working so damn hard, Miz Rose, that I've not 'ad a chance to get home much,' Reg said, his ferrety face looking tight and strained. 'But I went 'ome this dinnertime, wiv me mates, and . . .'

Jenny laid down the fish as Reg's mouth began to pull itself into odd shapes and her arms went out and caught him to her, hugging him fiercely, letting him hide his emotion from her while another part of her mind thought how odd it was that her arms had guessed what he was going to say long before her brain had caught on.

'The 'ouse wasn't even there,' Reg said, between gulps. 'Nor most of the street. Mum's awright and me two lickle sisters, but me dad's gone. 'E was a warden, and they don't take shelter, see? But, Miz Rose, we ain't got nowhere to go and me mum don't want to leave me 'ere and take the kids into the country, like they said, and Richie remembered that there ain't no one in Mr Nick's flat . . .'

'Well, you and your family must move in at once,' Jenny said, understanding. 'It'll be nice to have you close, Reg, and nice to have another woman besides Minnie and Val and myself here. We're out so much . . . do you think your mum would help out a bit with Marianne? Perhaps your little sisters could come round and play with her. There aren't any other children round here.'

She was speaking partly from conviction but partly so that Reg could recover himself before having to say anything else. He was pleased, she could tell, but she could also tell that he had never expected her to refuse.

'That's great. Richie said you'd let us . . . but what about Mr Nick's stuff? We ain't got nuffing left, but I wouldn't want to spoil 'is fings.'

Jenny gave him a little shake and moved back to the table, where she examined the fish furtively. Enough for one more? Of course!

'Nonsense, Reg, Nick won't mind. Just try not to break his precious gramophone records and he won't give a hang about anything else. Where's your mum now?'

'Oh . . . in the Fishers' place. Did you know they've

taken in anuvver of me mates?' Chap called Duggie
Dwyer. 'E was bombed out and 'is wife bought it.'

'Yes, Richie told me.' Jenny did more lightning calcula-
tions. 'Go and tell your mum it's fine by me and give her
the key . . .' Jenny reached it down from its hook above
the sink '. . . and tell her I'm cooking tea for us all tonight,
and can she be round here in about thirty minutes, please.
Do your sisters like fish and chips?'

'Not 'alf,' Reg said briefly, heading for the kitchen door.
'Fanks a lot, Miz Rose.'

'Jenny? I'm coming home for a few days. I wouldn't have,
but I've got engine trouble and for once we've more pilots
than aircraft, so I thought I'd grab the opportunity whilst it
lasts. Pleased?'

Jenny, cradling the phone blissfully against her cheek, let
a huge smile spread across her face. He was coming home!

'Pleased? Oh, Simon, you don't know how much. It
seems absolutely ages since I saw you last! When?'

'Tomorrow. About teatime, I think. And you know one
reason I'm coming back, don't you?'

'Oh, dear.' Ever since the raids had started, Simon had
been begging Jenny to leave London. But surely he
realised she could not possibly do such a thing? To leave
the city would have meant abandoning Val, her job at the
hospital . . . she could not do it!

'Don't oh dear me, my love! My mother's gone, did you
know? Went down to Norwich and stayed there. Mind
you, she's sure that the raids can't go on much longer, so
she hasn't opened up the house – she's staying with
Auntie Tina at The Pride – but nevertheless . . .'

'Oh please, Simon, don't let's argue; anyway, you
wouldn't want me to go back to Norwich, would you?
They've had some dreadful raids. That was why Val and I
went into Surrey that weekend.'

133

'I know, I know. We'll talk about it when I get home. How about cooking a man's favourite supper? Want me to bring anything back with me?'

'Just yourself,' Jenny said exultantly. Wonderful, to have Simon home for a few days, even though the nights would probably be spent in that beastly basement with everyone else.

'Right. Give the babe a big kiss from her daddy and tell her to watch for me around fourish. 'Bye until then, sweetheart.'

Jenny replaced the receiver and made for the kitchen. She was tired and everyone she knew was tired. Not with a healthy, ordinary sort of tiredness but with the slow and dragging lethargy of total exhaustion. The bombing had not let up at all. Every night for ages the siren had sounded and they had heard the throb of the bombers' engines, the whistle and crash of the high-explosive tearing to earth, and the roar of fires and blast. The noise made by the anti-aircraft batteries surrounding the city was welcomed, of course, but it did not seem to do very much good. Everyone was waiting for a list of enemy aircraft shot down, but so far they waited in vain.

She did not know what was worse, to be at the hospital and away from the baby at nights, or to be shut up with her head down in the basement. No one ever made the pretence any more of going to bed like a Christian, as Minnie called it. The moment dusk began to fall it was into sensible clothing and on with preparations for the night ahead. In Jenny's case, this consisted of making up several flasks – hot milk for Marianne, tea and coffee for the adults, and a smaller flask of brandy for near misses when the shelter shook and the whistle sounded right overhead and you were convinced that this was the one with your name on. Reg's mother, Dora Grundy, and the two little girls named Elizabeth and Margaret after the princesses but known to all and sundry as Liz and Maggie, seldom came down to the basement, which they thought creepy and dangerous. They went, as soon as there was even a hint of darkness, down to the tube station where they slept on the platform, on the escalators, even in the long, echoing corridors, wrapped in skimpy home-made sleeping bags and joining in singsongs, round games and, sometimes, fights.

'You oughter join us, luv,' Dora Grundy urged, once she discovered that Jenny dreaded being alone in the basement with Marianne. 'It's ever so deep, ever so safe, they say. And we 'ave a laugh, we do.'

'No, I daren't,' Jenny said diplomatically. 'You know what you said about the fights, and about the night when someone started a panic and they all surged up the stairs and people got crushed; Marianne's too small for things like that yet.'

She did not tell the truth, which was that the smell alone was enough to put her off, and that she hated crowds more than she hated the basement.

But she was not often alone. Minnie always used the basement during raids, and so did her lodger, and so did Richie when he was off duty. Val did too, though Jenny suspected that Val hated it just as much as she did. Val was awful, always popping up at the least sign of a let-up in the noise to see whether it was over yet, or to get another blanket, or to use the toilet. There was a discreet bucket in the inner cellar, which they used when they thought it unwise to go above ground, but Val always managed either to last out or to risk going back to the flat.

This evening, however, as she bustled round making preparations for the night ahead, Jenny did not mind nearly as much as usual. After all, Simon would be home tomorrow night, so she would be sure of some company. Richie and Val were both on duty, Minnie was staying overnight with friends who lived out Croydon way, and the Grundys would be going down to the tube. That left herself and the Fishers' lodger, and Mr Dwyer had already announced his intentions.

'Them bastards may kill me, but they ain't going to deprive me of another night's sleep,' he had said, when Jenny met him dragging himself over to the flats in the early morning. 'I'm 'aving a barf, then I'm getting into my kip and I'm going to bloody sleep the bloody clock round, until I stop seeing fires in me 'ead.'

Understanding the urgent, indeed imperative, desire and need for sleep, Jenny had not attempted to argue with him. After all, he was doing a terribly dangerous job – more firemen were killed than most people realised – and Reg had told her that they'd had two men blinded since he started regular work with the Service. It was the heat that did it, he explained.

She was pouring Marianne's hot milk into the flask when someone rang the bell. It was Liz, the elder Grundy girl.

'Just to tell you we're off, Mrs Rose. And Mum says that if the warden asks, Mr Dwyer's the only one in the flats tonight. He told her to say the place was empty,' she added earnestly. 'But Mum says it won't do, and even if Mr D. won't shelter they've got to know where 'e is. Might save a deal of trouble.'

'Right, Liz, thanks very much,' Jenny said, shutting the door as the pale-faced little creature turned and trotted down the stairs again. She saw why Mrs Grundy wanted the warden to know the truth. If the shelters were hit, or if the flats were hit and the basement knocked in, they would want to know exactly who was where. No use searching the rubble of a shelter for a man snoozing peacefully in his own flat; no use leaving a man buried in the rubble of his home because you thought him safe in the shelter.

But it was a miserable business.

Jenny turned to the kitchen and began making the coffee.

'Oh damn, the phone!' Jenny jumped up from the table where she, Val and Marianne were having breakfast and snatched the receiver off the hook. Pray it isn't Simon, cancelling his leave, was her first thought, but she was safe; it was only her mother-in-law ringing from Norwich.

'Jenny, darling? Lovely to hear you; how are things?'

'Hello, Mother, lovely to hear you as well. We're fine. And you?'

Sarah's warm, cheerful voice came over the wire for a few minutes, giving her daughter-in-law all the news and telling her, rather wryly, that Cara was bearing up very well to the fact that her husband had lost an arm and was in a German p.o.w. camp.

'Rather too well, in fact,' Sarah admitted now.' She's a spoilt little madam but I don't care for the way she behaved when she heard about poor William. She finds physical disability embarrassing and nauseating, which is why we haven't broken it to her yet that William lost a leg as well as his arm. Honestly, the way she carried on! She seemed to take the word 'lost' quite literally, and to hear her telling people you'd think the poor fellow had deliberately mislaid the thing to annoy her!'

'I can imagine,' Jenny said warmly. 'But she'll have to be told one day.'

'Probably,' Jenny wondered whether her mother-in-law knew that Cara was spending every spare moment with any member of the armed forces who could afford her company. Probably not – Auntie Tina certainly seemed to notice nothing amiss, and she was with Cara all the time whereas Sarah had only been down in Norwich for a few days. But in fact she wronged both women. Tina knew but hoped that, if she ignored it, the nasty knowledge would go away. Sarah knew, and intended to give her daughter such a wigging that she would think twice before being unfaithful to William again. If she was unfaithful. Sarah rather thought that Cara was far too selfish to give anything for nothing, particularly herself.

'Simon's coming home today.'

'Really, darling? How nice for you. Is he going to bring you down to Norwich for a while?'

Sarah never nagged, never interfered, but Jenny guessed that she must want her only granddaughter near her and far from the Blitz. She was reluctant to shatter hopes, but it had to be done.

'No, not this time. Last time we came down, if you remember, there was a bad raid and it seems irresponsible to take Marianne from one lot of bombing to another. She's used to the flat and she's got toys and so on down in the basement – not that we spend much time there during the day if we can help it. It's mainly at nights, and she sleeps pretty soundly then.'

'I suppose you're right, though we haven't had a raid for over a month. And perhaps Simon wants to see a bit of life, theatres and so on. Anyway, give him my love, won't you, and tell him to see if he can spend an hour or two with Uncle Con whilst he's in town. Poor darling, he misses me, though he says he'd rather have it this way and know I'm safe.'

When she had said goodbye and rung off, Jenny returned rather slowly to the kitchen. Val, spooning soft-boiled egg into Marianne, turned and smiled at her.

'Auntie Sarah? She's a darling, isn't she? It must be jolly hard for her having to choose between Uncle Con and Sebby all the time. But perhaps Uncle Con might get a job in Norwich, you never know.'

'Perhaps. Val, what do *you* think about leaving London?'

'I think you ought to go,' Val said promptly. 'I love living here with you, I'd miss you terribly, but I still think you ought to go. It's much harder on you than it is on me because you've got the baby to worry about. And the home to run and your job to fit in. But you aren't going to listen to me, so I shan't nag you.'

'No,' Jenny said thoughtfully, taking her place at the table again and beginning to butter a slice of toast. 'No, but I rather think Simon will.'

Chapter Eight

Although Jenny had assumed that Simon intended to spend his leave in London he had come home at four o'clock, taken one look at his wife and daughter, and borrowed all Val's hoarded petrol coupons to fill up his own car.

'Sweet coz, I know you won't mind. I'm appalled by the way Jen looks,' he told Val at the first opportunity. 'She doesn't just need me, she needs to sleep properly, to eat properly and to forget about danger, shelters and sick people.'

'Don't we all,' Val commented. She, too, was feeling the strain, though she knew she was not suffering as much as Jenny. She was out in the ambulance through the worst of the raids, moving through the streets, and no matter how dangerous it might be you could never quite convince yourself that a moving target was as hittable as something – or someone – who just sat there and waited for it. She was always far jumpier when she was in the basement and she could only imagine how Jenny must feel night after night at the hospital, telling her patients that the hospital was a steel construction (which was true) and almost indestructible (which was not).

So she watched Jenny climb into the front seat of the car, settle Marianne on her lap, and wave as they went, and knew that Jenny was smiling from her heart and would benefit tremendously from her little holiday.

She waved until they were out of sight and then

returned to the flat, and as she was sitting at the kitchen table, eating poached eggs on toast and reading the paper, propped up against the teapot, she had a sudden premonition. She had better get used to it, because the chances were that solitary meals were to be her lot from now on.

'We'll find our own peace,' Simon had said, as they drove away from London, and he was as good as his word. They spent the first night at an inn by the roadside, but next day he found just what he was looking for. A cottage in a fold of the Cotswolds with the hopeful sign 'Bed & Breakfast' swinging above the gate. The Harpers, who owned the place, told them that they mostly catered for walkers and cyclists these days, people who wanted to get away from the cities for a while. But they were given the best bedroom, with a tiny room leading off it which was ideal for Marianne, and the exclusive use of a brand-new bathroom, put in just before war broke out, Mrs Harper told them proudly.

They found the cottage at teatime and that first night Mrs Harper made them a dinner which seemed to indicate that rationing had not yet reached this remote and lovely spot, though Mrs Harper was quick to point out, when Jenny made a remark to that effect, that fish was not rationed for anyone, that fresh fruit would grow in most gardens that got sun and a good twice-yearly manuring, and that if the hens were in lay anyone with a bit of go about them could make egg custard.

For the second night running, Simon encouraged Jenny to go to bed at nine, came up with a hot drink, and found her dead to the world. His idea of a second honeymoon had not included a bride who slept for twelve hours at a stretch, but he was far too generous a husband to complain. He woke her with tea and biscuits at nine in the morning, and to her startled and guilty enquiries about their child assured her that Marianne had been up and about for hours, had eaten an enormous breakfast, and was at this very moment pottering around the garden with Mr Harper, feeding the hens, collecting the eggs, and talking non-stop.

Breakfast provided mute testimony to the hens, to the pig up the road which had been slaughtered to everyone's benefit, it seemed, and to the wisdom of baking one's own wholemeal bread. After the meal Simon packed them into the car and took them down to the coast. It was a bright autumn day and Jenny and Marianne paddled, built a huge castle and dug a deep moat round it whilst Simon lay watching them and soaking up the sunshine.

'What price West End shows?' he murmured as Jenny lay down beside him and rested her head in the hollow of his shoulder. 'What price four-course meals in big shiny restaurants? What price London, in fact?'

'A fig for them,' Jenny mumbled, snuggling up. 'Gracious, look, Mari's fallen asleep, and I thought she was perpetual motion!'

Sunbonnet askew, woolly bathing suit rucked up over one tiny, round buttock, Marianne slept with the abandonment of childhood, half on the rug and half on the golden sand. She did not wake when they got back into the car, nor on the drive, nor when they popped her into the cot in her tiny room.

'It's plenty of good, clean country air and proper food, that's what does it,' Mrs Harper remarked, as she served the two of them with a good, old-fashioned dinner – or what she said was an old-fashioned dinner – of fresh tomato soup, roast lamb with mint sauce and a black-currant pie and fresh cream that had Simon begging for seconds. 'It's no place for children, London, not even in peacetime.'

'I know, but my work's there,' Jenny said, rendered far

more uncomfortable by this homely woman's remarks than by Sarah's gentle questioning or Simon's pleas. 'I couldn't let people down by leaving, could I?'

Mrs Harper smiled at her and shook her head.

'No. But you don't perhaps think it's worse to let the little one down?'

'I don't know,' Jenny said. She was trying so hard to do the right thing, to keep working at the hospital, to run the flat, to do the shopping, take care of Marianne . . . above all, to keep going on when what she most wanted was to sleep and sleep in a proper bed. There was a solution, though, which would in a way answer both sides of the question. She could send Marianne down to Norwich, to be taken care of by someone else. She had worried quite a lot about the actual air in London, which was constantly dirty now as the bombed buildings and the fires filled the atmosphere with dust and soot. She could at least spare Marianne that if she sent her away.

She said as much to Simon when they were driving slowly back to the city, the following day. And Simon, as always, was fair.

'The decision must be yours, my love, but isn't Marianne a bit young just to be farmed out? I honestly think she needs her mother for a bit yet. If you feel you can't leave . . .

Through orchards heavy with fruit, past woods where the leaves were just reluctantly turning colour the little car sped, until they began to re-enter the suburbs once more. Here, too, hedges were turning, grass was wearying of its summer brilliance and taking on the softer tint of autumn, and the little gardens all had their apples, pears, scarlet-berried shrubs. And then the scene changed again as they entered London itself. They could smell burning, see the choking dust which flew whenever the car passed a pile of rubble that had once been a home. Jenny's nose wrinkled with distaste, yet inside her something welcomed it all. The friendliness she had known here, the feeling that, whatever came, they were all in it together, had been marvellous. People came into hospital who had lost everything yet they smiled, thanked you for what you had done, and went out again to make themselves some sort of life. And in their turn, they shared whatever they had salvaged with others.

It was not yet seven o'clock when they drove into Granville Gardens. Simon parked the car on the long frontage and then glanced across at their home . . . and stopped moving, puzzled. Something was different. Not wrong, perhaps, but different, not quite right . . .

'Why are the big doors closed?'

Yes, that was it. The big doors were left open all day so that the ambulances and the cars and buses could drive in and out, and they were left open at weekends so that the people cleaning and servicing the vehicles could see without having to use the electric lights. So why were they shut now, when it was still daylight and a sunny day at that?

Jenny picked Marianne up and tucked her arm into Simon's. The three of them went forward, a little uncertain still, and Simon opened the small door at the side which led into the garages – and stopped short once again.

The back gardens had been concreted over and were used to park the buses and any cars which were not hired out. It was immediately obvious that a bomb had landed there; a huge, still-smoking crater greeted them and half a bus lay in the bottom of it. The other half protruded from a pile of rubble. When you looked closely you could see bits of bus and car all over the place . . . and bricks, window-frames, a door with the glass panel still intact. A strip of familiar carpet hung from the poplar tree which grew against the back wall, and now you could see through the wall into the road behind, because part of it was no longer there.

Clutching each other tightly, Simon and Jenny stepped into the garden and looked up at the flats. There were six, and the backs of five of them had been sheered right off. Half their bathroom was on public view, half Val's room, half Marianne's nursery. The bathtub had two legs on the floor and two legs in space, and looked very unsure of itself, like a swimmer about to plunge into the sea yet not altogether believing that the water was warm enough.

'My God!'

Simon's whispered exclamation broke the silence and Marianne, pointing upwards, remarked: 'Teddy! And Rupert and Bajjy and Sailor Bill and . . .'

'That's right, love.' Simon took her from Jenny and held her very tightly against his shoulder. 'All your nice toys, eh? But not you, thank God, not you!'

'What shall we do?' Jenny's voice was small and scared. 'Where's Val? And where are the others? When . . .'

'It's all right, but we'll have to make some phone calls, find out . . .' Simon was saying, when a familiar figure came through into the garden. It was Minnie, reassuringly normal in her grey shopping coat and flat, sensible shoes.

'Back? Well, here's a horrible thing to come home to! Never mind, no one was so much as scratched, though poor Dora Grundy had a bit of a collapse. Understandable, when you think it's the second time she's had a home bombed out from under her, so to speak. Val's working, said it would take her mind off it, and Richie's with her, of course. The rest of us are in the end flat. The authorities came and did tests and said it was safe. Freakish, these blasts, it seems. It's crowded, mind, though once things are sorted out it'll just be them as has to stay near here what'll live there. Richie, of course, and Val; Duggie and the boy Reg. I'm to cook and make do for 'em, but everyone else will need to find somewhere else. Fire Station's only just down the road, see, and once the authorities have satisfied themselves that the building isn't about to come down they're going to bring the ambulances back.'

Minnie had been running on whilst they took it all in and collected themselves; now, she saw that they would be all right. She held out her arms to Marianne.

'Come to Minnie then, baby! We'll go up to the end flat and I'll make a nice cup of tea and we'll have some cake and then you can discuss what you're going to do for the next few nights. Oh, and I've got your post, Mr Simon, and yours too, Jenny, though it doesn't look important. Come along.'

They followed her up the familiar/unfamiliar stairs, into the flat that was the twin of theirs yet so very different. Some people called Wright had had the flat before the war, but they had taken all their stuff out of it when they went, leaving only odd wallpaper, a kitchen with the walls painted deep pink and the paintwork white and some multi-coloured linoleum. Minnie, it appeared, had been busy already. Nick's big, soft green sofa was along one wall, the two winged armchairs from their own flat stood on a strange square of carpet, and the curtains at the windows had once graced Minnie's kitchen.

'You've done wonders,' Simon said, looking around him. 'What about a stove, and beds?'

'We got quite a decent electric cooker from the council,' Minnie said with pardonable pride, leading them to the kitchen which already looked cosy and lived in. 'Reg shinned up your stairs and brought down that nice kitchen table and two of the chairs – the others weren't any good – and he and Duggie swung the rest of the stuff down on ropes. Blankets and things were easy, but we haven't bothered with beds, we just brought mattresses.' She led the way through into the first bedroom. 'See? A bit like a dormitory, but that's war for you.'

'Marvellous,' Simon told her. 'Now let's have that tea and a bit of a chat. When will Val be back?'

'Tomorrow morning.' They were passing through the hall when Minnie put a hand to her mouth. 'Oh, I nearly forgot your post. Here.' She fished it out from under the telephone and Simon took it, and then they returned to the kitchen. Minnie shot a shrewd glance at Jenny, who had not said a word. 'Come on, luv, you make the toast whilst I see to the tea, and Simon can read his letters.'

Halfway through the preparations, however, the phone rang and Minnie made her way into the hall, shutting the kitchen door behind her. When she put the receiver down she called through the door that she would be going out for fifteen minutes, and then they heard the front door shut.

Jenny took a deep, shuddering breath and spoke.

'All right, don't say it. I've made up my mind at long last. Marianne can't stay here, though I expect they'll find me something at the hospital. I'll send her . . . no, take her . . . down to Norwich tomorrow, and leave her at The Pride with your mother and Auntie Tina.'

Simon took hold of her and shook her gently. In his arms, she felt that she could almost sense the tension in him, which was being held in check for her sake.

'No, sweetheart, you're getting away from all this, both of you. I haven't said anything before, because I thought you deserved your chance to help with the war effort and to do what you wanted to do, but I'm going to tell you now just how I feel. How do you think I can fly successfully knowing that your danger is every bit as great as mine? That's the way to get killed, to have your mind on the ground when you're in the air. I want to fight to defend you and to preserve your peace, not your pieces.'

His voice shook a little and Jenny, winding her arms round his neck, knew that she would do anything to save him pain. She acknowledged, a little sadly, that she had not been sacrificing herself in remaining in London, she had been behaving very selfishly. The sacrifice would be to leave the danger and the excitement, the feeling of being at the centre of great events. She would go, as Simon wanted her to, and she would go where he wanted her to, and not just for Marianne's sake, either. She would go for Simon's sake, because she knew that he was right; he could not give his whole heart and mind to his work when he was worrying about her.

'I see. And you're right, of course. I'll leave. But where shall we go, Simon?'

She felt him relax, felt the tension drain out of him, and knew she had made the right, the only, decision.

'Where? I'll think of somewhere.' They heard the front door open and shut, and Minnie's footsteps approaching across the bare floor boards. They let go of each other and began to butter bread, to lay the table, to chatter inconsequentially.

They were halfway through their tea when Simon remembered the letters and got them out of his pocket.

'Better read them . . . hey, here's one from my best girl!'

'Curse those little blonde WAAF officers. They have all the glamour,' Jenny remarked, cutting Marianne's bread and butter into soldiers so that she could dip them into her egg. 'Which one is it this time?'

'It's little Rosie-posie.' Simon read, chuckled, read again, then handed the letter to his wife. 'She's a gem, that kid. Just read it and then Minnie can have a go.'

But Jenny had hardly begun to read the first page when Simon slapped his knee and exclaimed.

'Got it! Of course! Why didn't I think of it at first? You

can go to Devon, to the farm Rose was evacuated to. Bless me, why didn't that occur to me earlier?'

'Possibly because you guessed they wouldn't want an unknown woman and child thrust on them,' Jenny said with an edge to her voice. Devon was a very long way away! 'Darling, they've got Rose and another child from the orphanage; they won't want anyone else!'

'But they will – they do! You haven't reached the second page, but if you just take a look you'll see that Rose says she's going to have to move out of her big bedroom so that two landgirls can have it. Mr and Mrs Riley haven't actually done anything about getting the girls yet, but they'll have to, because the son who did most of the heavy work has joined up and is driving a tank, according to Rose, and their other worker is off in a week or two to an ack-ack battery outside Plymouth.'

'Well, yes, but . . . a farm, miles from anywhere? How could I help with the war effort? I wouldn't want to do nothing but mother Marianne,' Jenny pointed out.

'No, I know you wouldn't, but the Rileys want help on the land! Darling, wouldn't you like that? You're so energetic, you love being out of doors, and yet you'd be safe and away from the big cities. Those Rileys are good people, judging from what Rose says, and to tell you the truth I'd like you to be with Rosie-posie. That child has always been underestimated by everyone except us.'

Jenny gave Simon an uncertain glance. She knew he had always felt close to Rose and was almost as fond of the orphaned child as he was of Marianne. Ever since they had met, when Rose's orphanage walked through Granville Gardens on their way to school, there had been a special sort of feeling between Rose and herself and Simon, though Rose had been attracted to them in the first place merely because their name was Rose as well. The fact that hers was her first name and theirs a surname did not seem to matter much to the child.

But if it was really what Simon wanted . . . If it would give him peace of mind so that he wouldn't go getting himself killed . . . Jenny began to read the letter. Yes, it was true, the Rileys would be getting a couple of landgirls and Rose would have to give up her big room with the lovely fat feather bed and move into a small attic room. But she did not mind, not Rose! The attic was lovely, it had a view unsurpassed. She could even see the pond!

Jenny laid the letter down. 'All right, if you're sure it's the right thing to do. I'll write to the Rileys tonight.'

'No. Telegraph. Explain to Mrs Riley that you'll work, and pay for your keep and Mari's, what's more. Tell her to telephone if they can't have you, but otherwise say you'll be arriving . . . well, the day after tomorrow.'

'Oh, but that's too soon,' Jenny cried. She could feel tears welling up. 'And Simon . . . I'll be so far from you . . . No more forty-eights, it won't be long enough . . . And so far from Norwich . . . So far . . .'

He came round the table and took her in his arms. Over her head he smiled at Minnie. He could see she understood and approved.

'Darling, what makes you think that I'll be stationed in the south of England for ever? I may get posted abroad. I could end up miles and miles away from London. See?'

'Yes, I suppose so. But while you are here, will they l- let you save up your leave so's you can get down to us? Or can we come up to visit you?'

Jenny's voice was wobbly, but she knew Simon was right which made it easier to bear.

'I'm sure they will. Be brave, darling, the war can't last for ever.'

But Jenny, drafting a telegram to send to Mrs Riley,

thought that sometimes a couple of months could feel like years.

The trap carrying the children bounded across the rutted lane. There were four of them now – Rose and Roy, both bound for the Rileys' farm, and James and Denham, who lived 'up'n over' according to Mrs Riley, which meant that their house was on the other side of the hill. Earlier, there had been six – a bit of a squeeze but good fun nevertheless, especially for Rose, because the two who had just been dropped off were at her school, and what was more they were not native Devonians but Londoners, as thrilled by the marvels of the country as Rose and Roy were.

Not that Roy ever showed his excitement, of course, for he was thirteen and nearly old enough to leave school. Mrs Riley was having a running battle at the moment with the people who managed the orphanage, who thought Roy ought to start work. But Mrs Riley argued that when the war was over the country would need people with brains and qualifications, and she wanted Roy to get his school certificate, perhaps even higher. Matriculation was not beyond him, they said at the grammar school, and Mrs Riley's eldest boy, who had gone to Cambridge and had letters after his name, had done very well indeed for himself. Even Philip, who had been at the farmhouse when Rose and Roy had first arrived, had been clever. He had gone to agricultural college, Mrs Riley told her young guests proudly, and not only could he plough as straight a furrow as Mr Riley himself and help a cow with a breech birth, but he knew why he did what he did!

'Which is more than 'ee may do, my 'andsome,' Mrs Riley had remarked to her husband, smiling at him. 'Yet you do right, howsomever.'

The trap bounced over a couple more ruts and Roy abandoned his attempt to read. He stuffed the book into his blazer pocket and turned to his companions.

'I wonder who will drive us to and from school when Sizzle goes? Can Mrs Riley drive, do you think?'

Sizzle, sitting on the driver's seat and appearing to be half asleep, guffawed.

'The missus? Course she can, boy! But it'll be one of they landgals, you mark my words. Missus can't spare time cartin' 'ee to school an' back.'

'Landgirls? Yes, but suppose they can't drive?' Roy said. 'Or are you staying long enough to teach them?'

Sizzle, who seemed to find most of their remarks amusing, guffawed again. Rose had wondered what he would make of the army; now she wondered what the army would make of him. Her experience of soldiers was limited to the ones she had known in London, but it did occur to her that they all appeared much sharper than Sizzle, if sharp was the right word, and that they also laughed a lot less.

'No, lover, I bain't stayin' around. Mebbe li'l Rose's friend can drive a trap, eh, Rosie?'

'Which friend? None of my friends at school can drive at all, I don't think,' Rose said, considerably mystified. 'You don't mean matron, do you?'

Matron had called once to make sure her charges were settling in. Rose did not know to this day what Mrs Riley had said to her, but matron had left abruptly, red cheeks positively scarlet, lips nipped into a very tight line, and had not returned. Goodee.

Sizzle, predictably, guffawed for a third time. He also pushed his cap to the back of his head and tugged at a springy dark curl of hair.

'Come to think, letter only come today, so her won't know yet,' he remarked to thin air. 'Wait an' see, maiden.'

All the way back to the farm, therefore, Rose pondered

on her friends. She had lived here now for a whole year, so she knew lots and lots of people, but apart from the Rileys and Sizzle, none of them, she thought, could drive a pony and a trap. Well, Denham and James could of course, but they were still at the grammar school themselves, so could scarcely take people to school and then return trap and pony to the farm. And anyway, Denham and James lived quite near a proper road, so if the trap-transport was not available they could always go in by bus, though it would make them very late for classes.

Her reverie was cut short as the trap swung under the arch and into the farmyard. The children piled out, Denham and James to continue up the lane on foot until they had gone 'up'n over' to their own place, Roy and Rose to rush indoors and get their tea. Sizzle would take Toadflax into the stable and rub her down before he ate, but before he could do that he would have to unharness her and take her out from the shafts. This was well worth watching and Rose, who loved horses, usually lingered, but today it was a rush for the kitchen door, racing Roy, and a quick dash to the sink to wash hands. Mrs Riley, meanwhile, was already slicing bread and spreading it with clotted cream over by the table.

'Auntie Marjory, Sizzle said . . .'

'Oh, did 'un?' Mrs Riley applied more cream, spreading with vigour. 'Well, nothing's settled, no, nothing.'

Rose was a child highly sensitive to atmosphere of any description, due, no doubt, to the fact that her early childhood had been spent in the company of her very young and volatile mother. Now she could hear not just indecision behind Mrs Riley's voice, but very real distress. She hesitated, then went and stood close enough so that she could, if necessary, comfort.

'What is it? What's happened?'

'Nothing. Nor 'twon't, if I 'ave my way.'

Rose sighed and looked around for something that would change the subject; take her hostess's mind off her problem, whatever it might be. Her eyes alighted on an envelope with familiar handwriting.

'A letter! It's from Jenny!'

'No, 'twas a telegram . . .' Mrs Riley began, then saw the envelope too, shrugged, and began, happily, to smile. 'Dearie me, what us'll do in a rage! Even to deceiving one of His littl'uns.' She stopped spreading cream and turned to smother Rose in one of her huge, feather-bed hugs. ''Tes your friend, maiden. Her sent I a telegram. Her would like to come to we for a while, an' the baby, too.'

'Really?' Rose burrowed her head into Mrs Riley's ample bosom. 'But what would she do here?'

'Work on the land seemingly. Her 'ud pay for their keep, too.'

'But perhaps you'd rather have a real landgirl?'

Rose had not known how badly she missed Jenny and the baby until that moment, but she knew something else as well. Mrs Riley loved her. Not just the way people do love little girls who stay with them, but with a real, deep, proper love. A sort of mother's love, really, Rose told herself. And in some way, Mrs Riley did not want Jenny to come here and yet was ashamed of herself for her feelings. How odd people were! Rose could remember when she had first known Jenny and Simon that she had felt just like that over the baby Jenny was expecting. She just *knew* she would hate it when it came. Yet when Marianne was born she had loved her most dreadfully, because Mari had taken a baby's place in her parents' lives, and had not usurped the little girl place that was Rose's. Could not Auntie Marjory understand that if Jenny came here now it would be like that? That she, Rose, had places in her heart, too, and that nothing could ever push someone like Auntie Marjory out? Certainly not Jenny, nor Marianne, because they had their own places already; they didn't need anyone else's.

But to explain that one would have to be a great deal cleverer than Rose knew herself to be. Instead, she clutched as much of Mrs Riley as she could and hugged her tightly, saying words which Mrs Riley had never expected to hear.

'Auntie Marjory, I love you so much! If you don't want Jenny and you need a real landgirl, just you say so!'

Simon drove his wife and daughter down to Devon as he had arranged, taking two days over it. Jenny was a little quieter than usual, but that was understandable. She had lost her home and was about to lose her husband's company, except in the rare intervals when he would be able to get a leave long enough to manage the two-way journey in the time available.

She'll chirp up when we arrive, Simon told himself as they left the town behind and started to follow the directions they had been given to reach 'Riley's place'. She won't mope for long, not my Jenny.

As he drove, he examined the countryside and found it pleasant. Such gentle hills, such abundant trees, such sweet rivers winding between their high banks. It was all so leisurely, so clean, after the bustle and filth of the city.

He turned left into the lane. It was a bit of an eye-opener, that lane. Fortunately it had been a dry month, so it was only dust that rose, chokingly pink, as the car made its way over the ruts, but in the winter Simon could well imagine what it would be like. A morass, he thought rather guiltily. Still the Rileys were used to it and Rose seemed to get in to school every day, so it could not be *that* bad.

After half a mile the lane rose into a hump over a bridge. He slowed down and was glad he had done so, for ahead of him the lane seemed to disappear into a tunnel. Actually, at this point it became a good deal lower than the surrounding countryside, so that they were driving along between eight-foot banks surmounted by tangled trees and hedges which gave the tunnel-like effect. Marianne, who had been sitting on Jenny's lap absorbed in her own thoughts, glanced round her, her eyes black in the gloom.

'Dark,' she remarked. 'Very dark.'

'Not really, sweetie,' Simon said reassuringly. 'Here . . . see?'

They had emerged from the tunnel into a lighter part of the lane, where the banks were lower and where the hazel trees which grew on top of them reached out long fingers towards the trees on the opposite bank without actually mingling branches and shutting out the light. The last rays of sun fell through these branches and Marianne smiled. The hood of the car was down, so she could see the blue of the sky above and the fluffy white clouds.

'Nice,' she said dreamily, holding out her hands to the sky. 'It's nice.'

Jenny sniffed. The dive into the tunnel had filled her with foreboding; what sort of people were they, who lived in the wilderness and did not even trim back the hedges which kept out the light of day from their driveway, if a lane at least a mile long could be so described? But the lane led only to the Rileys' place, they had said in the town. Other dwellings, they had explained, were more easily reached by taking the main road.

The landscape changed again and Jenny sat up a little straighter. On their left the banks were topped by apple trees, laden with scarlet and bronze fruit. An orchard – the orchard which Rose talked about so often in her letters, no doubt. That must mean the house was not far ahead.

Even as she thought this the lane widened and there it was, standing end on so that very little of the house could be seen until you went through the arch and entered the farmyard. Simon slowed still more, because the farmhouse, whitewashed over the years until whatever its original building material might have been was hidden beneath a thick smooth coating of icing-like white, was actually built right on the lane, without so much as a pavement or a bit of hedge between it and the thick, pink dust. Jenny had time to see that the thatch came down to within four feet of the ground and that there was not a single window in the long wall facing the lane, and then they were swinging through the arch.

'Why an arch?' she said, but no one answered. And indeed Jenny herself never gave the matter another thought, for they were all too busy staring.

The farmhouse was beautiful, but it was not just that, it was the air of enchantment which hung over it. The house itself, the arch and the stables formed one side of the square; opposite it was a long, open-fronted building which housed a tractor and a variety of farm carts. Above that was a loft, and on the other two sides were more buildings, only the doors were closed so they could not see what their purpose might be.

The enchantment, however fleeting, was instantly recognised by Simon, at least. Rose had described this farmyard so many times and so lovingly that her own sense of wonder had touched it. A second glance showed the cow pats across the flagstones, the broken door swinging on the right, the moss-covered and badly hung gate through which the livestock must come. And yet . . . nothing could quite take away the enchantment, he discovered. This was a real, working farm yet there was still something of a play-farmyard about it. He realised that he knew, from Rose, that the buildings on his right were the cowsheds where the cows came to be milked, and the buildings on the left the dairy and the wash-house, where she and Mrs Riley and an odd assortment of cats held sway, churning butter, heating the milk to clot the cream, and lighting the fire under the huge boiler to get the sheets and pillowcases, the table cloths and the napkins, boiled whiter than white.

The cats, Rose had explained, kept down the mice and rats, and in return Mrs Riley provided them with saucers of skim milk and, twice a week, a sizeable washing-up bowl full of scraps.

As if thinking of her had conjured her up, the moss-covered gate swung open and Rose, with dirt on her nose and a stick in one hand, appeared through it. She was opening the gate for a herd of black and white cows which followed her placidly through it, but her own placidity did not last for longer than it took her to see the car and to recognise the occupants. Her stick went one way, her plaits flew out, and she rushed across the yard and hurled herself into Simon's lap, whence she proceeded to cover Jenny and Marianne with many kisses.

'You're here! You really are – Auntie Marjory didn't stop you coming, not that I thought . . . You're going to live with *me*, Marianne . . . D'you remember your Rosie, then, luv?'

Jenny returned the kisses, gave Rose a hug, and then surveyed the child solemnly.

'Darling, how you've grown! And plaits! I don't know that I like them, they make you look so grown-up!'

'Neater,' Rose said briefly, giving Jenny a glowing glance. 'Does Auntie Marjory know you're here?'

'Well, scarcely! We'd just driven into the yard when you shot through that gate like an arrow and landed on Simon's lap! Shall we get out, and you can go and prepare her for the worst.' Jenny hesitated. 'Is . . . is she going to mind us being here, Rosie? With Mari and everything?'

'She'll love it,' Rose said decidedly. 'I'll just . . . Auntie Marjory, it's them!'

Jenny and Simon turned as the back door opened and a big woman came out. She was as tall as Simon but her hair was fair, streaked with white at the temples. Her face was rosy from the heat of a stove, but her smile was warmer than most and there was humour in her small, brightly twinkling eyes.

'Welcome, welcome,' she said. 'Come in and sit down . . . Us've made 'ee a right good tea, eh, Rosie?'

'Everything you like, Auntie Marjory said, so I did my best to remember,' Rose informed them, preceding them into the kitchen. 'Simon isn't difficult to feed, is he, Jenny? He likes all food, just about. But I thought *your* favourite food was fruit cake, raspberries and cream, and shrimps with bread and butter.'

Jenny stared at the table to which Rose was pointing. Bottled raspberries, a big bowl of clotted cream, and another of pink shrimps. Her lips twitched, but she suppressed the smile and turned to her hostess.

'Mrs Riley, how can I ever thank you for such a wonderfully generous welcome? And please don't think Marianne and I will be fussy, because really, as Rose says, we simply enjoy our food!'

The table was spread with good things and Simon, who complained now and then of the sameness of RAF cooking, was already wondering how he would manage to sample everything. But Mrs Riley, inviting them all to wash their hands and then settle to eating, seemed to have no personal doubts as she sent Rose out to call the men in and took her own place behind the teapot.

'My husband says we'm to start without he,' she announced, as Roy and Sizzle came into the room. She chuckled, glancing with pride and with pleasure at her well-spread board. 'But as you see, no one's liable to go short in this house.'

'Darling, I couldn't be happier to leave you in such good hands,' Simon murmured that night, from the depths of the feather bed that had once so startled Rose. 'They're absolutely straight and honest, the pair of them. They'll encourage you to work, they won't take money for your board, and Mrs Riley could hardly keep her hands off Marianne. I shall go away from here tomorrow knowing that you're going to be busy and happy, and that was what you wanted, wasn't it?'

Jenny, snuggling against his cheek, nodded.

'Ye-es. Only it seems wrong to be working in such idyllic surroundings when poor Val and the others . . .'

'They haven't got a baby to look after. Damn it, Jen, *someone's* got to grow the nation's food, so why not you? And think how marvellous it will be for me, when I do get leave, to be able to come here and relax.'

'Yes, you're right. It's only my conscience, Simon darling, that keeps saying it's perfection, the country childhood I missed, and that I shouldn't enjoy myself when others are suffering – and dying – in the Blitz.'

'Then you'll stay? And no moaning at the bar?' He felt Jenny nod against his chest and rumpled her hair. 'Bravo, darling!' There was a pause and then he added thought-fully, 'That youngster, Roy; decent young fellow. Rosie seems fond of him.'

'Well, they're both from the orphanage,' Jenny pointed out rather sleepily. She had had a full day. 'It's only natural, Simon.'

'Perhaps. But she's special, is Rose. I wouldn't want her to get involved with someone just because he was the only boy she met.'

Jenny was so startled that sleepiness vanished. She sat

bolt upright in bed and stared at the dark shape that was Simon and the points of light that were his eyes, for they had pulled the blackout curtains back as soon as they had extinguished the candle.

'Simon Rose, what *are* you talking about? Poor Rose is only eight. She's scarcely likely to elope with the boy! And damn it, darling, if she did it wouldn't be any of our business! You sounded just like an anxious and rather jealous father!'

'Did I? Well, I feel a bit like that – we're *in loco parentis* with Rose, love, in a way more than we would be with a niece or something, because she chose us to be friends with, didn't she? And she's got no one else.'

Jenny lay back again.

'I suppose you're right. But Rose goes to school in town, don't forget, so she'll meet plenty of boys apart from Roy. And anyway, we aren't going to be here for ever!'

'No, of course not.' Simon gave his wife a rib-cracking hug and kissed the side of her neck. 'Go to sleep, woman, don't lie here talking to me!'

In their own room the other side of the farmhouse, Marjory Riley and Dan lay in a very similar feather bed. They lay cosily, sides touching, though they did not snuggle. Marjorie was a large woman and Dan, though he had been a big man once, had grown stringy with age; she always worried a little in case she might roll on him during the night, though it was not a fear she would have revealed to a living soul.

'Dan, are 'ee wakin'?'

'Yes, dear.'

'Baint young Simon like l'il Rose? Did 'ee mark the likeness?'

'Yes, you'm right. Mebbe they'm distant relatives?'

''Tis possible.' Marjory gave a gusty sigh. 'Likely coincidence, would you'm guess?'

'Likely.'

Neither of them was much given to speculation and the possible solution satisfied them both. Soon they slept.

Chapter Nine

Frank was in the yard working on *Gay Times* when he heard a vehicle slow, stop, and then continue on its way along the lane. He glanced at his watch wondering whether someone had brought Lenny back, but it was far too early. However, it was Saturday and people did come down to the Broad still at weekends, fishing or just wandering along in the peaceful sunshine.

He picked up his sander once more and began smoothing lovingly along the curve of a plank. The little cruiser was his now, since, believing her to be lost in France, he had insisted on paying her owners her full value. The ladies had protested, but he had found them another nice little boat even better suited to their requirements, and that had satisfied them. They felt they should not accept money, they explained rather shyly, when it was for their country.

And then *Gay Times* had come back. A telephone call from an official somewhere down south had alerted him to the fact that the boat had been found on a sandbank and had been towed into harbour; it awaited collection, the official said rather frostily, as though Frank had been deliberately negligent in some way.

Frank, who had seen the cruiser sink for the second time in two days under the weight of desperate men trying to get to safety, had never expected to see her again, far less to find that she had made her own way back, riding on the tides and currents of the channel.

'Just like Paul,' Lenny had remarked when he heard. 'Only how could a boat do it alone, Uncle Frank?'

'Tides and currents,' Frank explained, going into greater detail about sea and wind movements only when Lenny showed that he really was interested. Yet to him, it was more of a miracle than anything else. She was not the only boat who had crossed the channel alone after Dunkirk, yet he still found himself regarding her with loving awe; she had somehow managed to elude minefields, U-boats and enemy shipping, to say nothing of rocks and shoals. She had weathered, of course, and lost most of her paintwork, but she was whole; a tribute to her builder and to some secret spirit of homing which Frank knew was rubbish but which he believed in nevertheless.

He had offered her back to her former owners, of course, but they were quite content with their new boat and assured him that *Gay Times* was now his undisputed property. Accordingly, whenever he could do so, he was cleaning her up and polishing her, though for precisely what purpose he was not sure.

Perhaps I'll give her to Paul when the war is over, Frank thought, caressing a smoothed plank with the heel of his hand. Beautiful wood! Lenny was right, the little boat had a lot in common with Paul, for they had both made their own way home against all the odds. Paul was with the Norfolks in Wimbledon at the moment, defending the United Kingdom until such time as they were needed abroad, but he would be back one day and then, perhaps, he would be pleased to own the little cruiser.

'Frank, you shouldn't work on a Saturday, should you? You should tell the navy . . . Oh, I see.' Val strolled into the workshop, an emerald green silk scarf holding her bright hair back from her face, a casual jacket slung round her shoulders. 'That isn't naval work, I suppose.'

'No, not exactly. Actually we work straight through at weekends when we've got something coming up for completion, but then we take a day or so off when we're waiting for supplies, and this is one of those weekends.' Frank straightened, smoothed the wood once more with his hand, and grinned at his sister. 'Nice to see you, Val. On leave? How about a cup of coffee and a piece of cake? Madge doesn't trust my cooking, she's always popping in with bits and pieces to eat, but I am capable of coffee – or you can make it for me if you like.'

'Coffee will be fine. Who made the cake though?'

Frank laughed and ushered Val into the large kitchen where he spent most of his spare time. It was the end of April and the air outside was still quite chilly, but here in the glow of the Aga one felt at home.

'How unkind! You're remembering Lenny's scones! They were a bit grey, I admit, but not all that unpalatable. Anyway, he's got a lot better. Madge insists that he not only washes his hands but weighs ingredients. And with rationing it's as well she does or we'd have a full swill-bin every day instead of once a week. Did you know Lenny wants me (us, I should say) to keep a pig?'

'Why not? Mother's talking of doing just that. And don't change the subject, Frank. Who did make the cake?'

'Madge.' Frank pulled the kettle over the hot plate and it began to sing almost at once. 'Can you get the coffee down? It's that bottled stuff I'm afraid. And there's sugar in the tin marked biscuits, and biscuits in the old sweet-jar.'

'Don't say you still take sugar!' Val got mugs off the dresser, spooned coffee into both, and then dipped the spoon into the sugar. 'I gave it up at least a year ago.'

'I give it up regularly. About twice a week,' Frank said. He was a confirmed three teaspoons man. 'I'm cutting down at the moment, so just two big spoonfuls will have to be enough. Oh, I forgot the cake.' He disappeared into the pantry and emerged again clutching a large, very dark cake with icing on top. 'It's a chocolate one – want a bit?'

'Smashing. I'll have some of that *and* some of those biscuits,' Val said. 'Is it warm enough to take it outside?'

Frank had a rustic bench beside his back door and visitors liked to sit there sipping their drinks and watching the world go by across the water.

'It's in the sun and quite sheltered,' Frank said, taking the spitting kettle off the hob and pouring water into the coffee mugs. 'How long are you down for? You never said, but I suppose this is leave?'

'That's right,' Val said, following him out into the hazy sunshine. They both sat down and sipped silently for a few moments, gazing out across the placid Broad. On the other side was the village, and some boys were frolicking with a ball along the other bank. Their voices came over the water, very faint, rather mysterious.

'How long this time?'

'Six days. I used the first to travel down on and I'll use the last to get back, which gives me a clear four to enjoy. Mother spoils me and so do the aunts, so I should return to London fit for the fray, but I felt I'd like to come over here, get some real peace, and talk to my big brother.'

'I thought you wanted to talk,' Frank said complacently, taking a huge bite out of his slice of cake. 'Is it advice you're after? If so, just tell me, because I'm nearly old enough to be your father.'

'We-ell, it isn't advice, exactly. Frank, have you been in touch with Mabel, since Dunkirk?'

'Just about; she got one message through. She says she'll be all right since she's a French citizen with a French passport and so on. She had been nursing but she really wasn't needed once the BEF had evacuated so she was going to make her way to a farm on one of Matthieu's estates. She said she'd sit out the war there, amongst other people she knew and trusted.' He took another bite of cake, ate it, and then heaved a huge sigh. 'Sometimes I can't believe two people can be as unlucky as Mabel and I, but mostly I realise that we've been unbelievably lucky and I should be grateful.'

'Lucky? To spend your lives loving each other and never being together? I think that's terribly unlucky,' Val protested. 'Your Mabs is so beautiful and charming and such a dear that to be kept apart from her must be hell.'

'You've got it wrong, little sister.' Frank shook his head at her and finished off his cake. 'In fact, your words underline my luck. Your Mabs, you said, when she's another man's wife, lives in another country, and has a son by her husband. Yet despite everything, she's my Mabs and always will be.'

'Are you lovers though?' Val asked bluntly, and Frank saw with amusement that her skin had flushed a deep pink. 'I'm sorry to ask you, but I do have a reason for my cheek.'

'Oh, do you? Then you'd better tell me this reason and if I think it justifies impertinent questions I'll answer you. Fire ahead.'

'Oh dear! You'll have to be patient, Frank, because it won't be easy for me to explain. Do you remember me going to Germany to see the Olympics in 'thirty-six and staying with Minna and her family, the von Eckners?'

'Yes, of course. That was how we came to have Salka and the others here when things got too hot for them in Berlin. So what?'

'Remember me talking about Otto von Eckner? He never came to England but he was Salka's boyfriend – fiancé really as they'd intended to marry one day. Only they weren't in love. At least they couldn't have been because Salka's married now, to someone called Osbert Heldenberg.'

'So?'

'Well, after Salka finished with Otto I got very friendly with him. He'd been writing to me for simply ages, which you'd have known if you'd been living at home as I used to hang about waiting for the postman morning after morning . . . We met in the summer of 'thirty-nine, in Paris. Do you remember me going abroad with you, that summer? And I took myself off to Paris for a day? You thought I'd gone to see Ghastly Gaston. I was having a mild sort of relationship with him about then, only it wasn't him I met, it was Otto. I tried to persuade him to come back to England with me because I was terribly afraid – he loathes Hitler and all he stands for you see, which is dangerous – but he wouldn't. He explained that however he feels about Hitler, he loves his country and wants her free and what's more he loves flying . . .'

'He's a German flyer? In the Luftwaffe?' Frank put an arm round Val's shoulders. 'You poor brat, no wonder you wanted to talk about the difficulties of being apart! What you're going through is infinitely worse than what Mabs and I have suffered.'

Val's eyes filled with tears and she returned her brother's hug fervently, wiped a spilt drop away with one finger, and then grinned at him.

'It's so wonderful to be able to tell you and find that you understand! Mother thinks all Germans are child-eaters and wife-beaters; Jenny only sees them as people who might kill Simon; and to everyone else they are the enemy. But I love Otto, not his . . . his Germanness. We used to write through a friend in Spain, but then the letters stopped coming and mine were returned with "gone away" on the envelope, so I suppose the friend either got fed up or left. And now, it's all so awful . . . I can't help worrying not only about his safety, but whether he'll go on loving me! I shan't change, but . . .'

'Look, love, he isn't the casual sort, I can tell. Why should he change? Mabel hasn't, nor I, and you're very like me in all sorts of ways. Just remember . . .'

'But it's entirely different,' Val wailed. 'Frank, don't you see, I can't be sure? Our relationship wasn't like yours and Mabs's, tried and tested. It was still at the jelly-setting stage – you know, when you dare not turn it out of the mould for fear it will just flop all over the place. That's how we were, all new and uncertain.'

'How horribly unromantic! It wasn't like that at all, it was young and green and sweet, your relationship, like primroses when they first come pushing up through the moss in the spring or . . .'

'Or lettuces before they've developed a heart,' groaned Val. 'It's no use, Frank, I'm not romantic and actually I don't think Otto is either. You see we hadn't had much time or many meetings, we don't really know each other terribly well, not even well enough for me to picture a future for us. All I know is that I miss him so terribly that sometimes I wonder why I go on.' She looked shyly at her brother. 'And we . . . well, I don't know about you and Mabs, but we never had time to be lovers!'

'It doesn't matter,' Frank said slowly, after a thoughtful pause. 'When Mabs ran away we were just a couple of kids, though I know she wanted to marry me. She'd made it clear enough. But I couldn't make up my mind. I was pretty badly wrecked after the first war, you see, and I didn't think it was fair to saddle Mabel with the sort of man I'd become. And when I made up my mind that I wanted her at any price . . . well, she'd gone. I never found out why, either, she'd just left me without a note or a word and the next thing I heard she was in France and married.'

'Poor you!' Val said, awed. 'But even so, Frank, you'd known Mabel all your life, nearly. Otto and I . . .'

'What I'm trying to point out is that it really doesn't make much difference whether you're lovers or not,' Frank said patiently. 'We've no choice, you and I. All we can do is wait.'

'Yes. I pray quite a bit,' Val said diffidently. 'I don't suppose it makes any difference – I mean God's got quite a lot on His hands at the moment, one way and another – but that doesn't stop me nagging Him sometimes.'

Frank laughed, stretched and got to his feet.

'You're not the only one. It's about time I fetched Lenny. He's taking a badge in fire-lighting with the cubs, but I said I'd row over and fetch him about now. If you come along we'll eat out in style.'

'Goodee!' Val went down to the edge of the staithe with him and got into the small, sturdy row-boat. 'Where? At the Wherry, or will you go mad and take us into Lowestoft for a breath of sea air and a specially fine meal?'

'It'll be the Wherry, since Lowestoft is full of closed restaurants and warning notices,' Frank pointed out. 'What's more, my petrol's too precious to spend on an idle pleasure trip. And by the same token, how did you get here?'

'By train and then hitched a lift with Stedman, butcher of this parish,' Val said. 'Are you going to let me take an oar?'

'Not this way, we're in a bit of a hurry. But you can take both oars on the way back if you like, if you can persuade Lenny to hand them over. He's getting quite good, though he does splash rather.'

'I'll keep you to that,' Val leaned back and half closed her eyes. 'Row on, Macduff!'

*

170

'When's tea?' Cara came into the kitchen hurriedly, to see that everyone was busy. Ruthie was peeling a mound of potatoes, Tina was rolling out pastry and Beryl, with her hair in curlers and a cigarette drooping from her lower lip, was wrestling with the mincer, an awkward machine. There were tears running down her cheeks, Cara saw with detached interest, but this was by no means a rare phenomenon. What was unusual was the cigarette; Auntie Tina had absolutely forbidden smoking in her kitchen, and Beryl was using the mincer, which must make it even worse!

No one answered immediately so Cara spoke a little less demandingly. It would never do to set backs up so far that they made things difficult.

'I'm sorry, but I'm going out tonight and I'm in a hurry – I say, Beryl, are you smoking? That's awful in a kitchen. I know Auntie told Desmond off for doing it and he wasn't even cooking!'

Tina ignored her niece save for shooting her a very cold look, but Beryl reddened and took the cigarette out of her mouth. She crushed it out against a plant pot but slipped the stub into her apron pocket.

'I'm awfully sorry, I'm afraid I forgot . . . the onions are stinging my eyes and . . . well, I forgot.'

'It doesn't matter, Beryl,' Tina said distantly, equally annoyed with both women; with Cara for pointing out to her something that she had decided to ignore and with Beryl for being such a misery and for not brazening it out. She's old enough to be Cara's mother, Tina thought crossly, pummelling the pastry in a way which boded ill for the pie she was making. Why can't she stand up for herself and put Cara in her place? She turned to her niece.

'Since you're here, Cara, and doing nothing, would you please lay the table in the dining-room? We shall be a large party for tea . . . Ten people, I think I said.'

'That's right, Mrs Tina,' Ruthie said. 'Eleven if Caspar comes back.'

'I don't see why Auntie Ray's children are here for nearly every meal,' Cara grumbled, slamming out of the kitchen to fetch the trolley and raising her voice in the butler's pantry where it was kept. She wheeled it back into the kitchen. 'I don't mind giving a hand but I'm going out tonight and . . .'

'Just lay the table, Cara,' Tina said forbiddingly. She was getting really tired of Cara and was looking forward to seeing the girl's mother when she came for tea, for Sarah was in Norwich for a flying visit. I'll tell her that Cara's heading for trouble, Tina resolved. And I'll tell her that the only way out of it is for Cara to be forced to do some sort of war work. How they would force the girl, who was sheltering behind Mira, she had no idea, but Sarah said she would think of something and Tina had a good deal of faith in her sister-in-law.

Cara, piling the trolley with cutlery and crockery, must have sensed criticism emanating from her aunt because she said casually: 'Mira's got herself into a state this week. They're making them wear their gas masks in school for a few hours each day to accustom them to the feel of the straps and so on, and she's been having nightmares. I thought I might take her out into the country for a picnic tomorrow afternoon.'

Beryl murmured approvingly, but Tina was made of sterner stuff.

'Just you and Mira?' she said sharply.

'I haven't got a car, Auntie,' Cara said reproachfully. 'I've got a friend who would be quite willing to take us though. We could take Em and Edmund too if you'd like it, Beryl,' she added.

Tina took a deep breath. Now was the time to tell Cara that she did not want the children drawn into her niece's clandestine meetings with the young pilots she danced with, played tennis with, and met for brief amorous struggles at the end of the drive. But Cara continued to speak.

'She's ever so nice. Her name's Mrs Poll and she's got the use of a lovely car and the petrol because her brother's been sent abroad.' She turned limpid eyes on her aunt. 'You'd approve of her, Auntie Tina. She's one of those ladies who go round bombed sites serving cups of tea and hot pies to the heavy salvage workers.'

On those words she left the kitchen, letting the door swing closed behind her. Tina and Ruthie exchanged meaningful glances. Cara might not be very clever, but she certainly had a knack of either disarming or eluding criticism!

Sarah came swinging up the long, beech-lined drive wearing a neat grey suit with a navy blouse under it and navy walking shoes on her feet. She was forty-seven years old and looked ten years younger, which was nice because otherwise her second husband, Con, might have begun to regret marrying a woman eight years his senior. Not that he would – Sarah's marriage was one of the very good things in her rather pleasant and satisfactory life.

But right now, she was going to deal with an aspect of life which was less than satisfactory – her daughter. She only had to think of Cara lately and the years settled heavily on to her shoulders like a treacle-soaked blanket. Why couldn't the girl remember that she was a married woman? Why did she have to go through life offending and upsetting people? Sarah knew Cara was spoilt, but it was not her fault. She had done her best from the start to see that Cara grew up thoughtful, generous and sensible. But when the child had been young, Sarah's mother had shared the house with them and she had made life so difficult for Sarah that she had allowed the dictatorial old devil to get away with giving Cara everything she asked for and generally ruining her.

After that William had taken over. He had tried to change Cara, but he had gone about it the wrong way. Money and servants, an adoring husband and uncritical friends, had all contributed to the way Cara was now.

But Cara must change. She was a fool, Sarah knew. Foolish to play about with other men, and even more foolish to be so casual with her man, for William was one of the best. But was she so stupid that she would cast all her personal possessions, money and the position she held as the wife of a rich man into the melting pot for the sake of flattery and a few kisses from the young RAF officers she met when she went dancing? Sarah did not think so, but Con disagreed.

'She'll be flattered and cosseted into bed,' he warned his wife. 'Then who's going to face William, when the war's over and he comes out of that camp? Cara will weep and say she didn't mean it, but William isn't the sort to accept being a cuckold complacently. For all our sakes, my love, you must speak to Cara!'

Tina thought that war work was the answer and Sarah, who worked very hard indeed, knew that she was probably right. Part of Cara's trouble was boredom, for she did not like looking after children, she hated housework, and she managed to get out of doing either. With a job which needed regular hours and concentration, she might simply decide that it was not worth the effort to get into the city to meet her newly acquired boyfriends!

As Sarah reached the front door of The Pride she pushed it open and called out. Immediately the lounge door shot open and Sebastian appeared with a shout of 'Ma!', casting himself into her arms like a rugby player going into a tackle. He was a sturdy boy and Sarah staggered, kissed him, and then pushed him away from her.

'Darling, what a wonderful welcome! Where's everyone? I'm staying for tea, but I thought I'd have a word with Cara first, if I can find her.'

'She's laying the table for tea; we're having it in the dining-room because we're a crowd,' Sebastian said. 'I'll go and tell them you're here whilst you have a talk.'

'Good idea.' Nine-year-olds are seldom tactful but Sebastian, who detested his half-sister cordially, probably sensed that Cara was in for a telling off and so wanted to be helpful. 'Off with you, then, whilst I talk to your sister.'

As Sebastian trotted kitchenwards Sarah opened the dining-room door and went inside. Cara, looking bad-tempered, was slapping table mats on to the dark and gleaming surface, but her face lit up as she recognised her mother.

'Mummy! It's lovely to see you!' She hurried round the table, scattering table mats all over the floor, and kissed Sarah enthusiastically on the cheek. 'How are you? You look beautiful and smart, and not nearly old enough to be my mama.'

'Thank you, darling. Let me give you a hand.' Sarah picked up a handful of knives and forks and began to put them in place, talking as she did so. 'I've come down specially, Cara, to tell you I think it's time you took on some war work. You're being very selfish you know, living here in this lovely house and contributing so little. Auntie Tina never tells tales, but I'm bound to admit that she did say you were bored. She and Ruthie manage the house, I know, but I gather they manage Mira too, plus your share of the washing, ironing and so on.'

'Well, Ruthie does do quite a lot,' Cara said unwillingly, her small face flushing. 'But I get Mira from school, and . . .'

'Sometimes. Sebastian usually fetches her. He mentioned it in a letter. He's a good lad, despite the fact that he's also a devil.'

'Oh. Well, yes, he fetches her sometimes but I do help – look at me now, laying the table for ten people!' Cara managed to make it sound as if she was also personally making a twelve-course dinner. 'Don't you call that work?'

'No, I don't. Look at Jenny. You know she's pregnant again, but still working on the land, don't you? I should think she'd take laying a table as very light relief after that. And Val, driving ambulances through the sort of conditions that you can't even imagine. She's only been given a few days off because the authorities have come to realise that if people don't get right away every now and then they crack up. I want to see you doing real work.'

'I don't see what use I'd be,' Cara muttered, fiddling with the salt cellar. 'I can't drive because William said it was pointless when we had a chauffeur; I couldn't work in a hospital like Jenny used to because I hate sick people. Well, no, not hate, but they frighten me, and I'd only upset them. That's why I can't go out with ambulances, either. I'm not tough. I'm very fragile, William always said so, so I can't dig for victory, and I've never had anything to do with figures or business, so I can't do work like you do.'

'That's a fine list of can'ts,' Sarah said, laughing a little. 'Now what about some cans? Darling Cara, you're a very intelligent woman. There must be something you can do even if it's only working in a shop or a factory!'

'I don't see the point of all this since I'm not eligible because of Mira,' Cara said sullenly. 'No matter what you think, you can't *make* me work; no one can.'

'That's true. But I can tell Auntie Tina that I think you need more independence, and either take you back to

London to live in your flat there or let you go back to the flat here, in the city.'

'I wouldn't go back to London, not for anything,' Cara said quickly. She did, occasionally, read the newspapers. 'But if you're going to be mean to me, then I could move back into the Prince of Wales Road flat, though it's not terribly safe there and I'd probably get killed.'

'You'd be prepared to do that rather than work? But how would you manage with Mira on your own?'

'Oh, I wouldn't take Mira,' Cara said at once, not seeing the trap yawning beneath her feet. 'Really, Mummy, surely you wouldn't think I'd move Mira when she's so happy here and getting on so well at school? No, I wouldn't dream of upsetting her and I'm sure that however cruel Auntie Tina might be to me she wouldn't be unkind enough to send Mira away.'

'No, you're right, of course. And what, my dear Cara, do you think the authorities will say when they find you living in a luxury flat all by yourself, with someone else looking after your stepdaughter, several miles away? Do you think you wouldn't get called up for war work then?'

'Oh!' Cara goggled at her mother, a picture of astonished outrage. Then, surprisingly, she started to laugh. Between giggles she said: 'Mummy, you're awful – I never thought you'd descend to blackmail!'

'I never thought I'd have to,' Sarah said rather sadly. 'What do you say, sweetheart?'

'All right, you win, I'll get a job. In some ways I shan't be sorry, since I get bored to tears sometimes.' Cara turned the now empty trolley towards the door. 'I'll go down to the city hall on Monday and see what's on offer.'

'That's fine, darling, but don't get taken in by the lure of a uniform, because from what I've heard you work incredibly hard and can get sent anywhere at a moment's notice. You stick to local work – you can, because of Mira

– and you're sure of a decent home, Auntie's homecooking and Ruthie's excellent washing and ironing.'

'All right. Though I'd adore to wear the Wrens uniform,' Cara said, pushing her trolley out through the door that Sarah was holding open. 'What puts me off is strange beds – I've always hated sleeping in strange beds. I'll tell them I have to stay in Norwich.'

'I'm relieved to hear it,' Sarah said, hoping that her daughter's hatred of strange beds also encompassed the back seats of strange cars and the insides of strange air-raid shelters. She closed the dining-room door and caught up with Cara as she crossed the hall, putting an arm around her waist. 'I'm glad you're going to be sensible, darling, because you've worried Uncle Con and me a lot. Do you know that?'

'I don't see why, when there are all the others . . . Simon and Jenny, and now that other baby, the one she's going to have in the autumn . . . and Sebastian, little brute that he is. Why, compared to them, I can't have worried you at all! I know what a saint you think Jenny is, so how you can let her go off and slave on a farm, and waddle around probably doing all the things she shouldn't do, I don't know!'

'I worry about you the most,' Sarah said firmly, ignoring the spiteful note in Cara's voice when she mentioned her sister-in-law. Cara had never forgiven Jenny for being so generous and loving, Sarah knew. 'You're very young and William's a long way away, and you've behaved like an unmarried girl for too long. Your husband's a prisoner in a foreign land and he doesn't deserve, to be blunt, an unfaithful wife.'

'I'm not!' Cara exclaimed, blushing to the roots of her hair. 'I write every single week and I can't help it if my letters are dull – my life's dull! Anyway, William would be the last person to want me to mope just because he's not here, he'd say you go ahead and make some fun for yourself and those poor boys in blue!'

Sarah winced at this horrid phrase, but continued to attack.

'What an absurd remark. No husband could possibly even think such a thing, far less say it. And just tell me the truth now; when you are trying to find something to say to William, do you tell him that you go dancing at the Samson & Hercules ballroom in the city three, four, or even more times a week?'

'It isn't always at the Samson, they don't hold dances that often,' Cara cried, patently begging the question. 'It wouldn't interest William, but I don't mind telling him, because I never behave cheaply, never! I can't help it if I'm pretty and a good dancer and if boys like my company! If I couldn't go out in the evenings I'd die!'

She infused a pathetic note into her voice, but Sarah was not taken in for a moment. She shook her head reprovingly at her daughter.

'William married you when you were fresh out of school, so though you've had a lot of love and his friends' admiration, you've never had young men chasing you before and it's gone to your head. Don't you see that decent young married women don't behave as you are doing? What do you think people say about you?'

She expected more outraged squeals, but Cara looked suddenly thoughtful.

'Yes, I suppose people don't understand. But I can't give up going out, I just can't, and I swear on the Bible that I'd never do anything to . . . well, to break my marriage vows. To tell you the truth, though it's quite fun in a way, William was ever so much keener on that side of it than I was; I like the cuddling and the fun things – presents, lots of compliments, little kisses . . .

But all that grunting and bouncing . . . well, who'd want to do that with anyone they didn't know frightfully well?'

'I'm speechless,' Sarah said, struggling not to laugh. How different her two elder children were! 'Doesn't it occur to you, Cara, that a man doesn't give a girl presents and fun without expecting something back? Men, by and large, approve of the . . . er . . . grunting and bouncing.'

'Yes, but I really am awfully pretty,' Cara said with enough self-satisfaction to turn a stronger stomach than Sarah's. 'Honestly, Mummy, they just want to be the one to take me out and be with me! I'm awfully good at being reproachful and hurt if they try to go too far,' she added proudly. 'So I don't think you need worry about anyone trying . . .'

'All right, I'll do my best not to,' Sarah said hurriedly, fearing that another repetition of grunting and bouncing might completely wreck her composure. It would scarcely impress her feckless daughter if she began to giggle helplessly. 'And now, love, shall we change the subject?' She glanced around the butler's pantry. 'I daresay these walls are boggling over this conversation!'

'All right,' Cara said peaceably. 'Was there ever a butler, Mummy? And if not, why is it the butler's pantry?'

Sarah did not know the answer to that one and the two of them went into the kitchen and began to help with preparations for the evening meal, which was called tea these days since it scarcely merited the description, Tina felt, of dinner.

Sarah thought no more of the subject, save to tip Tina the wink that Cara had been spoken to and would go down to the city hall on Monday, but later that night it was brought forcibly back into her mind again.

She had been upstairs, saying goodnight to Sebastian, when Cara called her and she hurried out to have a word with her daughter, who, dressed in pale blue with the faintest of make-up, looked quite adorable. Despite everything, she was going out to a dance.

Having seen her off Sarah returned, to find Mira sitting solemnly on the foot of Sebastian's bed, apparently engaged in serious conversation. As Sarah entered she was in full spate.

'Yes, but why do you have to grunt and bounce when you get presents, and why do men do it and not ladies?'

'I don't know,' Sebastian was saying, his brow furrowed with thought. 'I think it must be a type of dance. They were talking about dancing at first, when I . . . oh, hello, Mummy!'

Sarah judged it better to ignore the fact that she now knew Sebastian had been eavesdropping on her and Cara in the butler's pantry; no good would come of it and it would only land her in the awkward position of having to answer some pretty pertinent questions. But as she sat on the end of his bed, telling him what she had been doing up in London without him, her mind was seething. Simon had been such a devil for the girls, such a virile exponent of the art of grunting and bouncing, and yet Cara was quite indifferent. What would happen when Sebastian reached puberty? The mind positively boggled!

Chapter Ten

Heat. Oppressive, damp, silent, the very air was hot. Nick felt that his lungs had ceased to be made of tissue and had become great, wet sponges, turkish bath sponges what's more, and that his skin was fast growing scales.

Was it the rainy season? He neither knew nor cared. He only knew that he had joined the army to fight against Hitler and all he had done since Dunkirk had been to hang about in England training, then take ship for India, and now swelter.

Bombay had not been too bad. Interesting, in its way. Colourful, vital, the crowds fast moving, the accents strange, the people friendly, and the animals and birds weird and wonderful. English soldiers moving amongst turbaned natives, bareheaded natives, high-class natives. Lectures on caste and its importance. A monkey glimpsed swinging high in a palm tree. Cheap bananas, brilliant sweetmeats, stalls full of silks, gold and jewellery. Yet an incredibly poor country. Beggars in the gutters, legless, eyeless, hopeless. Noise which battered your eardrums and assailed your senses, and those senses already reeling under a bombardment of smells and sights.

India was not, as he had believed, full of Indians. It was full of people so different that it was incredible that they were all natives of the same country. Black, brown, cream, their skin colours were all different and yet all, in their way, were beautiful. He had seen a woman whose skin was truly blue-black, making her hair seem merely brown in comparison. She had been lovely, with a proud, disdainful face and a walk that queens would envy. She wore huge gold bangles round her wrists and was tall enough to look over most of the heads of people on the pavement beside her. He had stared so hard that she had glanced in his direction and he had felt a small icy shock of surprise, for the eyes in that magnificent, blue-black face were green – Nordic eyes in a Queen of Sheba face.

They had heard about the rioting in Ahmedabad, Bombay, but had not taken any part in its quelling; they were a hot-blooded people, quick to anger, quicker to strike and to take offence, a proud people, they were told. Yet they were also told, far more subtly, that English soldiers should not fraternise. How can we fight side by side without fraternising, Nick wondered, then thought that the veiled remarks must refer to women. He realised it would not do to fraternise with women who might totally misunderstand any attempts at friendship.

Bombay had fascinated him, but this was not Bombay. This was what they called intensive training in jungle warfare. It meant that he must live in a tiny canvas tent in the heart of a tropical jungle, spending a great deal of his time when he was not actually slogging through the jungle itself underneath great, wet masses of mosquito netting whilst next to him lay his friend Dave on an identical camp-bed under identical mosquito netting. Too hot to sleep, naked but for a sweat-soaked sheet, they lay there and heard the thick drops of moisture fall on the canvas roof. They heard other sounds, too. Animal sounds. Monkeys gave weird, terrifying cries, and pigs snorted and grunted through the thick undergrowth. They weren't pigs really, of course. They were wild boar, but they did sound quite like domestic pigs until they saw you and grew fierce and wicked, little eyes gleaming, tusks erect.

Other creatures stalked outside in the steamy dark; creatures which Nick had read about in Kipling but had never really considered meeting – or hearing – in the long nights. You were not afraid, exactly, because it was still impossible to believe that you were hearing a real tiger, and that the growling, grumbling, old-man sounds which rumbled round the camp were the very noises which, once, had held a woodcutter helpless whilst Sher Khan stole a naked babe from the safety of a fireside.

But surely, it had never been so hot in *The Jungle Book*? Nor so sweaty? Mowgli, lucky chap, had roamed the jungle naked, Nicky remembered. He had gone down to the waterhole when there was a drought and had drunk the water, lain on the baked earth, and longed for the rains. But somehow it had all been beautiful, comfortable. Never like this!

'What a bloody awful country! I wouldn't mind if we were fighting the Hun here, but all we're doing is creeping through this filthy jungle with our bellies flapping and our bowels churning. And no mail, either, until we're back in civilisation – if you can call headquarters that.'

Dave was suffering from a mild dose of stomach trouble, brought about by eating fresh fruit two days previously from a bazaar. They had been warned to wash all fruit, but . . . it had looked so tempting, Dave told him pathetically, rushing past on his way to the latrines for about the seventh time in two hours.

Nick, though he sympathised with most of what Dave had said, now felt called upon to remonstrate a little. It would do Dave no good to start worrying about mail because he was quite right, there was no chance of receiving anything here, and probably what they did get would be weeks or months late and wildly out of date. It was worrying for them all and perhaps worse for Dave, three months married when they had embarked at Southampton for an unknown destination.

'Brought the bowel-churning on yourself, fellow! And personally I'd rather be trained to fight than fighting in these conditions. Ever done any history?'

Dave sighed and turned over so that the camp-bed sank a further two inches into the spongy leaf mould of the clearing.

'I did, once, several centuries ago. Why?'

'I was thinking about Old Nosy's campaigns. Do you remember how, during the Napoleonic wars, they all went into winter quarters as the weather worsened each year, and stayed in them until spring came? Summer was the time for fighting wars, when you manoeuvred and planned and chased the enemy or had the odd siege. But in the winter you holed up and held dances and card parties and went hunting, if you were a hunting man. Now that's how wars should be waged, if you ask me.'

Dave propped himself up on one elbow and stared through the netting at his friend. His expression was incredulous.

'You lie, Neyler! It stands to reason no one could have fought a war like that! No, come on, you're having me on!'

'I'm not, it's true as I'm lying here.' Dave guffawed and Nick grinned. 'Sorry, I mean reclining, probably. And it is true – that's probably why the war lasted twenty years, mind you. They never fought anywhere but in Europe though, or perhaps they'd have battled in the winter and found somewhere cool in the shade for the summer. Which, if you ask me, is what we ought to do.'

'Yes, but is this winter or summer?' Dave moved and grunted with disgust. 'By God, there's an ant the size of a bloody *cat* in my bloody bed! Ugh, look at the beastly great pincers on the brute! By golly, it's *threatening* me, the little swine! Look at it – brave as a lion and damned nearly as big!'

Nick leaned up on his elbow and peered at the ant. It was nearly as large as Dave had said, and every bit as fierce.

'Perhaps we could train 'em to attack the Hun instead of us?' he suggested hopefully. 'I wonder if it's a soldier ant? I believe they'll eat anything. Don't they just chumble their way through living flesh? Or am I thinking of piranha fish?'

Dave had flicked the ant out of his bed at the first mention of it being a soldier ant, but this appeared to worry him, for he leaned anxiously over the side of his bed and scanned the floor.

'Don't know. How did it get in with me, anyway? I'm not all done up like a bleeding bride just for fun, you know! What's more, I've scratched that bite on my leg and made it bleed – suppose the thing smells the blood and invites its mates in for a feed? I could be a flipping skeleton by morning.'

'I shouldn't worry, I think I did mean piranha fish. I don't think ants eat you alive – well, not unless you're covered with honey,' Nick amended, remembering an old Tarzan story that had made his flesh creep as a kid. 'If it wasn't so hot we might have a zizz, but I suppose that's out of the question? I want to sleep, because I might dream of my girl, and that would keep me happy for a few hours.'

'If I sleep and dream of Dora, with my luck she'll be in a compromising position with some damned flyer on top of her,' Dave muttered. 'What I think is, I was wrong to marry her. Gave her a taste for it and then buggered off, didn't I? And she's the sweetest, prettiest . . .' He banged his head with the heel of his hand. 'Here I go again! Take my mind off it, Neyler!'

'Don't worry, she's a grand kid, she won't let you down,' Nick said drowsily. 'I'm going to think about those carvings in that temple – blimey, the men were bad

186

enough but Sergeant Hough just couldn't believe his eyes. I thought his head would fall off when we marched away. It was screwed round over his shoulder long after the place was out of sight.'

'Temple? God, Nick, you're so bloody naive – that wasn't a temple, man, it was some sort of bordello. Why on earth should a temple have dirty pictures on the walls?'

'They may have been dirty to you, old man, but they were a heavenly vision to whoever put them there. And I assure you it was no bordello, it was a perishing temple! They've got some very rum religions here, and they worship some very rum things. I'm going to get a book about it.'

'Oh, sure. Get your girlfriend to send you one. Or that sister of yours, what's her name? The one with flaming hair – I fancy her like crazy . . .' Dave remembered his recent marriage '. . . or I would, if I didn't have Dora.'

'She's Val, my twin. The other one isn't a sister, she's Simon's wife, Jenny. Simon's my partner in peacetime.'

'OK, OK, I get muddled, you seem to know so many women. What's your girl called, then?'

'I haven't got one, I don't think,' Nick said rather gloomily. 'The war came along and things changed and I never got round to seeing her or finding her address. She was only a kid, anyway. We didn't know each other very well.'

'Then you're available.' Dave brightened up. 'You're OK, lad, they've got pretty nurses in the hospitals and there must be girls here as well as us; in the ATS for instance. And then there's all the local crumpet – brown they may be but if those temple drawings are anything to go by they'll make your hair curl! Get yourself a piece of the action, boy, as the Yanks say, and then you can fill me with envy by descriptions of her athletic prowess. Which these girls must have, if . . .'

'. . . those temple drawings are anything to go by,' Nick finished for him. 'Get your own thrills, you dirty little sod, and in the meantime just shut up and go to sleep.'

And presently, it seemed, Dave had done just that, for apart from the constant drip, drip from the trees and the background noises of creatures moving through the undergrowth and insects chirping, creaking and shrilling, his even breathing could be heard, gradually changing into a light snore.

Nicky lay back and thought about the only girl he had ever taken out with serious intent. Vitty. Of Italian birth, independent, perhaps rather too involved in how to live her own life to participate fully in a relationship with someone else.

He sighed and shifted on the narrow camp-bed. Why couldn't he fall asleep? His mind roamed restlessly about, trying to find an answer to the huge question mark that was India, trying to sort out his feelings for Vitty, trying to solve, in the end, the riddle of the universe, or at least that was how it felt when you just could not sleep.

His last conscious thought was regret though, that he had not managed to get her address so they could not even exchange letters.

William slept in a hut with eleven other men. They had tiered bunks with a thin blanket each and a thinner straw mattress. They ate dreadful food and suffered harsh, though not cruel, discipline. Life might have been boring without the escape committees, the classes in languages, in accountancy, in anything that someone in the camp was qualified to teach others, but now that the officers and men were into a full year of being shut up they knew the most important thing was to be kept physically and mentally alert, and made sure that most people had some interest, even if it was only in getting out of there.

Handicapped as he was, William could take no part in escape bids nor in the physical fitness side of things, but he did his best to keep occupied. He was learning German and perfecting his French, and he and another chap were attempting to learn Russian from books, though they found it far from easy. He had also learned to use his wooden leg well, so that he could stump about the yard, and managed to cope with only one arm since he found it better and easier than attempting to use an artificial one.

It was odd that he scarcely worried at all about his business now, though he had done at first. He got letters from his chief clerk which were always cheerful and he supposed that in wartime business either boomed or went under without a great deal of help from anyone. His, it seemed, was booming and, since this was so, he wanted to know nothing else because he was in no position to change anything, anyway.

He missed Cara dreadfully. He dreamed of her at night though, and such dreams were a great consolation. In dreams, his wife was everything he wanted and more, in dreams Cara had a depth and a warmth which she lacked in real life, though William no longer believed this. Distance had made Cara perfection itself and he longed to be with her again.

Her letters were always a bit of a let-down after his dreams, but he consoled himself by recalling that she had never been one for books or letters so the very fact that she wrote each week should represent a greater effort and a good deal more love than it would have done from someone more articulate. They were oddly dutiful missives, though he never put the thought into words in his mind. She said at least twice in each letter that she loved him and missed him, she told him what Mira was doing in school and talked airily about the bombings, always ending with how safe she felt at The Pride and how good

Auntie Tina and Ruthie were. She always mentioned that Uncle Des was an air-raid warden so despite the length of the drive they were always visited during a raid, which gave her added confidence. If there was space left, she filled it with big crosses and little ones – hugs and kisses. Oh yes, her letters were lovely to receive!

Yet much though he loved Cara's letters, he enjoyed Mira's more. They were so natural and unaffected, so full of her life, both its joys and its sorrows. School was wonderful, and Sebastian a genius and a dear friend. She had a sum book full of ticks and an English book full of stars. She no longer cried in the shelter when the teachers took them down and when the big bombs dropped near she still did not cry. She jumped, but she did not cry. She did not cry in the cellar, either, and when Uncle Des gave her a medicine-drink called bandy (William, with a smile, had mentally inserted the missing letter) she had 'spitted it all over the cellar floor not from badness but because it stinged and burned'.

In reply William wrote them both long letters, but it was always difficult to answer Cara and wonderful to answer Mira, which meant, he feared, that sometimes his letters to Cara were a trifle stilted. To Mira he could write without self-consciousness, harking back happily to his own childhood, telling her funny stories of p.o.w. life, imagining vividly her small, plain face as she scanned his words.

He had received a batch of mail this morning and thinking about it was keeping him awake long after the other eleven men had dropped off to sleep. It seemed to happen frequently that for some reason the mail piled up somewhere, so you didn't get any at all for weeks and then you got it all at once. And this time, with three letters from Cara and four from Mira, he had noticed something that, previously, had escaped his attention.

Cara's letters were almost interchangeable. In each

letter she had used the words 'Maxie bit the postman the other day', and in each one she had quoted Mira's teacher's comment that Mira had a vivid imagination. Why should this be? Did she really not know that she had said the same thing before? And was her life so empty, poor darling, that she had to repeat the same little snippets of information three times? Or could it be that there was an area of her life about which she did not wish to write? The thought forbade sleep. Could this possibly be why her letters seemed so dull, so very uninformative? That she only wanted him to hear about a tiny part of it? But he was being ridiculous, inventing bogies where none existed – anyone could write the same things three weeks running when they didn't realise their letters would all be read simultaneously! He was being bloody silly. The time to worry was when he had something concrete to worry about.

Like Badger. Badger had had a letter from his sister, telling him that his young wife was going out regularly with an air force officer. The sister was worried, she said, because she could do nothing about it. What in God's name did she think Badger could do? He could not even write and accuse his wife since his sister had begged him to say nothing in case she got into trouble for telling tales.

William rolled over on to his other side and hastily rolled back again. The stump of his arm was sensitive and if he lay on it in a certain way it retaliated by giving him frightful cramp in his missing hand; he could feel non-existent fingers curling into spasm, which was even more un-pleasant than it sounded.

He slept at last as dawn was lightening the sky in the east, and dreamed of Cara. In the dream she was just as he longed for her to be, faithful, intelligent and sympathetic. He felt vastly reassured when he woke. She was his darling child-bride still, but she was pining for him; that was why her letters seemed so dull. It was a compliment, really, that she should be dull just because he was not with her – he could have laughed at his own fears the previous night. Awful, what a few sleepless hours could do!

Cyril came off watch in a bad temper, which was a thing he was never prone to; a more even-tempered lad of sixteen would have been hard to find. But a midshipman's life is not an easy one at the best of times and when men are pushed, by danger and circumstance, to work twenty-four hours at a stretch, they tend to take it out on lowlier members of the human race. Cyril had been bawled at by the No. 1 because he'd been feeding the gulls with some crusts left over from breakfast, and then he'd been gibed at by a rating because he'd gone scarlet. The rating had made some remark about tomatoes being cheap this season and Cyril had known very well what he meant. Damn it, what a bind it was being fair-haired! No one could help blushing, any more than they could help having spots on their chins and foreheads (Cyril was cursed, just at the moment, with an unusually prolific and colourful batch), but people noticed such blushes much more when you were blond. Being six foot two inches didn't help much either. Cyril, thinking up horrid means of paying the rating back for that muttered comment, cracked his head on the top of the companionway and lost his hat. He grabbed it and crunched it down over his ears, but by that time he was convinced that the whole of the ship's complement was watching him anyway and laughing at his ineptitude, his height, his blond hair and his spots.

Which was why, when he blundered into the mess a few moments later, he was in such an uncharacteristically bad mood. And the greeting he received didn't help much, either.

'Hello, Chick! Foggy up there?'

Cyril growled something under his breath and flung himself into a chair. He was sick of it, that's what he was! All the ancient jokes he'd suffered at school seemed to crop up everywhere! Suggestions that the taller you were the nearer the sun; more suggestions that in cold weather icicles must hang from your ears because everyone knew it got colder as you went higher. Remarks about recognising the ship in dock when they saw this yellow mop mysteriously moving, high above the ground . . . He would have told them to pick on someone else, but that was the disadvantage of being the one and only midshipman aboard. There really was no one else.

'What's the matter, lad? I take it that it is still foggy, then. Dammit to hell, and we're due for leave this time when we dock, but you bet they'll take it out if we dock late.'

Scotty was the sub-lieutenant and a decent enough bloke really. Cyril, realising that he had asked a genuine question and had not been poking fun, felt rather guilty. Now that he thought back, it had been foggy when he'd first gone on watch, but it had cleared quite quickly and he had not given the weather a thought since. He cleared his throat and looked rather shamefacedly across the wardroom at the other man.

'Oh, sorry, I was miles away. It isn't foggy actually, the weather's quite decent. I think we're on time what's more.'

'Good.' There were only the three of them in the wardroom, Scotty, Cyril, and the navigating officer, a bridge-fiend who had spent a lot of his off-duty time patiently initiating the two youngest officers into the intricacies of his game. 'Now, Falconer, tell this young man what you were just telling me.'

'What?' Falconer was not very tall and very neat and precise. He was also an excellent officer and despite his predilection for bridge he was tough as old boots and as fast moving as quicksilver. Cyril liked him.

'You know, old boy! About the bacon.'

'Oh, that.' Falconer had been reading a paperback but he put it down, rubbed his eyes, and then spoke directly to Cyril. 'Did you know we were bringing home the bacon? Quite literally, I mean. We've got the entire nation's bacon ration in the convoy this time and if we let any of it slide to the bottom of the sea and waste away in Davy Jones's locker we'll have Winnie to deal with personally.'

'Is that true?' Cyril grinned. 'If I'd known I'd have nipped over and borrowed some. Crumbs, how long is it since we had our way with half a pig?'

'*Not* the best way to put it, young Neyler,' Falconer said repressively. 'However, if you want to win approval, just mention at home that you were escorting their bacon ration and I daresay you'll be overwhelmed with offers of hospitality.'

'Women will fall at my feet?' Cyril suggested hopefully. He sometimes suspected that he was the only virgin aboard, but it was a closely guarded secret if it was true, for to hear him talk one would have thought him a highly experienced, even slightly cynical, young man. Or that was what Cyril hoped they thought, anyway.

'Indeed,' Falconer corroborated. 'And of course, if you could lay your hands on some of that bacon . . . well, the mind boggles. You could probably have your way with half the ladies on the Southampton waterfront.'

'He could have his way with half of them for a Woodbine,' objected the practical Scotty. 'You should have said with half the girls in . . . What's the name of that hick-town you inhabit, Chick?'

'Norwich isn't a hick-town, it's a big city,' Cyril objected, but he was not defending his birthplace with as much enthusiasm as usual, due to his mind being on higher – or at any rate, different – things. 'Is it true, though? That if I had lots of rationed food . . .'

'True as death,' Falconer assured him. 'This run's been pretty mundane, but if you're escorting convoys from the mystic east, well, you can imagine.'

'Clothes are rationed, or they will be soon,' Cyril said dreamily. 'In twelve months they'd probably give their all in exchange for a pair of silk knickers.'

He leaned back in his chair, then sat forward again and reached for the fat pad of paper which he had flung down on the table very much earlier in the day. He got a stump of pencil out of his pocket, licked it, and began to scribble.

'Writing letters? To which lovely lady is this one addressed?'

'It's to Bella. I'm asking her what she'd do for half a pound of streaky,' Cyril said, scribbling away. It was another dark secret that Bella was his fourteen-year-old sister, and one which she shared with much enjoyment. Bella and he were close, best friends, just as Art and Maude were and, further down the family, Edmund and Emily. He wanted a girlfriend in a pleasant, dreamy sort of way, though he had not the faintest idea what he would do with one should he acquire such a luxury. But in the meantime, Bella was a useful blind to pull down over the ship's company's eyes!

Cyril wrote on, soon absorbed. He did not need to write, since this was a leave trip, but even so the letter would get back to Norwich before him because they usually managed to hold one up in port for a day or so.

As he signed off at the end of the fourth page, it occurred to him that though Scotty and Falconer had been mucking about, there might come a time when he could bring something back that was useful to his family. The thought of pleasing them gave him a glow. It did not occur to him that his own presence was the most pleasing thing of all.

'It's a bit below us, catching the bus, but since everyone's so bloody petrol-conscious at the moment . . .' Art paused as a figure loomed at his elbow with a reproving cough. 'Oh, sorry, miss. Two returns to the Regal, please.'

'From where?'

What a ridiculous question, Art thought sadly, considering that they had only just got on the bus and that the bus ran almost exclusively at this time of the day to get personnel to and from the airfield. But he did not voice these feelings, he just told her what she wanted to know.

'The airfield.'

As he said the words he glanced up, and got a pleasant surprise. This conductress was a poppet, a little darling, a sweetie! Curly blonde hair beneath her cap, a neat figure, well-applied lipstick. He smiled at her.

'We're going to the flicks, me and my friend. Have you been this week?'

The bus was nearly empty, but she glanced around as though walls had ears before she replied. New at the job, Art guessed, and afraid of being reported.

'No, not yet, but I shall do. It's *Gone with the Wind*, ever so good. My friend June went and she cried buckets.'

'Who's taking you?'

That was Harry, an opportunist if ever you met one. Art scowled at him and was disappointed that the conductress smiled.

'Who says anyone?'

'I'd be proud and happy . . .' Harry began, but the girl was turning her dial to the correct amount, running out the flimsy tickets and taking Art's money. She did not seem to be taking him seriously.

When she had gone off down to the other end of the bus, Art said: 'Cried buckets? I'm not sure that I want to see this flick, with or without a blonde beside me.'

'Never mind, darling. If it upsets you you can lean on me,' Harry said, in falsetto. Then, dropping to his normal tones, 'Why don't we get that girl to make up a four, Art? With that friend of hers, what was her name? June, that's right.'

'Well, we can't, we don't know her. She doesn't look the type you can pick up.'

'Oh no? All women can be picked up, if they like the man doing the picking. I'll have a word with her before we reach the Regal.'

They got down from the bus when it reached their stop, Harry with his self-confidence severely punctured. She had listened, smiled very sweetly, and then used such language . . . Harry claimed to have been shocked. Art, who had sisters, thought that 'Get stuffed' was nothing to what she might have said, and was not terribly sympathetic.

They saw the film through to the bitter end, though both would have much preferred a good Western, then had fish and chips, and caught the bus back to the airfield.

'Guess who's conducting?' Harry hissed, as they ran up the stairs to the top deck. 'You try your luck this time.'

'I'll do no such thing,' Art said at once. It was odd, he thought, how little self-confidence he had with women, though he flew a bomber over Germany and watched the eggs go down without many qualms. To change the subject he added, 'What about that raid on London last weekend, then? Think it was a reprisal for bombing the Berlin opera house?'

'Bound to be. Your lot all right?'

Harry had seen a photograph of Val and Maude, swimming down in Yarmouth before the war. Ever since he had hankered to meet them both, but so far Art had resolutely refused to mix business with home life. Nevertheless, it was decent of Harry to remember that he had a sister.

'Yes, I think so. Someone would have got in touch if they hadn't been, or so I tell myself. Tiddy went up for a weekend though, to see his folks, and said it was a miracle anyone was left alive. So it must have been a bad 'un.'

The conductress arrived alongside them and Art waved their return tickets, hoping she would go away before Harry started something, but she seemed in no hurry to depart. She clipped their tickets, cleared her throat, and then said: 'Good film?'

'You'll enjoy it,' Art said kindly, not wanting to say that they had found it pretty dull stuff. 'It's a women's film, really. My friend and I prefer something with a bit more action.'

'You do?' She moved round so that she could look down at him. 'Well, why don't *you* ask me who's taking me to see it, then?'

'Possibly because I don't want to get snubbed,' Art said truthfully. 'I hope you enjoy yourselves, whoever it is.'

'That rather depends on you.' She gave him a serious glance, but her eyes were sparkling. 'Would you like to see it again?'

'Not much, it's a helluva long . . .' Art stopped, stared, and then started again '. . . a helluva long film. Why?'

'I'm off tomorrow, after twelve. That's why.'

Art stared, moistened his suddenly dry lips with his tongue, and then, with his face getting hotter and hotter, blurted it out before he lost his courage.

'W-would you like to come to the flicks with me tomorrow, Miss – er – er?'

'My name's Pet . . . short for Petula. What's yours?'

'Art, short for Arthur.'

'OK, I've got it. Yes, Art, thanks very much, I'd love to come out with you. What time and where?'

'Outside the Regal? At t-t-two?'

She shook her head, her eyes still teasing him.

'No, Art, the big film starts at two! Tell you what, I'll be on the same bus as you came down on today; meet me on the bus! Tomorrow, at around one-thirty. All right?'

'Oh yes, very all right,' Art said, pushing his hands up through his hair. When she had gone he leaned across and hissed into Harry's ear.

'Harry, dammit, *she* picked *me* up!'

'I noticed. Art, you're the most clumsy, inept fellow who ever had the devil's own luck! I bet she's expensive, too – you'll find yourself in the one and nines for starters, and she's bound to want something more exotic than fish and chips. I bet she drinks gin and tonics.'

'What the hell? I don't grudge a girl a gin or two.' The bell rang for their stop and Art nearly fell down the stairs so fast did he descend them. Pet was swinging on the centre pole, advising the two people who were about to climb aboard that they should wait until the passengers had disembarked.

'Night, Pet,' Harry called, and was echoed rather less boisterously by Art.

'Night, boys,' she called back and then, a little self-consciously, 'See you tomorrow, Art!'

Jenny, feeling rather pleased with herself, climbed down from the trap, tied the pony up to the rails beside the telephone boxes, and went into the nearest. She looked at her watch, then up at the clock she could just see by stretching her neck and closing one eye – not a pretty sight, she reflected with an inward chuckle. Yes, it was going to be all right to telephone now. Simon had said that he would be in the office – where he was not supposed to be – from ten to ten until five past, so she should get him.

She picked up the receiver and arranged the coins neatly

beside the telephone. She knew the number by heart, of course, but she always carried it written out on a piece of paper in her handbag, with Simon's name and rank beside it. You never knew.

The operator repeated the number after her and then there was the usual lengthy wait, the clickings, hummings and long bleeps and moans which always seemed to happen when she rang Simon. Then the ringing tone and his voice.

'Don't tell me, it's my favourite poppet!'

'Simon Rose, what would you say if it wasn't?' Jenny tried to sound indignant, but it was uphill work; she missed him so much!

'It isn't!' He had a lovely, teasing, deep voice – oh, she adored him! 'How's things? And how are both my babies?'

Jenny touched her flat stomach with fingers that still refused to believe the evidence of a pregnancy test. She would have to get a lot fatter before people realised, yet she was five months gone now.

'We're well, all three of us. I felt junior give a teeny kick the other day. I remember what it felt like from Marianne, and it was just lovely. Have you heard from Val?'

'Circuitously. In a roundabout way, that means. I met Cyril on his way home for a long leave – we met in London. I only had a few hours but Cyril had seen Val and said she was well. Actually, he was fearfully worried about her, in a way. He said he'd never dreamed she could look so pale and haunted and worn out, but after he'd been with her for a few hours he thought she seemed better, more herself. I expect you know they were blasted again really badly about ten days ago?'

'Oh dear, I wish Val would get out of it! I did hear.' Jenny sighed deeply. 'Simon, darling, you'll find out sooner or later but I'll tell you now. I had a letter. Do you remember Flo?'

Flo had been Jenny's fluffy-headed debutante friend who had worked the same shifts and the same wards as herself. Simon had only met her once, but he had been impressed with her careless acceptance of the dangers and her complete belief that the war would end soon and in victory.

'Oh, Jen, not Flo?'

'I'm afraid so. A direct hit on the laboratories which weren't manned, except that Flo had taken a box of samples over for the day-staff. She was killed outright. Or so they told her mother. She wrote to me.'

'Darling, I'm sorrier than I can say. Does it make you feel very bad?'

'I'm ashamed to say that it doesn't. Simon, if you hadn't thrown your weight about . . . Well, I don't have to say it, do I? Poor little Marianne, she needs me. Only I do wish . . . I wish . . .'

'I know, love. Tell me about the landgirls.'

Despite Jenny's work, the Rileys had still been forced to engage a couple of landgirls, though as Mrs Riley said, it wasn't surprising. They had, after all, lost not only Sizzle but her two sons to the forces.

The landgirls, when they arrived, were not at first glance ideal material for hard agricultural work. They were sisters. Sue had carroty hair and unhealthily pale skin and Ruby had meek, mouse-coloured hair and acne. They were both thin as lathes. They came from Poplar in London where, Mr Riley remarked once they were well out of earshot, they might have lived under stones for all the weathering they had seen. However, both girls proved to have plenty of character and, although their mistakes were the subject of much side-holding mirth, Jenny soon noticed that they never made the same mistake twice. Ruby, indeed, had a fearless attitude to work which many a sturdier girl might have envied and seemed quite content to do any job, no matter how hard or dirty, provided that she was not 'fussed' as she put it.

Despite their slender figures, both girls ate like horses. They were completely indiscriminate, wolfing whatever was put on their plates with great enthusiasm, and no matter how hard their day or how tired they were, it seemed a matter of pride to them that they go out at least twice and sometimes three times a week. They were very young, of course – Sue was nineteen and Ruby eighteen – but even so they made Jenny feel old and jaded. Such amazing energy, such ebullience!

'They're both very well, thanks. I was very touched the other evening actually. Sue offered to babysit whilst I went out dancing with Ruby!'

To her surprise, Simon was not at all impressed by this evidence of large-hearted generosity.

'You didn't go? I should damned well hope not! I'm not going up there in the black of night to defend my woman only to find her out gadding with someone else.'

Jenny knew that Simon had transferred to some sort of secret place, where they were flying night-fighters. She had heard, with some amusement, that the pilots were being fed carrots to help with their night-sight, but had not believed a word of it. However, night-fighters were beginning to get results and to chalk up successes.

'Of course I didn't. Why on earth would I want to go dancing?' Jenny said, honestly amazed that he should even imagine she would do such a thing. 'I'd only have cramped Ruby's style, whatever that may be. A mother-image! No, I don't fancy it at all.'

'You aren't a mother-image, that's the snag,' Simon said gloomily. 'Oh, damn!' That was the operator, reminding them that their time was up. 'Any more money, sweetie? Oh, damn, you're fading! I love you! Kiss Mari for me! Write!'

Jenny, shrieking back above the static, put down the phone when the line went dead and left the box rather thoughtfully. The idea! How could Simon ever think she would go dancing like a single girl, when she was in fact a married woman!

I mean, she told herself, Simon wouldn't do such a thing. Would he?

In fact, nothing was further from Simon's thoughts than any sort of gadding. Though he had done his best to be comforting and nothing else, the news of Flo's death had turned him cold. To think that it might have been Jenny! He must not, would not, think about it. But of course he did.

The trouble was, he was off to London this very evening. He had not mentioned it on the telephone, knowing that it would upset Jenny to think of him in danger, but he was going up to take Val out. Laddy had wanted to go and see her, but things had not worked out right and then Simon had rung the flat and spoken to Minnie.

'She's fair wore out,' Minnie had said bluntly. 'She an' Richie both. That's just drive, drive, drive, and not a rest do they have when the raids are bad. Richie stands it better, being a man, but he've had his moments, lately.'

She went on to describe how Richie had fought his way across blazing London to a hospital, with three wounded adults and a child in the vehicle, and when he reached it matron herself had been standing in the foyer, purple with dignity and indignation.

'You can't bring those people in here, my good man,' she had told the astounded Richie. 'This is principally an eye hospital and I need my beds for genuine patients needing surgery.'

Richie and his mate had stared as she told them the

nearest route to a hospital which would take the wounded. It was miles away and it meant crossing areas which both men knew to be impassable.

'I cannot have men like you palming your responsibilities off here,' she had finished, and that had been enough for Richie.

'He saw red, see,' Minnie explained. 'He and his mate got the people out of the ambulance on stretchers and that, and just dumped them in the foyer. A coupla nurses come out of a side ward and said they'd see to 'em, and then the men walked out, leaving this matron person gobbling like a turkey cock Richie said.'

'And you think it would help if I came up? I'll come willingly, but will Val listen to me?'

'Ho no, she won't *listen*,' Minnie admitted. 'What you've gotta do, boy, is carry her off. Just insist that she hev a break for a day or two.'

So Simon, off to kidnap his cousin, was rather dreading the ordeal ahead.

'Look, Val, all I'm asking is that you come away for a weekend. No, not down to Norwich; they've had raids there too and besides, I think you want complete rest. I know a marvellous little cottage in the Cotswolds which would do you so much good! You'd come back better able to cope, really you would. Why don't you give it a try?'

'Too tired,' Val said simply. They were sitting in the kitchen of the only inhabitable flat. 'Too darned exhausted. Go away, Cousin Simon, and let me sleep.'

'You can sleep in the car. Come on, pack a bag.'

He got his way in the end, of course, and drove off triumphant, not knowing then how his bright idea was about to fall flat on its face in the mire.

When they reached the little cottage in the Cotswolds which Simon had remembered so happily, they knocked

204

on the door. Simon beamed proudly at Mrs Harper and announced that he had brought his cousin down for a weekend.

Mrs Harper plainly did not believe him. She stared at him whilst hot colour crept up her cheeks and her eyes got smaller and smaller.

'Beg pardon, sir?' she said at last. 'Did you say cousin?'

She managed to make it sound like a dirty word. Simon, feeling a bit hot around the gills, said that yes, he *had* said cousin, and he would be very obliged if Mrs Harper could let them have two rooms for the weekend.

Mrs Harper reminded him, in arctic accents, that when he had brought his dear little wife and child down into the country, not so *very* long ago, there had only been one room available, with a tiny slip of a place for the baby to sleep. Things, she said nastily, her eyes darting over Val in a thoroughly insulting manner, had not changed since then – not *here*, at any rate!

Simon apologised, but pointed out that he had not enquired about the number of rooms when he had brought Jenny and Marianne here, and had not been told. He was sorry to have troubled her.

In the car once more, he tried to apologise to Val and she said it didn't matter, that the woman was a silly old fool who didn't recognise sincerity when she saw it, and would he mind terribly driving her back to London since she had no desire to be taken for a floosie twice in one evening.

Simon felt that he slunk back to London. He and Val spent the first night on mattresses in the cellar with Duggie Dwyer snoring between them. Val slept, twitched, gulped, whimpered, and finally gave such a shout that she knocked her head on the wall and woke herself up. She was asleep again in seconds, and then she twitched, gulped, whimpered and cried out again.

Duggie Dwyer snored and snored and lashed out with his fists once or twice and talked nonsense under his breath.

Simon could not sleep. What must life be like up here, when you never got any respite; when every night you were hiding down here in the musty underground air, hearing the shriek and roar of the Blitz? No wonder Val had nightmares! No wonder she cried out like a child when the bombs fell close to rock the cellar. And, he thought with morbid humour, no wonder she twitched, gulped, whimpered and kept others awake!

Once, he grew concerned with the violence of her reaction and went over to her mattress, taking her in his arms. She quieted, moaned, and then her eyes blinked open and gazed up at him with such a look of wondering love that Simon felt, for one second, horribly embarrassed. But only for one second; with recognition the look faded and was gone, leaving hot-tempered annoyance.

'It's only you! Simon, you swine, I thought . . . I thought . . .'

Val slept again, and Simon laid her gently back on to the mattress.

The second night was, if anything, worse. The cellar was crowded since neither Richie nor Minnie was working, and halfway through the night young Reg added himself to the human sandwich down below. By dawn, Simon was only too eager to get out of there and complied eagerly with Val's suggestion that they get some air.

They walked out into what Simon afterwards thought of as Hell with a capital H. He had never seen or imagined carnage and destruction like it. They went along streets where fires still raged, past a bombed building where men with drawn and exhausted faces were digging out the dead. In less than half a mile he saw a child's body disinterred whilst a woman keened and clutched her torn and bloodied dress around it; a dog with only its head intact spread across the pavement; a man with a gaping wound in one cheek leaning on a scrap of a boy black with filth and weeping. What they had suffered one could not begin to guess.

When they found the café Val had brought him in search of they had a cup of tea and a doorstep of bread and margarine and then made their way back to the flat. Simon spent the journey urging Val to let him take her away, back to Norwich.

'Join the services, girl, work in the city . . . Anything but this! You've done your share and more. This will ruin your health and break your spirit! You've no reason for going on, battling against all this!'

Val listened and shook her head and finally, he suspected from sheer exhaustion, she told him why.

'I'm in love with a chap I met before the war, Simon. Otto von Eckner. Do you remember me talking about him? He's in the Luftwaffe.'

Simon had stared with anguish at her pale face and haunted, darkened eyes. He understood.

'Val, you poor darling, you can't take on responsibility for what your fellow does . . . Our chaps are doing the same to them, if on a smaller scale! Otto may be out in Crete or Greece or North Africa, he may fly fighters, he may never have handled a bomber in his life!'

'I know. Logically, it's absurd. But emotionally, it's the way I feel. Responsible in some small way for this; to blame, because I can't forget him. When the war's over I want to find him and stay with him, and I know the only way my conscience will let that happen is if I do my best for these poor bloody victims of Hitler's murderers.'

'I do understand, but, Val, you've done your bit! Can't you let it go, now? Go somewhere else, where it isn't so bad, where you'd get *some* let-up?'

Val shook her head.

'Can't. Would if I could. And you've seen me on two bad nights – I'm at my worst down in that bloody cellar. I'm far better out with my old bus, picking people up, *doing* something. It's the hanging around and waiting that I can't abide.'

So he had left her there. He had talked to Minnie again, explained about the fiasco in the Cotswolds, and Minnie had explained about the men in his cousin's life.

'Flits from flower to flower she do,' she said sagely. 'There's been two policemen, a conshie – ever so nice, he was – several auxiliary firemen and a banker or two. We call 'em Val's army, for they're all nice lads what would dearly like to be the only chap in her life. But I can tell why she does it; misses someone special, she does. Always been the same, our Val, never would upset anyone deliberate. So she smiles and goes dancing and jokes and laughs and underneath, she misses him – whoever he is.'

And Simon, with his new knowledge, agreed with her that she was probably right and wondered how long Val could keep going before she cracked. He hoped with all his heart that she would outlast this Blitz, which everyone knew – or hoped they knew – could not go on for ever.

Chapter Eleven

Maude came in from the ops room after the graveyard shift rubbing her eyes and longing for her bed to find Sandy waiting for her.

'Come on, I hung about knowing you'd be out any minute. Coming to the canteen for some brekker?'

'Oh, I don't know, I'm awfully tired.' Maude rubbed a bit harder. 'It was quite a night – but then when isn't it? Seen Alan? I've got this hazy sort of feeling that I promised to meet him in the canteen at lunchtime, but it might have been breakfast.'

'Then come with me, and you'll find out.' Sandy laughed as Maude nodded and trailed after her. 'Head up, shoulders back, you aren't dead yet!'

'Aren't I? You could have fooled me.' Maude was still yawning as they entered the canteen where an ill-tempered lady with an off-white turban round her straggly locks was hurling inch-sized bits of overcooked bacon on to plates which already contained iron-hard eggs. 'What, no Alan? I'll go back to bed, then.'

'Back? You're mad, woman, you haven't been to bed at all! Come on, taste the delectable grub that the delectable Phoebe has slaved to bring to this point of perfection.' The 'delectable Phoebe' sniffed and wiped the back of her hand across a long, reddened nose. 'Bacon and egg for two, please, Phoebe, and two cups of milky tea.'

Presently, with the food in front of her and the teacup already half emptied, Maude began to feel human. It even seemed possible that she might survive for long enough to climb into her bed; previously she had been convinced that she would barely make her bedroom. She crunched her portion of bacon and glanced round the room.

'No, no Alan. Never mind, it must have been lunchtime. I say, San, will you give me a yell at around half past twelve?'

'No,' Sandy said equably. 'You know very well, Maudie, that you need your sleep. You're off tomorrow, aren't you? Right, I thought so. Tell you what, if you're awake at lunchtime and in here, you can make any arrangements with Alan that you feel capable of, but if you aren't here I shall be. I'll explain that you're going to have your sleep out today but will contact him tomorrow. How's that?'

'Sandy, you're an angel!' Maude finished her bacon, dug her knife into the unyielding yolk of the egg and decided it was not worth the struggle. She replaced the cutlery on her plate and bit into the bread and scrape, as the girls called it. 'One day I'll do the same for you. Do tell Alan sorry, though, if I'm not around. Tell him its exhaustion that's keeping me and not a lack of interest in his company.'

'Of course. What, not finishing your nice egg?' Sandy speared it with her fork and lifted it across to her own plate, seeming indifferent to the fact that it neither bent nor sagged, but remained as immobile as a rubber trick-egg. 'My God, I must be desperate.'

'We all are,' Maude pointed out. 'I'd like a slap-up meal tonight – I wonder if Alan could run to it?'

'Alan might run to fish and chips, but I should have thought slap-up meals were out; he's got a car to run as well as a war, remember!'

'That's what I meant – fish and chips. After canteen yuck fish and chips *is* a slap-up meal. Hey, do you remember when we were kids, San, the comic papers and their slap-up meals? Desperate Dan and his cow pies, feasts in the dorm with the Bruno boys? Tiger Tim getting all the doughnuts except for one which got stuck down the ostrich's throat? By golly, those were the meals!'

'Just tell Alan that your idea of a slap-up meal is cow pie or a second-hand doughnut and he'll have you certified,' Sandy warned her. 'Those cow pies had the horns sticking out the top, usually . . . Isn't it funny the things you remember? Did you read Billy Bunter? He was the one for forbidden food . . .' She put on a squeaky voice. 'I say, you chaps . . .'

'Read, in the past tense? Dear girl, I read them still. My brothers' bookshelves are crammed with that sort of thing and my uncles were devotees of *Chums*, so we've got old copies of that going back way beyond the last war! Actually, they're jolly good.' Maude stood up, a piece of bread and scrape still in one hand. 'It's no good, I can't stand here discussing highbrow literature with you, woman, I'm dropping. Goodnight, goodnight . . .'

'. . . parting is such sweet sorrow,' intoned Sandy dramatically, holding out a hand and clutching her brow with the other one.

'. . . that if I don't go to bed soon it'll be tomorrow,' capped Maude, giggling at her own brilliance. 'Don't forget Alan at lunchtime.'

'I shan't. Off with you, then!'

Maude went into the WAAF hut and down the long, well-polished corridor to her room. She was in there, throwing off her clothes and telling herself that only sinners and dirty girls went unwashed to bed and knowing she was not being convinced, when someone tried the door. Maude had locked it when she came in and in her half-dazed state she did not reach it in time to stop the person who had rattled walking away, so she had to shout after the retreating, uniformed back.

'Hey!'

Penelope, for it was she, jumped and then turned.

'Sorry, Maude, I didn't mean to disturb you. I was just bringing in your post.' She blinked at Maude's near-nudity. 'I say, old girl, shove something on. Suppose an officer should come along?'

'Male or female?' Maude nipped back into her room and slung a dressing-gown round her shoulders. 'Hang on a mo, Penny. Since I've been jerked out of my daze I'd better come up and have a wash; we can walk up together.'

'OK. I'll hang on to your post until you've done the necessary.' Penelope looked at her friend and then smiled, shaking her head. 'Dear Maudie, what do you intend to wash *with*? And dry *on*? Look, you go on and I'll nip back and get your towel and spongebag.'

'You're a dear,' Maude said gratefully. She made her way along to the wash-room with its row of toilets on the left and washbasins on the right and poured some water into a bowl, grimacing at the lukewarmness of it. She washed her face and was flicking her hands free of water droplets when Penelope returned with her gear.

'You've got lots of letters,' she remarked, as Maude soaped herself. 'I don't know who from, of course, but they're quite fat and promising, except for one which is probably a bill.'

'I don't run up bills,' protested Maude. She finished her wash, attacked her teeth vigorously, and spoke through a mouthful of foam. 'It's probably from one of the kids. They don't run to much in the way of length.'

'Probably. Have you finished? Want me to walk back with you?'

'I've done, but don't bother, nosy, because I'm not going to open that lot yet. I'm going to sleep first.' Maude took her letters. Great, there were four of them. 'Off with you, Penelope.'

'I'm in no hurry,' Penelope said, sauntering out of the wash-room ahead of Maude. 'Anyway, I wanted a word with you. Are you seeing Alan today?'

'I might. Why?'

Maude knew very well why Penelope wanted to know. She had been going out with Alan now, in an easy, friendly sort of way, for a long time, and Penelope had recently been going out with one of Alan's friends. Penelope was considering getting engaged and could not understand why Maude and Alan did not follow suit. Alan was keen, and he was such a nice bloke, steady and reliable yet great fun.

'Well, Stan's off. We could make up a foursome and pool petrol and go out somewhere.'

'Can't, because I may decide to sleep through. Or at least, I may not have much choice, if I get to sleep early and deeply! I've told Alan that if I don't turn up in the canteen for lunch he'd better go off by himself.'

'Or with someone else.'

'Yes, fine,' Maude said equably. 'He's welcome to take other girls out. I wish he would. I'm not the clinging vine sort.'

'I know. I don't understand you. Alan's one of the nicest blokes on the station and he eats out of your hand yet you don't seem to care at all! One of these days he'll go off with someone else and you'll realise what you've missed.'

They had reached Maude's door now but Maude paused, her hand on the knob.

'I don't love Alan and I don't intend to pretend otherwise. What's more, I don't believe in this indiscriminate sex that's going on, because even if you don't have a baby and get chucked for that reason you'll probably find he gets posted, or killed, and that will just mean you're left with a broken heart. Remember Morella?'

Penelope nodded. They all remembered Morella. A silly

little thing, a fluttery creature with huge, trusting eyes and a bust which she hauled up so high that it was in perpetual danger of chucking her under the chin. An eyelash flutterer, a leaner, a crinoline-miss born into the twentieth century by some freak of fate, Morella had fallen for the charms of one of the pilots and he had been killed and Morella had tried to kill herself. Not very efficiently, because she wasn't an efficient girl, so she had been found before the bottle of aspirin had done any permanent harm, and had been taken to hospital in town and then sent away, none of them knew where. But she had left a pathetic little note. Poor, fluttery, desperate Morella, battering against the realities of life as a butterfly batters against a lit lamp. Swallowing and gagging and doggedly swallowing again, until she lost consciousness, because she was five months pregnant and because he had been gone for eight long weeks. She had no girlfriends. She did not seem able to make girlfriends. She was scared of the WAAF officers; scared of her parents; scared of the scandal she would create if she admitted her condition. It had been easier to die, to frizzle in the flame, bright wings becoming dust.

'But, darling, we aren't like Morella,' Penelope said at last. 'We don't have to go all the way . . . or if we do, we can take precautions against . . . Well I refuse to be classed with Morella. I'm quite different.'

'That's just where you're wrong. We're all Morellas, underneath. If I let myself fall in love with a fellow I daresay I'd think just like she did – that if you love him you should give yourself. I think Morella tried to kill herself not because of the baby, whatever she may have said, but because her life was empty without her man. You see, she liked boys a lot, but once she'd given herself she didn't care about the others. Everyone noticed – she never tried, once, to get another fellow, did she? No, it's a lot simpler

214

to blame the baby and I know they're a terrible complication, but I don't think they're nearly as dangerous as falling in love!'

'If you'd fallen in love you wouldn't say that,' Penelope said shrewdly. 'But I do get your point. You don't intend to be serious with Alan because you don't really feel much for him. Is that right?'

'More or less. See you later, Penelope, and don't let *me* put you off getting engaged.'

'Don't worry, you won't.' Penelope strolled off down the corridor again and Maude went into her room, shut the door, slung her dressing-gown on the floor and climbed wearily into bed. Smiling to herself, she pulled the covers up round her ears. She wondered whether Penelope *did* go all the way; if so she was not prepared to admit it to a couple of virgins like Maude and Sandy!

She expected to fall asleep at once but found, to her dismay, that Morella's troubles were going round and round in her head. At the time they had all been shocked that the girl had felt unable to confide in any of them, but now it occurred to her that perhaps she was cold, unfeeling, and that was why she neither fell in love with Alan nor felt that she ought. She began to have imaginary conversations with Penelope in which she justified her actions and feelings and assured the other girl that she was as hot-blooded as anyone else, given the right circumstances.

Sitting up with an exasperated sigh after twenty minutes of this, she reached for the batch of letters. She ripped open the first one and began to read. It was from Val, an excellent correspondent, and she giggled twice and felt much better for having read it. Darling Val! I'm like her. We both guard our emotions from the wrong people so that we'll have more to give the right one, she thought confidently. No one could call Val cold!

The second letter was from Desmond and though her father wrote rarely he had got in full measure the family ability to tell a funny story well, so his letter was amusing and cheerful.

The third letter was from Edna, her friend from school who had been posted, poor darling, to Scotland. Not that she was repining; she was delighted with her lot and particularly with the Free French, who thronged the nearest city.

Edna had met a smashing chap. He had a friend, another smashing chap. Both lusted after Edna, but so far she had remained Pure. She was considering Giving In, but had not yet done so. Had Maude got a chap worth Giving In to? Why didn't they have a pact that the first to Do It would write to the other and give Details? I bet it's me, Edna had added complacently and without a single capital letter, what was more.

Maude giggled and lay back on her pillow to consider Edna's proposal. The way she was heading, Edna was right, she would most certainly be the first to Do It! She would also be the first to describe in a letter what It was like, Maude thought with another gurgle. What a marvellous girl Edna was, completely without self-consciousness when out with a chap, so that she announced early in the relationship that she did not like French kissing and would not stand for it.

'You wait, Maudie,' she had written, 'until you Come Across a Frenchman. They think it is Kissing to open their mouths and Lick you! It is Quite Revolting; how very Foreign they are!'

But now only the last letter remained to be opened, the thin one, the one Penelope had thought looked like a bill. Maude's eyelids were beginning to droop but she opened the letter anyway and spread the thin sheet out on the bed. She glanced at the signature. Bill. Who on earth was Bill?

She didn't know any Bills! She began to read and immediately she knew that it was the bolshie rear gunner, even if he *was* a pilot now.

Dear Maude, the letter read *You'll remember me, I daresay. The chap learning to fly bombers at Kennet last year. I'll be down your way Thursday, and I'd like to see you again. About three in the Fisher's Arms, if you can make it.*

It was just signed Bill and she realised, with exasperation, that she had no recollection of his surname so could not write back and tell him she had other plans. She could, of course, ignore the letter, but that would mean standing him up and she despised girls who did that. To her surprise a number boasted quite openly about it, saying with a degree of glee that at such and such a time Fred or Frank or Phil would be walking up and down outside a cinema or a pub, waiting for her. She supposed it was a small revenge for the fact that a girl was still supposed to wait for a fellow to take the initiative in a relationship, but she still thought it a petty meanness which she would not stoop to.

It was not until then that she looked at the date on the postmark. It had been posted two days ago . . . heavens, and today was Thursday! Well, that simplified things. She would ring the pub at three, ask for Bill, and explain that she was busy. Good. That would be sensible, so he would not hang about waiting for her, though she did not think he was that sort of bloke. More the sort that waited thirty seconds and then invited the nearest woman out for a drink!

Smiling to herself, she snuggled down again and felt sleep stealing over her.

She was woken by someone coming into the room and saying her name in a small, scared voice. She opened her eyes reluctantly and stared into the round blue eyes of ACW Joan Myers, who pulled a sympathetic face.

'Sorry to wake you, but there's some chap been phoning you all afternoon and he's in ever such a temper, ever so rude he was and to Miss Taylor as well. She told him not to ring again, she said you'd get into trouble and she said she'd send the AFPs down to the pub he's ringing from if he didn't learn politeness. Only he rang again almost at once and when I rushed and answered . . . I knew you wouldn't want Taylor to get it . . . he barked at me to "Wake the woman, for God's sake!" and honestly, dear, I thought I better had!'

Her voice held the mingling notes of admiration, awe and envy; Bill seemed to make strong impressions, Maude thought crossly. She swung her legs out of bed, groped for her slippers and stood up.

'I'd better come, then. Is he still on the line?'

'Oh, no! I said I'd get you to ring him back. The number's by the telephone.'

'OK. Skedaddle, then. I shan't be a tick.'

Barely five minutes later she was in the mess, only to find the phone in use; but as it was Joan she went over and raised her eyebrows. Her guess had been right, it was Bill.

'Hold on a sec, she's just arrived.' Joan handed over the receiver thankfully, her colour even higher than it had been in Maude's room. 'Gosh, he's cross!'

Maude sighed, took the receiver and spoke briskly into it.

'Well? I'm here now, they came and woke me.'

'Got out of bed the wrong side too, by the sound of it,' Bill's gravelly voice said nastily. 'Did you get my letter?'

'Yes. When I came off the graveyard shift. I meant to ring, but . . .' she glanced at her watch, saw that it showed 3.30, and gasped. 'I've just looked at the time. I overslept. Sorry, but I don't see that you've got much to complain about. If I'd been on duty I wouldn't even have read the thing until five or six tonight.'

'Hmm. Yeah, I suppose I knew that. Look, can you come down to the main gate? I'll pick you up and we can have a chat.'

'Oh no, I don't think so. I'm still terribly sleepy, and . . .'

He cut across the sentence blithely.

'What? Sorry, the interference is awful, sounds as if there's a bushfire on the line. I'll be at the main gate in fifteen minutes, then. Try not to be late. I've still got the same old banger.'

His receiver clicked down leaving Maude a prey to various emotions. The line had been clear enough her end, but she knew this did not mean it had been equally so at the Fisher's. *Had* he heard though, and refused to accept the brush-off? It seemed quite likely. If so, should she be bulldozed into a meeting that she did not want and had not sought, or should she just stay here? She needed a cup of tea now, her mouth was completely dry, and she wasn't dressed – and besides, she wasn't one of his little WAAF pick-ups who would come running whenever he crooked a finger.

Yet fifteen minutes later she was down at the main gate in a cream linen dress with a tobacco coloured jacket over it. She thought she was being silly, but she had never stood anyone up yet and she did not intend to start now. However, if he was late she would walk straight back to the mess . . .

He arrived on time. In a scruffy little sports car which screeched to a halt far too close to her feet for comfort.

He looked just the same. Bristly dark hair, pale skin, sarcastic dark eyes.

'Well done. Hop in.'

'Bill, I came to tell you I couldn't come out . . .'

He got out of the car and took her arm. None too gently, what was more.

'Nonsense, I've come a long way to see you. We'll go

for a bit of a drive, it's a lovely afternoon, and we can talk.'

'But I don't want to hop in and we've nothing to talk about,' Maude said, infuriated with his calm assumptive air. 'I said on the phone that I couldn't meet you, but . . .'

'Look, you walked all the way down to the main gate so you must have a few minutes free.' It sounded perfectly reasonable put like that. 'I'm not trying to kidnap you, I just want a chat, and then I'll drive you back up to the station so you'll save the walk, see? If you've got to get back then I'll see if there's anyone still here from my old bunch, have a bit of a gossip.'

It seemed churlish to refuse so Maude got silently into the passenger seat. After they had driven a short distance she said crossly: 'All right, then, I'm sitting here; speak!'

'Why can't you come out and have tea with me? What's happening up at the station that's so important? I've come a long way to ask you something.'

'Ask away.'

'I will, over tea. Be a sport, Maudie.'

Rather reluctantly, Maude found herself laughing. After all, the chap had come a long way (or so she assumed), and he could scarcely eat her! She had told Alan to go without her if she did not turn up at lunchtime and he had done so; she had nothing planned. But on the other hand she did not want Bill suffering any illusions. Better tell him the truth.

'Look, Bill, I hardly know you, but what I do know I don't much like! When you were stationed at Kennet you were odd and rude and abrupt. You made absolutely no effort to be friendly or even to get to know me. When I got your letter I was astonished you could take it for granted that I'd remember you, let alone want to see you again. You could scarcely call meeting you once in a pub and being insulted, and then again in the canteen where the insult was a bit less obvious, a good start for any sort of relationship.'

'What about that night in your bedroom, then?'

Maude had grown up a lot since that night. She did not even begin to blush, though she turned an angry glance on him. He really was a boor, to make it sound as though he had spent the night in her room!

'Oh, that! I was in shock, I believe, and would have behaved the same with anyone else who came into my bedroom and started hugging me. I was glad you were alive, of course, which probably made me let you touch me in the first place,' she added conscientiously.

'Was that *all*?' He stared at her incredulously, taking his eyes from the road for a moment and then turning back to stare ahead once more. 'It meant no more than that?'

'No.' Maude smiled to herself. So this was the line to take! She had pierced his seemingly impregnable armour of self-satisfaction. She could actually see from a muscle that jumped by his mouth that he was grinding his teeth. Although the whole thing had happened ages ago, it hurt his ego to admit that she had not been bowled over by his embrace. The conceit of it! 'Why on earth should it? Tell the truth next day I thought it was some sort of crazy dream.'

'A dream? If that interfering cow hadn't walked in you'd have known it wasn't a dream.'

His voice was low but intense, and the threat in the words made her feel uncomfortable, but she was determined to show him nothing but an indifferent face. She laughed.

'I don't know what you thought you could do, with Sandy asleep in the bed three feet away! Or perhaps you had visions of carrying me off on your milk-white steed to somewhere a bit more private?'

He slowed the car to negotiate a bend, then drove it through an open gateway, bouncing over the rough track until they were forced to a halt by the luxuriance of a crop of standing hay. He switched off the engine and turned to Maude.

'I had visions, all right. Ever since. Not you?'

'I don't even know what you mean,' Maude confessed. 'I told you, I thought you disliked me, you were so rude and unpleasant. If I meant anything to you, that night, why did you ignore me and keep out of my way afterwards? Don't tell me you were embarrassed because you'd behaved so badly.'

'No, not embarrassed. I often behave badly.' His voice was unconcerned and Maude had to bite back a giggle. He was really incredible! 'You see, it's never happened to me . . . that I wanted something other than . . . well, a bit of skirt. I didn't like it, I didn't want to get involved, perhaps find myself going steady, and besides I'd got my posting so I knew I was leaving. But I was sure you were thinking about me, thinking about that night, wanting to see me again.' He stared at her, apparently genuinely puzzled by her resistance to his charm. 'And you didn't? You just dismissed the whole thing as a dream, or bad manners, or a bit of both?'

'That's right,' Maude said rather mendaciously. She had indeed thought about the incident long and hard at the time. 'You left and Alan began taking me out quite often, and he's such a pleasant, considerate sort of person that I put you and that night right out of my head. I think Alan's good manners and so on rather spoiled me for your . . . your less civilised approach.'

Bill stared at her for a moment, his gaze brooding and bitter. Then he leaned forward and started the engine.

'I suppose you want to get back to the station, then?'

'Yes, please,' Maude said, though in fact she was intrigued by the situation. Could it be true – as Sandy had implied – that men like Bill could only approach women through rudeness and a sort of restrained violence? And had he meant that he had dreamed of her all these months? Then commonsense reasserted itself; if so nothing would have been simpler than to telephone or write. No, it was all part of his approach, a softening up in this instance because she had not fallen at his feet.

He turned the car, not without difficulty. But in the gateway he hesitated.

'You sure? You wouldn't have tea with me? It's a good tea, and I have come a long way . . . I've booked in for the night so I can't just leave. They made me pay first, though now that I know you're involved with Cumnor . . .' He glanced at her, half shamefacedly. 'Would you?'

Maude looked at her watch, sighed, then nodded. 'Yes, all right, I'll have tea with you. I hope you don't feel that you've come all this way on false pretences, because you know I never do pretend what I don't feel.' She stopped; this seemed to be going all wrong. 'What I'm trying to say is that if you'd written or rung before I could have saved you the journey.'

'Fair enough. Can we be friends, then?'

It was said pleasantly enough, but to Maude's quick ear it did not quite ring true. It sounded as though Bill was imitating the sort of man he most definitely was not and did not want to be. Maude, telling him that of course they could be friends, was quite shocked by her own cynicism. How could she read ulterior motives into every word the fellow said. His pride had been hurt because she did not want to go out with him and he'd said some silly, rather conceited things, but that did not mean he was all bad. The least she could do was to take his offer of friendship at face value.

'Good. Then we'll go back to the Fisher's and have the very best tea they can put on, and then I'll run you back to the station. What shift are you on?'

She hesitated for too long to carry on and lie boldly as

she half believed she should have done. Instead she told the truth.

'I'm not on again until Saturday at eight.'

He said nothing, merely giving a little half-nod, but she was sure that beneath its set line his mouth was smiling.

'Maude Neyler, where *have* you been?'

It was late on Friday night and Maude, returning sun-kissed after a whole day in the spring sunshine, smiled rather guiltily at Sandy, then glanced quickly round the room, but the mess was empty save for themselves. After the things she had said about Bill, she had no desire to admit that she had spent the day with him!

'Just out.' She flopped into a chair and stretched out her legs. 'I'm tired, but we had fun.'

'We?'

'All right, as if you didn't guess! Me and Bill.'

'I thought so. And did he try to ripen the acquaintance? So to speak?'

'I don't know what you mean!' But Maude, colouring vividly, knew all too well. Bill had tried to make love to her every time he stopped the car, which had been often, and Maude, suddenly aware that however much she tried to deny it Bill was *not* like Alan or any other young man she had ever been out with, had been forced to a great degree of frankness before he would stop.

'I'm not going to give in, you know, because I don't want a sordid little affair,' she told Bill crossly, after his fourth attempt to kiss and cuddle her into a frenzy of passion, during which, she was very sure, he had every intention of seducing her. 'If you just want a romp in the hay then find someone who's game for it. I've got better things to do.'

'There is no better thing,' Bill said, against her neck. His hands were stroking her back, treacherously comforting. 'Maude, you've got the loveliest . . .'

His hand had slid round the front and was endeavouring to create a gap in her neatly buttoned blouse. Maude dug her nails into his knuckles and he stopped, looking – and indeed, probably feeling! – deeply injured.

'I said stop it,' Maude told him. She was breathing heavily and so was he, but for totally different reasons. 'For God's sake, don't you understand English? I won't be mauled and grabbed and squeezed unless I want to be, and I *don't* want to be! Is that clear?'

'Yes, it's clear, though I don't understand you. Maudie, you're a lovely girl . . .'

'Start the car.'

'With lovely . . . What?'

'Start the car.'

'Oh, but . . .'

'Start the bloody car or I'll get out of it and walk home!'

Bill, with a sigh, started the car. After a while, he glanced sideways at her. Amusement was beginning to banish the heavy, sulky look he had worn.

Maudie?'

'What?'

'Darling, sweet, sugar-plum Maudie, what are you thinking?'

'I'm thinking that the next time we hit civilisation I'm going to get out of your car, thank you for the drive and for the interesting talk, and go back to the station.'

'Oh! Why, for God's sake?'

'Because it's no treat to me to spend a whole day fighting a fellow off. Half a day is plenty. Come to that, an hour is too much. Bill, no means no in any language and you're becoming boring and exhausting.'

'Boring?' She had offended him again she could see, but Maude was past caring. Just what did he think she was, for goodness sake? 'Boring? What do you mean by that?'

'As if you didn't know! It's boring to keep repeating no

and to have you continuing to behave as though it was yes. And it's exhausting to have to wrestle with someone as strong as you.' She sighed. 'You cheat, Bill, I'm nowhere near your weight. Fight someone your own size!'

The car slowed and stopped. Poor Maude immediately sat up straighter and got her hands into a defensive position, but this time Bill just laughed and, leaning sideways, kissed her cheek.

'I'm sorrier than I can say. Why don't I think, instead of always hurling myself into action? You aren't like anyone else I know, that's the trouble. I swear I'll behave from now on.'

And he had. Which meant that they really had enjoyed their day, for even whilst behaving Bill was an amusing and interesting companion. So now, loyally, Maude had no intention of telling Sandy about her early struggles.

'He was good company, then? Are you going to see him again? Write to him?'

Maude shrugged and yawned.

'Heavens, it's been quite a day and I'm on at eight in the morning! I don't know whether I'll see him again. He's gone dashing back up north now, at any rate. He said he'd be in touch some time though.'

'Hmm. What about Alan?'

Maude stood up and collected her handbag and jacket.

'What about him? Look, I'm not serious with *anyone*, so why should it matter if I've spent a day with Bill? We chuntered around, had lunch in a pub garden, rowed on the Avon, had a so-called Devonshire tea at a place with frilly waitresses and coloured china. We just had a pleasant day out.'

'I wasn't criticising, I was only asking.' Sandy got up too and the pair of them headed for their rooms. 'How do the two compare?'

'They don't,' Maude said slowly, after a moment's

thought. 'They are so different – chalk and cheese are not in it. I suppose the main difference really is that when Alan's out with you he's thinking about *you* all the time, how to please you, what you'll enjoy, whether you're tired. But Bill only thinks about himself. Yes, though he was good fun and so on, underneath he's thinking what sort of impression he's making all the time, I guess.'

'Then you prefer Alan?'

'I didn't say that, because it wouldn't be true. I don't prefer either of them.' She glanced across at Sandy, her eyes sparkling. 'If you must know, Bill's a lot more exciting!'

Chapter Twelve

Cara was approaching the factory gates in a wicked temper. She had been woken at seven by Auntie Tina, though she had gone out and bought herself an alarm clock so that she might wake when she wished, and had warned Auntie and Ruthie not to bother with her. She had not set the alarm, of course, since she fully intended to oversleep and then to tell the foreman that she had been ill, but Auntie Tina seemed to have second sight and when Cara had exclaimed that she had forgotten the alarm, had said very sweetly and insincerely that she had been afraid of something like that, so had got up early anyway.

'I've brought tea and biscuits,' Auntie Tina had said briskly. 'The rest of the kettle of water you can use to wash, since the boiler is out now that the weather's better, and when you come down I'll pack you some nice sandwiches for your midday meal, since you said the food in the canteen was so bad. Do your best, dear, to be in the kitchen in fifteen minutes, then you can have some breakfast before the bus.'

Cara had dressed, shaking with rage at the sheer interference of the elderly. She *wanted* to be late, as late as she possibly could, because then they would see that she was no use and would, she hoped, tell her not to bother to come back. She did not need her wages nor want them, she just wanted to be sent to the manager and sacked. But she did not quite dare to tell Auntie Tina this.

Instead, she pretended, and pretending always came hard to Cara. She thanked her aunt for the tea, she ate the nourishing porridge, prepared overnight by Ruthie and warmed through each morning, and she graciously accepted the boiled egg, bread and margarine. But though she did her best to eat slowly Auntie Tina had her eye on the clock and on the dot of 7.25 she shooed Cara out of the house and actually watched her go down the drive. And it was not until then that Cara dared use one of her newly acquired words.

'Shit!' she muttered, slowing to a snail's pace. 'Shit, shit and shit!'

She had not known it was an expletive until the foreman had said it, and then she guessed at once, since he did not seem to know any ordinary words. He said it first on her very first day when he saw her pale grey kid gloves and the big bottle of handcream she kept by her machine. He said it again, louder, when he told her to take them bleedin' gloves off and she had refused, very politely, to do any such thing. He said it a third time when she complained that the tea was stewed and far too strong, and a fourth time when she asked him not to shout since she had a headache.

The other girls, who should have been on her side, had not been at all nice to her, either. One of them, Shirl, had warned Cara not to get on the wrong side of the foreman.

'He've got a foul mouth,' she explained. 'Blind you up hill and down dale, tell you things about your mother you never knew, and use words you can't even spell. You'll be better off if you don't give him no cheek.'

It was useless, it seemed, to explain that she had given no one any cheek, but had merely made sensible points in a quiet voice. They knew better. To answer back was bad, but to be cheeky, like Cara, was worse. Asking for trouble and making the atmosphere tense.

As with all new workers she was moved around the factory at first until they found a niche into which she fitted. It was speedily clear that this would not be easy. Working a machine, treadling away with one foot and feeding metal into its hungry maw with the other, might seem straightforward, but in fact it was not. The metal went in slightly on the skew, unless you were strong and careful, and Cara was neither. She had no idea what she had done wrong but the girl on the next machine knew whenever a piece of Cara's work came through. She would lean over and in broadest Norfolk tell Cara that she *must* feed the metal in absolutely straight and it must be held quite level whilst the machine gobbled it up. And then she would add that, in her opinion, Cara was 'a bloody fule', which did not do a lot for Cara's self-confidence.

So it was unfortunate that she had reached Newmarket Road when the 90 came in sight. There were other girls from the factory already on the bus, and they would be quick enough to tell the foreman that Cara had been fit and well that morning, if she tried to say she was sick. The conductress saw her and stopped the bus, shouting at her to run and Cara broke into what, for her, *was* a run. Breathless, she climbed aboard and sank into a seat, though not for nearly long enough. All too soon she was being decanted at the factory gates.

The girls were queuing up to sign on and Cara stood amongst them, her mood still far from sunny. She wished she might shock them all by using her new word, but alas, they knew many far worse ones and would hurl them back at her without the slightest hesitation. So she signed on and prepared to return to her hated machine, or would have done except that a woman with a camel's face and a scarlet turban on her straggly black hair told her in a raucous voice that she would be on the assembly benches today.

Cara soon proved herself extremely bad at assembling. One stood before a moving belt on which bits of machinery moved along at what, from a distance, seemed a slow enough pace. Cara had to pick her particular bits out, fix a gadget from an unmoving tray in front of her on to the bits, and replace the part on the belt so that the next girl might pick it up and insert her own trayload into it. Cara could see that it was easy, that a child could do it, so how did it happen that she could not? She fumbled, she dropped bits, and even when she got it right she was far too slow, leaving the girl next in line almost screaming with irritation.

When the tea-break came, the girl went and whispered into the ear of the gypsy woman who had introduced Cara to the assembly line, and the gypsy woman came over and told her harshly to take off her gloves since they were slowing her down and some were on piecework, whatever that might mean.

Cara thought about refusing, looked into the gypsy woman's wild black eyes, and decided not to bother. She shoved her gloves into her overall pocket and returned to the bench.

At lunchtime she had to go to the canteen again, since in her rush and flurry she had left her packed lunch on the bus. But she was glad she did, afterwards, for as she was pushed and jostled towards an empty table, she met a fellow-sufferer. A tall, elegant girl who looked vaguely familiar came over to her and asked if they might share the table.

'I've only been here a few days,' she confessed as they set down their trays. 'It's awful, isn't it? Some man keeps swearing at me for putting metal in wrong. I don't understand it at all, but I'm sure no one need speak to me like that! And when I apologised and asked him to show me how to get it right, he called me Lady Muck! I very nearly told him there was no need to be so fraightfully rude!'

Cara, agreeing eagerly, felt she had found a friend. Anne, too, assured her that she wanted to keep her hands nice, though she did not dare to wear gloves and her handcream was always tucked well out of sight. They agreed to walk home, or part of the way home, together that evening, and to meet again on the following day, and it was only as Anne turned to wave before making her way back to her machine that Cara realised where she had seen her before. Anne had been a manicurist at one of the better beauty shops in the city. Cara felt let down. Anne was not then truly 'one of us', but very nearly, almost, 'one of them'. Yet she was a lot nicer than most, and had been very kind. Cara decided to forgive her for her background and went back to her assembling in quite a good frame of mind.

Later, however, things went back to being bad again. The gypsy woman, whose named turned out to be Blodwen, called Cara a stuck-up tart. Cara gave her one of those looks, the sort of look you give someone so infinitely beneath you that you can't even bother to answer her, and Blodwen marched straight up to her and slapped her face hard enough to make her rock back on her heels. Cara had wept and the foreman, who was a pig of a man usually, put his arm round her shoulders and told her not to mind the old cow. Cara had cried louder, giving him such a piteous look from big brown eyes brimming with tears that he had actually told her to take ten minutes off to get herself a cup of tea.

The tea tasted better than it had all week and Cara returned to the bench more cheerful, even though the girls on either side of her looked murder at her and tried to speed up even more to show her that she'd done a silly thing.

Later, she and Anne walked home together, and Anne told her to be careful of the foreman, who had a reputation for doing more than pinch bottoms, if he got you to himself. The first-aid place, apparently, had been used for assignations, so if you cut your finger or stubbed your toe and he offered to bandage it for you, it meant . . .

'Does it?' Cara said, her eyes rounding with horror. 'How very stupid I am, Anne. I would have trotted off with him if you hadn't warned me! Oh dear, and I suppose if you get cross and tell him off . . .'

'My dear, it would be *fatal*,' Anne said solemnly. 'He'd not listen for a start, but if you screamed or something and made him stop he'd hate you worse than poison and pick on you all day until you let him have what he wanted.'

Cara could not imagine the foreman doing anything more physical than drinking tea and shouting at his underlings. She looked interrogatively up at Anne. Could she mean what she seemed to mean? Oh, surely not! The foreman was old, extremely ugly, and, Cara would have supposed, totally incapable! She had guessed, from the frequently overheard and totally uncomprehended range of dirty jokes and stories, that all men and most factory women had their minds on *That* all the time, but she had not for one moment suspected there was the slightest danger!

Anne, looking down at her new friend as light and horror dawned, nodded sympathetically.

'Yes, my dear, I know *just* what you're thinking, but it's the truth! He still wants his oats, old and 'orrible though he may be.'

Cara, making her way up the drive, pondered on this remark, and decided it definitely meant what she thought it meant, and that she was a fortunate girl to

233

have met Anne. Now, with hard listening and some judicious questioning, she might begin to understand a lot of the things she heard.

Mira thought it was heavenly, having Mummy working all day and too tired to interfere with her when she was at home. She had come to terms with school and had enjoyed her time there since she had discovered that reading, though it seemed tedious, was in reality a door to Daddy through which she alone might pass. Cara could – and did – write letters too, but she was not at all interested in what Mira wrote, and anyway she seldom had a chance to see them since Mira put them in an envelope which she then handed to Auntie Tina, who did the rest. Her letters were long, intricate and usually very blotchy and untidy, with many of the letters written backwards and the spelling chiefly notorious for its originality, but Daddy loved every misspelt word and every blotch and did not hesitate to say so and to urge her to write more.

With school, Sebastian was closer to her as well. He went to the big boys' school though not, yet, to the grammar, but he was not with her during the day. However, when baby-school was over the bus children waited in the dinner-room for the school buses to arrive and these, due to the exigencies of the war, were the same for big schools as for the little ones, which meant that if Mira waited too she would presently be despatched out into the great world in time for Sebastian to walk home with her.

Many boys would not have enjoyed feeling themselves responsible for a small, plain little girl, but not Sebastian. She was his special property, his nice little slave, and he was only too happy to have her along, tagging behind, agreeing with him, enhancing his opinions and never venturing her own unasked.

No one had ever picked on Mira or been mean to her, and she knew they never would whilst Sebastian took her to school in the mornings and picked her up in the afternoons. Sebastian was so tough he could knock oak trees down if he wished – she knew he could because he had told her so.

Then one evening Mira was sent upstairs to call Mummy down for supper, and she went into Mummy's room to find Cara sprawled across the bed, weeping steadily. She looked up as her small stepdaughter entered, but made no effort to stem the flood. Indeed, most uncharacteristically, she held out her arms and Mira, after the smallest hesitation, went into them.

'Oh, Mira, I'm *so* unhappy,' wailed Cara. 'How I wish Daddy were here! He wouldn't let them bully me and shout at me in that horrid factory! Why did he go to the war? He should have stayed here to take care of us.'

'Men must fight,' Mira said seriously, patting Cara's wet cheek. She knew that men did not always fight because Val had a friend who was what they called a conshie; he was looked down on by the family, so of course Daddy had to fight. Did Cara not know that? Mira drew back and peered into Cara's tear-drowned eyes. 'Daddy had to fight, but I don't think he wanted to. I don't think he likes fighting.'

'I know, you're right,' Cara muttered, resting her hot face against the child's smooth hair. 'I'm being silly. It's just that I miss him so very much.'

'I miss him badly too,' Mira said shyly. She put her soft little hands round Cara's neck and kissed the petal-smooth cheek. 'Never mind, Mummy. Daddy will come home soon. Ruthie says the war can't last for ever!'

It was the first time that Mummy had cried over Daddy, Mira thought wonderingly. Not even when she heard about Daddy's poor dear hand had she shed a tear.

Mira was quite shrewd enough to realise that a good part of her mummy's sorrow was for herself, her own predicament, but at least being unhappy in the work she did had made Mummy realise just how good Daddy was at protecting people. So in a way it was good that Mummy hated the work and that people were not nice to her.

But before Mira could be terribly tactless and break the new kindness between them, she remembered that she had been sent up here with a message. She put both her hands in Cara's and heaved her off the bed.

'Dry eyes, Mummy. Ruthie's made a beef pie and chips, and she says could you come down right now, please, before the chips go cold.'

In fact, Cara had not been crying merely because she hated her work and longed for William; she had just put on her dark green skirt with the pleats and found herself unable to fasten the waistband. So she had been crying, at least in part, for her dear little nineteen-inch waist which was no more.

She knew what had done it, of course. That damned canteen, that was what had done it. Masses of potatoes, pies with inch thick crust, great sugary buns! And because she was working so hard she could not resist, could not say no, and just smoke a cigarette and drink some tea. She was always tired, but she managed to eat everything that was put before her. Mealtimes were important, the only time at the factory when she dared to get right away from her work and relax for a few minutes.

Cara had been taken off assembling for obvious reasons – the war effort had been cruelly hampered by her presence there – and had been put on to different work. She spent all her day threading tiny little screws into the appropriate holes in very small tubes, then she screwed them tightly home with an assortment of fine little screwdrivers. The work was neither dirty nor tiring but it was demanding, something that not just anyone was asked to do. After she'd been at it two hours the foreman, who happened to be a very large lady but who was still called a foreman, had announced that Cara was ideal for the job. 'Neat, accurate, doesn't lose herself,' she said loudly, glaring at one or two of the other girls. 'Not fast, yet, but she'll pick up speed as she goes along.'

This praise was balm to Cara's battered spirit, and she responded to it the only way she knew how. She tried. For the very first time, she wanted to succeed, to build up speed, to stay in this quiet area of the noisy factory where it was important that you kept your hands clean and oil-free, your nails short and trimmed, and your voice low. Bertha, the foreman, was kind, what was more. She actually seemed to like Cara, to appreciate how very hard Cara worked and to give her praise when it was due. The other girls, taking their lead from Bertha, were nice as well. Cara was grimly determined that this time she would keep the job, this time she would not be moved on somewhere new, like a plague carrier or a locust.

However, the work did have to be done at a certain speed and that, for the moment, was just a little bit faster than Cara could manage. Which meant that in order to keep up she had to bolt her dinner with all speed, hurry back to her bench and then work straight through including tea-breaks, which she had begun to value. So though she was very much happier at work and far less inclined to plot to lose her job, she was always tired and that meant that, at home, she was frequently cross and more frequently tearful.

On this particular evening, however, she arrived in the kitchen to find her brother Simon sitting at the table, wedged between Emily and Edmund, who adored him, with Sebastian keeping a place for Mira. He adored his half-brother, too, but he would accept his place in the pecking order. Being a mere nine against his cousins' twelve and eleven, he would have to wait his turn to get at Simon.

Simon looked up, got to his feet, and then, as Cara squeaked a greeting, came forward and kissed her cheek. He looked concerned and affectionate and held her face between his hands for a moment, looking down at her.

'Cara, my dear! You're looking tired out.'

'Cara's working very hard making components,' Tina said tactfully, before her niece could antagonise Simon by starting to whine and complain. 'She gets tired of course, but she's looking very bonny otherwise. She's put on a bit of weight and has colour in her cheeks, and she sleeps so soundly that not a dozen alarm clocks can wake her.'

'Yes, of course, I forgot you were working,' Simon said, releasing her and taking his place once more. Cara pouted; Simon had never been very fond of her, but blood was obviously thicker than water since he had shown more interest in her than ever before. Why did Auntie Tina have to denigrate her tiredness and miseries? 'Work won't hurt you, Cara. Look at Jenny-penny, she works like a horse.'

'She's pregnant, so she won't be working,' Cara objected pettishly. Simon would push Jenny into the conversation and praise her to the skies no matter what she did. And anyway, she hadn't stayed in London for all her talk, not like Val.

Simon watched Ruthie ladle beef pie on to his plate and then turned to his sister once more.

'She is working. She couldn't join the land army because of Marianne and then the new baby, but she's working side by side with the Rileys' landgirls. Mrs Riley suggested I try to stop her in case it was bad for baby, but she said if she could stand up to winter jobs like muck-spreading and sprout picking, then summer jobs would be a piece of cake.' He smiled round the table. 'There aren't many like my Jenny,' he finished complacently.

'That's true, but Cara Dopmanns don't grow on trees, either,' Tina said tactfully. 'Help yourselves to vegetables, everyone – ladies first, Sebby! Cara works very hard, Simon. You should be proud of her.'

'Yes, you should be,' Cara said sharply. 'Everyone thinks I'm wonderful, to work the way I do in a factory. You should hear what the RAF fellows say when I . . .' she stopped, realised that this would make things worse and continued rather lamely, '. . . when I go out for an evening.'

Simon gave her a long, hard stare.

'Go out? Who with? Val said something, but . . .'

'If Val's been tale-bearing then I'll tell a few myself,' Cara cried venomously. 'Horrid cat, how dare she? She came down here and lectured me like a mother though she's hardly any older than I am, and the boyfriends she has are notorious. She hauls them in by the dozen, I should think! She came with me to the Samson last time she was down and honestly I was ashamed of her, smiling and flirting and dancing with everyone and making them all think she was so wonderful.'

Simon smiled maliciously but said nothing. Cara was in the middle of wondering just why he had not answered her back when she suddenly realised what company she kept. Tina would never allow evil to be spoken of her beloved youngest child!

'*What* did you say, Cara?' Her brows almost meeting, her nostrils flaring, Auntie Tina suddenly looked terri-fying and vengeful, a far cry from the dear little aunt pottering about the kitchen making delicious meals, getting up early to see that Cara left for the factory with hot food inside her! Cara, blanching, began to mutter excuses, but she might as well have saved her breath; Tina overbore her.

'Are you insinuating that Val would do anything to be ashamed of? How dare you, and the way you've been behaving, too! Acting like a spoilt child at the factory, insisting on wearing grey kid gloves and then weeping and wailing because the factory girls thought you were stuck up and put on airs. Well, you *are* stuck up and you *do* put on airs! What's more, Val is a single girl without ties and you're a married woman! She doesn't need to go sneaking off down the drive, taking advantage of the blackout to cuddle or worse any officer that asks her! She doesn't put her wedding ring on her right hand and pretend to be single – she doesn't need to, she *is* single! You're a scheming, deceitful creature, Cara, and Val's generous, loving and very moral!'

Tina came to a breathless halt, lacking breath for any more scorn to pour, and Cara began to mutter excuses, hoping that this was to be the end of her awful mistake. But she was not safe yet; Simon came in to the attack, guns blazing.

'I applaud every word that Auntie just said, Cara, but let me add a bit. William's a long way away, he's been badly wounded and he's a prisoner of war. But that doesn't mean he can't hear stories, find out what's going on. If you behave like a slut then someone – not me, but someone – may write a letter to him, telling him what's going on. And when the war's over and he comes home, you may find yourself without a meal ticket.'

Cara, weeping bitterly, began to positively howl at the thought of anyone writing to William and telling him wicked lies about her. 'Simon Rose, you're wickedly unfair to me, just as you always have been! I don't do th-

things to be ashamed of. I only took off my w-wedding ring when Val was with me for a j-joke, and because the men . . . They paid her such a lot of attention, it wasn't fair . . . She's got so much and she's single so they expect that she'll be more . . . you know . . . and why can't I be told I'm pretty and dance nicely? W-William's too f-far away to tell me how nice I am!'

It was not the moment, Tina considered, to break it to Cara that William would probably never dance again, but Simon, in white-hot rage, had no such scruples.

'Haven't they told you yet? You're a poor thing, Cara! William's lost his leg, and he won't do much dancing even when he does come home, so you'd better get used to it!'

There was a moment of silence before Cara cast herself down across the table and began to wail louder than before.

'A leg? He'll never dance again? Oh, oh, God is so unfair to me! I can't help it, people with bits missing frighten me! Oh, my God, my poor William!'

Mira, who had followed the conversation as someone watches a tennis match, began to cry as well. She hated rows, and now Mummy was saying Daddy had lost a leg, and she had thought it was an arm. She clung to Sebastian, gulping and making little lost dog noises. Whimpers.

'Take the child out and give her some tea and talk to her, Sebby,' Tina said briskly. 'Ruthie, could you . . .?'

Ruthie nodded, picked up the children's plates and led them out of the room. Emily and Edmund, used to the furious rows and remembering, dimly probably, the fights that their parents had once waged, continued, stolidly, to eat their beef pie. Simon still looked smoulderingly angry and only Tina felt horrified and shocked at herself. How could she have lost her temper so completely after having been careful and tactful for so long? She put her arms round Cara's heaving shoulders and pulled her gently into an upright position, holding on so that Cara could not collapse across the table once more.

'Now come along, dear, we all said things we regret, but we'll say no more about any of it, except that you must realise Simon had a point; people could easily put the wrong interpretation on all your gaiety down at the dance halls and some nosy, spiteful person could write to William.'

'Some people already have misunderstood,' Cara said, giving Simon a loaded glance. 'But they're wrong, everyone's wrong about me. I work terribly hard at that hateful factory so why shouldn't I have a little bit of dancing in the evenings? All the other girls do, really they do.'

'All right, don't start justifying yourself, old girl, because you can't,' Simon said heavily, helping himself to more chips and another spoonful of mashed swede. 'Let's forget it now . . . I think Ruthie's bringing the kids back.'

Ruthie was. Calm and collected, she swept in, with Mira looking happier and Sebastian chewing. Plainly, he had not neglected his dinner while taking care of one confused and tearful slave!

'We're back,' Ruthie said cheerfully, sitting Mira down in her chair and then going round the table to take her own place. 'What a fuss over nothing. This family's always been the same, I told Mira, blow hot, blow cold! Let's get this pie finished so that we can tackle my special pudding.'

Simon picked up a forkful of chips, ate them, and then addressed Cara.

'Look, I'm sorry, I expect I said things which I should

have left to Mummy. If you aren't too tired, how about coming to the gala dance at the Lido tonight? They're doing a buffet supper and spot prizes. I know there isn't much thrill in dancing with big brother, but . . .'

Cara lifted a glowing face.

'Oh, Simon, would you? It would be marvellous!' She had not touched her meal but now she took a huge bite of pie and spoke through it. 'I've got such a pretty dress. It's got puffed sleeves and inserts of lace . . . I've never been to a Lido supper dance but I've heard the girls talk about them. They say you have ever such a good time!'

Tina and Ruthie exchanged a glance more complex than one would have believed possible. *There, if she's so thrilled to be going out with her brother then she couldn't have been up to much*, it said. *There's good in the girl, I always knew it*, it said. *She's growing up quite nicely*, it said, for both ladies had told each other many times that Cara was just immature. There was also a touch of *I told you so* from them both, which was also true. Tina and Ruthie had salved their respective consciences when they had their severest doubts about Cara with frequent assertions that she was not liable to let anyone have his way with her. Now, it seemed, they both thought they had been proved right.

Simon, intercepting the look, had only read approval – it said a lot for Tina and Ruthie's closeness that such a brief look could convey such a multiplicity of meanings!

'In his last letter Simon said he'd taken Cara dancing when he was down for a forty-eight.' Jenny sighed and took another slice of toast, then glanced down at her waistline. The trouble was, she had been on early milking this morning, and getting up before it was fully day and tramping about in that wonderful, misty morning-time when the world seemed young and new was certain to give her an appetite.

''Twas a brotherly thing to do,' Mrs Riley said, pouring more milk into her tea. 'Fond of she, is he?'

'Not specially. In fact he rather dislikes her. But he felt sorry for her, and I'm glad he did it, because when she was with him she wasn't with anyone else. And nor was he, of course.'

'Her's the lass whose husband's only got one arm, isn't her?' Mrs Riley clucked sympathetically and stuck another slice of bread on her long toasting fork which she then held out towards the open front of the range. She and Jenny were both partial to hot toast and farm-made butter. 'Poor toad – and as for Simon's feelings towards she, 'tes not uncommon in brothers and sisters, I believe.'

'The fact is, I think Simon felt guilty. You see, William, Cara's husband, lost a leg below the knee as well as his arm, but no one dared tell Cara. She's got a thing about disability. And then someone mentioned that Cara was gadding off dancing and Simon lost his temper and told her that William would probably never dance again. She was upset, and so he promised to take her dancing.'

Mrs Riley tutted, but with the comfortable air of one who had heard very much worse stories in her time. Despite the fact that she and Mr Riley had their two fine sons, they had surprisingly few other relatives. Both had been only children, both had been the product of only children and perhaps it was for this reason that Marjory Riley was so fascinated by tales of Jenny's numerous relatives by marriage. Jenny herself, with only one brother and a mother widowed young, had been brought up with the Neylers and the Roses. Living next door to The Pride, her houseproud, snobbish, introverted mother had been only too happy to have Martin and Jennifer next door, making whatever mess they liked in someone else's house and on someone else's lawns.

'Oh, well, I daresay there's no real harm in Cara's carryings-on,' Jenny said, pouring herself more tea. Whoever did the early milking had the rest of the morning free and that always meant a deliciously extended breakfast. 'She's very beautiful, Marjory. I must try and bring a photo back when I go back to Norwich next . . . or I could get Auntie Tina to send me one. But I felt such a horrid stab of envy when I read the bit about Simon taking her dancing. I miss him so much, no one knows how much, and to think of him at a dance, holding Cara in his arms, humming the tune against her hair as he did when we were courting . . . well, it was hard.'

'You'll see he, when he gets a good leave.' Marjory brought in the toast fork, examined the end critically, and decided it was toast. She flicked it towards Jenny, who fielded it dextrously. 'There you are, maiden; more tea, to go with it?'

'Well, I should be watching my weight, but it doesn't seem to soar. Yes, please. Is there any marmalade left? If not, honey suits me every bit as well.'

Marjory pulled the earthenware pot nearer and examined the contents judiciously, then helped herself to a generous spoonful and pushed it over to Jenny.

'Us won't be able to replace this, seemingly, so 'ee take plenty. When her's gone her's gone.'

Jenny was spreading her own marmalade thickly over the buttered toast when the back door gave a preparatory rattle. For some reason best known to themselves the Rileys' doors had no letter slits in, so when the weather was fine enough the postman came down the lane and in through the back door to deliver the mail. When it was bad and the lane poached by cattle or frozen or snowed in, the mail was left in a wooden box right at the road end, but Mr Gumley usually made the effort and came the extra mile on his rickety old bike. Once at the house he rattled the door handle so that anyone standing between the door and the table could move out of the way, then he hurled the door open and shot the post across the intervening space and on to the table. However, on one never-to-be-forgotten occasion Mr Gumley had not seen the big earthenware bowl of skimmed milk standing on the table and the entire packet of mail disappeared into it with a plop. Mr Gumley, being a little deaf and very short-sighted, noticed nothing and left. By the time Marjory came to use the skim the letters were little more than unidentifiable pulp – Jenny was only grateful that there had been nothing from Simon amongst them. So now, remembering his mistake, Mr Gumley usually tried to come when someone was in the kitchen to take the letters and failing that he put them in a tidy heap just inside the back door. There they were a prey to passing feet, to adventurous puppies and to the greedy old hen who occasionally popped in to search for crumbs and porridge oats between the floor tiles, but unless a puppy actually absconded with a letter they should remain reasonably readable.

Having done his warning rattle, Mr Gumley opened the door. His wrinkled brown face appeared round it, tortoiselike, and he smiled, revealing long, yellowing teeth.

'Letters, my dears,' he announced. 'Late breakfast?'

'That's right, my dear.' Marjory had the teapot raised over the large empty cup with the blue and white pattern. Mr Gumley's cup. 'You'll join us?'

It was a rhetorical question and treated as such by Mr Gumley, who was already out of his gumboots and scraping out a chair as Marjory finished the sentence.

'Gladly, gladly. Left home at five and not a bite since then. Here's your letters.' He produced them and put them down on the table, favouring Jenny with a wide grin. 'You'm a lot to answer for, maid,' he reproached her. ''Fore you come here, no more'n a letter a week did I bring up the lane. Now 'tes every day, just about.'

'I know. I'm bowed down with guilt,' Jenny said, smiling at him as she sorted through the letters. 'Mind you, the girls get mail too. There's something for them here . . . just a card. One from my fond mama, one from Minnie, she's holidaying in Norfolk, and one from Val – goodee!'

'Nothing from Simon?' enquired Mr Gumley, who had long ago dispensed with formality so far as Jenny was concerned.

'Not today. I had one yesterday, but hearing from Val's the next best thing.' She opened the envelope and spread out the sheet. 'Excuse me, folks, whilst I have a little read.'

Marjory and Mr Gumley, old friends, talked easily of life and mutual acquaintances whilst Jenny read, but they both stopped and looked hopefully at her as she gave a squeal.

'Gracious! Val's coming down to Devon, Marjory, for a whole week! She says there was a terrible raid on London last weekend, unbelievably bad. She thinks it was one more than the people could stand. They seem dazed and lethargic and she feels she has to get away. She isn't afraid, but she says she needs to be fresh and hopeful herself to face their despair. She says to book her a room somewhere locally.'

'She'll stay with we,' Marjory stated with placid firmness. 'Gladly us'll have her. No question.'

'You are good! I'll ring the flat when I go in to fetch the children from school and leave a message for her if she's not in. I'll work twice as hard to make up, too, I promise you.'

''Ee do very well,' Mr Gumley remarked. He eyed her thickening waistline with interest and without a trace of embarrassment. 'Many 'ud make 'scuses over the event, but Marjory says you work harder than ever.'

'Good practice for when the baby's born,' Jenny told him, opening the next letter, which was a long grumble from Mrs Bachelow. 'Val doesn't say how she's getting here – surely she'll come by car? If so, thee and me and she will have an outing or two, Marjory!'

Mrs Riley's eyes sparkled and she permitted herself a big, delighted smile. It is the very nature of their work that farmers' wives do not get out as much as they would like and, though the farm had a stall in the indoor market once a week, the days when Marjory had reigned over it were long gone.

'All this rationing, takes three of we now to fill the stall,' she told Jenny. 'So that's market-day every third week; sadly thin of people the market be, too.'

Mr Gumley supped his tea in one long swoosh and then, reluctantly, got to his feet.

'If her don't bring the motor, you three young things could take the pony-cart around and over,' he reminded them solemnly. 'Best beaches in the world, Devon beaches, and reachable with a good pony they do be.'

'We'll go, one way or another,' Jenny promised him. 'We'll have a good time when Val's here. You'll love her, Marjory; everyone does.'

Chapter Thirteen

SPRING 1942

It seemed strange to walk down the Neue Friedrichstrasse again, strange even to see pavements that were not covered with snow, but Otto, looking round him, thought that it was good to come home. The bushes were showing green and before some of the houses great troughs of spring flowers were blooming. Berlin did not look war-torn, not after the sights he had seen in Russia.

But despite the sunshine and the flowers, you could not think this was a city at peace. The pavements were whitened at the edges so that neither vehicles nor passers-by should mistake the walkway for more road in the blackout, and he had passed bomb damage, as yet unrepaired, as he came down from the station. Yet though one would have known that this was a city at war you could not see even at second glance that this was the capital city of a country at war with half the world. Ever since the United States of America had entered the war Otto felt, and supposed most German people felt, lonelier and more cut off than ever. The Italians were allies of course, but they were not exactly a breed of warriors, and the Japanese, who were definitely a breed of warriors and were also allies, could not be said to be giving much . . . much comradeship to the German people.

So here we stand, Otto thought sarcastically to himself as he walked briskly towards his home, here we stand with Wops to the left of us and Nips to the right, expecting to crush the rest of the world with the same ease with which we crushed Poland and Holland. With the most optimistic expectations in the world, it still could not lead one to sleep soundly at nights.

Unless you were like Franz, of course, with his infinite belief, not in Germany perhaps, but in the Fuehrer. Franz trusted their leader as younger children had once trusted Jesus. Otto had seen quite a bit of his brother, since he had been ferrying supplies to the army during the winter, and Franz's faith had never faltered. He was doing well, too. He had started the war as an officer in charge of a platoon and had speedily risen to greater heights. The fighting on the Russian front had been hard and brutal – Otto had heard stories of outrageous cruelty, needless mass killings – but Franz was well thought of and respected by both his men and his senior officers. But could Franz *really* not see what an impossible position the Reich was being placed in by his beloved Fuehrer? Perhaps not, and perhaps it was best that he could not, for Otto had heard that the army at Stalingrad was not to withdraw but would remain where it was or go forward during the campaigning months to come. It would be hard for Franz and his men as the supply lines lengthened; perhaps belief in one's leader was necessary in order to continue to function at one's best.

Otto had been on the Russian front for almost a year, ever since Hitler, with a treachery greater than some had believed possible, had invaded a country with whom he had recently signed a peace pact. It had been a brilliantly clever and cunning attack too, for he had invaded simultaneously along the enormous length of the Russian borders from the Baltic to the Black Sea, and had caught the Russian air force quite literally asleep. Otto had flown ahead of the bombers on this occasion, to provide cover for them should they be attacked by Russian fighters and to get to the airfields first. When he reached the nearest of the aerodromes, he could scarcely believe his own eyes and nor could the pilots, navigators and gunners of the great armada of bombers which followed him across the frontier. The Russian aircraft were set out neatly in rows in the open, not camouflaged, not under cover, not protected. They might have been put there for some grand inspection – or for the speediest annihilation the German Luftwaffe could arrange.

It had been 3.15 a.m. on a Sunday in June of the previous year, and of course the planes had been annihilated, almost deservedly. What on earth had the Russian leaders been thinking of, Otto had wondered at the time, to leave their planes so powerless? As wave after wave of bombers droned over, some pilots did try to get their aeroplanes off the ground, but not one succeeded in getting airborne. For the Luftwuffe, it had been like some sort of marvellous game; unreal as a board game, too, with none of the blood and guts, the him or me, of more realistic air battles. Bomb the toy planes, machine-gun the toy buildings, watch the toy fires burgeon into beautiful life, and then fly on; on to the next neatly set out board.

When he got home though, full of his own tale, Otto had heard an even stranger and, in a way, sadder story. Despite their certainty that they had destroyed every single Russian aircraft, a flight of Russian bombers had flown over towards evening, to attack the German airfields.

'Poor blighters, they hadn't a chance,' one of the men who had witnessed the attack told Otto. 'Like the charge of the light brigade they came in, riding their great, clumsy winged horses into our smoking guns and weaving, quick-striking fighters. They didn't have a clue, they didn't know about ack-ack fire or tactics or height – not a thing. If I hadn't seen it with my own eyes I'd never have believed it was possible. They just came on, wave after wave of them, got shot down, crashed, died . . . and made way for the next wave, until the sky had emptied.'

That had been nearly a year ago, though. Then, it had been easy to see why Franz believed in the Third Reich, thought it invincible, armoured in light. Now, despite the fact that Russia was in a desperate position, things no longer looked so bright. The Luftwaffe had destroyed an incredible number of aeroplanes and ruined aerodromes and buildings. The army had besieged cities, attacked strongholds, laid waste the countryside. And yet . . . and yet the Russians were still fighting back! Because of the tactics wished upon the Luftwaffe by the army they had not done as their leaders thought they should have done, they had not annihilated the factories which had produced that awe-inspiring number of aircraft, nor the factories which were churning out other weapons of war. Instead, they had spent their time and used up their advantage in supplying their troops with food and equipment. What would happen when the Russians, bowled over by speed, surprise and – face it – treachery, struggled to their feet once more? No pilot knows at first how to fight a war – the English had done foolish things in the early days through ignorance, but they had learned, and learned quickly. Russian pilots would have been the same, and there were such numbers of them!

Franz, who still had faith, had let slip to his brother several times that in his opinion, and in the opinions of several of his fellows, mistakes were being made which could prove costly.

'Moscow should have been attacked and broken whilst we had the advantage of surprise; if the army had been allowed to continue its advance the capital would certainly have fallen,' he told Otto. 'It would have taken the heart out of the Russians, to know that their principal city was in our hands. If only the Luftwaffe had been allowed to smash it by air . . . but they say the bombs that fell on the Kremlin just bounced off! Still, I shouldn't grumble. We are winning, which is the main thing.'

Winning? What was winning? To be sure the German army was still in Russia, still holding its positions, and the Luftwaffe, too, had not withdrawn. But the cold had been so intense during the winter months that flying had almost stopped, and the army had been in no position to consolidate its successes. If anyone could show a real victory, it had been winter! The Russians were used to their weather and understood how to deal with it. They had the right fuel for their aeroplanes, the right clothing, even the right sort of food. Not so the German army or the Luftwaffe.

But still, they had survived the winter one way or another, and now spring was on its way again. And I, Otto reminded himself, am going home for a well-earned leave and should not spend the first few hours of it thinking about what I've left behind me. He positioned his kitbag more comfortably on his shoulder and smiled as his own home came into view. The railings outside had gone – to make guns for the war effort, probably – but the doorsteps were scrubbed white and the curtains at the open window waved in the breeze. He could see the blackout blinds stacked inside the bow window, but it was still a good place to be. He took the steps two at a time and banged the brass lion's head knocker resoundingly. It was good to be home, and to find that home whole and sweet still. He was longing to see his father, to tell him about the newer and bigger aeroplane that he would soon be handling. A Junkers still, but a four-engined one which they called a transport because it could hold forty troops or an equivalent weight in equipment and stores. He would be a much more useful part of the airlift with such a plane and that was the reason that he, Hans and Uri had been given leave; so that when they got back they could begin training on the new machines.

He was glad, he told himself buoyantly, that he would not still be in Russia for the autumn, as he waited for the knocker to bring someone running. The troops had gone in, struck a devastatingly hard blow, somehow survived the 1941–42 winter, and now they would strike a few more blows, prove their undoubted superiority, and withdraw before another winter began to bite. That was the way to fight a war, that was what Blitzkrieg meant – in, hit hard, out. He was glad he had had the distinction of flying through a Russian winter, but even more glad that he would not have to face a second. Once was indeed enough.

He had volunteered for the Russian campaign because he dreaded and hated the thought of fighting against Val's people, and his application had been greeted with great enthusiasm. His ability and experience had been in his favour as well as the fact that he knew his machine as well as most mechanics. Indeed, it had been his ability as a mechanic as much as his pilot-craft which had kept his machine in the air when many others were grounded in that bitter weather.

The door opened a crack; it was held by a chain so that he could not get further until the opener had identified him. Otto smiled to himself. A new servant, perhaps.

'I am Otto von Eckner; son of the house. Get my mother, and she . . .'

The door opened and his mother stood there. She was beaming from ear to ear.

'Otto, my darling boy! Come in, come in. Why did you not let us know you were coming? Vater will be beside himself with joy . . . Minna will be delighted.'

As Frau von Eckner pulled him over the threshold and closed the door behind him, Otto had a long look at his mother. She had aged. Her hair was streaked with grey and her skin had softened, was now the crumpled petal of a rose. Her mouth trembled, then smiled, then trembled back into sobriety. He kissed her, and felt that the tremble was now a part of her. He had not seen her for two years, but she seemed to have grown older by a decade in his absence.

'Mutti, you are fashionably thin, but it suits you.' It did not suit her, but he could see that nothing could stop the ageing process that had fined her down, faded her skin and hair. 'Where is Vater? Not working, surely, on a Sunday?'

The family firm had made cars before the war. Now it was tanks, armoured cars, field vehicles. Herr von Eckner wrote when he could, but he could not openly discuss his work though they had a code, of course, as every other family must have had in wartime. Otto knew, therefore, that the factory was producing at a phenomenal rate, that vehicles were streaming out steadily to take their place on various battlefields and that his father was highly thought of amongst the hierarchy of the Reich. He was looking forward, however, to a real talk, to being able to discuss the other side of the war as well as his own side. But his mother was answering him, taking his arm, leading him out of the hall.

'No, not today, thank God. We were about to have a light luncheon, which we will share, and then you and Vater can have a chat whilst I get out all my hidden stores of good things and make a really first-rate cake to celebrate your return.'

They were almost at the kitchen door when it opened and Herr von Eckner came out, chewing. The two men embraced, then Otto held his father at arm's length to take a good look at him, as well. Herr von Eckner had aged too, but with his ageing had come more strength and a certain acceptance. He would work against things he thought wrong but he would not struggle mentally to accept them, as he had once done. He was a good man forced into a situation where he would do his best, go so far along the path the Reich had chosen for him, and then say *no more* when he felt this was the right moment.

'Otto! My dear boy, my dearest son!'

He meant it. Otto knew himself to be tall, dark in a fair family, scarred, not by duels but by an unfortunate meeting with the sharp edge of the nursery fender when in hot pursuit of an enthralling puppy. He believed himself plain, thinking that fair Franz was handsome, fair Minna beautiful. He was not plain, for his face reflected the sensitive strength of him, the mind that thought for itself and did not obey blindly, as Franz did. In the way one does, he knew his father understood and appreciated him though he assumed, wrongly, that this was fatherly prejudice.

'Now, dear, let us continue to get luncheon.' Frau von Eckner bustled them all into the kitchen, a room Otto had scarcely entered since it was the domain of the domestic staff, or had been, before the war, and sat her son down in a chair close to the kitchen table. She began to slice a large home-made loaf. Home-made? His mother had rarely cooked. 'I'm making a few sandwiches, dear, and there's soup cooking on the back of the stove, and we've managed to make our coffee last out . . . then I can spare some Krummeltorte, just a small slice each. That keeps the wolf from the door until evening, when we have our main meal. I manage rather well, for I've become a clever housewife, have I not, Fritzl?'

Herr von Eckner assured his son that his mother was positively revelling in the rationing, the shortages and the dull food available, because of her newly discovered abilities as a cook and household manager.

'She does it all herself too, my son, though she gets some help from Minna . . . You'll see why I don't . . . ah, Minna, my dear!'

Otto had not much cared for his young sister, but as soon as she entered the room he could see that she had changed. She had lost weight and looked gawky and raw-boned, for she was a big girl, but that was not it. She came into the room apologetically, with her head ducked down, looking round at them through her pale eyelashes. And her eyes! Clear and blue and a little staring, now they were haunted, set in dark hollows in that once round and self-confident countenance. She smiled at Otto, and it was a timid smile which begged for understanding and gentleness; a far cry from the condescending sneer which had passed for a smile before.

'Hello, Minna,' Otto said as gently as even this new Minna could wish. 'Where have you been? Mutti has a good luncheon for us today!'

But this, it seemed, was a mistake. Minna glanced from her mother to her father and back again and then said very quickly. 'Only to the officers' club, really, that's where I've been, that's all, to the officers' club to help with the teas. Truly, that's where I've been.'

Her voice was like a child's high-pitched chatter – a child who fears that it has unwittingly done wrong. Otto was frightened into silence. He took the coffee his mother handed him and saw that her eyes were filled with tears, that his father's hands, as he carved ham to make the sandwiches, shook.

'Er . . . it's good of you, Minna, to help,' Otto said at last. 'Is it nice, the club?'

'Yes, very nice. I make them coffee and sometimes tea, and I slice bread for sandwiches, only the bread must be very thin and I'm not . . . Some of them are nice to me. Only some of them, though.' She looked hopefully at her mother. 'Is there cake, Mutti?'

'Yes, dear. I thought I'd cut the Krummeltorte; do you remember, the one you and I baked yesterday?'

Minna glanced nervously across at Otto, then scraped a chair close to the table and sat down on it.

'I think I remember. I bought apples for it in the market.' Again the blue eyes scanned the three people nervously. 'That was all I did, I just bought the apples, I didn't speak to anyone or . . . I just bought the apples.'

'Of course you did.' Herr von Eckner patted her head as he offered her a sandwich. 'You're a very good girl and always do just as you should.'

'Yes I do!' Minna beamed at them. 'I do just as I should.' She bit at her sandwich, then addressed Otto directly for the first time. 'I've always been good, haven't I, Otto? Franz always said how good I was and how I did as I was asked.'

'Yes, Franz always says how good you are,' Otto said soothingly. 'I've seen Franz quite a lot lately, and he sends you his love.'

This blatant lie – for Franz had never so much as mentioned their sister – was received with the only genuine smile Minna had yet given. He saw that Minna's eyes actually warmed a little from their anxious coldness.

'Oh, that was so kind – I love Franz! Of course I love you too, Otto, but you always did frighten me a little bit. Franz is such a beautiful brother, he always . . .'

'That's right, Minna dear. Would you like a nice hot cup of coffee, like Otto's?'

'What's happened to her, Father? She's twenty-two years old but she's behaving like a child of ten – no, younger!'

Father and son were at last alone, having left the two women to clear up after the meal whilst they went for a walk in the nearby gardens to settle their digestions. Herr von Eckner knew what Otto meant, but he sighed, hesitating.

'We aren't sure. We'll probably never really know what happened to her. Actually, the unexpectedness of seeing you has made her regress again. She hasn't been quite as childish as that for some weeks, but even at her best she isn't normal. Strangers can sometimes unhinge her mind completely, though we can build her up to a certain level until something happens to prick the bubble of her self-confidence and she descends to childhood again.'

'Father, you must have some idea what did this to her . . .'

'She just disappeared. She was gone a fortnight and the most diligent enquiries met with nothing but blank stares and denials. I did my best and then, when I could see that your mother was almost insane with worry, I went to the top. To someone very important and rather frightening, who I thought could find out what had happened. I saw him in a tiny, bare little office and he was shocked at what I told him and said he would do his best for me, though he held out little hope, not after two weeks. Yet within eight hours she was found on our doorstep. She was in a bad state, had been beaten – perhaps worse – but at least she was home, with us. We got her a nurse and had intended to put her into hospital, but it was soon plain that the sight of anyone other than myself and her mother put her into a state of almost mindless terror. Very very slowly, over the past year, we've brought her round to seeing that no one will hurt her. She goes to the officers' club always with Frau Gremm, or your mother, or with Annelise, and they make sure that she never goes off with anyone or becomes upset. At the first sign she's brought straight back here.'

'That's appalling,' Otto said slowly, as they strolled round the lawns. 'What's wrong with this country? Ever since before Gustav died . . .'

'Yes, I know.' Herr von Eckner shook his head. 'But it doesn't do to say too much, though you're safe enough here, out in the open. Berlin's thick with informers, you see. Every apartment block has at least one, sometimes an obvious person and a hidden one as well. Every street has its secret information box – you must have noticed them. All you have to do is post a letter voicing doubts about someone and the next thing you know the Gestapo have called on them and they've disappeared. Your mother and I count ourselves fortunate to have got Minna back.'

'Even as she is?'

'Even as she is. At first, you see, she was so ardent, so sure that following the Fuehrer meant salvation. And then doubts began to creep in. After her young man was killed in the attack on Warsaw she was very unhappy, but then Hermann came along, and I do believe she really loved him with all her heart. He flew in a bomber, not as pilot but as a rear gunner, and he was killed over Russia in the early days of the campaign. I know Minna voiced doubts, then . . . only to your mother and me, but it is possible that she made her feelings more widely known.'

'What did she feel? That their deaths were due to bungling?'

'No, not that. Simply that those who lived by treachery might die by it. If you remember, there had not been any declaration of war, not the slightest hint of aggressive intentions, before we invaded Poland. And Russia was worse, since we had a peace pact with her. Minna said what she thought and then became withdrawn and bitter. She no longer wanted to dance or to meet young men. Something in her died with Hermann, I believe.'

'And we can do nothing, say nothing?' Otto said slowly. 'Father, what is to become of us?'

'I don't know,' Herr von Eckner said simply. 'Evil begets evil as good begets good; you are better on the Russian front risking your life for what is good in your country than living soft on the sufferings of others.'

'I know it.' Their steps had taken them back on to the pavements of the city once again and without a word exchanged the talk became general – and harmless – once more. 'I meant to ask you, Father, whether you ever hear from Trudl?'

'Cousin Trudl? Why, certainly, for she's determined to marry Franz, you know, despite his rather obvious lack of interest! She knits him socks and scarves and writes him long letters – does he never mention them when you meet?'

'Yes, once or twice he's said she writes; he always looks positively tortured by her attentions though!'

The two men made their way back to the Neue Friedrichstrasse.

Otto's only other chance of a long and private talk with his father came ten days after his arrival in Berlin. Herr von Eckner had to go to a nearby township to buy some material needed at the factory, so he took Otto with him for the ride; and when the purchasing had been completed he drove his car out into the country, parked by a river, and the two of them walked along by the murmuring water and talked freely, perhaps for the last time before Otto returned to Russia.

Otto had been three times to the officers' club and had seen that despite her nervous illness, as it was called, there was still a young man prepared to be in love with Minna. As fair as she, but a good deal less strong and healthy, Willi Kettermann had wild, pale blue eyes and a tiny flaxen moustache. He was not strong enough to fight for he had been badly wounded in the back and legs two years earlier and he would never be completely fit again. He walked stiffly and slowly with a decided limp and he could not stand for long, but he was fond of Minna and in his gentle and compassionate company she could appear almost normal. Certainly a far cry from the terrified child she had appeared on Otto's first day home.

'I think if Kettermann proposes and Minna accepts, they'll both be all right,' Otto told his father as they strolled along. 'He's a good fellow; he'll take care of her as far as he is able. I still wish to God I could find out who was responsible for what happened to her. I've watched her at the club and it's pretty clear that one uniform in particular has a very adverse effect.'

'Naturally. But the bully-boys do all the dirty work. She may have been handed over . . . Dear God, sometimes I'm more afraid of knowing than of ignorance! For her sake and for your dear mother's, Otto, you've got to stop wondering and stop guessing. Do you understand me?'

'Yes, and I'm bloody glad I'm going back in a few days,' Otto said, his voice harsh with suppressed emotion. 'That poor kid, her life ruined . . .' He tore at a clump of irises and then yelped as the sharp, spear-like leaves sliced his fingers.

'I know. I wish I could get the women somewhere safe, but the truth is they're only safe with me and I have to stay here. Only whilst the factory continues to produce at its present rate am I valuable to the Reich.'

'With slave labour? Is that what you mean?' Herr von Eckner had taken his son round the factory, so he knew that Otto knew all about the workers there, but nevertheless the remark must have hurt him. His shoulders sagged, though he nodded.

'With slave labour. I treat them well. That's why I get the sort of production figures that everyone envies, but it would be impossible to convince the Fuehrer of that. He advises everyone to work the slaves to death and then he'll send others to replace them. If you were here, you'd see that it is all I *can* do, just stay here and see everyone is treated equally. If I were to leave, what do you think would happen to the little Jewish tailors, the Dutch, the French, the stupid, brave Poles who toil in the factory? They wouldn't last long. Even now I've foremen who I know damned well are informers, waiting their chance to find something wrong they can report. I tell you, Otto, it takes me all my time and energy to see that my factory isn't turned into another torture chamber for the so-called enemies of the Reich. And to keep your mother and sister safe and reasonably happy. Once, I had hoped that you and Franz would be here to help me, for whatever his faults Franz would be sickened by the slave labour, but I'm glad, now, that you both decided to serve your country on the light side of its dealings. We who hover between the light and the dark see things that we would rather not know about, for we can do nothing to help. I wouldn't want my sons in this filthy business.'

'You're a braver man than I, father,' Otto admitted. 'I'd flare up and get myself shot, which wouldn't help anyone. I wouldn't have the courage to do it the way you do, by scrupulous fairness and by intimidating those who would destroy you by sheer force of character. I'd rather go through another winter on the Russian front than face even two days in your factory.'

He had seen the slave workers in their grey rags herded into corners to have bread flung at them by overseers. Seen later, when the overseers went to the canteen for their own food, how Herr von Eckner had collected the slave labourers round for a meal of hot soup, black bread and some fresh vegetables. He had said to them in a perfectly calm and matter-of-fact voice that no workers who were on his premises should go short of food because a tired and hungry man was a careless man. He made it sound as if the overseers were the guilty ones, for neglecting the people in their charge.

Otto could see that he walked a lonely and slippery

tightrope, and that it was a rope which could easily break, plunging him into a desperate situation if things should go wrong. But so long as output was high and the standard of work equally good, they would let him be an eccentric, as he heard one of the foremen call him. Why not? He might even be right!

'Talking of preferences,' Herr von Eckner said suddenly, breaking the silence that had fallen between them. 'What made you volunteer for the Russian campaign? I was told you had volunteered and that the Reich needed more young men like you – I was high in favour that week, with two boys in Russia, I can tell you!'

'I went because I didn't intend to bomb Britain,' Otto admitted. 'Do you remember that girl Minna had to stay before the war? She came to watch the Olympic Games in 'thirty-six.'

His father's face lightened a little and a small, reminiscent smile touched his lips. Val, Otto reflected smugly, had that effect on people.

'Who could forget her? Val Neyler, the little redhead. A lovely girl, warm and intense; a good friend for Minna. I always regretted that my girl never accepted their invitations to visit them in England, but she was too bound up with what was happening here, too narrow in her outlook. So?'

'I wrote to her until war broke out. We met. I hope that after the war we may meet again. You must see that I could not continue to fly over Britain, knowing that she might be in the town or city I was helping to attack.'

'I see that. But the Russian front . . . never mind. No doubt you'll soon be back for good now that we've set out to do what we intended to do and crushed them.' His glance was interrogative. 'Or so the papers say.'

'I don't think we've crushed them so much as astonished them; I think they'll rally, but possibly too late to hit back. I hope so. Franz thinks we'll get to Moscow this summer and be back in Germany, triumphant, by autumn; he's on the ground so he's probably got a much better picture than I, up in the air. Anyway, I hope he's right since I've no desire to have to go through another Russian winter.' He shuddered expressively. 'What a climate – why anyone should want to invade such a country is beyond me.'

'Well, next time you want to avoid bombing Britain, choose a warmer theatre of war – God knows, the choice seems to be widening all the time,' Herr von Eckner said dryly. 'North Africa is warm, I believe, and Greece is downright hot.'

'Yes. To look at our record you'd believe every word of the propaganda that we can't lose. We've driven the Russians back, the Japs have cleared Singapore of the British and they're on the run in Burma. We've crushed Greece and Europe is under our heel. Yet there's a saying that Val flung at me once when we were talking about history. She said, "The British lose every battle but the last." Possibly, Germany will do the opposite.'

'When France fell and the rest of Europe were on their knees I listened to the English radio,' Herr von Eckner said. 'Some chap was going on about having their backs to the wall . . . how they'd fight on the beaches and in the hills but they'd never surrender. It doesn't sound much now, but I can tell you at the time it was stirring stuff. Well, now that's our position, Otto. First Britain, then Russia and now America are ranged against us, and it's we who are alone. But there will be no wall at our backs, no pity for us, because we are the aggressors; the attackers of innocence.'

Otto did not answer because there was no answer, but he took the older man's arm and together father and son walked on across the crisping grass beneath the innocent blue of the sky.

'I don't know that I'd describe it as volunteering, exactly,' Val said with a giggle to the man sitting beside her. 'We fought to get sent out here! I was lucky because I drove an ambulance all through the Blitz so when I joined the army I said at once that it was what I did best and that I wanted to go on driving ambulances. When I heard a detachment of drivers was being sent to Egypt I kept pointing out to everyone that I was ideally suited for the job – driving under fire being something I'd done more of than most – and someone, somewhere, must have agreed, so here I am.'

'Here', at that moment, was sitting on the step of her ambulance beside Billy Ross, who was what the powers that be described as 'walking wounded' although his shattered leg was incapable of walking. But he had made himself crutches and had hopped up into the ambulance cheerfully enough when Val and her co-driver, Annette, had picked up a batch of wounded from the Western Desert. They had stopped, inadvisable though it was, because the ambulance was elderly and needed a rest to cool the overheated engine. Val, who had done a lot of handing tools and shifting from foot to foot in London when Richie was servicing the ambulance engines, had only recently realised that she had assimilated a good deal of knowledge during those sessions, which she was now being forced to put into use.

'But this isn't Egypt,' Billy said, stretching and yawning. 'Not that I'm complaining, mind.'

'No, but I started out in Egypt. Since then, I've just gone wherever I've been ordered; Lebanon is fantastically beautiful at this time of year, in case you didn't know it, because it's the time of the wild flowers. Annette and I took a picnic up into the mountains a week or so ago – we went on horseback from Beirut – and we felt guilty at dismounting and sitting down to eat our food, because the ground was carpeted with tiny, exquisite little wild cyclamen. Yet the roads through the high passes are often blocked by snow in the winter months! You'll be with us for a while, until your leg is fixed. You must get me to take you out into the country. If I can find someone with a car, that is.'

Annette, who had been sitting in the back with the stretcher wounded, put her head round the doors.

'Val, we've been here half an hour. Do you think she's cool enough to start again?' Val glanced at her own wristwatch. Annette was right and it was asking for trouble to stay here any longer than they need; she got to her feet and walked round to the driver's door, waiting whilst Billy heaved himself cheerfully into the cab beside her. Annette would stay in the back now for the rest of the journey, doing what she could for the wounded.

'Right, we'll give it a go,' Val shouted through her open window. She pulled the starter and the engine roared into life, with only the slightest of coughs to show that there had been a good reason for stopping. Overhead they heard the roar of a plane's engines, but it ignored them, continuing on its way, so either it was friendly or it had decided to respect the red crosses on the ambulance's sides. Or, alternatively and far likelier, it had not even seen them.

Val glanced at her passenger. He looked all right, and it was better for the wounded in the back to have Annette back there rather than this cheerful young captain who could do so much less for them. Seeing her eyes on him, Billy smiled at her and tried, more or less successfully, Val thought, to appear painfree and untroubled. But she could see from the lines etched on his brow and from the corners of his mouth that he was in a good deal of pain.

'Well, Val? Just why did you want to drive an ambulance

under fire? Wasn't the Blitz enough for you? You could have spent the rest of the war in Blighty, driving fat generals or cooking food for the air force, I daresay.'

'I wanted to be really useful,' Val said slowly. 'I wanted to feel that I'd done something concrete towards winning the war. And I *am* useful here, you know. I'm good with engines – better than I guessed I could be – and I've got a way with cars. I can coax more speed out of an ancient Dodge than some can get out of a brand-new one. Though that's a mixed blessing, since I always get given the cranks instead of the trouble-free vehicles.'

'And you'll stay? You won't run out on us, go to somewhere a bit more glamorous?'

'No. I mean yes I'll stay and no I shan't fret for glamour! If you ask me, there's nothing as glamorous as Lebanon – if you can stand the fearful heat in the summer, that is. Though I hope I never forget the pyramids. Have you seen them?'

Billy shook his head. He had closed his eyes against the glare but now he opened them.

'No, I haven't. Go on talking, there's a darling; there's nothing more relaxing than a beautiful woman's voice talking entertainingly when you're half-dead on your feet but too uncomfortable to sleep.'

'That was a nice, if inadvertent, compliment,' Val said, laughing. 'I shall continue. When we first landed in Egypt I thought the pyramids so beautiful by moonlight that I never tried to see them at any other time. They take on colour from goodness knows where in moonlight – sometimes they are rose and the sky is cobalt, sometimes the sky seems black and they are silvery-blue, sometimes the sky seems sapphire and they are a magical turquoise. But then you see them as dawn flushes the sky pink and gold and they're mysterious blood-red rubies, or they're great solid blocks of twenty-two carat gold . . . I tell you, anyone can persuade me of anything about the pyramids. Outer space, magic, anything!'

'What were you doing, pyramid-viewing at dawn?' Billy asked idly. 'I thought you drove ambulances there as well.'

'Oh, we did, and that's how we became so familiar with the pyramids! At first we went out deliberately rubbernecking, but later we got really familiar with them at all times and all seasons. And it was then, I think, that I grew to realise just how wonderful they are and how they change. Shadowed or clear, in moonlight or sunlight or twilight, they seem to find colour and power.'

'They sound special. What about the Lebanon? Apart from the wild flowers, that is.'

'Well, in winter there's skiing; you can climb right up into those wild mountains . . . come to think of it that's the most fantastic thing of all. Once, a few of us climbed right up to the top of one of the highest peaks and reached it as dawn was breaking. We stood there in the snow while the sky flushed from the very palest green, the colour of a duck's egg, through into aquamarine into blue. We'd slogged up, of course, carrying our skis over our shoulders, and we began to ski down, whizzing along in minutes over terrain that had taken us hours and hours to climb. And it got hotter and hotter as the sun rose, and then the snow was gone and the ground was carpeted with wild flowers. You don't have an experience like that often.'

There was no reply from her passenger and Val, glancing across at him, had to smile. Her poetic descriptions had sent him to sleep at last!

Left to herself, she considered her life and found it good. It might be dangerous, driving out into the desert and around this land which was a man's land and had little time for women, but it was unforgettable. And here at least she was free from the terror that the man aiming the bombs might be Otto.

She had met plenty of men, of course; Billy Ross was only one who would convalesce and probably want to take her around until he was well enough to return to his own war. But though several of the men were charming, delightful company and intelligent conversationalists, no one touched her heart. Sometimes, when she was very tired and very lonely, she wished they would.

Chapter Fourteen

'All right, pet? Casper and I will join you later. He's getting on with his homework and I really must take Daddy his flask and sandwiches; it isn't like him to forget them, but the warning went unexpectedly.' Rachel blew Coppy, curled up in one corner of the Morrison shelter, a kiss and headed for the dining-room door. 'If you want a drink or anything, wait until the All Clear sounds. Nightie night.'

Coppy said goodnight and pulled her blanket over her shoulders. The Morrison was taking up most of the spare room in the dining-room even now that they had situated it close to the fireplace – that had been done after Daddy had warned them about flying glass from broken windows. Though it was a godsend, for the Siegals' modern house had no cellar, Morrison shelters did take up rather a lot of room and made it just about impossible to live any normal sort of life around them. Which was why the Siegals had put theirs in the dining-room which was seldom used these days for its usual purpose. Food was scarce and dull and usually eaten in the kitchen and, now the radio was in there and it was warmed by the Aga, it was usual to spend most of the day in the kitchen.

Indeed, Norwich had been free from raids for months, but Hitler, in his nastiness, had decided to bomb historic cities – the newspapers were calling them the Baedeker raids, since it was popularly believed that Hitler's hit list was culled from his Baedeker – and so the Morrison, long-ignored, was coming into its own again.

Coppy quite liked the Morrison. She had adored living at The Pride with all the family whilst the Blitz was at its height, but now that she was home again it was a good deal better to be curled up snugly in here than making the best of the smelly public shelter on the corner of their road. They had an Anderson in the garden, but it kept flooding and Daddy did not like to think of them going down there during a raid. He much preferred that they should crawl into this object which was a bit like a rabbit's cage, with a wire floor, wire walls and a solid steel roof. It would, the experts said, stop the house crushing you if it fell, so as soon as the warning sounded all four of them were supposed to get into it and stay inside until the All Clear went.

There was not room for them all at nights though, lying down. Since Daddy was a warden he was off as soon as the siren sounded, which left three of them, and Mummy had decided that it was just as safe to snooze on the steel roof whence, she assured her children, it wouldn't take her half a second to dive to safety should they hear the house beginning to collapse. Coppy was small and skinny and did not take up much room, but Caspar was a great, leggy sixteen-year-old and he had uninhibited sleeping habits. He spread out and bagged all the blankets, and despite the cramped space he kicked like a frog. He sometimes shouted in his sleep as well, and many a time Coppy, lying awake and battered at her end of the cage, wished that she could change places with Mummy out there on the roof. Safe as houses, Mummy had said when Caspar had queried her choice of sleeping place and Caspar had laughed at her ineptly chosen phrase. If houses were safe, he pointed out, there would be no need for anyone to have a Morrison in their dining-room.

It was a secret from Daddy that Mummy did not come into the Morrison, because when he was at home during a raid he and Mummy always took their blankets and pillows and slept under the big, solid kitchen table; Daddy said it was as good as the Morrison any day, and he was probably right. At any rate, that was where Caspar and Mummy would be for the rest of the evening until they decided to come to bed. Caspar would be studying for his school certificate and Mummy would be knitting for victory.

Coppy sighed as the thrum of engines overhead grew louder. It was lonely in here – suppose the house was bombed and did fall down and she was trapped! If Caspar was in the Morrison too it wouldn't be so bad, but she didn't much fancy being shut in her cage underneath the house all by herself. The planes were right overhead now and she could see a faint line of light shining underneath the curtains. She crawled to the end of the cage, pushed open the bottom bit and slid through, then struggled into her school cardigan and stood up and shambled kitchen-wards. She just wanted a word with Caspar, that was all, she told herself.

Caspar lay under the table on his stomach, with an oil lamp illuminating the huge sheet of graph paper he was working on. He was alone.

'Where's Mummy, Cas?'

Caspar rolled over and stared at her, then sat up and clonked his head on the bottom of the table. He swore and rubbed it, making his hair stand on end at the back.

'I wish you wouldn't creep, Coppy, you gave me a helluva scare. You look like Lady Macbeth, all great huge black eyes and bloodstained hands. Mummy's gone down to the post to give Daddy his flask and sandwiches, or at least I suppose she has. She went down to the gate hoping to see a warden, but she's been gone so long she must have had to take them herself.'

'She shouldn't, not during a raid,' Coppy said, ignoring

the bloodstained hands bit until she had more time for questions. 'Daddy's always saying we should stay indoors and under cover until the All Clear goes.'

Caspar gave his head a last rub, rolled on to all fours, and crawled out from his retreat. When he was well clear of the table he stood up, stretched, then held out a hand.

'All right, baby, we'll go and take a look out of the front door. If she's in the road we'll give her a yell, make her get a move on.'

Together, brother and sister went to the front door and opened it. It was bright as day outside, with the parachute flares dropped by the advance aircraft hanging like beautiful chandeliers in the dark sky and making the moonlight seem pale and insignificant by comparison. From the east they heard the sinister throb of the approaching bomber squadrons which would be on them in a matter of moments.

'It's going to be a bad one,' Caspar said uneasily. 'I've seen flares before, of course, but never so many. And that sounds like more than half a dozen bombers to me.' He glanced down the street towards the wardens' post. 'I wish Mum would come back.'

'I wish she would, but perhaps if she's reached the post or one of the street shelters she's better staying there until it's over.' A high screaming sound that both children knew well stopped the words in her throat. The bombs were starting to drop. 'Oh, Cas, I'm frightened!'

'Back to the Morrison,' Caspar said. His voice sounded firm, but Coppy knew him well enough to guess that she was not the only one who was scared. 'Run, Coppy!'

'Come with me! Don't go back to the kitchen!'

'All right, I'll tuck you in.'

They ran. As they dashed through the hall and into the dining-room Coppy realised that they had not shut the front door, but at least if Mummy was near then she wouldn't have to waste time out there fumbling with her key in the lock. She dropped to her hands and knees and crawled into the shelter, then turned, to see Caspar fixing the end-piece in place. He was still outside. It was noisy now, so noisy that she had to raise her voice to a shout.

'Don't go! Cas, please!'

'I won't be a mo, Coppy, honestly. I just want to fetch my maths; I'll have to do 'em in here for once. I can't just leave them. I can just see Mr Mossman letting me get away with that!'

But Coppy had opened her cage and was dragging at her brother's legs with all her strength.

'No, Cas, they're right overhead . . . please come in now, you've got to get across the hall and right across the kitchen too, please . . .'

Her words were cut across by an explosion so terrific that for one horrible moment she actually thought she had gone deaf. Then she saw, in slow motion, the walls sag inwards like huge, expanding balloons, saw the wallpaper rip, saw the ceiling bulge downwards and the light bulb explode. Then there was dust in her eyes and mouth, the world was rocking crazily, noise drowned thought and total darkness enclosed her. Something hit her, hard, across the head and she knew no more.

'There are two of them. The boy – my son – is sixteen, my daughter's twelve.'

Rachel was shaking so much that she could hardly stand upright. She had been trapped in a shelter a quarter of a mile away having delivered Adolphus's flask and sandwiches, and had sat there in an agony of apprehension in case the children should have come searching for her whilst one of the worst raids it had known rained down on the city.

When she had emerged it was still dark, and would be

for several more hours. Adolphus was still at work in his own sector, but Rachel had come home to find the house a pile of rubble with roaring gas jets lighting the scene into uncanny clarity, aided by a full moon and by the flames from someone's wooden garage which was burning furiously.

The warden she had found was an old man. Kind, no doubt, but ill at ease in the face of her anguish and obviously with no idea what to do. If only Adolphus were here! Agonising guilt and self-disgust was tearing Rachel apart, for she knew very well why she had gone out in the teeth of the raid with the flask and sandwiches. Partly because Adolphus would want them of course, but more because she dreaded being shut in the house when things were going on outside. More than once, lately, she had felt claustrophobic under that wretched kitchen table, had longed to take a more active part in the battle against the bombs. So she had seized her chance and left her children alone, and the house had been bombed and they were somewhere underneath it. And she did not know what to do, where to dig, whether to dig!

Someone took her arm and shook her, not unkindly. She looked, and it was another warden, a much younger woman with thick fair hair and a sharp, intelligent face. To be sure her ARP uniform was covered in dirt and her face was soot-smeared, but that only gave Rachel more confidence in her. This woman knew what she was doing!

'My children . . . in that house . . . my house . . .'

'Yes. Whereabouts in the house? Front or back?'

'When I left the boy was in the kitchen doing his homework. He was under the table. My little girl was in the Morrison, in the dining-room. That's in the front. It was such a violent raid, though, that I think they'd have moved together. Possibly in the front.' She followed the warden, who was shining a small and pretty useless torch in the general direction of the house. 'Where should we start? What should I . . . Oh, my God!'

She had seen the kitchen table. Some freak of the blast had lifted it, torn it in two and deposited it against the leaning rubble of the wall at the end of the garden.

The warden followed her eyes, then patted her shoulder.

'Doesn't mean a thing, love. Where's your husband? In the forces? Got sisters, a mother, someone you can call on until we dig the children out?'

'My husband's ARP,' Rachel said. 'Can I telephone my sister?'

'Not round here,' the other woman said briefly. 'But if you walk to the post they'll phone round, try to get hold of your husband. And someone there may know where there's a call-box standing.'

'I can't go, not whilst I know the children are under there. I have to stay, I should never have left them you see, I took my husband a flask . . . I have to stay. Can I move . . . begin to dig . . . ?'

'If that's how you feel. Tell me your name and I'll go down to my post to get reinforcements and tell someone to fetch your husband at the same time. My colleague will stay with you.'

The elderly man smiled timidly and nodded, as though acknowledging that he would not be much help, but at least he would be here.

'Right.' Rachel took a deep breath. 'The gas . . . the way it's burning like that . . . it worries me . . . is there any way of turning it off?'

'Not yet. If you look, you'll see that the main cracked outside the house at the front and again around the back. Was there a gas fire in the dining-room?'

She did not ask about the kitchen and Rachel knew why. If the children had been there . . . Rachel wrenched her mind back to the layout of the dining-room. Absurd, but she was having great difficulty in remembering.

'A gas fire? Yes . . . no . . . no, definitely not. Not in the dining-room.'

'Then they should be safe enough. In a Morrison? Yes, I thought so. A lot of people round here put them in the dining-room. That's where mine is, not that I use it much.' For the first time, Rachel looked at the warden as a woman, and recognised Sylvia Platt from further along the road. How odd, she simply had not even thought of the woman as a woman, but only as a figure of authority. 'Look, don't touch the rubble, my dear, it's too dangerous; you might start something sliding. That big beam . . . see? A good few of the downstairs walls are still standing and that beam may be keeping the weight of the upper rooms off . . . well, anyway, I wouldn't move anything. By the way, do you have a household pet?'

It seemed a stupid and inconsequential question, but Rachel understood at once. She had heard wonderful stories of cats and dogs locating their owners under piles of rubble and leading the heavy-rescue people to just the right spot. They even seemed, these animals, to know where it was best and safest to dig. If only they had allowed the children to have a dog – goodness knows they had asked for one often enough. If they had let Coppy have that kitten she had pleaded for. But they had not.

'No? Oh well, we'll have to try . . .' the warden stopped as Rachel clutched her arm. 'What is it?'

'My sister has a dog, Maxie. He adores Coppy and she adores him. Do you think . . . ?'

'Is it far? Could you fetch him, do you think?' For the first time Rachel realised that Sylvia Platt was genuinely afraid of touching the rubble because if they tried the wrong place for the children and dug there, they might do more harm than good. She clutched her brow, trying to make herself think logically. Just how far from here was The Pride? A mile? Half a mile? Three miles?

'Go and get Maxie,' the warden said gently. 'I'll go and phone for the heavy-rescue people and my colleague will stay here. Now you go and fetch the dog.'

'I will,' Rachel said. It helped, having something definite to do. 'I'll be as quick as I can. And please . . . if you can get my husband, Adolphus Siegal, he'll be more help than I could be.'

'I'll do my best,' the warden promised. 'Off with you now and bring the dog.'

Coppy recovered consciousness to find herself in total darkness. It was horribly hot and stuffy, yet her legs were freezing cold and her hands lay on her chest like two little blocks of marble. She moved, and found herself restricted in all sorts of nasty and frightening ways. Was she in bed? It was totally dark, nightmare dark. Usually, despite the most stringent attempts at blackout, you would wake, peer about you, and realise that *there* was the window, there the door, there the picture of the St Bernard puppy, the glass reflecting the telltale light cracks around the blinds. But now there was only complete, unreflective black.

She tried to move again and found that something lay across her icy legs, pinning them firmly to the ground, and suddenly recollection came flooding back. She and Caspar had been alone in the house, there had been an air raid and she had watched the house fall on them before it went totally dark. Where, then, was Caspar? She had been right inside the Morrison she was sure, but had her brother got in before the house collapsed? She could remember crying out, clutching at some part of him – and then the house had begun to close in on her.

She felt around, but nothing made much sense to her

seeking fingers. She could not touch the wire sides though she had been sure they would be close and when she put her hand up to feel for the steel roof it was lower than it had ever been before, and slanted. There was earth or dust or something all over her, gritty and horrible, in her mouth, eyes, nose and thickly caked on her lips. When her fingers stole out to find the comfort of blankets all they came into contact with was layers of thick gritty dust.

'Caspar? Where are you? I'm frightened.'

Her voice sounded small and there was a dull echo to it that convinced her she was alone in her tiny prison. She was still feeling about her, and just as she was about to stop for a rest, for even this tiny exertion was tiring, her fingers closed over something. A shoe? Yes, and it was Caspar's, and where there was a shoe there must be a foot! She tugged it hopefully, repeating his name.

The shoe came off in her hand giving her quite the worst moment of her life so far. The hair rose on her neck and she felt awful, clammy sweat break out all over her. Had Caspar's foot . . . ?

Desperately, she checked the shoe and it was empty. She gave a strangled sob and tried again to find out what held her legs, but she could not sit up so she lay back and tried to think rationally. She was in the Morrison, she was all right, she felt bruised and shaken, but felt sure she was neither dead nor gravely injured. Caspar had been either in the shelter or half in when the house fell down, she was nearly sure of that. If she was right and Caspar had got mostly into the Morrison then it might well be his weight pinning her legs down. She tried to visualise where the shelter had been and how it had looked, and succeeded fairly well. Then, her hands and mind got to work on what had happened to it. After ten minutes of earnest thought she knew what had taken place and where she now lay. The house had indeed collapsed and some part of it had brought its full weight down on the shelter. Because the end section had not been in place – she had, she remembered, been trying to pull Caspar through it – the weight on it had pressed the end of the Morrison almost flat so that she lay, not in an oblong cage, but in a sort of longish triangle, with her feet trapped where the steel floor met the steel ceiling. Where Casper was she had no idea.

She knew she must not panic, she remembered some man telling them at school that panic killed, but darkness was terrifying and she did long to hear Caspar's voice, to know he was alive as well. She thought about calling out, but her mouth and throat were so dry and dusty that it would be foolish to waste effort. She did give one little cry, but it sounded so flat and dull and odd in her echoing prison that she felt quite sorry for it. No one could possibly hear a little squeak like that beneath the tons and tons of rubble which must separate her from the real world.

It did not do to think about those tons of rubble. Just one small thought and a scream bubbled in her throat. She took her left wrist in her right hand and began to dig her nails into the flesh as hard as she could – anything to take her mind off being buried alive – and then an odd thing happened. Ticking away there in her wrist, as if this was just another day, she felt her own pulse. Keeping time, steadily, with her heartbeat and her breathing, showing her that, to a pulse, this was just another day, another awakening. It was not racing or jumping, it was simply keeping time, ticking.

Then she realised that she could *hear* her pulse, and that seemed rather clever too, until she thought again and decided that it was also impossible. No one, no matter how alone, how terrified, how buried alive, could hear her own pulse. So if it was not her pulse, what was it? She had no wristwatch, and there was no clock in the dining-room . . .

Caspar had a wristwatch. It had a luminous blob on each of the hands and a very handsome expanding bracelet which went round his wrist. She could hear a ticking and, if it *was* the wristwatch, she might be able to pick out the luminous blobs.

It was difficult to keep calm but the feel of her own pulse, still behaving perfectly rationally beneath her fingers, kept her cool. She stared and stared into the darkness, but she saw nothing but more dark. Then she closed her eyes and listened, and only when she was almost sure she knew where the sound was coming from did she open them again to stare into the blackness once more. Where was the sound coming from? Where, where, where? About . . . there! And she was right! Exactly where her ears had guessed, exactly where her eyes had focused, there it was, a tiny greenish point. She felt down that way, and at last found Casper's hand. It was very cold and still. She felt his wrist, the cuff of his shirt, the beginning of his jersey, up to the elbow. Then, nothing.

Coppy gave a huge, shrieking gasp and began to scream.

'Ray, darling! What on earth . . . ?'

Tina had been the first to respond to the desperate knocking, the desperate ringing, and she had come padding barefoot down the stairs to fling open the front door. Now, with her bedtime plait over one shoulder, she stared unbelievingly at her sister. Then, pulling herself together, she stood back so that Rachel could enter the hall.

'Come along in, dear, then you can tell me in the warm. We'll go into the kitchen, and . . .'

'We've been bombed. The kids are buried. Can I have Maxie?'

Tina had always been quick-witted and, although it was

282

the middle of the night and she was still thick with sleep, she understood at once.

'He's in the kitchen. Hold on, you go and grab him whilst I get some clothes on.'

She headed for the stairs and Rachel hurried kitchen-wards.

Maxie, suddenly seized around the middle and lifted from his basket, began to growl, recognised Rachel, and changed it to a yawn. He supposed, rather reluctantly, that a relative had a certain right to wake him, though the hour was uncivilised, to say the least. When she stood him on the ground he staggered and thought about simply curling up and going to sleep again, then decided against it. He looked up at Rachel, squinting against the light, yawned again, scratched an ear, shook himself and then trotted out of the kitchen and into the hall. Plainly, things were afoot for just as he reached the bottom of the stars Tina and Bella, both pulling on clothing as they came, began to descend the flight. He grinned at them, though they addressed their remarks to his companion.

'We've woken Mummy, Auntie Ray, so she'll cope here whilst Gran and I come with you. Actually, we haven't been in bed long ourselves, we were down in the cellar, so she probably wasn't asleep, just dozing. Gran and I will do what we can to help.'

That was Bella. She picked Maxie up when she reached the hall, then changed her mind and stood him back on the floor, rather to his relief. Terriers were not lap-dogs even if they were a trifle undersized.

'We'll just get coats and things on . . . Gran, this is your warmest . . . who's bagged my striped scarf? I expect it's cold out and so I'd better wear it. What about gloves . . . Gran, do you remember the gloves you knitted me for Christmas . . . Oh it's all right, panic over, here they are.'

Bella was chattering for a reason, Maxie reflected, as he felt his lead clipped on to his collar. He was tugged towards the back door though, which seemed strange, until Tina spoke.

'You won't mind driving the Rover, will you, Ray? The keys are by the back door and it'll save a bit of time, but as you know I've never learned.'

'I'm game,' Rachel rejoined. 'Anything, so long as we get back soon!'

They left the house and walked across to where the cars were garaged. The sky was growing lighter in the east and the stars were paling. They bundled into the car and drove fast, over bomb craters and round piles of rubble; Maxie thought it an exciting ride and growled beneath his breath every time Rachel slowed to negotiate a bend. Presently the car drew up and they all jumped out. Tina ordered Bella to remove something called a rotor arm from the engine which they then hid in the nearest hedge. Then they began running up the road towards where the Siegal house had once stood.

People were standing around. There was a huge lorry with a crane on the back. A woman in uniform hailed them.

'Well done, you were quick. Got the little dog?'

Maxie, star of the moment, looked round with deep suspicion, a growl beginning in his throat. What on earth had these people done to the place? Where was the house he had visited so often with his old friend Coppy? Where the neat garden, the chicken-run, the lamp-post against which he always cocked his leg?

But Bella was kneeling down in the dirty street, taking his face between her hands, looking deep into his eyes. He looked back, as eager as anyone to understand what all this was about.

'Coppy, Maxie, old boy. Where's Coppy? Find Coppy!'

Maxie shook himself free and glanced round. Stupid question! A halfwit could see that Bella was the only child here. All the rest were large men or women. He wandered over to the opposite side of the road, where a house still stood, but before he could so much as sniff the wall Tina had grabbed him by the collar and dragged him towards the great mound of rubble that someone had put down in the Siegals' garden.

'Coppy's there, Maxie! Find her, there's a good boy, find Coppy!'

Maxie sniffed at the air which was full of brickdust and soot and smelt pain and fear, too. He hated it. He backed away from the doomed building. What did they mean? Why were they all staring at him, even the total strangers? Coppy?

But now that he was close to the rubble, he could hear something. Faintly, far below, something stirred. He cocked his head first to one side and then the other. He no longer noticed that he was the cynosure of all eyes, that the watchers were drawing closer. He stalked, stiff-legged and ridge-backed, over to one particular pile of rubble. He pressed his nose against it, inhaled deeply, then sneezed. No one laughed or indeed moved; this was much too important.

Maxie sniffed again, then backed; the smell of pain and fear came worst and strongest from this part of the had-been-a-house. And then, without any more messing about, he began to dig, shovelling earth, half-bricks and muck out between his back legs, yelping on a high, excited note. So that was what they had meant – this was hide-and-seek and Coppy, cheat that she was, had some-how managed to pull the house down on top of her and was hiding underneath. He would find her! He would show her that she could not hide from him for long, no matter where she might tuck herself away!

When huge men suddenly appeared beside him and began to dig as well he thought about objecting, telling them to find their own place, but they were right, he could not get through all this lot without some assistance. Anyway, they were polite and deferred to him. Whenever he stopped digging and whining they stopped too, and waited for him to proceed. He did not have to explain to them that, as he dug, he could smell that this way would prove impossible, or that if they continued just here the whole lot would come down and might hurt Coppy worse than she was hurt already. They were not a bad lot at all.

Also, he was enjoying himself. Usually, no more than a paw's depth into some decent spot and an interfering person would come along, scream, grab his collar, and start moaning on about bulbs, roses, or the difficulties of growing leeks. Even the most understanding person seemed to have some objection to his employing his talent for digging. But this time they were actually encouraging him, letting him go first, helping him when he reached a beam or some masonry that he could not shift but which he felt should be moved.

Once, he raised a dirt-covered face, his eyes shining, and saw that his audience had grown. Coppy's father was here too, and a policeman and an ambulance – all sorts. Maxie grinned at them, and then dug with renewed vigour.

He was undoubtedly the star!

The scream which had been torn from Coppy's throat had two results. One was that in her terror she actually managed to move so that when the scream died out into a low, sobbing moan she was a couple of inches or so to the left of her previous position.

She was still shuddering from the shock of finding what she took to be Caspar's severed arm when she realised the moan was not hers. She held her breath, trying to ignore the thunder of her heartbeats.

'Who's there? Who is it?'

Her voice came out very small and frail and was answered almost immediately.

'Coppy? Wa-as tha-at yo-ou?'

His voice sounded strangely dragged out, slurred and slow, but even so totally recognisable. Her own voice, when she answered, rang with joy.

'Cas! I thought you were dead! Where are you? It's pitch dark, I can't see a thing.'

'Under . . . something . . . heavy.' There was a long pause, filled only by his rasping breaths. 'Can . . . you . . . move . . . it?'

'I don't know where you are or what you're under,' Coppy sobbed, breaking down now that she could at least talk to her brother. 'Are you in the Morrison with me, or out of it?'

The deep, dragging breathing rasped on for a moment, and then Caspar spoke again. He sounded a lot less strange and frightening, he sounded almost amused.

'I know what it is – you're sitting on my bloody chest!'

In fact, she was not sitting on him at all, but they were both crammed close to the mesh of the Morrison and Caspar, at the back, was greatly eased when Coppy managed to move forward a bit so that he could draw his arm out from underneath her and, as he said, breathe more easily. With a good deal of effort, grunting and muttering, they managed to roll a tiny bit apart and then Coppy confessed that the arm which had been round her had seemed, at the time, to lack a body.

'That was why I screamed,' she explained. 'I thought you were in bits.'

'Screamed?' Caspar's voice had gone thin again, and far away. Coppy was suddenly terrified that he was hurt badly.

'Yes, didn't you hear me scream? Shall I scream again, and see if anyone comes?'

He was a long while considering it. Then he said: 'No. Save your breath. Lie still and we'll talk.'

He was afraid too, Coppy thought wonderingly. Caspar, who was afraid of nothing, did not like being buried alive any more than she did. She took his hand and they both tightened their fingers on the other, glad of the contact.

'I saw your watch, that was how I knew some of you was in here,' Coppy said conversationally. 'Oh, did you hear that?'

'No; what?'

'A dog! Honestly, I'm not just saying it, I heard a dog bark. Well, not bark, making that high, through-the-nose noise that Maxie makes when he's shut out of a room he wants to get into. Listen!'

Next time they both heard it.

'OK; we'll give a shout just so they know we're here and keep trying to reach us. Ready, steady . . . go!'

The shout sounded quite loud with the pair of them, Coppy thought gladly. Strange how different she felt now that Caspar was with her and help close at hand. It was jolly nearly an adventure. And she was absolutely sure now that the dog not only sounded like Maxie, it was Maxie! She adored him, always had, and she knew his little noises as well as she knew the voices of her friends. She sighed happily.

'That's Maxie out there, Cas. He'll find us. He's a very clever little dog.'

'That's right, keep your pecker up. I'll give that dog all my next month's sweet ration if he gets us out, whether it's Maxie or one of the sniffer dogs the police have been training. I think we'd better keep quiet now though, and conserve our strength; once the light begins to come through they may need directions.'

'Right. Cas, are you hurt anywhere?'

'Can't tell, but my chest hurts. I daresay it's cracked ribs. And you?'

'No, I'm all right. Only I can't feel my feet at all, hardly, they're so cold. They're at the far end, where the roof's come down, or at least I think it has. Where are your legs?'

'Up round my bloody neck by the feel of 'em,' Caspar said gruffly after a short silence. 'Can you move your legs, honeybunch?'

'No, because of the steel roof being on them,' Coppy said. 'I think it's holding me down.'

'I get it. Right then, let's just lie here and think encouraging thoughts for a bit.' He paused. 'We might even say a prayer, I suppose.'

Brother and sister lay quiet, as the dog's whines got closer and the rescuers began to go with increased care. If they prayed, it was silently.

They prayed.

'Just let me read my mail and I'll be with you.' Maude sank on to the bucket seat of Alan's small car, opening her letter with less than care. 'It's from Gran – she writes a smashing letter.' Her eyes skimmed down the page while Alan, the soul of tact, polished the wing mirror by leaning out of the lowered side pane. 'I say, listen to this!'

'Listen to what?' Alan said plaintively, as she then proceeded to read the rest of the letter to herself. 'I'm not a nosy bloke, but you did say listen!'

'My cousins' house was bombed, and Coppy and Cas were buried. Gran says they were in the Morrison which goes to show that there's good in all things.' She chuckled. 'She didn't have much faith in Morrisons, but if they've saved Coppy and Caspar their stock will rise immeasurably; we're all very fond of the brats. Anyway, they got Maxie, Gran's horrid little terrier, and he sniffed them out and led the heavy-rescue blokes to the very spot. What do you think of that? I bet Maxie's head is so swelled he isn't worth talking to!'

'Were the kids all right? Apart from scared to hell, of course.'

'Gran says they were bruised and shaken and Coppy's legs were broken, but she'll be all right, though she may always walk with a limp.' She folded the letter and put it into her handbag. 'I hope they get Coppy straightened out. She's one of those kids who's always on the go – skinny, active, good at games and hates lessons. You know the sort.'

'I do.' Alan revved the engine and drove slowly off down towards the gates. 'I've been meaning to ask you, Maudie, would you like me to take you home the next time you get leave? No strings, if that's the way you want it.'

Maude glanced affectionately across at him and patted his knee.

'I'd love it, Alan. It's high time you met my family, and that includes Coppy and Caspar. Well, it'll have to, since they've moved into The Pride, probably for the duration. I think you'll love my family and they'll love you, so it's time we put it to the test.'

'Wonderful.' Alan's face brightened. 'What about doing some shopping, then? You know what sort.'

He had asked her to marry him twice since they first started going out together fairly regularly and Maude had said no the first time and that she would think about it the second time. She knew that there would not be a third time; Alan had said that three times came perilously close to nagging. Now, as he slowed the car and drew up on the verge, she went straight into his arms and returned his kiss. When he put her away from him he raised a dark brow at her.

'Well? What do you say?'

'I say what's wrong with a few strings? I need strings, to keep me down to earth when I'm with you.' Maude touched his cheek. 'Dear Alan, let's commit ourselves like crazy. Life's too short to waste.'

Alan gave her one last, exuberant hug, a kiss on the nose and then restarted the car.

'You won't regret it, darling,' he shouted above the roar of the engine. 'You won't regret it!'

Chapter Fifteen

'We'll get our heads down for a couple of hours and then we'll move on.' Nick spoke with the calm of utter despair. Retreat is never good for morale and losing one's company and finding oneself and one's platoon alone in the jungle with an enormous river between you and safety and no boats is enough to make the boldest despair. And the fighting in Burma had been bloody, desperate and one-sided, with the Japanese here in enormous force and fighting in their type of conditions, thoroughly at home with jungle warfare. Nick thought that they loved it and were good at it, for it fitted in with their ruthless animal outlook on life and death. He hated the Nips, hated every little yellow face that he saw, and he fostered the feeling, because it was better than the other prevalent emotion, which must be fear. They were so totally callous, so bloodthirsty, so inhuman.

They had killed Dave, though he refused to remember the manner of Dave's dying. It was enough that his friend was dead, would never be reunited with his Dora, never fight beside Nick again, with his cheery attitude, his colourful language, his secret contempt for any country that did not contain Dora.

Both his platoon sergeants were good chaps though, Johnnie Black was grand and so was Devlin; they were a team, now, though for obvious reasons Nick had to lead the team. Even so, when things got tough it was good to know that one would be able to guess with amazing accuracy how the other two would be acting, so that they could, like good whist players, take advantage of each other's tricks.

Looking around him at the tired and grimy faces of his platoon, Nick thought that they were all lucky. They had been pretty green when they started but now, after months and months of fighting, those of them that were left – their numbers had shrunk to eighteen – were hardened fighting machines, from eighteen-year-old Freddy Folkes to Erin O'Toole, who was twenty-eight and the grandfather of the platoon. And not only that, but there was not a man present who would not have risked his life for the others – indeed, *had* not risked his life for the others would not be putting it too strongly. Once the retreat had started they had covered some ground, all of it dangerous, from the jungle to the river plains, from the mountains to the lowlands. And now, with only the Chindwin between them and the border country, they had even more reason to take care for surely the enemy would mass here, knowing that every company, every platoon, every man, even, would have to cross the border somewhere, to reach India and safety.

But now the platoon had stopped in a forest because it was not yet night and they were nearing civilisation. A Burmese village could be a refuge, a trap or just an obstacle. No one could tell which until they had spied out the land for a good few hours, and this Nick felt they did not really have time to do. However, they were nearly out of food and their water flasks needed replenishment, so he had decided to sleep in the trees until dusk deepened to dark and then he, Snowy and Sergeant Black would make their way forward, using a banana plantation which lay conveniently close as cover, until they could see how the land lay. Then the three of them would either go forward, to see if the villagers were friendly and not infiltrated by the Japanese, or they would return to the forest edge and find a way round the village.

Meanwhile, there were the two hours to spend. Everyone curled up the way they found most comfortable and tried to sleep, but though the main heat of the day had passed it was still pretty warm, and Nick found that the village, and the prospect of presently stealing towards it, was not exactly sleep-inducing. Looking round, he saw that Johnnie was awake, as was Snowy. He lifted an eyebrow at them and they both nodded. Might as well make for the plantation now, at any rate, since this was the time when most activity would be making itself obvious; people would be herding the skinny cattle into the corrals for the night, feeding stock, calling to children . . . odd that they could hear nothing whatsoever from here, save for the tinkle of the pagoda bells.

Devlin woke when he heard the three of them moving out, but just nodded to them and then rolled over, to sleep once more. He knew that they needed to get what sleep they could, when they could, for who knew when they would next meet Japs and be forced to fight, or to hide?

Though their faces were darkly tanned and dirty, they rubbed earth across all visible skin surfaces before setting out, and they made their way to the banana plantation in a series of short rushes, each man going separately, covered by the other two. Long experience had taught them to move silently, to keep low and to watch everywhere for the least movement – movement meant life and life, all too often, meant lurking Japs.

They reached the plantation safely and with plenty of light still to show them what was going on. They were very near the village now, near enough to see the fairytale pagodas, pink and white and roofed with gold leaf, with the bells which tinkled out their guiding notes to anyone passing whenever the breeze blew. They could see the well, and the fields full of crops, and some of the thatched huts, each one built on stilts so that it was clear of the ground. They could even see that each hut was surrounded by its own neatly fenced vegetable patch. Yet where were the villagers? Nothing moved, not a stray dog, not a child, not a hen, picking for grain. If there had been a raid in the vicinity in the past twenty-four hours they might all be down in the shelters, but there had been nothing, and anyway from here one of the shelters could just be seen. The Burmese dug themselves deep air-raid shelters and then roofed the pits with branches, with blocks of solid earth or with bolts of wood. They were useless in the case of a direct hit, of course, but then so was the most sophisticated of Andersons; however, they were safer than the huts when it came to blast, and if a marauding band of Japs passed through a village shooting as they came you stood a better chance of being overlooked or at least not shot by accident if you were in a well-camouflaged underground shelter.

Yet the huts were intact, the fields and crops not pocked with bomb craters or flattened by soldiers' feet, so why were they deserted? Or perhaps not deserted, but why were the villagers so afraid that they had not ventured out of their huts? On the other hand, the villagers could have been driven out so that the Japs could use their homes as a stalking post to search out the last pockets of the British army, trying to make its way towards India. Or it could be a trap – and that was likeliest of all.

No way to find out from the banana plantation though; he would have to walk up to the village and find out the hard way.

When dusk deepened at last there was no need to talk, just an exchange of glances and then the three of them set out. Crawling now, almost flat with the earth, pushing through crops so that there would be no sign, trying not to break or flatten anything. Under the post and wire fence which kept out – or was meant to keep out – the villagers' own scrawny cattle as well as wild animals, across a paddy field, which was mucky work, between tall ears of maize and then into the main village street, thick with pinkish dust. Still not a sound of life – you could not count the faint chimes of the pagoda bells as they caught the night-breeze – and yet no signs of violence either. Nick rose slowly to his feet. They were in the shelter of the huts now, but he had the feeling that they were empty and anyway, standing or lying, if the place had been occupied someone would have shown themselves by now. He gestured and silently the three of them took a hut each and walked into the dark and cool interior.

Nick's hut was empty, but the fire had not been dead long and there was a cauldron over the fire with some sort of vegetable stew in it. Nick's finger only proved that it was blood-heat, which was not surprising, the temperature being what it was, but he did not think the stew had been cooked long. Not today, perhaps, but not many days ago. The most cursory glance round showed every sign that the owners of this hut had left, not in a wild hurry, but knowingly. They had banked the fire, left the stew on, and gone. Where, and to what? Impossible to say, but Nick found his unease growing. He left his hut and rendezvoused with the other men. In the shadow of the next hut Black muttered his own findings.

'Don't understand it, there was cooked rice – these people respect food, they don't just abandon it without good reason.'

'Aye. Reckon they've all left, but should we check 'em out?'

A nod, and the three of them went their ways in the deepening dusk. Nasty work this, now, spine-chilling stuff, because you went alone and in the dark into the interiors with no one at your back in case of trouble. Nick's shirt was sticking to his back with sweat by the time they reached the far end of the village and he would have sworn that his pupils had completely swallowed the iris, so hard had he strained to become cat-eyed in the empty, terrifying dark.

They met in the last hut. Every one had been exactly the same. It was a Marie Celeste village, left deliberately clueless to worry and puzzle whoever came after. The three men stared at each other, the very absence of obvious danger proving more frightening now than a danger which could be seen, touched. Nick found that his hair was prickling upright and sweat-drops the size of farthings were running down his spine, the sensation as nasty as though his shirt were inhabited by big spiders.

'What next, Nick?'

Sergeant Black's voice was softer and slower than usual; Nick knew it was a sign of considerable tension when Johnnie did not crack out his comments, even when he was whispering them.

'There's food and shelter here . . . tools, too. We've got to pick up some stuff to make rafts when we reach the river. The villagers might have left en masse for a wedding in a nearby village – if things like that happen in Burma – or they may have been driven out by Japs who used the place and then left it as the war moved on.'

'No.' Snowy's voice was firm on that one, at any rate. 'Remember the place Ginger christened Jap-pong?'

The other two men nodded. No, Snowy was right on that one, at least. A Burmese village which has been occupied by Japs bears definite traces. Nick felt that he wanted to get out of here and far away, if possible before daylight. He felt that it had to be a trap, that they were probably being watched right now. He felt that the enemy knew his problem, knew how desperately tired the men were, how they would welcome even a few hours spent under a roof with food in their bellies which was not tinned. It was a gamble to stay, and one he was not prepared to take. Better worn out and stumbling with fatigue but alive, than rested – and dead.

'We'll leave. There's a smell about the place for all it's so clean,' Nick said, and saw by his companions' faces that they were relieved by the decision. 'What about the food? Think it's all right?'

'Take the rice,' the sergeant decided. 'There's a good bit in a sack inside the last hut. Let's take it and scarper.'

They did just that, and wasted no time in getting back to the fringes of the forest where the men sat on the ground, packs on backs, ready to move. Nick explained the situation in terse short little sentences; he still wondered whether he was doing the right thing or just acting on impulse, but even so the feeling of wrongness was strong enough for him to refuse rather brusquely to let anyone brew-up. They had made the decision that the place was not safe, it therefore behoved them to put as much distance between the village and themselves as they could, and in the shortest possible time, too.

There were some good-natured moans from men who had been on the move for uncounted days, but they shouldered their rifles and kit, tilted their bush hats to the back of their heads, and set off. No one even thought about marching, they skulked, with two men on their flanks to watch for someone watching the platoon. Each man had learned to treat the landscape as though it seethed with hidden foes and they knew every inch of it was possible enemy territory.

About a mile on the further side of the village they came across one of the deep gorges known as chaungs where, in the rainy season, a stream would tumble and chatter over the rocks on its bed. Now it was dry, but where the stream would have been there were not just rocks. There were bodies. The smell came to them, sweetish and sickening, before they even knew the gorge was there, but once they did they slowed their pace, spread out, and searched for what they knew, but dreaded, they would find.

Johnnie Black found first and signalled the men to get back, into the trees, where he crawled over to them.

'They've wiped out a couple of platoons of the Indian army by the look,' he muttered once they were under cover. 'Our division, too. I saw the shoulder flashes. I'd think the fellows were lured into that village, slaughtered, and then their bodies were dumped here. Monsoon will break in a week or two, then they'll be swept away, not a sign left. The Japs probably forced the villagers to clean up and make it all respectable again and then they drove them out and withdrew into ambush somewhere, until another lot went in.'

'Thank God we didn't fall for it,' Nick said briefly. 'Skirt the chaung, chaps, but after about half a mile we'll drop down into it. All chaungs lead to the river eventually, and if it's a small one and well foliaged we might be able to lie up there during the heat of the day.'

They followed the chaung until midday, rested up until early evening and then set off once more. As dusk was falling they saw, ahead of them, the gleam of water. Presently, they could see that it was a mighty river, too wide to be anything but the Chindwin.

They found a fairly respectable grove of trees and used the axes they had pinched from the village to fell one or two. They went for the smaller timber, not only because of the difficulties of tree-felling if you are not used to it, but because Nick was reluctant to leave the sort of scar on the forest which might be spotted from overhead. Aircraft were always passing and re-passing above them and he had no desire for a quick-thinking pilot to put two and two together and radio his control to send a patrol out because someone had been cutting down trees. No, it was best to do everything as unobtrusively as possible, as though the Japs were everywhere.

Once the wood was felled they decided on four smaller rafts rather than a big one, which would be horribly cumbersome both to carry down to the water's edge and to guide across the fast-flowing waters of the huge river. The men split up into parties of four or five and made the raft that they would endeavour the crossing on, which seemed a fair way to make sure that you put your utmost effort into its safe construction. They had to be made quickly because food was short, though it was a relief to be able to brew-up with river water whenever they had a rest period, but even so they were made as riverworthy as was possible. If they sank the men on board would drown because a raft built for four or five would be incapable of carrying survivors and the river was too wide for any but the finest swimmers to cross and probably too fast-flowing anyway.

The two sergeants took a raft each, Erin O'Toole the third and Nick the last. Nick, Ginger, Ernie and Smiffy would push their craft out first, then everyone would make as directly for the opposite bank as they could. Useless to make plans, but they would do their best to stay together and to make landfall together as well, if possible. The river was the obvious place to watch for escaping troops, which was why they saw aircraft overhead, but it was a very long river and very thickly forested, which was no doubt why they did not see foot patrols. When they were hammering and using the axes the noise, after weeks of near-silence, sounded criminally and foolishly loud, but it could not be helped. They had to cross the river.

Once the trees were felled they worked fast, though Nick supposed that it would be hard luck indeed if the small gap they had made in the tightly curled parsley of the jungle actually showed up from the air. He had flown over jungle and knew that it was boring work, that one's eyes rarely strayed from the sky; only over clearings, where the gold-leafed pagodas stood out so well, did one's attention return to earth.

The rafts were finished at last, and there was nothing to choose between them for good ideas had been pooled, weight had been taken into account when choosing crews, and the results of their hard work looked businesslike and sturdy.

Now it remained to wait for dusk so that they could carry the rafts down to the river, and get them across.

They set off as soon as it was dark and made the river bank when stars were spangling the night sky. A huge, coppery moon cast much too much light on the water. They would stand out like sore thumbs should a wandering aircraft pass overhead. It did not much matter whether it was an enemy or one of their own aeroplanes because whoever it was would undoubtedly think they had come across a raft convoy of troops belonging to the other side and would bomb and machine-gun them accordingly.

However, just as they reached the sandy strip a cloud floated across the moon's face. And then another, and another, until the moonlight was constantly interrupted by cloud shadows. Crouching by the rafts, the men all watched the sky. They wanted to cast off when the sky was overcast so that they had as long as possible beneath the cloud cover for the crossing, and it did seem as though the clouds were coming across more and more often.

They were. After five minutes of not seeing the moon other than fleetingly, Nick pushed out his raft and gestured to the others to do likewise. They got them well out into the stream before climbing aboard since no one wanted to find himself high and dry on the wrong shore. As the current tugged his legs almost from under him, it occurred to Nick that just as they got aboard a Jap patrol might appear, having watched the entire business from some hidden spot, and open fire on them, killing them all with oriental glee at the surprise. It made him hunch his shoulders and squiggle aboard pressed flat to the round logs, but nothing happened. It was just the natural fear of one who had got so far on a long, long journey. It did not seem possible that they were to leave the Jap-infested jungles so easily.

The river, as they tumbled aboard the rafts and did their best to steer them towards the opposite bank, was incredibly noisy after the comparative quiet of the jungle, but the noise was mainly caused by the obstruction of their bodies in the water and the splashing and fuss of getting aboard. Once they were all on the rafts and beginning to paddle towards the distant shore, the river-noise seemed far less obtrusive. The paddles were home-made and each man had one; Ginger, Ernie and Smiffy used their muscle to keep the raft moving across-river and Nick did his damnedest in the stern to see that they steered more or less straight. But despite their best efforts the current would not be conquered and every now and again it waltzed them round in a couple of circles or carried them further downstream than they wished to go.

They must have been nearly halfway when Nick saw Johnnie's raft and Devlin's somehow manage to get into the same whirlpool effect and crash nose to nose so that the kneeling men lurched and swayed like drunks on a Saturday night, sprawling across the logs, cursing and laughing, unable, at first, to get to their knees again and start to paddle for the shore. Both craft got out of the current though, and Johnnie's backed since in the confusion the men were paddling frantically irrespective of each other and of the general direction they wished to take. Backing . . . if you could even pretend to yourself that a raft had a front and a back . . . meant that it just caught the edge of Nick's paddle, so that he stopped digging desperately into the water, and when he stopped the men did not, since they could not see what was coming. There was an awful moment when the raft tilted, then somehow it straightened, and they were heading for the shore once more.

Without Smiffy. He had disappeared into the fast-running water without trace, without even a splash, just going straight under and not reappearing.

'Keep paddling,' Johnnie hissed across the space that separated them. 'We've got Smiffy over here, but just keep going.'

Nick risked a glance and saw a body humped in the middle of the other raft. No one dared let go his paddle to give Smiffy artificial respiration but he had only been in the water a few minutes. If he could last until they reached the shore he would probably be all right.

They were in midstream when the most appalling flash and crash occurred, causing everyone to flinch and cower, expecting to feel the smash of bullets in suddenly cringing flesh at any moment. So they had been seen, then, despite the clouds! Then a flare lit the scene as bright as day and the explosion that followed nearly caused Nick's heart to stop. All round him he saw confusion; men flattened on the rafts, men dropping their paddles, men ducking, grim-faced, and then continuing to dig their paddles into the turbulent water.

Nick was still on his knees, still steering, but now he felt something warm and wet trickle down his face. Blood? And then there was another appalling crash and the scene leapt into brilliance once more, including the face of the man next to him. It was Ginger, his dirty face grinning from ear to ear, his bright orange hair flattened to his head and darkening by the minute. He shouted in a hoarse but muted voice which Nick could just catch above the sudden noise.

'Bit of awright, eh, sir? A good old thunderstorm!'

Nick, agreeing with a grin and a nod, felt about two inches high. Not an enemy attack then, but nature doing its damnedest to help them, or so it would seem. He looked around him, and he saw smiles breaking out as the huge drops of tepid rain began to fall, faster and faster, until they could scarcely see more of each other than dark shapes in the occasional lightning flashes. The storm must be right overhead and they had not heard its approach because of their own noise and the noise of the river.

'Watch out for sandbanks,' someone sang out, no longer bothering to hiss or whisper, for the rain was a curtain against prying eyes, and Nick saw the banks, barring the way to the shore. But it proved a fairly simple matter to beach the rafts on the sandbanks, to drag them down to the shore side and then to relaunch them. Smiffy was shaken and turned upside down until he vomited and then they were off again, into the teeth of the storm, heading for India.

They reached the further bank in good order. Not a man lost, though they were a pretty pathetic sight. Drenched to the skin, with their camouflaging dirt washed off, they dragged their tired bodies on to land, if not dry land, and then watched as the rafts went spinning downriver, no doubt to end up as matchwood somewhere.

'Now we're on the same side as India, I think we can afford to sleep for the rest of the night and all day tomorrow. We'll find somewhere tucked away and hope that the rain lifts by the following night,' Nick shouted above the roar of the storm. 'Pity we're all so bloody wet, but we've almost made it.'

There was not a face without a grin, and the widest was Snowy's. He was the only non-swimmer in the platoon. But it was Devlin who suddenly turned to Nick and grabbed his arm.

'It's not a storm, Nick . . . well, it is, but it's more than that. I reckon this is the monsoon – it's broken at the best time for us!'

'I bet you're right, at that.' Nick led the way up from the bank by the lightning flashes until they found a chaung with scrub growing thickly on the sides of its steep banks and a little river curling and splashing over its stony bed. 'Come on, find a relatively dry spot and get some shut-eye; we'll face tomorrow when it comes.'

Nick woke because the great lantern of the Burmese sun was gonging down on his head. His clothing had dried on him, his mouth tasted foul, and he could smell cigarette smoke, which meant that at least one other member of the platoon was awake. He opened his eyes and glanced round him and even as he did so, something else occurred to him. They had no cigarettes left. No one had been able to smoke for days and days. So if it was not one of his chaps smoking . . .

Then he remembered they were on the right side of the river now, so it might be a patrol of Indian troops, perhaps the Gurkhas, or another division of the 14th Army. He sat up, intending to climb up the bank to spy out the land, then decided that he had better wake the men first, because someone might stir or cry out and if by some freak the cigarettes were being smoked by an enemy . . .

They woke well and silently, but there was a crackling air of eagerness in the way that every eye strained towards the top of the chaung which worried Nick. If it should be the enemy, might that very intensity of feeling draw them to this hiding place, as a magnet draws a pin? Of course, it would only be a small patrol, skulking, as they themselves had skulked, hoping to grab a few prisoners, but the element of height would be theirs if they came over to the chaung and saw the platoon crouched below them.

The breeze was coming towards them for as the smell of tobacco strengthened so did the slight noises. The uninhibited tramp of booted feet, the clink of small arms, the sound of men chattering. It *had* to be friendly troops, probably Indian; he doubted that they were British, the voices seemed a little too shrill for that.

Nick squirmed up through the thickish cover to the lip of the bank and stared. Then, with one neat movement which probably told his men more than words, he slid back, as deep into cover as he could go. He lay utterly still, his face in the dust, scared stiff that if he looked up the light might catch on his face or eyes or teeth and give their position away. He dared not glance round to make sure that his men had read his movements correctly. All he could do was to lie there with his face as far into the sandy soil as he could get it and pray. Don't let them move, God, or sneeze, or glance upwards. Don't let those Japs look down, don't let them leave the track, keep us hidden, dear God, now that we've come so far!

He had seen, over the lip of the chaung, a long column of Japanese troops with heavy artillery towed by mule teams – that was the jangling sound he had heard. The men were not marching either, so much as sauntering. Some were smoking, they were all talking, and the dust they were kicking up must have been visible for several miles.

Even in his lowly position, Nick could not stop the inevitable reflection that things were a lot worse than he had thought, if the Japs could stroll around in long, untidy troop columns on the Indian side of the Chindwin. He had thought they were safe now, or reasonably so, but this proved all too conclusively that such feelings would be the death of them if they continued to trust in the river and the closeness of India. They would have to go on hiding and scuttling and crawling, if need be, until they reached India proper – for longer, if the Japanese had managed to penetrate that country.

The sound of moving men and mules seemed to be lessening and he risked a quick peep upwards, then froze. Damn it to hell, of all the rotten things to happen, the men had been told to fall out, fill their water containers! He could hear the laughter and splashes as men waded out into the shallows and right above him, on the very lip of the chaung, an officer on horseback was sitting his mount, apparently gazing right down at Nick. Even as Nick watched, unable to move or breathe, the officer's hand went to the rifle hanging at his horse's side.

Nick remembered the games of hide-and-seek he had played when he was young. One of his favourite hiding places had been the trough between the asparagus beds and he remembered one particular occasion when he and Val had taken up their places in that trough whilst the others searched.

After a good ten minutes one of the other children had come over to the asparagus fern and stared in. He and Val had been convinced they were spotted and afterwards they confessed to each other that with the conviction had come an absurd desire to leap from cover and admit that they had been found.

Nick had that feeling now. The chap had seen them, of course he had, so why not jump up now before he fired? He could put up his hands and try to surrender, or he could chuck a grenade – there was one at his belt – and see how many he could kill before he was killed himself.

He moved his hand; only a fraction of a fraction, yet it was as though the movement brought back his commonsense, killed the mesmeric feeling that the officer's un-moving gaze had engendered. Keep still, don't breathe, keep *still*!

He kept still. He had been looking towards the officer when he froze and he continued to look, though through eyes closed into the merest slits so that no movement of lash or eyeball would give him away. He told himself how thick the foliage was here, how the sand was churned, not by their footprints but by a thousand animals' paws. The rafts were far away and probably in pieces by now. Such equipment as they still owned was sand-coloured. There was nothing to show the Japs that a platoon of British soldiers lay unbreathing in the chaung, scarcely six feet below the polished hooves of the officer's horse.

The man continued unmoving for a second, still apparently staring at them, then Nick saw his fingers close convulsively on the rifle even as he jerked it up and fired . . . not just one shot, but half a dozen. B platoon continued to lie as they had fallen. Perhaps they did not know that the Jap officer had fired straight across the top of the chaung, though they had most certainly heard the shots. The sound was followed by some shrieks, more splashes and some high, half-scared, girlish laughter. Women? But Nick knew that Japanese soldiers do sound rather like girls when they laugh.

The officer shouted and Nick could hear the soldiers coming up across the strand. Calling and jabbering, they came and Nick waited, heart in mouth, for the officer to send them down into the chaung to search for . . . what? A noise? A flash of light which should not be there? A smell, even?

But they went. They formed up with more jabbering and more giggling and then the sounds grew faint, fainter, fainter, until once more the only noise was the soft rustle of the wind in the trees and the distant river.

Even then it was an age before Nick slithered back up the bank to a point where he could scan the countryside. But he did it at last, taking every possible precaution against booby traps or treachery. It was so difficult to believe that the officer really had neither seen nor sensed them, trapped in the chaung below.

By staring, he could just pick out, very far off, the dust of their departure, and then, scanning the rest of the terrain, he realised what the Jap officer had fired at. He slid down back into the chaung and addressed the men.

'Remember dragging the rafts across those sandbanks? Take a look up there – slow and careful, mind. We don't want any accidents now that we know the Japs are over here in force.'

A wicked-looking crocodile was slumped across the nearest sandbank. Dark blood puddled the sand beneath its snout. No wonder the Japs had come splashing out of the water so rapidly, and had not wanted to linger here, after all. The platoon stared, then grinned and then, as though the sight of the dead beast had released some unbearable tension, everyone began talking at once, telling each other how they had thought it was all up this time, how the officer had been staring straight down into each man's eyes, how . . .

'For Christ's sake keep it down,' Nick said urgently. 'Don't you see what this means? Those Japs weren't bothering to keep quiet, they weren't marching like men in hostile country, they were sauntering like men who know very well there isn't an enemy who can touch them for miles.'

'How bloody wrong they were,' Ginger said feelingly, earning a laugh all round. 'Not that we could have done much – how many did you see, sir?'

'A couple of hundred; too many, anyway,' Nick said briefly. He glanced overhead to where the blazing sun was making its way down the sky. 'We'll move with the dusk, going straight inland and avoiding all human habitation. If you ask me, the Nips are on the verge of invading India.'

'This ain't India yet by a long chalk,' Snowy said stoutly, getting to his feet and shaking dry sand out of his clothing. 'Still, we'll go careful, like. Having got this far, I reckon we all want to reach India alive.'

It took them nearly a month to reach India and know themselves safe. It was a gruelling month and the men that reached safety were thinner and less impeded by equipment. They were all bearded and even Nick, who next to Ginger was the fairest in the platoon, was tanned to a Cherry Blossom darkness. And their number had shrunk by three. Sergeant Black covered the last few miles in a recumbent position since he had been bayoneted through the shoulder, the weapon entering at the back and emerging through the hollow of his arm, but he was still grinning as they carried him to safety.

He had been surprised on patrol, but there had been two of them out and the other man, Ernie, had killed the Jap before he could give the alarm and the platoon had scarpered.

'I dunno where they came from,' Johnnie had remarked at the time, as Nick bound his wound as tightly as he could with strips of torn off shirt. 'But I know where he's gone, and it's even hotter there than bloody Burma.'

When they finally staggered into the frontier post they sent Ginger ahead of them, since despite the sun his hair remained unrepentantly red and his skin, though well-freckled, undoubtedly white. Fortunately the sentry saw that he was British before shooting and not after, so the rest of the platoon somehow managed to drag itself to safety. India, it seemed, had not been conquered by the little yellow men, even though the 14th Army had been forced to evacuate Burma.

The men were debriefed and sent to the hills, where Nick immediately became ill with dysentery and malaria, as though the diseases had decided not to pounce until the miserable specimen had crawled home through the monsoon-sodden jungles. And in his hospital bed he tried to comfort himself with the words he had used to Dave, months and months before. *The English lose every battle but the last*. He knew why they had been chased out of Burma, of course, as British soldiers had been chased out of Singapore and Greece and Western Europe. The enemy had been infinitely superior both in equipment and numbers. The question was why had men been sent into situations which they could not possibly control?

All over the world, he suspected, soldiers, sailors and airmen would be asking that question. It would be a while before they found the answer.

An odd thing happened whilst Nick was in hospital. He was getting better, the malaria which yellowed his skin – or was that the tablets he was fed? – was retreating and the dysentery was long gone. He was feeling weak but very much better, could actually see that he would not die here, as he had feared in the first weeks of his illness, when there was a commotion at the far end of the long ward for fever patients, and a nurse came into the room carrying an enormous pineapple. She was laughing, speaking to another girl over her shoulder as she came and Nick eyed them, enjoying the sight of young girls, carefree, clean, smelling of flowers and of clean hair and not of sweat or disinfectant.

They came level with his bed. The first girl had lovely rich golden brown hair which lay loose on her shoulders in deep waves. He turned a little, to look after her, enjoying the sight of such beautiful hair, very different from the black, shiny locks of the native nurses. Which was how he very nearly missed the second girl, until he heard a soft gasp, and someone sat down on his bed with a thump.

'Nick! Nicky Neyler, is it really you?'

Small, heart-shaped, wide-eyed, with dark curls framing it, a face he had once thought he loved. Vitty's face.

'I can't believe it! Vittorina Magrelli! What on earth are you doing in India? And in *here*, what's more?'

She smiled at him, a smile which showed that her pleasure in this reunion was every bit as great as his.

'I'm a nurse, now, though I'm on a surgical ward so you wouldn't have seen me, you having . . . what, malaria . . . ? Yes, I guessed it, most of the fellows have. Oh, Nicky, it's marvellous to see you. I thought I never would again, or not until the war was over.' She bounced gently on his bed. 'Look, I must go now, Antonia's waiting for me, but I'll be back and we'll tell each other everything.'

She danced down the ward after her friend, waving until she was out of sight.

Chapter Sixteen

'It's for you, Miss Neyler.'

The girl who had hurried across the mess so eagerly to answer the shrilling of the telephone bell held out the receiver towards Maude, who came quickly across to take it. She was expecting a call from Alan, who had been away on a course.

'Thanks, Saunders. Hello?'

A voice which for an instant was strange to her sounded in her ear, making her stomach turn in the most peculiar way.

'Maudie?'

'Who the hell is *that*?'

A chuckle. 'Aw, come off it, you know very well who it is.'

'I thought you were dead,' Maude said cruelly. 'What do you want?'

It had been nearly two years since she had spoken to Bill Richards, and on that occasion they had had a furious quarrel. He was so possessive, so sure of himself, and Maude, two years before, had been neither. Now, at nearly twenty-one and an officer responsible for the well-being of others, she was different, she reminded herself. What was more, she was engaged to Alan, so nothing Bill could do or say could hurt her. A pity that butterflies with elephant feet were dancing around in her stomach, but that was just the shock of hearing his voice after so long.

'To see you. What else?'

'Why? After all, we've existed – rather happily, on my part – for more than a year without so much as a glimpse of each other. Or a word.' She hoped that this did not sound as if she had missed him; it certainly would not sound as though she had counted the days. She had not, anyway, not quite. She only knew that it had been twenty-three months. 'Where are you, anyhow?'

'London. Why don't you ask me where I've been until now?' His voice held a trace of peevishness she was glad to hear. 'You didn't think I'd just ditched you, did you? After what we'd had?'

'The fight, you mean? My dear chap, I can fight with someone and forget them the next moment. Really I can.'

He was obviously determined to aggravate. Instead of flying off the handle or slamming the phone down he chuckled again.

'You can't fool me, my love. Remember that night when . . .'

Maude tried another tack. She infused deliberate patience into her voice. 'Bill, it's nice of you to ring after so long, but I'm awfully busy. Did you just want a chat or have you something to say?'

'I've *told* you. When can we meet?'

'I don't think we can,' Maude said slowly. 'Bill, things change in two years, believe it or not.'

'Ha!' It was a triumphant exclamation. 'Two years now, is it? A moment ago you said a year!'

'Did I?' Curse him for being so quick on the uptake! 'Well, it really doesn't matter that much. I'm engaged to be married, apart from anything else.'

'Does that prevent you from meeting an old friend? All I want to do is tell you what I've been doing these past two years.'

Maude sighed. Heavily and into the receiver, so that Bill would be in no doubt as to how she felt.

'All right. When and where?'

'When are you off? I'm on leave. Do you have a forty-eight or shall I come down to you?'

Maude considered. She did not want Bill down here, that was for sure, because he was quite capable of hanging around and making things difficult for her. Alan was marvellous and very understanding but he had never liked Bill, had blamed the other man for Maude's uncertainty over her feelings when he had first proposed to her, and would not be at all pleased to find that Bill, like the proverbial bad penny, had turned up again. No, it would be better to go up to London, give him the nicest brush-off she could manage, and come back here again. She could do it all before Alan got back off his course, what was more. And if Bill was a gentleman he would take one look at Alan's small sapphire and diamond engagement ring and leave her alone, anyway. Keep off, private property, that little ring said.

The silence had dragged on too long. Bill's voice had an edge to it.

'Maudie? Shall I come down there?'

'No. I'll come up to town. Meet me . . . gracious, it's hard to think of somewhere fairly central that isn't bombed flat . . . meet me by Nelson's column. On Saturday morning, at eleven. That'll give me time to get there.'

'Why? I can come to the station. Or if you're coming up the previous night I can pick you up at your hotel.'

'Bill, it's either Nelson or nowhere. And frankly, in the circumstances, I'd just as soon . . .'

'Nelson, then.' Bill did not sound at all cast down by her briskness. 'At eleven. Bye, Maudie.'

Maude came off the phone wondering whether she had done the right thing. After all, she knew Bill of old, and he could be damned difficult. She knew Alan, too, and he was far too good a man to blame her for Bill's strange attachment, if such it could be called after a two-year gap! But the truth was he hated Bill, because he had come into his own with her during the period of almost suicidal depression which had followed Bill's flinging her down. He had not dropped her, she still felt that he had flung her down, for after their quarrel he had simply disappeared out of her life. Not a word, not a line, just silence. Alan had taken her about, seeming to understand her sudden fits of wild gaiety, her moodiness and even the dreadful, dragging depression. When her defences finally broke, when she wept in his arms and begged him to find out what had become of Bill, he had been marvellous, had even understood that. Bill had been posted to the Middle East. Alan had never pointed out that there was a postal service, albeit an unreliable one, he had just cherished her until she had come to her senses and pushed Bill out of her mind. Or at least to the back of her mind.

If Alan were here, she supposed that he would advise her to leave it alone, to let Bill go on and break someone else's heart. Not because he thought her vulnerable any more, but because he knew how the sight of Bill might rake up old memories, old agonies. Alan was a giver, happy to give, to be a shoulder to weep on. He had never taken advantage of her loneliness, not even when she had practically suggested that they should become lovers. 'When you're ready we'll get married, darling,' he had said. 'Until then it's my pleasure to take care of you.'

Maude knew that dearly though she loved Alan, she did not have the same sort of feeling for him that had nearly torn her apart when she had thought herself in love with Bill. And a good thing too, for if that was a sort of love, it was a terribly uncomfortable sort. And then Bill had staged the row because she would not go to bed with him. Even then she had known that it would be fatal to give in, to let him sleep with her. She did not quite know why, she just sensed that Bill would not value what he possessed as much as the seemingly unattainable. But when she had said no, he had not behaved well. He had told her she was a snob, a tease and a conceited little bitch and then he had walked out on her, leaving her alone in a big hotel with a bill for two dinners about to be handed to her by an embarrassingly understanding head waiter.

When she remembered all these things, and the uneasy peace which she had attained after months of very real suffering, she wondered all over again why she was prepared to reopen the healed wound, let Bill into her life again, no matter how peripherally. Or was she now so indifferent, so armoured against him by her love for Alan, that she could meet him without a qualm?

No. She knew very well why she was meeting him. She hoped that seeing him again after so long would mean that she could see him for what he was – sexually very attractive but not a nice person at all. What was more she knew he would pester her if she refused to see him, perhaps might pester Alan, might turn up here at the station, at her home . . . anything. She was very sure he would not let himself be dismissed without a face-to-face encounter.

'Was it Alan, Maudie?'

Maude had been standing by the telephone for five minutes just staring into space and now Sandy, who was knitting and listening to jazz music on the radio, wanted to know what was happening. Maude blinked herself back into the present and shook her head.

'Sorry, I was miles away. No, it wasn't Alan.'

'No? Who was it then?'

No apology for curiosity was needed between them, but Maude shook her head reprovingly at her friend.

'Curiosity killed the cat! It was a voice from the dead, actually.'

'Maudie, not Bill?' At Maude's half shamefaced nod Sandy whistled her amazement. 'What did *he* want? That type always wants something.'

'Only to meet me.' Maude sat down in the chair she had vacated earlier and picked up her own knitting. 'I told him I was engaged to Alan.'

'Cheeky blighter. I hope you sent him off with a flea in his ear.' There was a pause. 'Maude, love, you didn't agree to meet him?'

'Oh hell, I knew you'd nag. Yes, I did.'

'After what he did to you? You're mad! He damned nearly broke you two years ago. You do know that, I suppose?'

'I know what you mean, but imagine what would happen if I'd just refused to see him. He'd have come down here hellbent on trouble, and I can't involve Alan; he would want to break Bill's neck just for a start.'

'Yes, I see that, but . . . look, do you want me to come along?'

'I think not.' Maude laughed. 'He'd be impossibly rude to you and make us both so uncomfortable that I'd regret having involved you. Bill has no conscience; that's part of his charm, I suppose. Look, I've promised to meet him and I'll go through with it, but I'm a different person, Sandy, you should know that. I'm not the meek little Maude he knew and bullied and I wouldn't go through being in love with Bill again for all the tea in China, no matter how I was tempted.'

'Don't lose sight of that,' Sandy advised shrewdly. 'Because you and Bill had something going . . . perhaps it was just first-love in enormous dollops, I don't know. But I do know Alan never got to you quite like that.'

'No. But Alan's the steady, insidious kind of bloke that creeps into your heart and takes possession of it by kindness, not by storm,' Maude said serenely. 'I'll be quite safe, this time. Bill's day is over.'

'I thought you'd stood me up. I thought . . . well, I remember you as smaller and . . . thinner.'

They stood beneath Nelson's column in bright sunshine with the sky blue overhead. As promising a day as ever I saw, Maude thought to herself, smiling brightly at Bill. He had changed too, but she did not intend to tell him so.

'I've got taller, probably, and more self-confident,' she said briskly. 'As for you, you're just the same.' He was wearing a sports jacket and flannels with an open-necked shirt. The collar of the shirt was outside the collar of the sports jacket and Maude's fingers itched to tuck it inside, where it belonged. Instead, she linked arms and pulled. 'Come on, let's go and have a cup of coffee somewhere and you can tell me what's been happening to you.'

Sitting on opposite sides of a window table with two cups of improbable looking coffee and an even more improbable mock-cream cake between them, Maude summed him up in her own mind. He seemed taller too, but it was only because he was thinner. His chunky look had gone and his belligerence, which usually made itself felt inside the first thirty seconds of being in his company, seemed to have become toned down, gentler. He had let her lead him into the café she had earmarked as suitable without one single grumble, for instance. But it would not do to stare; instead, Maude asked her first question. It was a simple one.

'Well?'

'I got sent out East. I did think about writing, but then things were difficult – we were maintaining our own aircraft and between ourselves I never thought I'd get back alive. I put it off. I've never been good at letters and all the explaining bit was too frightening. What could I say? Leaving you cold like that. Then when I did decide to write I'd left it too long. There wasn't an "in", if you know what I mean.'

'It doesn't matter,' Maude said. She smiled slightly, her eyes fixed on the coffee swirling muddily in her cup. 'I had a pretty awful time around then, myself, so I can understand in a way. There were times when I thought you must be dead, but somehow I never actually could believe it. You didn't seem the type. In the end, Alan came along and I stopped thinking about you, or where you'd gone or what you were doing.'

'Really?' She pretended to concentrate on cutting the cream cake into slices but she could see his quizzical expression change to annoyance at her apparent obliviousness. 'Aw come on, Maudie, if I'd had the faintest idea that I was going to be posted that row would never have happened, but as it had happened I couldn't think how to mend it, not in letters. And anyway, it took us a while to get out there, and then as I said things were tough. I shouldn't have just let it go, I should've written, but that's hindsight. I thought at the time that I was doing the best thing for both of us.'

'And so you were,' Maude said bracingly. 'And now we can be friends and forget the past couple of years.'

'Well, yes, but look, you aren't going to try to shut me out, are you? It'll be as it was, won't it? Maudie, you may not believe me but I've thought of you every day since that day we quarrelled. And wanted you. You wouldn't kid me that you weren't the same?'

Maude held out her hand, with the little ring twinkling on the third finger.

'Getting together again in any sense just isn't possible, I'm afraid. I'm going to marry Alan when the war's over and in the meantime I'm going to be faithful. Sorry, Bill, but there it is. I mean every word of it.'

His expression was dark, the line of his mouth grim. 'And if I had got in touch? Apologised and so on? Would that have made a difference?'

Maude shrugged. 'Who can tell? Probably, though whether . . . anyway, we'll part friends, I hope.'

'I see.' No argument, no bullying, no fuss? He *had* changed! 'Well, let's drink this vile coffee and eat our cake and then we'll go off and see what's happened to London since I saw her last. Any place you'd particularly like to see?'

Maude, drinking up her coffee, was almost fooled, but not quite. Bill had changed, but not that much; he would not give up what he wanted without a struggle and she had known from the moment she heard his voice on the telephone that it was still her, for some weird reason, that he wanted.

'No, nothing particular. I'm an easy sightseer.' She stood up as he did and let him take her hand. 'Off we go, then!'

'You love me still, Maudie, and I love you!' It was late evening and they were sitting in the lounge of Bill's hotel, the only people there. It was dimly lit because of austerity and well blacked out, and the fire in the grate could easily have been mistaken for someone's cigarette end, thrown into the grate to perish, so small was it. But Maude scarcely noticed her surroundings. She and Bill were squeezed into one armchair, and Maude was fighting a game retreat.

'I don't love you, I love Alan.'

'Then why don't you tell me to go to hell? If we part right now, do you know how miserable you'll be? How miserable we'll both be? Come to bed with me, Maudie, stay with me! It isn't just lust, I swear it on my mother's life, it's the only way I'll ever convince you that we're made for each other, that we'll never be truly happy apart.'

'I love Alan, and we're going to be married,' Maude

321

said, as she had been saying all day. The words had ceased to sound even vaguely convincing after such dogged repetition. 'I'm going to spend the night with my friends in Bloomsbury.'

'Look, love, if you come with me now and still say you're in love with Alan and going to marry him in the morning, then I'll leave you alone and never bother you again, I swear it on my mother's l –'

'Shut up. I happen to be rather superstitious,' Maude said. She had no wish to feel uneasily responsible if Bill's mother should take it into her head to drop dead. 'Can't you see that I'm well aware you have some sort of attraction for me and that I also know it's based entirely on sex! That, dear Bill, is all very well for a bit of fun, but it's no basis for breaking up what I'm sure will be a very happy marriage. I might enjoy it no end, I shouldn't be surprised if I did, you already know that I enjoy your kisses and cuddles, but I shall still know Alan's the man I want to spend the rest of my life with, and I shall have cheated on him. How can I explain that I slept with you to get you out of my system?'

'You don't have to explain to anyone. I'll make sure you don't get pregnant, and . . .' he stopped talking and stared at her, his eyes suddenly searching. 'Maudie? Are you trying to tell me you're still a virgin?'

Maude felt blood sweep across her face and neck, hot as fire. She knew only too well how she blushed and guessed that through her fine, ash-blonde hair her scalp would be as scarlet as the rest. Useless trying to hide her red cheeks, but how could he be so . . . so crude?

'I wasn't trying to tell you anything,' she said coldly. 'I'm going.'

She stood up and he followed suit, then took her in his arms. This time, his kisses were harder to resist, because she felt vulnerable, foolish, but after a few moments she tried to draw back and then, as suddenly and unexpectedly as it was possible, the longing for him which had never entirely been banished swept over her, making it madness not to stay close, to give. She lay weakly against him, and when the tingling magic started she made no effort to defend herself and push him away. Why not go through with it, she asked herself, with the remaining shreds of sanity which still lingered. He had met her for one reason and one reason only and once he had got what he wanted he would probably never trouble her again.

He led her, unresisting, up to his room, locked the door and began to undress her. Maude shivered beneath his hands but made no effort to escape or to argue. She would never be free from Bill until she had discovered that he was just a greedy and selfish lover, as he was a greedy and selfish person. He wanted her for the worst reasons and if she was being honest – and she was – it was for the worst reasons that she wanted him. It was, quite simply, lust without love, without respect, without admiration, even. So they would purge themselves of their unworthy emotion – if it could be termed an emotion – and then they would be cured of their madness, free to go their separate ways.

When she was naked she lay on the bed, watching him as he stripped off his own clothes. He had not taken his eyes off her since they entered the room and he did not do so now. Maude thought he looked nice with nothing on; broad-shouldered, broad-chested, yet slim; muscular where he had once been chunky. She supposed, from his gaze, that he thought she looked nice too, but then he was kneeling on the bed, looming over her, and it occurred to her for one quick, frightening moment that if this was what she thought it was, then she should not feel like this; so at ease with him though they were naked in each other's company for the first time. Not just body-naked either, she thought as he began to smooth his hand tremblingly along the line of her hips, but soul-naked. His mouth and eyes were gentle; it was as if with his clothes he had shed the old domineering, womanising Bill. Could this man who touched her as though she was infinitely precious to him, whose eyes on her were tender, could this be grabbing, guzzling, greedy Bill?

In the same thought, she knew that she, too, had shed her defences. Her sharp tongue was stilled, her defensive movements were quieted, her shyness and indifference gone, cast unregretted into the void. Instead she lay with him, pleasured by him, eager both to please and to be pleased.

His possession, when it came, was a crescendo of feeling which made her cry out, clutch him and admit for the first time in her life that she loved . . . loved . . . loved him! She could not have held back at such a moment though death had been the penalty for truth.

Later, he cradled her softly in his arms and she dived into sleep as one dives into warm water and slept without a dream until morning.

'Maudie rang. She sounded ever such a long way away, but she's coming home for a few days. I love having her home, the dear girl!'

Beryl sounded enthusiastic, but there was something more. She was bright-eyed, pink-cheeked, as though she had heard good news. Tina, eyeing her shrewdly, wondered what was biting her daughter-in-law. She, too, adored having Maude home, especially if she brought her fiancé with her. Every member of the family and all their friends approved of Alan and thought Maude a lucky girl. He was so nice, so handsome, such good fun – and, thought Tina nastily, so *English*! With the city full of American servicemen, at least half of whom seemed set on bringing Cara to ruin, it was nice to see a decent Englishman being properly appreciated.

'Lovely. Is she bringing Alan? What time will they arrive? Did she say?'

'Yes, she said "we", so she's bringing Alan. Well, she would be, since . . .' Beryl stopped, blushed a yet deeper shade of pink, and ploughed on. 'Mind you, it may not be for long, because . . . oh dear, I think I've said enough.'

Tina turned ostentatiously away from her daughter-in-law and continued to water her pot plants, humming under her breath. I give her three minutes, she thought. And in fact it was less than a minute later when Beryl spoke again.

'I really don't think I should say anything, but, Mama, Maudie said they were on their honeymoon – I think she said that though the line was bad . . . it could have been holiday she said, but she sounded so bubbly . . . Anyway, I do think they've been and got married.'

'Well, my first granddaughter married and me not there! But I know young people these days don't set much store by white dresses and pomp and ceremony.' Tina carefully cast into the back of her mind her own elopement, the lonely marriage in Inverness, the yellow silk of the teagown she had worn as a wedding dress. 'In wartime, young people act on impulse. She did say that Alan might be sent abroad, so I daresay they're snatching what time they can have to be together.'

'Yes, I suppose you're right, but it would have been nice to have a wedding here,' Beryl said wistfully. 'Doesn't it seem ages, Mama, since we had a real party at The Pride?'

'Very true.' Tina finished the last plant and turned towards the doorway. 'I'll tell Ruthie there are two extra for lunch and perhaps we could run to a special pudding? There's lots of nice soft fruit in the beds.'

*

The small sports car roared away down the drive, and the family, who had somehow managed to keep smiles on their faces throughout Maude's visit, allowed themselves to relax. Beryl immediately looked as though she were about to burst into tears, Tina looked angry, Desmond and Ray puzzled, the children released from unbearable curiosity. They turned, with one accord, to Tina.

'Mama, what on earth . . .' 'Gran, I thought you said . . .' 'Auntie, why did they . . .' 'Tina, you could have knocked me down . . .'

Tina turned as the car disappeared from view and stalked majestically back into the hall, followed by her family. Once the door had been closed behind the last child, she turned and faced them.

'Well! And I thought she was such a sensible girl! She's gone and married the wrong man! And of course you, Desmond, had to go and put your foot in it, to say nothing of you, Rachel!' She glared at her sister. '*I hope Alan likes stewed lamb*,' she mimicked crossly. 'Honestly, Ray, of all the names to choose . . .'

'It was a natural mistake,' Ray said ruefully. 'But I'm sorry, the silence did rather speak! And Des was a lot worse than me, weren't you, Des?'

'No! Well, a perfectly natural mistake. After all, no one told me what had happened and so when I walk into the room and see a perfect stranger there, I naturally assume . . .'

'That Ray's brought a friend round to meet Maudie and her new husband,' Tina said, glaring at him, a tiny, grey-haired autocrat with eyes bluer than the skies despite her years. 'Why didn't you hold your tongue?'

Desmond, despite himself, began to grin.

'Well, Mama, if you must know, I nearly said something a bloody sight worse; I nearly asked him if he was Alan's best man!'

The family stared at him, goggle-eyed. Tina recovered herself first.

'You didn't! Well then, we haven't done so badly as we might have. But that doesn't change the fact that the poor child's married to that fellow, so there's nothing we can do about it. No use trying to talk her out of it or wondering what she sees in him, it's a *fait accompli*, damn it. And that reminds me, Desmond, don't ever let me hear you swear in my company again.'

Ray's lips twitched, but Desmond knew when to be humble and when to tease.

'I'm sorry, Mama; it must have been shock.'

'He's probably very nice . . .' Rachel began half-heartedly, to be interrupted rudely by her daughter. Coppy was still not walking as well as the doctors hoped, but she had nothing wrong with her critical faculties!

'He's awful, Mummy, absolutely awful. Rude and pushy and sneering; I can't imagine why such a darling as Maudie married him.'

'Maudie isn't always a darling,' Eddy put in. 'Cooer, she can whack and scream when she's in a bate. Perhaps she scared Alan off.'

There were outraged howls at this brotherly remark; the family valued their Maude, even Em, a stout defender of her brother as a rule, casting him a reproachful look.

'Alan wouldn't, he was ever so nice. I didn't like that Bill either, I thought he was sarky. I hate people who're sarky to little girls like me.'

'Well, love's a funny thing,' Beryl said feebly, endeavouring to give her daughter some support at least. 'I daresay Bill's a wonderful person really. It was just that we were expecting Alan, and of course Bill was probably shy. There are so many of us and Maudie said he's an only child . . .'

'Love?' Tina snorted, her eyes flashing. 'She's no more

in love with that dreadful man than I am, and I think he's totally horrid and abominable. She's infatuated!'

A chorus of agreement broke out amongst the adults and Tina led the way back into the kitchen where Ruthie, her mouth set tight, had finished the washing up and was making economy scones with dried egg and grated carrot. She looked up when they entered and heaved a sigh, then picked up her rolling pin and flattened the scones a little more.

'Well, Ruthie? What did you think of him?'

'I've met that type before,' Ruthie said heavily. 'He'll be very attractive to women, there's no doubt of that. But they don't make a girl happy, that type. Maudie's too good for him and no error. She'll live to regret it.'

Coming from Ruthie, who was never one for rash and unconsidered judgements, this was condemnation indeed. Tina slumped down in a chair, then straightened her poker back and glared at her assembled relatives.

'Very well, we all think the girl's made a mistake, but that doesn't mean we've all got to sit around wringing our hands and lamenting. Beryl, put the kettle on! I need a strong cup of tea!'

In the little sports car, with the roof wound down so that they could enjoy the summer sunshine, Maude and Bill watched the Norfolk countryside unfold before them. Now and then, as if for reassurance, Maude touched Bill's arm and he, quick to respond, patted her knee.

'It wasn't easy, was it? Meeting my people, I mean. I wonder what your parents will think of me? After all, you were a great shock to mine since I was a fool and forgot to tell them I hadn't married Alan, but a bloke they'd never even heard me mention. But it's a bit different for yours. What sort of girls have you been bringing home, Bill?'

Bill shrugged. 'My sort. Not your sort.'

'And just what do you mean by that? Floosies? Bits of fluff?'

'I haven't been home for two years, remember. Before that it was what you could loosely class as good-time girls who happened to be good lays as well, I suppose.'

There was a short silence whilst Maude looked speculatively at his profile.

'And what would you loosely class me as, pray?'

Bill grinned lopsidedly and shot her a quick, rueful look.

'I didn't marry any of the others, remember. You're different. You belong to me.'

'That's nice. I think. I wish you had some brothers or sisters though. It wouldn't be so important for your parents to love me if you had brothers or sisters.'

Silence fell between them. It was a comfortable silence, even though it was tinged with Maude's very real apprehension. They reached the outskirts of the town and Bill drove through it and down a narrow street, where he brought the car to a halt outside a narrow house. Maude, suddenly stiff with fright, sat where she was until Bill came round and opened her door, taking both her hands and pulling her out to stand beside him. He put his arm round her shoulders and led her towards the front door.

'Here we go, then. Chin up, sweetheart!'

Together, they waited for an answer to Bill's knock.

'Big blow, Bobby! No, darling, not too much spit or no one will want to try your cake.' Jenny turned to the children standing watching her small son endeavouring to douse the solitary candle on his cake. 'Better give him some help, girls, before he takes it literally into his own hands! Rosie, be a dear and move the trifle before Marianne dives head-first into it.'

Marianne, a big schoolgirl now, gave her mother an indulgent look and moved the trifle herself, then leaned forward and gave a huge blow which sent the candle flame into instant oblivion and caused Bobby to crow with pleasure.

'There you are, Bobby, no more candle. Now we can eat your birthday tea! Auntie Marjory and Uncle Dan will come out soon with the hot sausage rolls.'

Tea was being eaten, on this glorious September day, in the orchard and though like most country people the Rileys saw no sense in eating out of doors, they knew how the children loved it and so made allowances for the odd tastes of townies. Indeed, barely had Jenny got Robert's bib in position and Marianne and Rose demurely seated than the others began to come out. The landgirls had been working in the harvest field, but Jenny had given herself an afternoon off to help with her son's first birthday tea. Marjory was a wonderful woman, but Jenny did want to contribute something to the festivities, and because Marjory was a wonderful woman she had understood, and had allowed Jenny to make and ice the cake almost without a word of advice, despite the fact that cooking in the Aga was not much like the cooking Jenny had done previously. And the cake had turned out beautifully, so that was all right!

'Well here we are then, all ready and raring to go,' Jenny said, when the sausage rolls were steaming on their plate and everyone was seated. Marjory and Dan had deck-chairs since Marjory said it ill became her years – or her knees – to try to fold her bulk down on to the grass, but everyone else just sat around, taking sandwiches and sausage rolls and talking as they ate. Roy was still at school with Rosie, though a couple of classes higher and at the boys' school and not the girls', and Ruby had proved to have other characteristics beside meekness. She had her own baby bouncing on her knee, a mere month younger than his playmate whose birthday was being celebrated.

Sue was engaged, though her fiancé was not present since he was a sailor and away for long periods at a time. Otherwise, things were very much as they had been throughout the time that Jenny and her children had lived at the farm.

Rose was handing cake when someone called from the farmyard; a man's voice, deep and familiar. Yet it could not be Simon, Jenny thought, jumping to her feet on the words with a hand flying to her throat. No, it could not possibly be Simon!

Rosie scooped Robert into her arms and flew across the grass towards the gate with Marianne hot on her heels. Jenny was just behind them, and she reached the farmyard in time to see Rose flinging herself at Simon, Simon fielding his son and Rose, and a dark, rather saturnine looking young man reach for Marianne and lift her up to hold her out to the pale, beautiful blonde who stood very close to him. For a moment she could not believe her eyes. Simon was here, without a word to her, and could that possibly be Maude? If so, the dark young man must be her new husband!

Jenny began hugging and kissing Simon, hugging Maude, and then, belatedly, turning to the young man. She was smiling.

'Forgive me. It was such a surprise to see them. I didn't even know Simon was coming this way! It *is* Bill? Yes, I thought it must be – I've heard about you, of course, though I'm afraid merely as Maude's husband.'

'That's good enough,' Bill said gruffly. 'Beautiful children you have – the eldest is so like Simon it's almost laughable.'

There was a tight little silence before Jenny assured him, laughing, that the likeness was purely coincidental; that Simon and Rose were not related at all so far as they were aware.

'Really?' The dark eyes were suddenly inscrutable and Jenny felt her hackles rising. It was so infuriating that everyone took Rose for Simon's daughter, yet no one ever remarked on the likeness between herself and the little orphan. It was only colouring, of course; Simon and Rose both had that combination of very dark blue eyes and almost black, curly hair that drew the eye, as well as the very clear skin. And they had certain ways in common, if you could call it that. Jenny tried not to notice, but it was impossible not to, when you loved both the people involved. Simon smoothed down an eyebrow when he was deep in talk and he stroked his chin with the knuckle of his left index finger when he was puzzled. So did Rose, but of course she adored Simon. She must have noticed these small idiosyncrasies and copied them, that was all.

'Come and share the birthday tea,' Rose was urging them, and all at once they were sitting down on the grass under the trees and eating and talking and laughing, and Jenny was perfectly happy and she could see that all was well with Maude, who watched Bill all the time, and who kept touching him as though to make sure he was still there.

Simon explained that he was down for a couple of days and had suggested to Maude that she might spend a day or so in Devon, and then the three of them could share the car and the petrol. Maude had very sportingly agreed, considering that it had meant taking Simon with them on the last little bit of their honeymoon.

'Are you on your honeymoon?' Sue asked, giggling, and Bill cast her a smouldering glance and said that he was. Marianne, wide-eyed, asked what a honeymoon was and Simon, who was marvellous with the children, began to explain to both the girls since Rose also admitted ignorance.

Simon, explaining with great delicacy despite Sue's

attempts to be more frank, was betrayed into stroking his chin with his knuckle; and Rose, honestly puzzled by the contradictory remarks made by Simon and Sue, stroked her chin with her knuckle. And just at that moment, Jenny *knew* . . . So, she thought with a flash of intense dislike, did Maude's new husband, and he found the knowledge amusing . . . So, though Jenny did not know it, did Marjory Riley. Even the landgirls would speculate afterwards.

The only people totally oblivious, of course, were Simon and his daughter.

Chapter Seventeen

SUMMER 1944

Jenny was almost asleep when she heard their train called at long last. Somehow she managed to wake herself up, get to her feet and shepherd the children across the platform to where the train stood. It was hours late, she was too confused and weary to work out how many hours, but at least it seemed that it was about to leave now.

The children were equally worn out of course. Rose was holding Marianne's hand and carrying a bulging hold-all, Marianne was lugging an earless, eyeless teddy bear as well as a carrier stuffed with odds and ends and Jenny herself had Bobby, two more carrier bags and the big brown suitcase. This she dragged along the platform, careless of the fact that she was probably ruining it completely, until she reached the steps leading into the nearest carriage. Here, temporarily beaten, she stopped to consider how to get her motley crew aboard, but she need not have worried. A soldier took Bobby and both carrier bags, an airman hefted her case, and a motherly looking WAAF helped the little girls aboard and then gave Jenny a conspiratorial smile.

'Don't worry, love, the fellers'll save you a seat. Just you git yourself aboard.'

The WAAF was right; someone had saved her two seats, a corner one into which she herself immediately slumped and another, which the girls could share. Jenny, thankfully settling in, saw that her case, the bag and the paper carriers were already aloft in the overhead rack, that

Bobby, restored to her arms, was still sleeping peacefully and that the little girls were both beginning to nod again, and then the train gave a lurch and a snort and they were leaving Liverpool Street station at long last.

Jenny leaned back and closed her eyes. What a day! It had begun so early, too, with the Rileys waking them at four, getting them a huge breakfast, and driving them down in the trap to the little station. Goodbyes were hurriedly said in the misty dawn because the cows still had to be milked and the pigs had to be fed on time, even though a way of life was being torn apart by their departure.

For the Rose family had left the farm today for good. Standing on the platform after the Rileys had gone, breathing in the country smells mixed with the railway ones, Jenny could scarcely believe that this was the end of it all; of the hard work and the idyllic pleasures of a Devonshire farm. In future, she would be working to build up the company which Simon and Nick had made, she would be bringing up her children, teaching them to be the sort of people she could be proud of. But never again would they know the kind of happiness they had known over these past years.

But Jenny knew that once the need to stay on the farm was gone, so her pleasure in the life would fade. Conscience told her that she should go back to The Pride, not just for holidays as they had done in the past, but in order to start getting the children used to a more normal way of life. School, here in Devon, had been dictated by the weather, by the state of the harvest, by all sorts of things which would not affect it in Norwich or London. Gaps in their education had been large, though Rose and Marianne were bright children and did not seem to have suffered very much for it. There were other things, however, which they were missing, as Sarah had told her daughter-in-law when she had last written.

'Nearly all the children are living at The Pride now,' she had said. 'They're getting to know each other so well, in a way which may never come again. Cousins sharing bedrooms, huge gangs of Neyler-connected children setting off to collect wastepaper or to dig for victory. All at the same schools, all with one aim – to win the war. And things are easier now that the bombing is over; you could come back, Jenny, without feeling you were letting either Simon or the children down.'

Sarah and Con both accepted Rose completely, despite the fact that Simon and Jenny had only actually taken the big step of adopting her eight months previously. Simon had jumped at the chance and so, though for a different reason, had Jenny. That one moment of certainty on Bobby's birthday had been replaced by doubts soon enough, but, as she had suspected it would, the very fact that Rose was now officially theirs had made such doubts and questions immaterial. Rose was their daughter now, a tower of strength, a loving and giving child who would immeasurably enrich their lives.

Jenny had agreed with Sarah that it was right for her to go back, and in many ways she was looking forward to being with the family again. Yet there was another part of her which dreaded relinquishing her free and independent life. The mushroom mornings when sunrise saw you out in the meadows with the sun the wrong way round and the shadows long and blue on the dew-spangled grass, finding the little white cushions and the bigger, brown-based umbrellas, picking them with care, putting them gently into the basket, proud of your skill in collecting this bounty. Afternoons in the harvest field when your nose peeled and your hands blistered and your muscles screamed from strain when you finally finished the work. Evenings when you milked the cows, ate a huge tea and then walked up'n over, to meet friends in the tiny inn, drinking cider in the garden with a rose loosing rich, scented petals on to your head and shoulders, watching the colours sucked from the sky as night came, marvelling at the velvet dark pricked with a thousand stars.

She remembered other days, too. Days when you walked along the lane through ankle-deep puddles, the water richly brown and muddy around your Wellingtons, the rain pattering on your cape. Seeing fat snails out on every broad-leaved blade of grass, passing the old, ivy-covered wall where they lived, and parting the tough stems to look inside at the cobwebbed cracks where the rain never seemed to penetrate. A secret world, that wall . . . a wren lived beneath the curtaining ivy, woodlice curled in some of the lesser cracks, and bats hung in the miniature cave where missing stones had made sufficient room.

There were snowy days, too, and days when gales whipped the blackberry brambles across your cheek so that the scar was there for life. Taking a great cushion of hay off the top of the stack, whirling it away on its harsh breath, the wind could be jolly or cruel; an opponent or an enemy.

Then there were the animals. The feel of a horse's muscles rippling between your knees as you rode it bareback up from the pasture, the smell of the horses in their stalls, the touch of a velvet muzzle moving hopefully across your open palm. And the cows' rubbery teats, their sweet breath, feeding a calf in a bucket of warm, watered milk, feeling your fingers taken by the baby thing, gently sucked.

Others, Jenny knew, had not been so lucky. Simon and Nick, both in their different ways battling to try to drive the Japs out of Burma, one in the air and the other on the ground, said little about the pleasures of their situation, though Simon did wax lyrical, from time to time, about temples and ancient cities, hip-waggling dancers and extraordinarily beautiful half-caste girls. Jenny liked to think that the cousins were partners in war as they had been in peace, both striving for the same end though both attacking it from their very different angles. She could tell that Simon, in the air, had a more pleasant task than Nick, on the ground, but it was nearly over now, she was sure of it. Soon they would come home and start their ordinary lives once again.

Thinking about the car-hire firm which the cousins had run brought Jenny's mind back to their arrival, two hours late after an engine breakdown, at Paddington earlier that day. And halfway across the station forecourt the sirens had started and an elderly porter had shepherded them into the nearest shelter.

'That's the doodlebugs,' he told them, almost proudly it seemed to Jenny. 'Ole Hitler may be done for, but 'e's givin' it to poor ole London afore he goes under. When the engine stops that means it's fallin', and you're best hunderground.'

When they eventually reached Liverpool Street, it was to find that trains were being delayed by a doodlebug, which had landed on lines running into the station. That was why they had been forced to sit on that hard bench for hours and hours, snoozing and waking, until a train could get through to take them the rest of the way to Norwich.

Now, actually on what would have been the last leg of their journey, it struck Jenny that there was absolutely no chance of the family meeting them at the station, as had been originally planned. Sighing, she listened to the train's tickety-boosh, tickety-boosh, and reflected that when they did arrive at Norwich Thorpe, instead of being able to relax and hand over responsibility to Uncle Des or Uncle Con, she would be forced to make phone calls, or whistle up a taxi or even knock up a hotelier, since it would be nearer breakfast-time than suppertime before they arrived, judging by their present pace and their extremely overdue departure. The children, no matter how they might snooze now, were going to be very weary indeed by the time she got them into bed.

She glanced down at them. Bobby slept still, rosy-cheeked, even snoring a little because his nose was pressed against her once white blouse. He was secure enough in her arms, and next to them Marianne and Rose slept too, leaning together like a couple of small, tipsy bookends. Next to Rose a tanned sailor slumbered and next to him, an equally tanned soldier. Opposite there were a couple of WAAFs and a Wren and last of all an elderly civilian, grey-haired, grey-faced, with a paper bag on his knee into which he surreptitiously dipped from time to time. His sweet ration? At any rate, he was the only one, apart from herself, who seemed to be awake.

Jenny closed her eyes. The dim blue bulb overhead gave out only the most subdued radiance and the windows were papered over save for a diamond-shaped cut-out in the middle through which one could, in theory, see the stations as they glided past. Jenny sighed and let herself relax. Everyone else slept; why should she not get a little rest as well? The sounds of the engine and the occasional clickety clack as they crossed points became soothing, soporific. Jenny slept.

She awoke, abruptly and rather frighteningly, certain that someone had said her name. She opened her eyes and sat up, not knowing for an instant where she was or why; scarcely who, even, since she imagined herself, for a split second, unmarried and in bed in a mountain hut where she had once been taken by the school on a climbing holiday in Scotland.

But she was still in the carriage, still jolting

339

Norfolkwards, still surrounded by sleepers. Everyone around her slept; even the civilian had crumpled his paper bag in one hand and his head rocked with every motion of the train. Yet . . . yet she felt that she was being watched, that she had been deliberately awoken by someone in this carriage and that the waker was observing her now. It was an uncanny and rather unpleasant sensation.

She looked hard at the faces opposite, since it could scarcely be either of the men on her own side of the carriage. The elderly man? No, she was very sure his unattractive sleep was genuine. The WAAFs? One had a round, fat face and pouting lips and was sleeping and snoring, and anyway Jenny was sure she did not know the girl from Adam. Or from Eve. The other had a weasel-face and was very spotty and her greasy hair was bundled untidily into her cap. Both girls, now that Jenny thought about it, looked as though they had slept not one night but a dozen in their blue skirts and jackets and grey stockings. Poor things, they must be terribly tired to sleep with such adandon.

The Wren, however, was quite different. She was enchantingly pretty, for a start, with ash-blonde curls clustered beneath her little cap. Her skin was clear and she slept – if she slept – neatly and attractively, her mouth closed, her light lashes lying demurely on her smooth, pale cheeks. What was more, now that Jenny was concentrating on her, she realised that she *did* know the other girl. Was she an ex-schoolmate? Or a neighbour? A friend of Val's? One of Martin's old girlfriends?

Jenny stared and stared, at the shapely figure in the smart, uncreased uniform and at the lovely little face. She *did* know her. It must have been that, subconsciously, she had recognised the girl earlier, tied her in with her own past, and then the moment she let go her subconscious had woken her not unfortunately with the Wren's name but with her own maiden name, the person she had been when she had known the little blonde.

After a few moments' perusal, though, Jenny saw the Wren's lashes stir on her cheeks and it occurred to her that one could wake someone through staring, so she decided to carry on wondering with her eyes closed.

It was, of course, fatal. Within moments, she slept.

Pixie Hopwood had recognised Jenny the moment the older girl got into the train, and had thought seriously that she ought to move away into another carriage until it occurred to her that Jenny was most unlikely to recognise her. After all, they had only met once, at that tennis party more than twelve years ago. Simon had invited her to the party and now she looked at Jenny's children and was sure all in a moment that they were Simon's children, too. The boy was the image of him, rosy, handsome, and the girls, who both had their heads together and their faces half-hidden, had his colouring. It would be nice in a way to ask about Simon, to discover what he was doing and how he was getting on. She had always had a soft spot for her very first lover and the father of her only child.

However, the fact that she had deserted her daughter held her back. No one knew, there could be no disgrace in the fact, but it was probably the only part of her very full and exciting life that Pixie regretted. If only she had known! But she had left on the spur of the moment, run away with Fred leaving little Hazel with her friend Elsie, fully intending to send for the child as soon as she was settled.

When Hazel was two Pixie had married an acrobat named Milton Mackay – might have stuck with him, too, had he not fallen off his trapeze one night when a trifle the worse for drink and broken his neck. That sad loss had sent her back to her friend Elsie Threadgold, and it was there that she'd met Fred, another girl's boyfriend. She'd run away with him only to discover that he was also a third person's husband, which meant, he told her, that in order to marry they would have to leave the country.

Pixie was willing. She thought it a great adventure to go to Canada with Fred so that he could bigamously marry her there. However, it had not turned out like that at all. Fred drank and when he was drunk he beat any woman within arm's length. Pixie was not the type to stand for that sort of behaviour and she left him, stealing sufficient money for a train ticket to another city, and there she got work, since she liked this large, generous new country that fate had landed her in and decided that she would not return 'just yet', but would send for Hazel.

Three months after arriving in Vancouver, however, she met and married a refrigerator salesman. He was fifteen years her senior and the steadying influence she felt she needed – only unfortunately he was also grimly boring and terribly self-righteous. Pixie, who had changed her name to Stubbs when she thought she was going to marry Fred, had married as Lynette Landry – she had found work as a chorus girl which called for an elaborate name – and when she decided that her refrigerator salesman was a mistake she simply changed her name back to Mackay and took another long train journey, this time to New York.

Once in New York, she was earning for herself again and so began saving up to send for Hazel. She was a talented dancer with natural charm and bounce and it did not take her too long to save up the money, but though she sent it off, care of Elsie, of course, her daughter did not come and neither was her letter acknowledged in any way. Pixie began to realise the years that had passed since she had left Hazel with Elsie, and, for the first time in her life, she worried. When war was declared in 1939 she decided that she must go home.

But it was easier to go home than to find a child who had been left with someone like Elsie Threadgold. Blank stares met her in the haunts which had once known Elsie well. She had left there, oh, years before! It was impossible, of course, to go to the authorities; Pixie did not intend to get into trouble for abandoning her daughter, let alone for the fact that someone to whom she owed money might catch up with her if she made enquiries through official channels. So Pixie worked in the London theatres all through the Blitz and continued to ask questions.

Then she got her answer, because Elsie was killed in one of the underground disasters in 1940; questioned as to whether she had a child with her at the time she was told that Elsie had had several. And Pixie stopped looking for her daughter.

She had cried for Hazel longer than she had ever cried for a man, and then she had gone home one weekend to her parents in their little cottage in Blofield. Not a word did she say about dead children, bigamous marriages or refrigerator salesmen, though she had to admit to the acrobat since she seemed to have saddled herself with his name. Otherwise she just told her mother a convenient fairy-story, which was accepted happily enough, and slipped back, for one whole weekend, to being Pixie Hopwood at home again.

But she had not the slightest desire to stay there. She just wanted home as somewhere she could return to when the going got rough. And after two whole days of placid talk, she had told her parents that she was going to see if she could join the Wrens. Nice uniform, lots of sailors, and office work.

She did it with ease. Bright and attractive, she passed an intelligence test and then told the officer examining her that she was quite a good shorthand typist. This was true, since Mr Refrigerator Salesman had taught her speed writing and had bought her a portable typewriter so that she could do his books at home, and this training now stood her in good stead. She became a personal assistant to a high-ranking naval officer, persuaded a boyfriend to teach her to drive and was now very nearly indispensable.

Sitting in the rain opposite the now soundly sleeping Jenny, Pixie found herself wanting to wake the other girl up so that they could talk. After all, Hazel was dead, Jenny was obviously Simon's wife, and she had taken the keenest and liveliest interest, once, in the Rose and Neyler families and their doings. It would be so nice to know about Simon! She hardly ever thought of him, to tell the truth, as Hazel's father, just as a friend from her far-off childhood, who had admired her and treated her well. That was why she had breathed Jenny's name, earlier – so that Jenny would say 'Why, it's Pixie, isn't it?' and they could talk. But the moment Jenny's dark lashes had lifted she had taken fright and closed her own eyes firmly. No, it did not do to unbury the past.

It occurred to Pixie, fleetingly, as she composed herself to doze once more, that had things been different the child leaning against the small girl might well have been her own daughter. But it was no use wishing. She, too, began to dream. There were two men interested in her at the moment, either would make a good husband; she would lie here and consider whether to make Paul or Jimmy the happiest man in the world. The future, after all, was what really mattered. And she was quite glad, really, that Jenny had managed to catch Simon. She had certainly tried hard enough!

At Holt everyone woke because one of the WAAFs and the soldier and sailor left the train and in the resulting bustle, with luggage being brought down from racks, overcoats donned, goodbyes said and scarves pulled from beneath fellow passengers, it was impossible to continue to sleep. Even Bobby mumbled awake, began to cry and was soothed with the remnants of a bottle of blackcurrant drink which Marjory Riley had made before they left. Jenny was so busy with her responsibilities that she scarcely thought about the Wren, so she did not notice how totally the other girl was taken up with Rose. Rose, on waking, had turned full-face to the blonde for the first time, and the Wren could not take her eyes off the child's small countenance.

Jenny might be preoccupied, but Rose could not help noticing. There was something about the fair-haired lady in uniform who looked at her so hungrily. It was someone she had once known, she was sure of it, only who? A stage-lady, she thought suddenly, for Mum had brought home lots and lots of stage-ladies, and they had all been very pretty and quite a lot of them had been very blonde as well.

This solution only half-satisfied her, however, for the *way* the lady stared was rather worrying. It made Rose long to say, casually, of course, that she was Jenny and Simon's girl now, their very own daughter, and no one could take her away from them. Not that this lady was likely to want to do that . . . but she did stare so!

Presently it occurred to Rose that the staring lady was really very like her remembered picture of her mum. She had the same pert nose, the same big, blue eyes, and the same laughing mouth. The hair was wrong though. Mum's hair had been lovely gold hair, not nearly white, but otherwise the resemblance was quite remarkable.

Rose closed her eyes firmly. So that was what it was, the Wren looked like Mum! Suppose it *was* Mum – what would she do? How would she behave?

Once, Rose had searched the streets, the parks and the underground stations for her mum. But that had been long ago, when Mum had first gone off and left her all alone. So if this *was* Mum she knew exactly what she would do. I would get off this train and never let on I knew, she told herself triumphantly. She didn't want me, once – well, I don't want her, now. I'm not her little girl, I'm Simon and Jenny's. I would say she was lying, she was not my mum, and I'd go off. Not that it was Mum, of course, it was just another of those stage-ladies.

Jenny was awake well before the train drew in to Norwich Thorpe. She was miserably worried about their arrival, which was silly, but she was so tired! What a fool she would feel, after this awful, jolting journey, if she should fall asleep just as the train got into Norwich and find herself carried on to Great Yarmouth! Presently her anxiety got so bad that she left her own corner seat, which was the wrong side, and went and sat on the other side of Rose so that she could keep bobbing up and down to peer through the gap at the darkness outside.

Watching, she saw hedge outlines become roof outlines. She looked at her watch and it was ten to three – what a nightmare journey! She began to get stuff down from the rack and it was as the Wren was reaching down her own bag that something about her profile clicked the memory into place in Jenny's mind – the extended arm should have been holding a racquet, reaching up to whack a tennis ball instead of clutching at a kitbag. The soft, goldy-brown curls had been cut short and bleached and the pretty, girlish profile had hardened into womanhood, but Jenny was now certain that the Wren was Pixie Hopwood, who had once made her miserably jealous because Simon had liked her.

Should she say anything? Make some joking remark about tennis? She might have done so but at that moment the train shunted all along its length and they all stumbled and bumped into each other, and then Marianne was

346

shouting that she was sure they were in the station and hadn't they better hurry, because there was a man outside with a torch, she was sure, and give me my teddy . . .

They all surged towards the corridor, Jenny in the lead. Time enough, she told herself as she wrestled to let the window down so that she could reach through it and open the door, time enough to say hello to Pixie when they were safely on the platform. The window gave in to her struggles and cold night air blew briskly through it. Jenny peeped out, then handed Bobby to Rose so that she could climb down first and then take him. She swung open the door, stepping down, and then someone whisked the platform from beneath her shoes, there was a warning shout from the darkness, she felt herself twist and fall. Something slammed her across the head and shoulders, the paving beneath her feet was writhing like a boa constrictor, and then she hit the platform like a stone and darkness blotted her out.

The small girl was wailing, the taller girl was comforting the baby. Behind them, the middle-aged gentleman was saying fussily that the train had not stopped and their mother had been very foolish and was probably bruised but otherwise, he was sure, quite unharmed. And what was more they must all stand sensibly still until the train was quite stationary, and then he would help them to search for her.

Pixie clung grimly on to the elder child's shoulders, and applauded all this good sense, then she took the baby in her own arms, watched the elder girl carefully down on to the platform, and jumped down herself, handing over the baby so that she could get the little girl off, and help the elderly gentleman with the carrier bags, the suitcase and the tartan hold-all. Only then did she bend over Jenny, supine on the platform but breathing normally.

'Mummy's all right, kids,' she said bracingly. 'What a bruise she's got on her poor old napper, though! Hang on here with her and I'll fetch help.'

She could see a tall, fair man standing beneath the light at the top of the platform and thought, ruefully, that you could tell a Neyler a mile off. She did not know which particular specimen this was, but it was a Neyler all right.

'There's been an accident, Mr Neyler,' she said briskly, as she drew level with him. 'Jenny jumped off the train before it had stopped and knocked herself cold on the door. The children are with her, though, all round her. Can you go up and give her a hand?'

'My God! I say, thanks . . . look, come back with me and I'll give you a lift to . . . I'm afraid I can't . . .'

'It's all right, you go to Jenny,' Pixie recommended, shouldering her kitbag. She grinned at the tall man. 'See you sometime.'

She set off across the station forecourt and out into the road. It was a good seven-mile walk out to Blofield and the thought of a lift had been tempting, but she still felt it was better not to get involved. That girl – she was almost sure it was Hazel, for all she had thought her daughter dead in the Blitz. The thought gave her a lovely lift of the heart, for after all she was Simon's daughter as well as hers, and if he had her he would see to it that the child was all right. She wondered if Jenny knew; odd, to think that Jenny, who had been so jealous of her once, would perhaps bring her daughter up as her own and never know . . .

She walked on, into the darkness which was never quite as dark as you think. By the time she reached open country, indeed, she was rather enjoying the walk, the swing of her arms, the sturdy strides of her legs. Nevertheless when the big lorry came grinding up the slope from the Thunder Lane crossroads, she paused and glanced behind her. His lights were dimmed, of course, but from the sound of the engine she would bet he was taking heavy equipment of some sort out to one of the aerodromes. She was right out of the city now, with open country on both sides of her, and she stopped as the huge lorry roared out of the darkness. She could see him clearly enough and guessed that he would see her, especially as the sky was beginning to lighten in the east. He was quite near, now, and much though she had enjoyed the first two miles of her walk, the last five would be hard going unless she got a lift. She stepped confidently out into the road, pushing her cap to the back of her blonde curls; men never could resist her hair!

The lorry driver was tired after a heavy day and night of driving and looked forward to getting to his destination. He was well used to this particular stretch of road having driven over it constantly, and told himself that he knew it like the back of his hand. Just about here he saw a fox, night after night, slinking across the road from a copse on his left to the broad sloping meadow on his right. He always imagined it was going home after a night's hunting and once he could have sworn he saw the droop of a wild duck in its mouth.

His attention was temporarily taken off the road at the point where the fox usually crossed by a train, travelling along the lines to his right. It made enough row, he thought crossly, to take anyone's mind off their rightful business, for it had made his heart jump with its sudden – and unusual – appearance just there. Showers of sparks came from its firebox and he could see the fellow shovelling fuel into the heart of the fire.

There was a bump and a thump on the nearside of the lorry and he jerked his concentration back to the road. Damn it to hell, he'd gone and hit the fox, thanks to that damned train which shouldn't have been on the lines right now, anyway. He glanced in his mirror and was almost sure that there was a darkness, sprawled on the verge. Poor little blighter; awful to kill an innocent animal, out on its hunting trip. Perhaps it had a vixen and a litter dependent on it. But there, war was war; better things than foxes were dying in this war.

He pressed his foot harder down on the accelerator and thundered on into the night.

The fox, about to cross the road just as the first pale fingers of dawn were touching the eastern sky, paused by the bloodstained dead thing and drew back, his lip curling, terror bringing his hackles high on his neck and shoulders. Uneasily, he moved forward, nose whiffling. It was dead, it could not possibly hurt him, and yet . . .

The fox moved off, not attempting to cross until he was a good five hundred yards further down the road. He would never cross there again, where the dead thing had reminded him of his own uncertain and danger-ridden existence.

'I'd swear it was Pixie Hopwood,' Jenny was saying as she climbed into the camp-bed set up in Ray's room. 'I don't think you ever met, Auntie Ray, but Simon had a real thing about her when he was fifteen or so. I used to get frightfully jealous. They haven't met for years, since she ran away soon after I met her, but he'll be ever so interested to know that she's still around, and even prettier, I think. She's bleached her hair, but it suits her.'

Rachel, who had stayed up to welcome the returning Roses, kicked the blankets off her feet, for it was warm with three of them in the small bedroom. Coppy was asleep and she envied her, but nevertheless she answered Jenny politely for she appreciated that the younger woman was probably too tired and too tense to sleep.

'No, I don't think I met her though I certainly heard about her. Why not pop over to Blofield – she was the girl who lived next door to the Butchers, wasn't she? – and have a chat? She'll probably be delighted to find out all about you and Simon.'

'Oh, we were poles apart as kids and we'll be even more so now, ' Jenny said comfortably, snuggling into her pillow. 'She's in the Wrens – didn't I say? – so she's probably only on a forty-eight and she'll have little enough time without me interfering. But I'm going to look up lots of my other friends now that we're back for good. Well, until the war's over and we can go back to Granville Gardens. Nick said, sort of casually, in one of his letters, that it might be an idea to keep an eye open for old cars, and for parts, and to put out a few feelers about work, so I'll do that too, of course. I daresay I'll be pretty busy.'

'Yes, I expect you will. When we heard you were coming home I think it made us all realise it's nearly over, with our chaps pushing the Germans back across the continent, and Val writing about the French people crying with happiness as they move forward. I don't think it will be long now.'

'Nor me. Nick and Simon are both caning the Japs back out of Burma. It's frightful there, Simon says, but he does feel very definitely that they are winning.'

'That's right; an end to the road,' Rachel said drowsily. 'Peace by Christmas, do you think?'

'Well, by next summer,' Jenny qualified. 'Poor Ray, I am mean, talking on and on. Goodnight.'

Rose, sharing a bed with Marianne, put her arms round her little sister and tried to push away the sudden feeling of unhappiness which filled her. Why should she feel unhappy – guilty, almost – just because she had imagined a stage-lady on the train might have been her mother?

Ridiculous! If the unhappiness did have any reason other than sheer exhaustion, it came from the fact that she had just realised a long and important chapter in her life was closed. Devon was not her place any more, though Jenny had promised that they would go back to the farm for holidays, once the war was over. She should be pleased and excited to be in Norwich, which she had heard so much about from the Roses but had never before visited. This was the start of her lovely new life, and this new chapter of it would be every bit as exciting and delightful as the farm chapter had been.

Rose sighed, hugged Marianne again, and drifted off to sleep.

Chapter Eighteen

1945

Art glanced sideways and backwards at his crew as the Lancaster droned on over Germany. Everyone was quiet, concentrating on their own jobs, but all Art found he was feeling was frustration and distaste for what he was about to do. Damn it all, it was a fact that the war was nearly over, everyone knew the Huns were as good as beaten, they were backing out of France and the other occupied countries so fast their heels were smoking – so why this? Why raid Berlin, their capital city, not searching for factories or arms dumps but in order to bomb homes and shops and schools? Someone had said the other night that it was supposed to make the Germans cower as they had tried to make Londoners cower, but so far as Art could see it hadn't worked with Londoners and it wouldn't work with Berliners. All it would do was kill people and terrify them and bring them grief.

On the other hand, they had to do something, because of the doodlebugs and those even nastier things, the V2s, which had been sent over Britain. So why not concentrate their bomb-power on the places where they knew the V1s and V2s came from, instead of starting reprisal raids? He could not help thinking of those poor devils down there, in the bitter cold and snow, having to put up not only with losing the war and being perpetually hungry, but with bombing raids, too.

Someone spoke to him and Art answered, then began to concentrate on his job once more as they neared their destination. But unfortunately, at that moment the memory of that phone call two days before came into his head. His father had rung to say that Cyril's ship had been torpedoed and that Cyril was posted as missing. Twice before, Cyril had been on a ship that had been sunk, had been picked up and brought home. But this time it seemed the ship had gone down faster and the water had been very cold. This time, the chances of his kid brother suddenly reappearing were not so good.

Nineteen! Cyril was only nineteen, but he had packed some living into those years! The ship had been hit at night and it was thought that Cyril had been on watch, but survivors who had got home could give no news of him. He might have been picked up by some foreign vessel, or even by a German one; he might be making his way home this very moment or in a prisoner of war camp. Or the unimaginable might have happened, but Art did not want to think about that. Not think about that bright, lint-fair head, bobbing, lifeless, far out to sea.

Twenty-three, on the other hand, seemed a good age, yet Art was aware that apart from war, he had done little enough. He was a year older than Maude and she had been a married woman for a good few months now. Art had only met Bill once but he had felt such an immediate, hair-prickling antipathy that it had quite startled him. Odd, because he and Maude were so close and usually they liked each other's friends. He rather thought, in retrospect, that he had sensed the difficulties which Maude was just beginning to have with her new husband. He could not understand why she had ever married Bill anyway, and was completely at one with the family's freely aired condemnation. Not Maude's type, not their type. The sort of fellow that girls chased after and then regretted marrying.

He had had several girlfriends since Petula and had

enjoyed his time with all of them, but he had not yet met anyone that he wanted to spend the rest of his life with. Or even a few months come to that. Girls were pleasant company, but he was concentrating, now, on getting the war over with. Sometimes he wondered what he would do when he was out of the RAF; sometimes he thought that twenty-three was quite an achievement and that twenty-four would be a better one. He believed that the war would be over before his twenty-fourth birthday, so just to achieve twenty-four . . .

'We'll be over the target in four minutes,' his navigator said. 'Flak and searchlights in three.'

He was right almost to the second. The big aeroplane managed to avoid some of the lights, but it had to drop lower to void its bombs and then it was buffeted by the flak and Art had to use all his skills and concentration to keep them at the right height and in the right place. He heard Harry call out when the bombs began to go away but he never looked down to see what, if anything, was hit. Not that you could miss targets, slap over the city like this.

'Right, eggs all gone!' Harry's voice was carefree. 'Head for home, fella.'

The tension always eased a bit once you'd got away from the target and the lights and were heading home, and that was dangerous, because that was the moment the fighters waited for, knowing you were less alert, tired out, wanting the time to go so that you could get to bed. But the guns were silent, in both the fore and rear turrets, so presumably they had escaped the squadrons immediately surrounding Berlin.

'Quiet night,' someone called over the intercom. 'Jerry's got plenty to keep him busy elsewhere, I daresay.'

'Too true.' Art chuckled. 'Just in my family alone he's got enough to keep him occupied. Val's driving ambulances with the occupying forces. Nick's attacking the Japs in Burma along with Simon, Caspar's flying night-fighters from Surrey somewhere, Bella's driving generals, Maudie's plotting and warning our chaps when bandits approach . . . and her husband, Bill, will be flying his bomber somewhere right now, I daresay. Bombing the Ruhr, perhaps.'

'What about the youngster in the navy? Cyril, isn't it? Any more news?'

'Not yet.' But somehow, Art could not believe that Cyril and his bright hair and gangling body could have been blotted out. No, he would *not* believe it. Cyril had been ditched twice and had come home grinning. It would happen again – it must!

'Well, plenty of time,' Harry said. 'Takes a while for news to filter through, in my experience.'

Art was agreeing with him when the aircraft bucked like a horse that sees a fence too late, then he felt the nose sink. He fought to lift it and heard a hideous noise; all the demons of the air seemed to be howling and shrieking just behind his left shoulder. He glanced at his navigator who was clutching his shoulder; blood spurted between his fingers.

It had all happened so suddenly that there was not even time to be afraid as the earth hurtled towards them. The last thing he saw was a great chrysanthemum of gold and scarlet flame flower before his vision. Then screaming blackness enveloped him.

Nick had had a letter from Val that morning, and was still trying to believe the bitter cold and snow of which she spoke whilst he fought here in this hell of heat and noise. He squatted in the bottom of his dug-out trying to will himself to feel the cold which she had written about, and to forget, for one moment, the burning heat – and the fact that in ten more short minutes, he and his platoon had to leave the doubtful shelter of this dug-out in order to lead an attack on the main Japanese guns outside the perimeter of the small town they were besieging.

Someone slithered into his trench. It was Captain John Sumner, who was organising this particular attack. He grinned at Nick.

'Right, old boy? Smoke bombs at the ready? Now what you want to do first is to reach the bunkers and then no heroics, just get down below the level of the firing slits and throw phosphorus bombs in on 'em. That'll liven 'em up a bit, and when they come rushing out, then's the time to mow 'em down.'

'Yes, the fellows know. But what about snipers, though? You said you'd fix them, but they're still pretty active.'

'Fletch says he's got two of 'em sussed; we'll do our best to put them out of commission before you go. All right? Everyone happy?'

The grim, dirt-smeared men of B platoon might not be happy, exactly, but they all nodded. They knew what they had to do and they would try to do it, though every man amongst them appreciated just what a risk they were running. Even with the bunkers out of it – if they reached them, if they could put them out of commission – there was still the main body of the Japanese army behind them, in the town.

Captain Sumner made off, leaving Nick watching the men and his watch. The battle raged all round them, the noise made speech next to impossible, so when the time was ripe he collected the men round him by glance, then jumped up over the edge of the trench and set off towards the Japanese bunkers, doubled up, tacking nightmarishly across the ravaged paddy field and through the torn and scattered maize which lay between them and the enemy. If they could get near enough to throw their smoke bombs

357

. . . If they could then see far enough through their own smoke to reach the bunkers undetected . . . If they could get the bombs through the gun-slits before they were seen and killed . . . War, Nick reflected, was just one huge question mark.

The township boasted three fine pagodas and as he squirmed and slipped across the paddy there was a lull in the noise, probably only of a second or two, but during that lull the sound of the temple chimes came clearly to his ears. It made him grin because it sounded plaintive, puzzled almost. You could not wonder at it, either. Snatched out of the quiet of the middle ages into the twentieth century, blasted by evil, by the roar of war, the Buddhist monks who had tended the pagodas dead, it was no wonder the chimes sounded so lost.

Then he and most of his men reached the bunkers, with the smoke screen of their flung bombs hiding them until the last moment, and threw the phosphorus bombs through the gun-slits. As soon as he had posted his, like bulky letters, he flung himself round the back of the bunker, crouching with his gun at the ready so that he could blast anyone emerging. The side against the bunkers was safe enough since there were, for obvious reasons, no gaps this side, but his other side, exposed to any Jap who might glance this way from the town, crawled with suspense whilst he kept his gaze and his gun steady on the end of the bunker where the Japs would emerge. Smoke poured out of the bunker, thick and evil-smelling, but no one came out and the noise of firing, the sounds of shells as they whistled overhead, gave him no clue as to what was happening inside the well-built shelters. He was pretty sure, however, that the main batteries inside the township were unaware of B platoon's attack. In jungle green, filthy anyway from mud and war, there was little enough to choose, at a distance, between himself and a Nippon warrior.

Just as he was wondering whether to ignore the bunkers and lead what would have been a suicide charge at the main batteries, men began to emerge. Small, yellow . . . and on fire. Screaming as they came, more animal than human, they rushed out, jostling, fighting to be first, and Nick began to fire, feeling hatred come easily now he needed it, feeding the hatred with pictures from a memory crammed with horrors. Even so, he felt relief when the bunkers appeared to be empty; smoke-filled and silent, stinking of phosphorus, human excreta and death.

As he turned to gather his men once more he saw Sumner ambling across the paddy. He walked over to him as he neared the empty bunkers.

'I think we've cleared 'em, sir, though we haven't been through them yet. Do you want us to do that before you start the main attack?'

'Is that you, Nick?' Nick grinned and nodded, realising how the blackening effect of the smoke must make them all look alike. 'Well done, old fellow! Yes, get your chaps to go through the bunkers and I'll get Freddy's lot to make sure the dead really are dead. Then come forward with the rest, will you? Many casualties?'

'Only one. Travis got a nasty wound in the shoulder; can someone take him back?'

'Only one? Well done indeed! Yes, send a couple of your chaps back with him.' Captain Sumner turned back to where the men were waiting by the openings into the bunkers. 'Can you get them cleared pronto, chaps? The company'll be coming across for the main attack in five minutes. A Jap with a machine gun could do a lot of damage from there.'

It was true, so Nick sent two men back with Travis and then the remaining troops got into pairs to search the bunkers. They skirted the piled-up dead since they had all seen a 'dead' Jap get to his feet and kill three Tommies before he could be overpowered.

Nick and Devlin took the bunker they had bombed. It was empty save for a body sprawled at the far end and Nick, with his gun very much at the ready, walked down towards it. When he got near enough he saw that the body was naked, and his stomach turned protestingly. He went nearer, however, and saw that it was, or appeared to be, a girl, lying face down on the dirt. He glanced at Devlin, then turned her over with the point of his bayonet. She was a Burmese girl of about fourteen or fifteen, very beautiful and very, very dead. Nick knew that the Japanese had been holed up in these bunkers for at least three days . . . it seemed that they had brought their own amusement with them.

Just to make sure, Nick examined her for bullet wounds, but there were none. Her face was flower-like, white and innocent; death had taken the fear and smoothed away the cruel knowledge. Now she lay like the child she was, needlessly dead, caught up in a war that was none of her making, none of her caring.

He did not know quite how he got out of that bunker, he only knew that he was more hurt and shocked by that dead little girl than by all the other atrocities which had scarred his mind. And he would never forget her, not if he lived to be a hundred.

Otto was digging. The worst of the winter seemed to be over, or at least March had arrived, so he felt he could dig and perhaps even plant something, though he was not too sure what.

He had another scar on his face now, making him look piratical, for it crossed the fight-with-the-fender scar which people took for duelling, but he was not unhappy. In fact, glancing around him, he knew that he was almost as lucky as he had thought himself, three months ago, when he had first been taken prisoner. Not that they had known he was a prisoner, for by the oddest of coincidences he and a Mustang had both been shot down at more or less the same time and he, thrown from his machine into a lake and with most of his clothing burned off, had been taken for the pilot of the American aircraft and had been solicitously invalided out of France into a hospital at Southampton, where he had been marvellously nursed back to health.

Then, of course, he had been sent to a prisoner of war camp, where he now was. It was in Norfolk, in the flat eastern side of the county, and although in the bitter winter it had been cold enough for anyone it had been a healthy, bracing cold which did none of the men any harm.

Otto, indeed, had thrived on it, growing sturdy on rations which were a considerable improvement, he was assured, on what the ordinary British people ate since they had to feed their prisoners according to the Geneva Convention even when they could not manage to treat their own citizens so generously.

He was happy, too, because this was Val's country. He could not get in touch with her, not while their countries were still at war, but he was as sure as everyone else that the war would not last much longer. He had seen Germany and knew what condition she was in. Sometimes he and the other pilots talked of their experiences, marvelled at the fact that they were told there was no fuel for the aircraft so they could not fly sorties after the enemy when they could see the fuel dumps for themselves, fairly overflowing with the stuff.

Everyone on the camp knew that Hitler was a madman and knew that their fellow countrymen, the people who held back the fuel supplies, knew it too and wanted

Germany to suffer as little as possible from a war which was being artificially prolonged by Hitler's determination not to admit defeat. Just before he was shot down Otto had heard Hitler's speech, in the course of which he had admonished his people to 'fight like werewolves against the aggressor', which Otto had thought rather ingenuous even at the time.

In deep contentment, Otto learned English, worked in the garden and around the camp, and wrote home to his parents. He was worried about them, but worrying did not help. Minna had married her young man and Herr von Eckner had bought them a little farm in the country. I want your mother to go there when the worst happens, he wrote.

It was hard on his parents, having a son in a prisoner of war camp and their only daughter sick in her mind. Otto believed that Franz was dead – wanted to believe it. He had ferried supplies to the troops outside Stalingrad and from time to time he had met Franz and been shocked by his brother's appearance. Gaunt and red-eyed, Franz had admitted quite openly that they were beaten, that they could not even break out from the surrounding Soviet troops because they were too weak. He told Otto that he and his men caught and ate rats, when rats were to be had, and still they waited for reinforcements which did not come, for a change in fortune which they no longer believed in.

Every day, Otto and his companions flew in what supplies they could, but it was drops of water against a desert. The day came, as they had known it must, when they flew over the ruined city in the cold dawn and saw not one movement. Not a rat, not a soldier stirred.

Otto had seen the Russians in action, so he hoped that Franz was dead. Better by far to be dead than to be a prisoner of a country like Russia.

After that bitter campaign, Otto had been glad to get back to the fatherland, though he had fought in the Western Desert for eighteen months, and had found that heat, sand and sweat were, in their way, as bad as cold, frostbite and thick ice.

And now, he was at rest. For you, the war is over, the catchphrase went, but Otto revelled in the truth of it for him, at any rate. He was waiting out the rest of the war, learning English so that he could talk to Val in her own language, learning how to use the land to its best advantage because experts were here to teach him, learning how to take defeat on the chin, to accept it, and to turn it to one's own advantage.

He dug his spade into the soil once more, and eyed the pile of tiny spring cabbage plants. This was his own plot, but tomorrow was Monday and he would be out working properly, at his own request, for a farmer who needed help on the land. Hard physical work and a quiet conscience, Otto reflected, were not regarded nearly highly enough. They could make a man contented faster than most things.

'Can you get a few more sticks, Val? Without some dry fuel, I'll never get it to light!'

Annette, Val's co-driver, was kneeling on the brick floor of an enormous fireplace, though the fire that she was endeavouring to light was very small indeed, no more than a tiny wigwam of twigs set up in the draughty old grate. But fuel was scarce, as was everything else, for the army was pushing through occupied France, liberating as it went. It sometimes seemed to the girls that by the time they had brought the wounded back last thing at night anything eatable had been swallowed, anything wearable had been donned, and anything combustible had been burned. Quite often, indeed, there were no suitable billets for them, so they slept in the ambulances through the freezing nights, getting up at regular intervals to run the engines so that their vehicles would start next morning.

However, on this particular evening they had been lucky. They brought the wounded back to the first-aid station, which varied every night, for it would have been useless to have left the station far behind them. It had to dog the army's footsteps, so to speak, in order that casualties might not have too far to travel to reach hospitalisation. The first-aid station was supposed to be out of reach of enemy shells, but it almost never was. However, tonight the army had suddenly decided to move on and the first-aid station, being almost full, had decided to remain, so when Val, Annette, Sara and Jeannie brought their ambulances back, laden, for the last time before darkness fell, they found a whole cottage free for their occupation. What was more, they had a bit of fuel, an oil stove to cook on, and a big kettle in which to heat up their washing water – luxury indeed!

'More sticks? You're a glutton.' Val was still in her greatcoat but she had shed her helmet; she now slapped it on her head again since the shelling had not ceased with the coming of darkness and made for the street. Perhaps someone would have 'won' some wood, and be willing to share? The soldiers admired the girls who drove their ambulances into the thick of the bloodiest battles, and would always hand over a fair half of anything they had managed to obtain, but the girls tried to be as independent as possible. However, with the snow two feet thick and the air like iced water, independence was a luxury few of them could afford. Val looked hopefully up and down the street, and waved as a man she knew emerged from a bombed building further up; he was carrying what looked like planks.

'Hi, Chris – is that burnable?'

'Yes, indeed it is. Since that house is nothing but a shell I decided it would be fair enough to ferret around, and I found a cupboard with slatted shelving. Want some?'

'Oh, please, if you're sure no one will mind.' Val gratefully allowed her arms to be filled with the thin wooden shelves. 'Want some wine in exchange? We were given four bottles by a grateful gran this morning – we took her little baby into the station and the doctor operated on a great big ear-abscess, poor mite. The baby's relief was tangible and so was Gran's – the kid had cried non-stop for sixty hours, she reckoned.'

'No, we're all right for wine, thanks,' Chris said. 'Where are you billeted? Not in the ambulances, I trust?'

'No, we've been lucky tonight, we're in that big cottage on the end,' Val said, waving towards it. 'We've really had some luck – we were allowed to garage the ambulances in that big barn and a couple of chaps who are going to run truck engines, an hour on, two hours off, say they'll do the same with the ambulances, so that we can all have an undisturbed night for once.'

'You deserve it. You kids are marvellous,' Chris said warmly, heading for his own billet. 'Night, Val.'

'Night, Chris, and thanks a million for the wood.'

Val re-entered the cottage and handed her armful to Jeannie, who promptly gave it to Annette who received it with gurgles of appreciation.

'Clever Val, all this – the fire will be roaring presently. Jeannie found some sort of cake stuff which she swears is fuel so we'll burn that once it's going strong, though I've got my suspicions . . . Join the hot-water queue, Val, and then once that's over we can start heating the grub.'

The nightly wash and clean up was something which the girls carried out no matter how tired they were since their commanding officer, a redoubtable woman who ruled them all with kindness and tact, assured them that no man wanted to find himself being taken care of by a woman who smelt of dirt and diesel fuel, who wore no make-up and whose hands looked like a mechanic's. Knowing the importance to their morale and to their passengers', therefore, the girls hoarded their tiny supplies of lipstick and face powder, begged, borrowed or stole soap, and always managed, somehow, to have a clean towel and clean underwear somewhere in the cab of their vehicles.

Sometimes, though, it hardly seemed worth it. When you had been struggling with an engine that would not start, when you had been lifting heavy, bloodstained young men in and out of your ambulance and slogging through mud and snow and icy temperatures, when you were hungry and exhausted and had spent the last three nights sleeping on the hard floor of your ambulance, then it was a terrible temptation to skip the nightly beauty treatment. But no one ever did. Sometimes they had to shout and yell and shake each other awake until the water was hot and they could wash, sometimes they were too tired to eat, but they always went to bed clean and sweet-smelling and woke up to put on make-up, to brush their hair until it shone . . . and then to work until they were ready to drop once more. Pride is supposed to be a dreadful thing, Val thought sometimes, but it saves us from sluttishness!

'It's going to be another noisy night,' Jeannie remarked as she handed Val a kettleful of hot water. 'I'm filthy – I must have picked up a dozen men with a leg blown off today.'

'Yes, I know, we did as well.' The retreating Germans had sown the countryside with landmines as they went, but because they were hurrying they frequently blew up their own troops, and, of course, it was terribly dangerous when you were driving if you happened to swerve on to a hidden verge. If you stopped to get a wounded man lying in a ditch you were supposed to prod every step of the way before treading on it yourself. You did, too, after seeing a man turn to speak to the man behind him and in so doing touch the verge, which immediately exploded, taking his leg off in a welter of screams and blood. But no use to dwell on what the day had brought, or what tomorrow might bring. Val glanced at her watch as she took it off and laid it down beside the wash-basin. 'Any more coming in tonight, or are we the team?'

Sara had washed her hair and was drying it by fluffing it out with her fingers in the firelight. Jeannie was crouched over the fire too, heating up her rations in a large saucepan. They both shrugged.

'Who can say? But probably it's just us, since no one's turned up for an hour or two.' Jeannie, who had spoken, turned to Val. 'What's it like outside? Still snowing?'

'No, it's stopped, but it's terribly cold. If only the guns would stop we might actually get a decent night's rest for once.'

As she spoke there was an appalling crash, the oil lamp flickered and nearly went out and Jeannie uttered a shriek. Val saw the fire suddenly go out and then, as the oil lamp's flame steadied, she realised that everyone was looking as though the snow had somehow managed to penetrate the roof of the cottage. The lath and plaster ceiling had crumbled and showered them with 'snow' – except for Jeannie and Sara, who surveyed the world through masks of soot. Everyone shrieked, swore, and began to try to clean themselves up by vigorous dusting down.

'Goddammit!' Jeannie said, whilst Annette cried that she was starving and just look at the stew. Sara, giggling, was trying to scoop a thick fur coat of soot off the stew and dusting herself down at the same time and Annette, ever practical, was opening more stew and emptying the tins into another pan which she was balancing on the oil stove.

'It's too bad. They always say we'll be out of firing range this time and we never are,' Jeannie said tearfully, surveying the stew and the loaf of well-blackened bread. 'My fire's out, too – that bloody soot! Look, I'm going begging. You know what the fellows are like. Someone will have something over, they always do. I'm damned if I'll go to bed hungry.'

'I'll come with you,' Sara said, casting her pan of sooty stew down on to the floor. 'Jimmy Parkes is further up the road and he had a hen, only I said we'd be all right because we'd got our rations. Now I'll tell him what's happened; ten to one they invite us to dinner. We've still got the wine, so we shan't be a burden on them.'

The two of them struggled into their greatcoats and helmets and left, but they had scarcely gone before they were back, wide-eyed and scared. They opened the door very gently and their faces appeared in the aperture. Val and Annette, crouched over the oil stove tending the stew, glanced over to the doorway rather crossly. What now?

'Come out for a moment, would you?' Jeannie's usually brisk and rather impatient tones were oddly hushed, almost reverent, Val thought, but she got to her feet. As she went to the door she saw that Sara's rosy face was quite pale.

Val and Annette left the cottage and emerged into the crisp coldness of the night and once they were in the roadway and turning back towards the cottage they could see the reason for their friends' sudden reappearance. The place must have received a direct hit. The entire roof and upper storey had been crushed to nothing, the chimney had fallen and was lying across the side garden, and what was left could only be described as distinctly tottery.

'When we looked back and saw what had happened we

nearly *died*,' Sara said earnestly. 'I was terrified that it would go before we got you out. Come on, let's go and report this to someone.'

'Not till I've gone back for my stuff,' Val said determinedly. 'I'm not leaving my kitbag and my one and only pair of clean knickers in there. And my tin hat's there, and my greatcoat, and all our food, and . . .'

'Val, don't be silly, you can't go back.' Jeannie's eyes were black with fright. 'It isn't worth it, it's worth more to be alive; that place could cave in at any moment, you'd be crushed . . . just for a pair of clean knickers!'

'And my soap and lipstick, my greatcoat . . .' Val turned back to the cottage. 'If a shell landed on me now, without my tin hat, I'd be dead anyway. Hang about.'

To her three companions it seemed an age before she reappeared, dragging everyone's personal possessions along through the snow behind her. She looked like a one-man band, with kettles, pans and bedding festooning her person.

'There! Everything's out and all we've lost is a fire, our stew, and a night's lodging,' Val was saying as she reached the gate, when there was a rumble and sigh behind her, and the remains of the cottage collapsed in a cloud of dust.

Val looked over her shoulder and squawked, but Annette, who had been facing the scene, gave a little sigh and fainted clean away.

'Oh well, someone else will have to carry her,' Val said stoically, clanking off down the street like a knight in armour. 'Come on, who's for spending the night in a nice, familiar ambulance?'

Cara came dreamily up the drive in the sweet, late April sunshine with the lightest of light breezes lifting the hair from her forehead. Once, she had hated this walk, associating it with war and with the work at the factory, but now, she very nearly loved it. She thought, with rare sentiment, that she had known some good times through her work at the factory. She would miss it all when it stopped, the work, the companionship of other people and particularly Anne, and the feeling that she had attained a degree of expertise and independence solely through her own efforts.

Of course, it was much easier to appreciate the walk now that spring was almost turning into summer. Earlier, during what had seemed at the time an interminably long winter, she had very nearly had to dig her way up the drive, and that had not been so amusing after a long day's work. It had not been too bad, however, once she had made it clear that someone must meet her at the bottom of the drive to help her through the thick, deep snow. In fact she admitted that it had been fun – several times she and her escort, whether it was Uncle Des or one of the cousins or a friend, had laughed so much that they had arrived at The Pride quite weak with mirth. Whoever was meeting her brought the sledge, and though the meeter had the fun of coasting down the drive, he then had to tow the sledge up again, with Cara enthroned on it. Because it was fun, she had quite often put her shopping bag on the sledge and helped with the pulling, and perhaps had fallen in the soft snow, and laughed helplessly, and arrived at the front door all in a beautiful glow, to be greeted by the biggest fire they could manage to build, and hot toast, and some of Ruthie's nicest cake.

She had begun to be aware of herself at this time, as a person who was not only beautiful and rather glamorous, but something more. Once the GIs had arrived in Britain, of course, she was assured of her beauty and her glamour, but it was this something more which particularly intrigued her. She found that because of her new, stretched life at the factory, she was able to share Maudie's jokes, and Bella's, too, when she came home from driving her fat colonel about London. Uncle Des's fire-watching stories had more point to them when she could cap them with what had happened to *her* on a late shift.

She knew, of course, that her relatives disapproved of her friendship with the various GIs that she brought to the house, but Cara had never cared what other people thought and did not intend to start now. She was a little taken aback to discover that Anne, by now a close friend, thought her foolish to get up what she called 'flirtations' with the American servicemen and then to expect people to believe that she was not just one of the girls who would do anything in exchange for a pair of nylon stockings or a box of candy. To be sure, she speedily became the recipient of many pairs of nylon stockings and boxes of candy, to say nothing of swathes of dress material, warm woolly scarves, kid gloves and silver bracelets to show off her slender wrists. But whatever anyone believed, she had given no more than sweet words and a few kisses for all this bounty – as well as the pleasure of her company, of course.

People were also rather shocked at her attitude when one of her American friends was replaced by another. I am *not* fickle, Cara had assured Anne on one occasion. The boys fly those aeroplanes over Germany, and I can't help it if they keep getting shot down! Nor she could, of course, but it was, in a way, convenient – though she told herself that she would much rather they were not killed. Still, it did mean that a young man barely had time to begin to wish she would start a more intimate relationship with him before he was gone and another was walking up the long drive with her, taking her dancing, bringing her candies.

The tenor of Cara's thoughts was interrupted. A shout from behind her brought her head round, and there was

Coppy, nipping along with almost no sign of the limp that she carried to remind her of her particular bomb. Coppy was sixteen now, and unless Cara was very much mistaken she was going to be another charmer like Val, only with more conventional looks. Coppy's lovely, coppery curls were well-cut and always shining, her skin was pale and clear and her eyes, though Cara thought grey eyes dull, were almond-shaped and so sparkling that she always seemed on the verge of laughing.

'Hello, Cara! I've been suffering all the slings and arrows of a violin lesson – *when* will Mummy see that it's quite useless and I'll never have Caspar's way with a bow?'

'You're very good,' Cara protested. 'I thought you'd been meeting your boyfriend. I didn't realise it was violin night.'

'It isn't . . . Well, it's an extra lesson because I've an exam coming up,' Coppy explained. She threw the older girl an indulgent glance. 'As for boyfriends, I leave that to you, my dear cousin. Milton may think I'm charming – well, he does – but I think he's wet!'

'Coppy, how can you say such an unkind thing! He's delightfully good-looking, he's very intelligent, and he's at your feet. All he wants is one word and he'll whisk you back to the States with him when he goes and make you a filmstar!'

'He's just a boaster,' Coppy remarked. She glanced rather shrewdly at Cara. 'Do they say things like that to you? Well, I'm sure they must, but you don't *believe* them, do you? They're awful schmoos, you know, they'll tell you anything because they know they can get away with it. I take every word they utter with a pinch of salt.'

'Well, perhaps some of them . . . but Sholly's different, he wouldn't lie to me,' Cara said defensively. 'Anyway, he wouldn't talk about whisking me back to the States. I'm a married woman.'

'You wouldn't think so,' Coppy said, adding hastily, 'And I didn't mean that nastily, whatever you may think.' Endeavouring to change the subject, she continued, 'The war's nearly over and Val's halfway to Berlin, she said so in her last letter, which means that your William will soon be home. Don't you get terribly excited when you think of it? It will be wonderful, won't it, to have him back? Mira can hardly sit still when you mention that they'll bring the p.o.w.s back first. She sits jiggling around and beaming at everyone. I guess you must feel the same.'

'In a way I do,' Cara said cautiously. 'In a way . . . Well, it won't be the same, Coppy, will it? I'm different and so will William be. He'll be crippled, for a start, no matter how you may try to dress it up, and I've always felt uneasy with cripples. Then he'll be an invalid too, and I absolutely *hate* sickrooms and hospitals, though I'm sure it's much easier than factory work and the uniforms are *lovely*. I'd have looked really sweet in one of those big white aprons with a wide dark belt.'

'A man isn't crippled just because he's lost his arm and his leg,' Coppy said scornfully. 'You do exaggerate, Cara! And anyway, after what he's been through you should be glad to take care of him.'

'Hmm. Actually, I dread him coming home,' Cara said in a burst of confidence. 'People have gone on and on about him, how marvellous he is, how brave, how wonderful, until I think I'd rather live with a plaster saint! And I suppose he won't let me see Sholly any more, or any of the other fellows I've got friendly with . . . He'll expect us to manage on our rations with no little extras . . . I bet he'll disapprove of the black market and everyone *knows* that it's the only way to live decently . . . No, Coppy, if I'm honest I'm dreading his return, not longing for it.'

'I daresay other women are feeling a bit like that,' Coppy said, taking Cara's arm. 'No, really, not just because their husbands have been hurt, either. Think of our family. We've got men coming home who've been away for five whole years, and in that time the women have changed terribly because they've been Daddy as well as Mummy to the kids, and they've learned how to manage money instead of turning to their husbands for advice all the time, and they've had interesting jobs which they may not much want to lose. And the men – it's been ever so different for them, too. They've been in foreign countries, or in command of big numbers of men and they've been taking life-and-death decisions. Now they'll come home to being clerks in offices or fathers of children they may feel they hardly know any more. Oh yes, it'll be hard for people, even if they don't realise it just yet.'

She turned, to find Cara regarding her with open-mouthed awe.

'Coppy, you're a very clever person, do you know that? I've often wondered what good it would do you, being so clever at school and getting matric first go when you were so young and all that, but now I can quite see. I bet no one else your age could even imagine all the things you've just been saying! I bet you're right, and it isn't going to be *joy and laughter and peace ever after*, the way that songs says. I bet it will be hard going for lots of men and women, not just for me and William.'

The conversation ended as they arrived at the house and during tea and afterwards, when she got herself ready to go dancing with Sholom Mittelmann, her latest conquest, Cara put the matter right out of her mind. But later, on the dance floor with Sholly's arms around her, the thought recurred. It would be difficult for her, next to impossible, when William came home. A saintly figure she saw him now, thin and frail and expecting her to wait on him hand and foot. Disapproving of everything about her, the way Auntie Tina disapproved. Tight-lipped if she laughed or cried, expecting things from her which she could not give.

But there was a way out. Sholly talked about his flat in New York, his ranch in the country, his big, happy Jewish family. They ran a chain of bakery shops 'coast to coast' as Sholly put it, and had so much money that they almost did not know what to do with it. And Sholly adored her. If she told him how much she dreaded the moment when William crawled or crutched or whatever a one-legged man did over the threshold and back into her life, surely he would . . . do something?

'You happy, honey?'

Sholly's dark brown voice, like chocolate, double cream or rhum babas, caressed her ears even as his big, respectful hand caressed the small of her back. He squeezed her fingers and Cara squeezed too. Yes, Sholly Mittelmann had distinct possibilities; if things got unbearable she would remember this moment and the thoughts that had risen, unbidden, into her mind.

Chapter Nineteen

'The war's over, Bobby! That means Daddy will come home, and Uncle William, and all the others!' Marianne hugged her little brother and then leaned over and hugged Rose too. 'Isn't it odd, Rosie, that Bobby can hardly remember Daddy at all? I remember him perfectly well, of course.'

The three Rose children, Eddy and Em Neyler, Sebastian and Mira were all crowded on to the swing seat in the garden. The sudden end of the war was highly exciting, with fireworks in the market the following evening, grown-ups crying and giving out food and treats they had been hiding and hoarding for months, and schools simply taking it for granted that holidays would be handed out all round. Of course it had been very aggravating for people like Stuart Bachelow, because he had been about to go into the air force and now no one knew whether he would be wanted or not, but even Stuart was taking it very well and joining in the fun and games.

Bobby was not yet three, but he was still chattering away rather well for his age. Now he swung his fat little legs out and asserted stoutly, 'I does remember Daddy; I does, I does!'

'He doesn't really,' Mira said loftily from the height of her eight years. 'Babies remember Daddy-shaped gaps; I heard your mummy saying so yesterday, when someone asked how much Bobby remembered.'

'It's been a long time for all of us,' Em remarked. She

was not so much affected since her own father had spent all the war being an air-raid warden, but she had sadly missed her elder brothers, so she felt that this counted her as almost a war-orphan. 'Mummy keeps saying Chick will turn up, but it's been a long time. And then Art's been in a German hospital and a chaplain wrote Mummy a letter which had her howling into her cornflakes. Art's been badly burned and the chaplain says he'll need all her love and fortitude. Well, I think that's what it said and I can tell you, it made her howl, didn't it, Ed?'

'Everything makes her howl,' Eddy said acidly. 'She's a ninny, Mummy is. Though she can't help it, I don't think. Fortunately none of us take after her in that way. Even when I heard about Chick . . . well, we didn't cry much, did we, Em?'

'Bella did,' Em asserted. 'But then she dried her eyes and said she was *sure* he'd turn up and she's usually right about him, so we'll keep on watching the news. Maudie was jolly cut up about Art, too. She cried for ages when she heard, and then she went off and phoned that Bill fellow, and I don't know what he said, but she suddenly screamed rude things at him and slammed the phone down. Serve him right, I bet. I can't stand that fellow. He isn't good enough for our Maudie, everyone says so.'

'I wish I'd met him,' Rose said wistfully. She hated to be left out of anything to do with the family. 'I wish I'd met Chick, too. Though I'll see Art when they send him home.'

'If we're still here,' Marianne reminded her. 'If Daddy's back, and Uncle Nick, we might be back in London by then.'

That shut Rose up. She loved Norwich so much that the thought of returning to the flat and London was not as exciting for her as it appeared to be for Marianne. Sebastian took pity on her; he and Rose were exactly the same age having been born within minutes of each other on the very same day of the year and he felt an affinity with her. He often came to her rescue when there was an argument, though Rose was a real little peacemaker and turned many a squabble into a friendly chat despite the antagonists wanting to get at each other's throats!

'How much do you remember about before the war, Rose? We'll have to get used to peacetime, and I daresay it'll be easier for us who can remember something about before. The little ones have never known anything but war, when you think about it.'

'I don't remember anything,' Marianne announced importantly. 'But all this war ending reminds me of a big clock winding down. It's all right whilst it's being wound *up*, all very exciting and that, but when it goes down and finally stops it's going to be awfully dull and horrid. I mean, at the moment we've got fireworks and parties and people coming home and lots of fun, but when all that's happened, what will we have left?'

'If I remember rightly, we'll have lots of sweets, and all the nice sort of fruit like bananas which we don't see now,' Rose observed. 'And colours – I think people wore prettier clothes and there wasn't such a fuss about making do. And best of all, they won't be able to say "Don't you know there's a war on" whenever they want to stop you doing what you want.'

'I remember the sweets and the fruit all right, and no blackout and parties in the garden with little lights strung on the trees,' Sebastian said, tugging at Rose's hair ribbon, which was hanging by a thread anyway. 'What about you two? What do you remember? You're the oldest, Ed.'

'Not a lot more than you,' Eddy remarked. 'The food was good though. Lots of meat, as much as you could eat, and cakes with real cream and currants in buns. Car rides were fun, going down to the seaside for picnics . . .'

He was interrupted. The seaside had been out of bounds

for such ages that only he and Em could really remember it, though the other children talked constantly, and wistfully, about playing on a beach.

'Shut up, Ed. I think I can hear . . . yes, I can!'

Rose jumped to her feet and tore off towards the house with the others close on her heels. Sitting still had never appealed to them much and now they enjoyed the opportunity to run as Rose hurtled through the conservatory and across the hall towards the telephone which she, and now the others, could hear ringing. She snatched the receiver from its rest, beating Eddy by a hair's-breadth, gulped hello into the mouthpiece, then listened intently.

'What? Oh, sorry, I'm a bit breathless, I've been running. Yes, of course I'll do that, Uncle Frank. Right. Right. Yes, don't worry, I will, the moment I put the phone down. Yes, the others will come with me. Oh, give our love to Lenny as well – shall I ask them to come up here and ring you back? All right, I will. Bye!'

Rose replaced the receiver and turned to the others, her face glowing with importance and excitement.

'Come on, we've got to go down to Ada's cottage with a very important message. You'll never guess who's come back, and one of the first, too! Come on, I'll race you down there!'

Frank had been on edge for days knowing that France had been liberated and expecting Mabel to ring when she could, or write at least, but there had been nothing, no word, no message, nothing. He had a deep, calm inner certainty that she was not dead though, and he absolutely refused to let himself worry. She would come to him when the time was ripe, he knew it, and until she came he would work hard and look forward to the moment.

Nevertheless, his ears had become so attuned to listening for the telephone and the doorbell that they had become almost indifferent to other sounds. Which was how he came not to look up when he heard the sound of oars in the water at around four o'clock in the afternoon. He knew it would be Lenny, who had taken himself off earlier in the day intent on helping with the firework display which was planned for later in the evening; if Frank knew his Lenny, he would be accompanied by a couple of his dearest mates and they would swarm over the yard and sheds, go and eat all the bread Madge had left for tea and then look injured if asked to row back to the village for more provender.

The bedraggled scrap of humanity which had turned up on Frank's doorstep more than five years ago, announcing itself to be Lenny Cripps, was now a sturdy fourteen-year-old, tanned and muscular, who could row, swim, fight and play almost any game you cared to name. He was Frank's secret pride and joy – and Madge's, for Frank's housekeeper swore that without her to care for them both Frank and Lenny would have been dead of starvation and neglect years since.

Frank lifted his head and grinned across at Ben, working away with a plane on the opposite side of the boat they were making.

'That'll be Lenny and he can make us a cuppa; I'm dry enough to drink the Broad, but a cup of tea would go down even better. In fact, since he's early, he can . . .'

Ben was looking over his shoulder, towards the open door of the boatshed. His eyes were getting wider and wider, and a sort of half-smile was beginning to curve his mouth. Frank swung round and stood perfectly still, one hand still resting on the boat. He felt that if he moved his heart might stop.

Mabel. If she was worn and weary, he did not notice; if her hair was streaked with white, he did not see it; if her clothing was that of a French peasant, he could not have told. She was just Mabel, the woman he had loved for half a lifetime and lost for half of it as well. Just Mabel, which was like saying just perfection.

They both stood there, staring, until Mabel spoke.

'Good afternoon, Frank, Ben. Forgive the intrusion.'

Frank crossed the shed in a couple of strides and took her arm. His fingers were trembling so much that she shook too – or she told herself that this was why she trembled. He mumbled something about putting the kettle on and hurried her across the yard and into the cottage. Then, he closed the back door. Firmly.

Inside the cottage, they stood a little apart and smiled at each other and then Frank pulled the kettle over the fire and, with his back to her, spoke for the first time. His voice sounded croaky, almost unused.

'You're back. For good this time, is it?'

'For good.'

She did not qualify the remark with the conventional sophistry of *if you want me*; she did not explain that she had been widowed nearly four years ago and was now free to marry again. It was not necessary and they both knew it. The years between had fallen away for them both as if they had never been. This was the same Frank and the same Mabel who had shared so much and had intended, a quarter of a century ago, to share much more. Things had gone wrong and twenty-five years had been wasted through no fault of theirs. They had both lived other lives. But they both knew the other lives had been false and hollow, that their lives from this moment on would be enriched simply by their togetherness. Two halves of a perfect whole, they could ignore the wasted years now, and exchange slow smiles.

'Darling Mabel!' He took her in his arms then and for the first time they kissed. She was still in his arms when the door burst open, and Lenny cannoned into the room. He stopped and stared but Frank only tightened his hold on Mabel, though he grinned at the boy over the top of her smooth, dark head.

'Kettle's on, old boy. This is Mabel. You haven't met before, but she's going to live with us. I'd introduce you properly, but I suspect she's having a little blub – you know what women are. So if you'll go and make up a tray and cut Madge's cake, she can tidy up whilst you're gone.'

'You're kiddin', aren't you?' Lenny said incredulously. He looked at Frank again. 'Oh, no you're not. Well, that'll give us another ration book when we're shoppin' for food, that's one good thing.'

'And that,' Frank told Mabel as she dried her swimming eyes and tried to powder her nose whilst still in his arms, 'will probably be Lenny's only comment on my changed circumstances.'

It was.

Nick and his platoon greeted the news that peace had been declared with only moderate enthusiasm, since it was clear that the Japanese intended to fight on. But they were being hard-pressed now, the British forces were doubled and it was pretty clear that, even if the Japs did fight on, they were being driven out of Burma.

So Nick, greatly daring, wrote to Vitty. It was not a long letter, but it was an important one because it said what he had not liked to say before.

'Wait for me, if you possibly can, so that I can propose the moment we've cleared the Nips out of Burma,' he said at the end of the letter. 'Don't go getting yourself repatriated yet, there's my darling girl.'

After the letter was sent, he felt wonderful; clear-eyed and bold, almost capable of fighting the Japanese army single handed. He and his sergeants toasted his declaration of intent in strong tea and both Devlin and Johnnie told him he was a lucky man.

Later, of course, Nick felt conscience-stricken that he had said anything, when he had vowed to himself that he would not burden Vitty with the knowledge of his love. But he salved his conscience by writing to Simon and telling him to take care of Vitty should anything happen to him, and asking Simon to 'see her all right' when she got back to Britain should he not be in a position to do so himself.

After he had despatched the second letter, he felt even taller and stronger; he had committed himself and was happier as a result and more determined to survive. He had a lot to live for.

The day that Cara heard William had set sail for home she made up her mind. They had been on at her again, the aunts and the cousins, to say nothing of her sister-in-law. William was a wonderful person, he deserved better than to come home to a wife who was still spending nearly all her time with Sholom, no matter how delightful a friend that young man might be. She had done nothing about the flat, so plainly she expected William to move into The Pride until things were sorted out and that was fine by them; William was a great favourite with everyone. But the least she could do now that she was no longer working at the factory was to help a bit about the house! Everyone else was busy bottling fruit and making jam, letting the children's clothing out and patching sheets, cleaning down the walls and floors, digging the garden, searching for bits and pieces at all the jumble sales which would make the place look what Auntie Tina called 'less austerity'.

So Clara made up her mind.

'I'm going to open up the flat,' she told the assembled

family one night at supper. 'Sholly will help with the decorating and Jack says he knows where he can get hold of some white emulsion paint, so at least we can make the place look clean. I'll wash all the upholstery and the curtains and so on, because they're in a good state, they don't need replacing. But the place is filthy, so it'll take me all my time. I'll leave Mira with you, of course.'

Sholly Mittelmann, however, heard a different story.

'I just can't face William when I want to spend the rest of my life with you,' Cara declared passionately. 'Sholly, I'm the only person in the whole country who's more miserable because the war is over than before it.'

Sholom, a true gentleman, clasped her to his heart and assured her that there was no problem.

'I'll buy you a ticket, honey, and you'll be in Noo York before you know it,' he declared. 'You can live with my folk until I get demobbed, which will be purty soon, I guess, and then William will divorce you and we can get married. Only I don't reckon we'll say *that* to my parents; they're old-fashioned about divorce. We'll let on we got married in Britain, and that'll suit them fine. Then, when your divorce comes through, we'll go off somewhere real small and quiet and get ourselves married official.'

'Go to America alone? Oh, dear!'

But this, it appeared, would not be necessary. Sholom, who really did love Cara, gave a small party at which he introduced her to three other GI brides, who would sail on the same ship. Cara, reassured, found them good company, agreed to travel with them and went back to a lonely night at the flat a good deal more cheerful.

At least, she thought it was to be a lonely night; but Sholom, *such* a gentleman, seemed to feel she owed him something more substantial than a goodnight kiss. Cara, regretfully playing her part in the grunting and bouncing, thought that at least this would mean she had burnt her boats. She would probably have a baby, and lose her figure, and go through awful agony just so that she could spend the rest of her life looking like an inexpertly filled potato sack. She was paying expensively for her ticket to that brave new world which Sholly assured her was waiting for her, but at least she was escaping from the horrors of living with a crippled husband. And a saint, to boot – she was not sure which was worse.

Otto had been released from the camp and had been given a ticket and all the necessary documentation to send him home; only he wanted to see Val first. He was rather touched, in fact, to find that the tickets were all for a two-way journey, so that if he got home and found the situation there impossible he would be able to return to Britain. He had worked hard here, to be sure, but they would not really want him back, he knew. They would have enough to do to find all their own returning servicemen work. But it gave him a good feeling to know that he was half expected to return, and he knew it was how the other prisoners felt as well. When he explained that he had a friend in England that he wanted to visit he got a good deal of sympathy over that, too. One of the officers from a nearby RAF station who had taken a good deal of interest in him was contacted and offered to accompany Otto to Norwich. According to what he found there, he would decide whether to go or to stay.

'I shall have to go back, of course, to make sure that my people are all right,' Otto told the camp commanding officer. 'My father has been imprisoned and until he can get a trial and can prove his innocence things will not be easy for my mother. Though once I am home, I hope to persuade her to go and stay with my sister in the country. Things are very bad in Berlin, I believe, but in the country it will probably be better.'

Thus it was that Otto and Tony Marchman arrived on the doorstep of The Pride at eleven o'clock one sunny August morning; Tony took one look at the size of the house and gave the other man a jubilant thumbs-up sign. He plainly thought that for a prisoner of war, Otto had not wasted his time! But then their ring was answered by a motherly looking woman, who stood in the doorway eyeing them questioningly.

'Can I help you, gentlemen?'

'I would like to see Miss Val Neyler, please,' Otto said stiffly. Suddenly his heart was beating far too loudly, thundering in his ears. He thought the woman must be able to hear it and must wonder at his nervousness, but she was shaking her head, looking apologetic.

'Miss Val's not back yet,' she said. She looked as though she might close the door on them. 'I'm very sorry.'

'Is she . . . She is in Norwich, perhaps? When is she expected home? It is very important that I see her, you see, before I go back myself.'

Tony, sensing that the woman was puzzled by them, put his oar in.

'My friend needs to see Miss Neyler rather urgently,' he said briskly. 'Is she in England, or is she abroad? And do you have a date for her homecoming? Would it be worth my friend remaining in Norwich overnight, for instance?'

'Come you in, and I'll fetch Miz Neyler – Val's mother,' the plump one decided, apparently having more confidence in Tony's obvious Englishness than in Otto's equally obvious foreignness. She crossed the hall with the two men in her wake and flung open a door. 'Wait you here.'

She left them in a small but pleasant room with a large desk, book-lined walls, and a few comfortable chairs which they were both too shy to take. The study, Otto thought approvingly. Val had described it and said her mother spent quite a lot of time here. There were fresh flowers on the windowsill, which was pleasant, and the smell of cared-for books permeated the air. He turned from his perusal of the room as the door opened.

'Good morning.' A tiny woman with a great air of busyness and competence entered, smiling and holding out her hand. 'I'm Tina Neyler. I'm afraid Ruthie didn't give me your names, but . . .'

'Otto von Eckner,' Otto stammered, taking her hand. 'And my friend, Tony Marchman.'

Tony, smiling, shook hands as well but left Otto to do the explaining this time.

'I have come to see Val . . . Miss Neyler . . . your daughter. But the maid she say Val is not in this house . . . I have tickets home to go, but first I want very much Val to see . . .' His English, crumbling under the strain, came to an abrupt halt, but Tina was equal to most things.

'Yes, I do understand. You're being repatriated and would like to see my daughter before you go. Sit down, Mr von Eckner, Mr Marchman. I'll just organise coffee and biscuits and then we can talk, but before I do I'd better tell you that Val isn't here. She's serving with the armed forces and to the best of my belief she's still in Berlin. I shan't be a moment.'

She left the room and Otto, who had taken a seat, jumped to his feet, his face working.

'She's in Berlin! I must go, Marchman, I must leave at once, otherwise I'll miss her! What a twist of fate, that she should be in my country when I am in hers!'

'Sit down, old fellow,' Tony Marchman advised kindly. 'You can't rush off here and now, even if it was a polite thing to do, which it would not be. Look, when Mrs Neyler comes back we can ask the important question, which is when will the daughter arrive home. Until then, just relax.'

Tina came back presently, bearing the tray complete with coffee, cups and a mouthwatering array of Ruthie's home-made biscuits. She sat herself down, dispensed coffee and biscuits, and then raised her brows at Otto and spoke to him in German which, though not as fluent as her French, was still above average, and a good deal better than his painfully acquired English.

'Otto, I've heard Val speak of you, of course, both after her visit to your parents' house and later, when she was corresponding with you. She writes home whenever she can and in her last letter, which I received only this morning, she was very excited because she was in Berlin and intended visiting your parents to get what news she could of you. By now, she will probably have been told that you are in England and, since she has already said that there is no work for her there, I imagine she will waste no time and will return at once. You are almost certain, therefore, to miss her unless you are prepared to wait here for some considerable time, which I doubt will be possible. It would probably be better if you corresponded with her.'

'Corresponded? Ah, but, madam, you cannot understand! Val and I had hoped, when the war ended . . .'

'Val was one of the first people to go into the concentration camps with her ambulance,' Tina said quietly. 'What she saw there has hurt and horrified her so much . . . she cannot speak of it to me, her mother. What I'm trying to say to you is though you may still want a . . . a relationship with Val, my daughter may feel differently. A face-to-face encounter, therefore, might be painful and useless. Why not write first, see how she feels?'

Otto stared down at his knees.

'I must speak to her,' he muttered, still in German. 'If it is as you say, it's more important than ever that I see her. But of course I cannot wait here; I have a duty to my parents, too.'

Tina raised her brows.

'Indeed? Then surely you had better go home and write from there. I trust, incidentally, that your parents are well? Val was worried about them but did not put her worries into words.'

'My father will have to stand trial for employing slave labour,' Otto said quietly. 'That he did so cannot be in doubt, but had he refused not only would his life have been forfeit but he would have been condemning that same slave labour to concentration camps or immediate death. He had no choice . . . but his workers, slave and free, will speak for him when he's brought to trial. Others, too, were helped by him and they say they will do their best. However, even if he's released without a stain on his character all his lands and property will be forfeit.'

Tina nodded and leaned forward.

'That, unforunately, is the penalty of losing a war,' she said briskly. 'More coffee, gentlemen?'

Berlin was worse than Val had imagined, a city full of grey and frightened people who had not had a decent meal for longer than they cared to remember. Val found her way to the Neue Friedrichstrasse as soon as she was able to do so and was shocked by the dirty, neglected air which hung over the once busy and bustling thoroughfare, by the bombed buildings, the boarded up windows, the listless, shifty-eyed people.

She paused outside the von Eckners' flat, wondering whether it was occupied or whether the family had – wisely – fled to the country to escape from this gaunt ghost city, but then she rang the bell anyway; a servant might have been left behind.

Frau von Eckner answered the door timidly peering at her visitor, and then, realising it was Val, she burst into tears, flung the door wide, and dragged her in.

'Dearest Val, my dear little English friend! How miserable and lonely I am now that they've taken Father away to stand trial because he used slave labour in his factory! A sin, they call it, to give people good food and to refuse to work them to death as the Fuehrer wished him to! He did it for the best, all, all, and now he is suffering for his goodness. Our country homes and estates, all our land, even this flat, except that no one wants it, is forfeit. And he is in prison, Val . . . dear, good man that he is, in prison with villains and murderers . . . He'll not survive it, I'll never see him again, I wish I were dead!'

'Now come along, Mutti,' Val said, gently steering the older woman across the bare and echoing hall and into the kitchen, where she sat her in a chair. 'The worst has not happened, for Herr von Eckner is not dead yet! Cheer up and I'll make you a nice cup of coffee – I didn't know what your food situation might be, so I brought a packet of coffee, a loaf and some rather beastly sausage meat. Oh, and some tins of corned beef and some sugar – it's very difficult to know what to bring, not understanding your circumstances.'

Frau von Eckner's eyes glistened as Val upended her shoulder bag on the kitchen table and the food rolled out.

'Food! Wonderful, wonderful! I can make you a meal, now, and a drink of coffee. Sit down, sit down, and I'll tell you all the news – Minna is married and living in the country. She and her good man have a dear little farm. I don't think that will be taken from them for Willi was badly wounded earlier in the war and so had no part in it, really, and poor Minna . . . did Otto mention Minna to you when he wrote?'

'He couldn't write once the war started,' Val reminded her gently. 'Before, he just mentioned that she had some nice boyfriends . . .'

'No, of course not, how foolish of me. It's just that in his letters he mentions you sometimes as if . . . but I'm being a silly old woman.' She had lit the gas and was filling a kettle. 'Minna had a sort of illness and it has taken her a long time to recover from it. She is well whilst they remain in the country, quietly living and working with their animals and in their fields, but it would never do for her to have to return to the city, oh dear me, no.'

'I see. A-and Otto? Is he back home now? Living with you?'

She knew the answer must be no as she glanced around the kitchen. The room was empty enough, but there was only one chair pulled up close to the grate, only one cushion on that chair. No, this was a room where someone lived alone.

Frau von Eckner stared at her.

'Otto? Don't you know, my dear child? Why, I suppose I thought, in my heart, that that was why you had come! Otto was shot down quite six months ago, and . . . Val, dear, are you all right?'

Val forced herself to smile, though she had been unable to prevent her legs giving way beneath her so that she had sunk on to one of the ladder backed chairs. She tried to look cheerful, interested, but she had felt the blood drain from her cheeks and guessed that she looked ghastly.

'I'm quite all right, thank you, but I've had a long walk and no food since last night. I just felt a little faint. You were saying . . . ?'

'I'll make the coffee.' Frau von Eckner fussed with the cups and with what she had been about to say. 'Oh, yes, Otto. He's in England, dear, he was shot down and taken to England last October! *That* was why I thought he'd have written to you, of course it was! Yet you say he didn't?'

'No, he didn't, or if he did the family didn't forward the letters. When's he coming home, Frau von Eckner? I – I very much want to see him.'

'I really couldn't say, dear. I've written to him explaining about his father and begging him to come back soon, but I've not yet heard when to expect him.' She passed Val a cup of steaming coffee and drew the second cup towards her. 'My, I'm looking forward to this. Coffee's a real treat in Berlin!'

Presently Val helped the older woman to make a meal with the food she had brought and then she suggested that it might be for the best if Frau von Eckner went into the country and stayed with Minna and Willi until such time as Otto was home, but Frau von Eckner shook her head.

'No. I won't leave until Father is set free,' she insisted. 'Not unless Otto gets home first and takes over for me, here.' She turned to Val, hope lighting her small, crumpled face. 'Val, my dear, will you wait for him here? Stay with me? I know it won't be much fun for a bright young thing like you, but . . . oh, Val, if only you could!'

Val wanted to go home very badly. Ever since the day when she had driven into that first concentration camp she had longed for home with a sick and terrible longing, to get the sights and smells out of her mind before they drove her mad. Knowing that there was good in the world had seemed, for weeks, an impossible dream; she felt that in her own home with her own people around her, she might begin to acknowledge that the madness which had infected Germany and left such suppurating sores was not universal.

But this was Otto's good little mother, clutching her arm, smiling hopefully at her. And Herr von Eckner was a man of conscience, a man to admire and help, not a man to desert in his hour of need. Something had happened to Minna so that the great strong Amazon of a girl could not take care of her parents as she could have done, once. And she might be able to offer some sort of guarantee of goodness for Herr von Eckner. She could visit people he had helped, get them to come forward . . .

She would have to stay, for Otto's sake. He would expect it of her and, had the situation been reversed, she would have expected it of him. Besides, no matter how she might feel about the German race, she loved Otto with her whole mind and heart and that was not likely to change.

'I'll stay willingly,' she heard herself saying. 'Can you billet me officially, do you suppose? Then I can pay for my room and share my rations with you; it will make shopping very much easier.'

And soon, perhaps, Otto will come home, she added mentally. Please God, let it be soon!

Chapter Twenty

'What do *you* want?' Cara bent over her case, straightened and glared at her sister-in-law with something akin to hatred. She could not imagine why, but this running away, which was to have been such a glorious and sensible adventure, seemed to have gone cold on her. And one of the worst parts of it was that everyone else seemed to be enjoying themselves so thoroughly. They went to coming-home parties, planned their own, welcomed relatives and friends with enormous gusto and still managed to keep up an incessant round of harvesting the fruit and vegetables which were ripening in such abundance. Never had the trees at The Pride groaned beneath heavier loads of fruit, never had the Rhode Island reds laid larger eggs, never had the river resounded to merrier shouts when the children went bathing.

Jenny, entering the room in a hurry, seemed for once to resent Cara's spiteful reception. She reddened slightly, but still answered calmly enough.

'Want? Well, I only wondered if I could help. You're off tomorrow, Mother says, so I thought . . .'

'I can manage quite well by myself,' Cara snapped, not even pretending to be civil. She stuck her nose into the wardrobe and muttered something that Jenny was supposed to hear about interference, then turned back into the room again, carrying one of her evening dresses gently in both hands. 'If you want to help, why don't you go and pick plums or whatever it is Auntie's bottling now?'

'Oh well, I just thought that as William would be back in three or four days you might be glad of some help,' Jenny said. 'Anyway, you can't deny, Cara, that you've taken your time over this packing. You've been threatening to go for a good three days yourself, and I thought . . .'

'Well, don't. Jenny, *do* go away. I can't concentrate with you standing there staring like a stuck pig.'

'Don't be so bloody rude!' Jenny, stung out of her customary kindness, glared at her sister-in-law and Cara, who had wanted to annoy the other girl, found herself on the defensive, backing across to her suitcase, with an apology almost on her lips. But Jenny had not finished yet. 'May I just give you a bit of advice, Cara? If I were running away to my lover, I'd get *on* with it, I wouldn't hang about making excuses for not packing.'

'Running away wi . . . Really, Jenny, I think you must have gone *mad*. The prospect of having Simon back tomorrow really must have gone to your head,' Cara said. But not even she could prevent the hot blood from coursing across her face and dying her skin scarlet. 'You shouldn't say things like that even in a temper.'

'Look, Cara, you can fool your mother, you can fool Auntie Tina, maybe you'll even manage to fool Uncle Con when he comes down tomorrow, but frankly, I doubt that you'll ever fool me, I've known you too long. It's clear as crystal that you're going to run off to America with that fat Jewish lad whose bottom is too big for his breeches. That Sholly you've been dancing attendance on. I think you're a fool, but I also happen to be very fond of William, so I wouldn't prevent you going for the world.'

'I hate you, Jenny Rose, and you're a damned liar,' Cara screamed, in a whitehot rage. 'You're making up evil, wicked tales about me and may you be forgiven . . . No, may God forgive you, for I never shall. You'd like to see me in disgrace with everyone, wouldn't you? Oh yes, I can see it all, the saintlike Jenny telling the saintlike William what a bitch I've been. Well, you shan't, you shan't, because it's all lies and I can prove it's all lies and . . . '

Jenny grabbed her by the shoulders and shook until Cara's curls danced across her face and she stopped screaming.

'Look me in the eyes, Cara Dopmann, and swear you aren't going to run off to America and I'll go down on my knees and apologise to you for what I've been thinking. Go on, look me in the eyes.'

But Cara could not. Instead, she burst into tears, ran to the bed and flung herself full length on it.

'Go away!' she howled. 'You're wicked, and you've always hated me, and if I *do* go, then I'll have been driven to it by people like you.'

Cara cried for a long time; when she had started it had been full afternoon, by the time she finished she could hear someone downstairs turning on the six o'clock news. She knew she would have to go now, she could not bear to spend another night under this roof. And besides, she was as good as ready. She had just been putting off the moment when she would have to move back into the flat. Partly, she knew, because she was afraid that Sholly might reassert his rights the moment she moved back, but mainly because she hated to burn her boats.

Now, however, Jenny had forced her hand. Cara got up off her bed, shut the big case and glanced round the room. A nice little room, she had been happy in it for a good few years now, but happiness had fled once she had made up her mind to go away. She went downstairs, rang for a taxi, then lugged her big suitcase down the stairs into the front hall where, presently, the taxi-driver carried it out to the car for her.

Being Cara and being an upset Cara furthermore, her farewell was, to put it kindly, casual.

'Cheerio, everyone,' she said, putting her head round the kitchen door where the family were crowded round the table eating. 'I'll be pretty busy at the flat for the next two or three days, so please don't let anyone come interfering and thinking they're helping, because I shan't be a bit grateful.'

'Not even me?' Mira said hopefully. 'I could help you, and I would like to do something for Daddy's welcome-home party.'

'Oh, that'll be held here at The Pride, I'm sure,' Cara said quickly. 'Just you keep out of my way, Mira, until Daddy's home; then you're welcome to come to the flat as often as you like, of course.'

She left the room, slamming the door behind her, and reflected that, since she would be on her way to America by the time Daddy got back, she had never said a truer word.

William was to arrive home on Friday, but on the Wednesday Art came back, so they had decided between them that they would postpone an actual party until the following week, when Simon should be home as well.

'We might even put it off a bit longer, since Nick surely will have finished driving out Japs by the end of the month,' Tina said hopefully as she and Ruthie performed miracles of culinary art with the rations available. 'Art looks very well, if you can . . . Well, you've just got to get used to his poor face.'

Art had been badly burned and though plastic surgeons had done their best, the right side of his face was oddly shiny and stiff and his right eye seemed permanently half-closed. Tina had been charming with him, cheerful, optimistic and loving, but she had cried herself to sleep that first night. He had been such a handsome boy; no one would call him handsome again, but she did hope that

397

some nice girl, somewhere, would marry him and take care of him! Jenny, an understanding little soul, had come to her room and put her arms round her while she sobbed, and brushed out her hair, and had assured her that Art was still a very lovable person and would make his way well enough once he was stronger, but she still needed convincing. Poor, poor Art!

So now it was Thursday and teatime, and the family were assembling for high tea at six o'clock, as they did every day. They had a sort of supper at about nine for anyone who was still up and still hungry, but otherwise they just had breakfast, a light lunch, and high tea. Since everyone was at home, Tina had got her second table out and the children were sitting at that whilst the adults assembled round the big kitchen table, with Ruthie, who always maintained that she liked eating on her feet, moving between the two.

Somehow, Ruthie had managed to acquire enough cheese to make a cheese sauce, which she had poured over two huge cauliflowers, and they were to be eaten accompanied by the delicious home-made bread which she baked weekly; everyone was concentrating on their plates, therefore, when the kitchen door opened and a man came into the room.

'Hello-ello-ello! What, no welcome for a returning hero? Where's my best girl, then?'

'Daddy!' shrieked Mira.

'William!' shrieked Tina and Jenny, whilst everyone abandoned their food and fell upon the wanderer who, with a shout, sat down on the nearest chair and pulled Mira on to his knee.

'You're not supposed to be back in England until tomorrow,' Tina said presently, in a dazed voice. 'Oh, William, Cara's down at the flat getting it ready for you, she'll be *so* upset not to have been the first to greet you!'

'I'll give her a ring, tell her to come straight round here, catch a taxi,' Jenny said resourcefully, jumping to her feet. She kept going hot and cold as she remembered what Cara was probably doing at this very moment, unless, of course, she had already fled the country, which was quite possible. No one had dared to ignore her command not to go down to see how the flat was coming along.

'No. Please don't ring, anyone. I told the taxi to wait, just in case, so now I'll get into it and drive straight down to the flat.' William smiled at them all. 'Please don't ring. I would much rather not admit I'd miscalculated and come here first.'

Everyone laughed, everyone agreed, but Jenny ran out first and hopped into the taxi.

'I'm coming with you, just as far as the front door of the flat,' she told him. 'Look, William, be sensible. Cara might be out, you haven't got a key . . . and although I don't suppose it's occurred to you, the lifts aren't working yet because there are only two flats occupied, which means there isn't a porter, either. I swear that I'll make myself scarce the moment you get in there.'

'Well, I might be glad of an arm on the stairs,' William said, gracefully conceding defeat. 'Off we go, then!'

'What's more, knowing Cara I bet she hasn't got anything much to eat in the place,' Jenny continued as the taxi purred off down the drive. 'And you must be hungry. If she's willing, it would be better to come back to The Pride and have a meal there, where Mira can see you, rather than trying to get something in the city.'

She continued to babble as they crossed the city, but when they reached the flats her courage nearly gave out. William looked so tired yet so excited and happy – she was very sure he was in for a horrid time and he did not deserve it at such a moment.

'If I'm not out in ten minutes, you'll know Cara's home

399

and everything's fine,' William said as they got out of the taxi. 'Stay here, there's a good girl.'

'No. I'm coming up, just to make sure she's there and not out.'

William gave in, but halfway up the stairs he whispered: 'Look, love, don't think I don't know what's been going on, because some so-called "friends" have been only too eager to tell me. But that's all past. I love my wife and I intend to keep her, so . . . ah, just let me ring the bell and if we hear footsteps please scarper, there's a dear.'

They reached the well-remembered front door and William rang the bell, but Jenny was already halfway down the first flight, for Cara had the radio playing. She called back softly, 'Good luck!' and then she was out of sight although, above her, she heard the door begin to open.

Cara was making pancakes when the bell rang. She had just fancied pancakes and since Sholly had managed to get her a lemon from somewhere and she had wangled an egg from the milkman she was rather enjoying her bakery session. It filled the flat with a lovely, homely smell, which the flat could jolly well do with, since Cara had been here for a couple of days without even bothering to unpack.

The ringing of the bell annoyed her, though. Had she not given Sholly a key? Why couldn't he use it instead of ringing in that infuriatingly humble way all the time? So she took her time answering, dragging across the kitchen and hall, rubbing her nose with a floury finger and snatching irritably at the door. She was scowling and, since she was enveloped in a vast print apron left by some long-forgotten charwoman, she was neither looking nor feeling her best.

'What do you mean by . . .' she began and then stopped, one floury hand flying to her mouth and the other to her throat.

'W-William!'

'Darling!'

'William! Oh, oh, William!'

She did not know how she got into his arms, she just knew she was there. And it was arms, not arm. Two arms enfolded her, and he stood steady, taking the weight of her as she flung herself against him. She buried her head beneath his chin and felt something begin to happen to her heart. Slowly, painfully, the hard shell she had built round it to guard her against regretting William was cracking across. It hurt. She clutched William harder and began to cry.

'Oh, William, it's been awful! It's been such a long time, and I did want you so! I'd forgotten how safe you are, how right you make me feel when I'm with you! Oh William, hold me, don't let me go!'

William turned and still in each other's arms they stumbled back into the lounge and collapsed on to the little mouse-satin chaise longue that William had paid such a lot of money for, because he told her it had once belonged to a child-bride like her, only that first child-bride had been a homesick young queen. The queen had been no prettier than she, William had said fondly, and her day-bed was pretty too, even though it was three hundred years old. Now, as they cuddled on the chaise longue, Cara felt the crack widen across her heart, and caressed his face with fingers that trembled.

'How handsome you are, William! I'd forgotten how beautifully your face is made.'

He was stroking her curls, kissing her wet cheeks, her eyelids, and the softness of her lips.

'Sweetheart, until I felt you in my arms I was old and worn out and terrified. Now I'm young again and nothing matters but you.'

'You haven't changed! They went *on* about how you

401

would have changed and what you'd suffered, but you're just the same, only better. You have lovely silver hair which suits you, and your face is thinner, but that only shows those dimply lines up better in your cheeks.' She patted his thin cheek. 'I'll make you good food and fatten you up, even though I like you thin!'

He laughed, but the words had reminded Cara of something else, something she had forgotten. Could she say nothing? But no, the new, soft heart which was painfully emerging through the crack in the old, hard one did not approve of deceit, it seemed. Not with William, at any rate. Other people were fair game.

'William, I have to tell you that I've been very silly and rather bad whilst you've been away.' Cara swallowed nervously. 'I'm afraid I'm going to have a baby and it isn't yours. I was going to run away . . . I still will, if you want me to. But I don't want to, I want to stay here with you and make you love me like you did before.' She snuggled against him, still sure of her welcome. 'You see, they kept on about how you would have changed and how you'd disapprove of me and all my ways and I thought I couldn't bear to have to live with a saintly person who would think me wicked, so I told a fellow I'd go away with him. So he . . . he bought me a ticket for America and then I suppose he felt . . . The ticket was *very* expensive . . . and I couldn't very well agree to marry him and not do the other thing, could I? So I did, and I wish and *wish* I hadn't, because I can see you won't be pleased about the baby.' She heaved a deep sigh and turned in his arms, trying to see his face. 'Will it be all right? Will you forgive me and let me stay with you?'

'That's a bit of a facer,' William said after a few moments. 'Cara, tell me one thing; why should I accept another man's child when everyone will know it's not my baby?'

'Isn't that unfair and just like a man?' Cara pouted. 'I accepted Mira, didn't I? She was yours and not mine and everyone knew it, but I accepted her, so why shouldn't you accept mine?'

'Darling, I was married to Naomi before I even knew you! She'd been dead two years before . . .'

'Well, you'd been gone five before I did anything with anyone else,' Cara pointed out. 'I waited longer than you did, William! And I only did it because I'd started thinking of you as an ogre and I got scared, so when this fellow wanted me to go away with him, and he was very kind though pretty dull really, I just couldn't . . .'

'Cara, how pregnant are you? When's the baby due?'

'How should I know?' Cara stared up at him, wide-eyed that he should expect her to trifle with dates at such a time. 'If you mean when did he buy the ticket, it was . . . oh, more than two weeks ago.'

'More than two . . . Have you had a pregnancy test, then?'

'Well, no, but he did it, William. I thought you understood, and you said that if people didn't take precautions that was how they got families, and so . . .'

'He didn't take precautions, then?'

'I never asked him,' Cara said truthfully. 'Oh, William, do you think he did? Do you think I might not be having a baby after all?' An enormous beam of relief spread across her face. 'Wouldn't that be *wonderful*? I was dreading getting all fat and bulgy.'

But William, it seemed, had not capitulated. He held her away from him and his expression was stern.

'Cara, that is *not* the attitude to take. Look, you haven't told this chap you aren't going away with him after all, have you? What's he going to say if, and it's a big if, I let you stay with me?'

'He'll be cut-up, of course, but then he'll go back to the

States and forget all about me,' Cara said reasonably. 'Why not? After all, I *am* your wife. He can't expect me to leave you when I find I've made a dreadful mistake, and I still love you so frightfully. I'll send the ticket back if you like. I'll ring him up and tell him it's in the post.'

William detached her clinging hands and stood up. His face was haggard.

'Cara, ring the bloke up and have a chat with him whilst I go for a walk round the square. You're my wife and I love you, but I won't take you back if you're not a hundred per cent sure you want me and not this other chap. And remember, I'm willing to let you go if that's what you want.'

'But it isn't!' Cara cried, jumping up too and trying to cling to him. Her face was crumpled with anxiety and tears began to course down her cheeks again. 'William, I don't want to go with Sholly at all, not even a bit, I'd rather stay here all alone. But what I really want is *you*, to love me and take care of me like you used to do.'

'Right. Then ring whilst I'm gone.'

William walked slowly under the summer elms and into the square garden, then his strength gave out and he slumped down on to the bench by the lilac bush and contemplated the sparrows and his problems from a prone position.

He had not been surprised to find that Cara had been unfaithful. Even his friends had written guardedly enough to make him suspect that all was not as it should be with his wife. But . . . another man's baby! It was odd how you could tell yourself that she was young and heedless, had been taken advantage of, yet the thought of fathering another man's child stuck in your craw.

On the other hand, few women would have been as straight with him. He believed that she did love him,

404

though she probably had not known what love was until he had entered the flat that afternoon. As for Sholly – what a name! – it was pretty clear that she had no more intended to sleep with the fellow than fly. It had just happened, and Cara, having agreed to run away with him, had been unable to find a good enough excuse to stop his lovemaking.

But it had only been once, and she'd come straight out with it, confessed everything. Was he really going to let her go off to America just because his pride would not stand for a secret knowledge that her baby was not his? Because it could easily *be* his, since she had conceived so recently. If at all. He could not help grinning to himself at her naive assumption that she must be pregnant because she had let the fellow have sex with her. Dammit, he loved her!

He was still contemplating the sparrows when someone sat down on the bench beside him and a soft face was pressed against his. Cara spoke in his ear.

'I've done it. I've told him the ticket's in the post, and it's all right, William! I'm *not* having a baby! He was very offended. He said no gentleman would get a girl in the family way when he was sending her off to foreign parts.'

'Cara, did you ask him?'

Cara nodded emphatically.

'Of course, once you'd put the idea into my head. I thought you'd be happier knowing one way or the other. But it's all right, you see, I'm not going to get horribly fat, so . . . can I stay?'

William sighed and stood up, pulling her with him.

'Yes, you can stay, you terrible creature, but you *are* going to get horribly fat; I shall see to it personally.'

Cara dragged him to a halt and looked suspiciously up into his face.

'William? What do you mean by that? Do you mean that you and I will have a baby? On *purpose*?'

'That's right, young woman. You're quite old enough to be a mother, and I'd like another child.'

And Cara, instead of moaning or arguing, just hugged him tightly, with eyes like stars.

'All right, William,' she said meekly. 'If it's what you want . . .'

'I'm determined that this wedding will be the best the family has ever seen,' Tina remarked across the kitchen to Ruthie. Both women, flushed and elated, were baking for the great day. 'A September wedding is my favourite, because there are beautiful flowers and leaves and, of course, lots of fruit.'

'The family've missed most of the weddings,' Ruthie pointed out, 'so Nick deserves the best we can manage. And that,' she added, looking around the crowded room, 'is going to be almost pre-war!'

It was not put into words, but Ruthie had been as disappointed as Tina herself to miss Maude's wedding and then to hear, by telegram what was more, that Val had given no one a chance to express an opinion, but had simply married Otto and was now Frau von Eckner. They told themselves that they had understood and sympathised with Frank and Mabel's desire for a quiet and private ceremony, though at the time Tina had shed a few tears. She had gone along to the register office with Mr and Mrs Walters, and she had kissed the bride and the groom and wished them well, but she *would* have liked white, and flowers, and a fuss and a big party!

'Yes, it's going to be quite a do,' Tina agreed contentedly. 'Though what we'd have done without that marvellous Marjory Riley I just don't know. What a genius to send a dozen cockerels as a wedding present!'

'Tha's true, we wouldn't have put on much of a spread without 'em,' Ruthie acknowledged. 'Though I'm glad it waren't me as had the killing of 'em. Black market's all very well, and a wedding's a better excuse than most . . .'

'Yes, well, we won't go into that again,' Tina said hurriedly. When the family were assembling she thought it was only natural to want better for them than she could get with her ration books, and someone would buy the stuff so why not her for once? She did not grudge the money when she saw Art and Simon vying for the last lamb cutlet, or Maude tucking into liver and onions. But when they found out how she got them . . . ! I don't understand the younger generation, she told herself now, transferring hot scones from the oven to the wire cooling tray. Look at the nasty things they'd said when the Jap war ended and I was honest enough to say I was glad of that big bomb that hit Hiroshima, if it meant that the Japs would sue for peace and stop fighting! The children were perfectly horrid to me and it was very hurtful being made to feel like a mass-murderer. Jenny had said that exploding the big bomb would go down in history as one of the wickedest things mankind had done to itself; she said that anyone who applauded the bombing of Hiroshima was denying God . . . Awful, embarrassing things like that.

Tina for once had not been able to marshal her arguments sufficiently to beat down the waves of younger generation disapproval so she had taken refuge in tears. Weeping, she had told them she only wanted her boys home again alive and unharmed, and then they had forgiven her, and Maude and Jenny and Bella had hugged and kissed her and told her she didn't understand and that when she did she would agree with them.

'Have you had all the answers to the invites, yet?' Ruthie was making sponge cakes for the bottom layers of the dozens of trifles she intended to put before the guests. Tina, who had a promise of cream on Saturday, had marched very stiffly into the kitchen the previous day and told the assembled family that if anyone at all queried any of the food at the reception, then she personally would never speak to that person again. Duly chastened, the family had sworn indifference on this one occasion at least, so she had been satisfied that she might cheat a little.

'I think so. Everyone's coming, though Val, poor darling, won't arrive until quite early on Saturday. It's a shame, because she'd love helping with all the preparations, but that's life. I suppose we're lucky that she's managed to get here in time. After all, we couldn't give anyone much notice.' She smiled indulgently at the scone mixture in the big yellow bowl. 'Nick's so impetuous, and Vitty, too – isn't she the dearest little thing, Ruthie? I loved her the moment I set eyes on her.'

'Yes, because she's so like you were at her age, I know,' Ruthie said, smirking. 'I'll be bound she int as wilful, not if my memory serves me well.'

'At her age I had children and responsibilities,' Tina said vaguely. 'She's more like I was at seventeen or so. Ah, she's a pretty thing. She's very nearly good enough for Nick!'

'True. That gal who's bridesmaid, did you notice how . . . ?'

'Betty, you mean? I did notice, and I must say, it would be wonderful if . . . no! I shan't talk about it, it's too important. I think you've done enough sponges, dear, but if you go to the fridge you'll find some very hard lard and we could start making the puff pastry next.'

Betty was staying in the house, sharing a room with the bride and the other bridesmaid, Coppy. Betty had volunteered to go shopping with Art, to see if there was a big-hearted butcher in the city who might be persuaded to part with some liver, since Tina felt that her returning war heroes and heroines were almost certain to be on the brink of pernicious anaemia, if not worse. Not only had the pair returned with the liver (thanks to Bet's shameless ways, Art had said with a grin), but they had returned like old friends, laughing together, making allusions that no one else could follow, and planning quite openly to see more of each other once the wedding was over. Betty, fortunately, lived a mere ten miles outside the city so it would be a simple matter for them to meet.

'When I get a car . . .' most of Art's remarks seemed to start, and Betty parried with 'I can always catch a bus!' which did rather seem as though their friendship would continue.

'She don't even seem to notice his cheek,' Ruthie said, from the depths of the fridge. 'Though it int as bad as it was; nor the eye.'

'Puff pastry, dear. Let's concentrate on *this* wedding before we start thinking about the next!'

Maude had not wanted Bill to come to the wedding, because he and she had agreed to live apart and it seemed unnecessarily painful to share what was obviously going to be a wedding in a thousand. But it was no good saying things like that to Bill, because, though he agreed things were not right between them, he had not wanted her to move back to her own home, leaving him with his parents in Lowestoft, thirty miles away.

'You're not giving it a chance, Maudie,' he had said, but Maude thought that chances were all very well. She had given Bill enough of them, God knew, forgiving him for affairs with other women, days when he just did not bother to speak to her from dawn until dusk, and even trying to understand and sympathise with his odd behaviour once the war had finished and he had been demobbed and was living with her officially. It had been bad enough when he had stormed into lodgings, got her into bed with his usual mixture of loving and bullying, and stormed off again in the dawn; that had been understandable in a way, because he was stationed eighty miles away and was still working though she had been demobbed. But when he was at home all day, with nothing to do, he could at least have been halfway nice to her! But instead he had been touchy, abrupt, spiteful and generally impossible. He talked about a place of their own but did nothing about getting a job. He despised his father's work as a fisherman yet toyed with the idea of distant-water trawling, which was hard work, dreadfully dangerous, and would mean he would be away for long stretches of time.

Finally, Maude had come home for a weekend – she had offered to take him as well and he had refused scornfully, saying that her people were snobs and happier without him – and had been offered a job as sales assistant-cum-clerk in a grain warehouse. She took it, and only went back to Lowestoft once after that, to tell Bill that their marriage would never work and that she thought a legal separation was a good idea, until one or other of them met someone else, whereupon they could talk about divorce.

The family were very supportive, except, oddly enough, for Art. He had stared at her for a long time, with his injured eye giving him an accusing, bird of prey look. And then he had said, 'Oh, Maudie, my love, it's a helluva thing to be cast adrift. Can't you give him another chance?'

'But you didn't even like him,' Maude had cried, bewildered by this apparent volte face. 'You never even pretended to get on!'

'Liking's got nothing to do with it,' Art had assured her. 'It's just the way you feel when the ground's cut from under you – no job is bad enough, but it's the feeling that you're not really wanted any more, that your sole reason for being born was to win the war and now that you've done it you're so much scrap metal. See what I mean?'

'No,' Maude had said honestly. 'I don't, because I worked too, remember, and I was chucked out, and I didn't feel like scrap metal.'

'It's easier for women, because they've got a traditional role to play which doesn't include fighting a war; that's the untraditional part. But a man . . . dammit, I can't explain any better than that. But don't do anything hasty, will you?'

She had promised not to, and that was why she had reluctantly agreed to Bill's being invited to the wedding, though she had not expected him to come. When he telephoned to say he'd be along and would come to the house first so that they could go together, she had felt a happy throb at the sound of his voice, immediately nullified by the dreadful thought that, being Bill, he would probably turn up with some horrible little tart on his arm just to show her.

So Maude, getting into bed on Friday night, was not looking forward to the wedding a bit.

'All right, darling? You were good to agree to the midnight train! It means that we'll be at The Pride in time to say hello, and I'll be able to get my cream and gold taffeta out of my wardrobe.' Val squeezed Otto's hand as the train thundered on through the night. 'I look *fabulous* in that dress. You'll be thunderstruck!'

'You look fabulous in everything, from your uniform to your birthday suit,' Otto muttered, returning the squeeze. 'God, I'm dreading this affair! Not only do I meet your beloved twin for the first time, but I shall be held up for inspection by all the rest of the family and found wanting, naturally. No job, no prospects, my father still under a cloud for all they've dismissed the charges against him . . .

I'm a stateless nomad. They'll curse me for daring to marry you.'

'Really, Otto, you are stupid! We agreed the moment we met, both of us, that what mattered was love, and you can't doubt mine for you, any more than I doubt yours for me. You said you'd like to work on the land, and I've got a bit of money . . . Though I don't know about buying property. From what that man said, I gather we can't, not in England, not right now. But, darling, we'll find something we can both do, I promise you!'

'Where shall we live? Not with your family, that would be doomed. My nationality alone means that I'd be fighting prejudice . . . Oh, God, Val, let's get off the train at the next stop and run away and hide!'

'No.' Val shook her mane of red curls. 'I love Nick next to you and I wouldn't let him down for the world. I vowed I'd get to his wedding if it cost me my last penny and you, my lad, goeth where I goeth, so don't think I'm going to let you cry off and show me up! Let's have a snooze now, or we'll be chewed rags by the time the train gets in.'

Nick, in his demob suit, was preparing to be a beautiful bridegroom. He had a crisp white shirt and was knotting his dark tie around his throat; he thanked heaven that the demob suit was dark too. He would have felt wrong in a light blue or a brown, but this charcoal grey could not be better.

Simon, humming to himself, was already dressed, as befitted the best man who had a good bit of running around to do. He was fiddling with his carnation, though, uneasy because it showed a tendency to tilt gradually to starboard whenever he moved quickly. The war had not changed Simon very much physically, but Nick knew they were both changed by it. He tried very hard not to keep jerking his hands, but he had not yet succeeded in recapturing serenity and nor had Simon. They both moved incessantly, lost their tempers easily and, shamingly, found that tears were no longer a phenomenon confined to women and children.

Nick checked his appearance in the glass; thin as whipcord and as tough, he looked older than his years and had not shed the watchfulness which Burma had brought to a fine art. But Vitty did not mind. She had known him a little before the war and she knew him very well indeed now, and she told him that she loved both the Nicks, so that was all right.

'What do you think of Val's chap? Bit of a shock, eh?'

Simon spoke casually, but Nick knew that Simon thought Val might have found an Englishman; damn it all, there were enough of them in love with her! Why marry a *Hun*? Even gentle Jenny had admitted she felt the same, and Auntie Tina and the older members of the family had been shattered. Still, Val was Val – neither to be driven nor led. She had made her choice and very awkward it was for them all, but she had had a worse war than most women. If she could still love Otto after what she'd seen then it must be a very real, solid sort of love. And the other sort, based on a mutual physical attraction or on sex, didn't last. Look at Maude and that Bill!

'A shock? Oh, you mean that ferocious scar.' Nick chuckled. 'He's very shy and speaks very little English. But he must be OK, you know, or Val wouldn't have married him. You can't say she fell for his stunning looks, because, though he is good-looking despite the scar, think of the fellows who were falling over themselves to take her out when war broke out! And during it, come to think.'

'So you think it will work out? Not like Maudie and Bill?'

'I think Maudie and Bill would have made a go of it if they'd had something to start on, so to speak. Living in that tiny little house with his parents was doomed from the start, but Maude was sure she could be happy anywhere, so long as they were together. Oh well, she's a lesson to us all not to fall for a pretty face and a good line-shooter. Are you ready to go down yet? I said we'd walk to the church; it isn't far and it's a lovely day.'

When Vitty came up the aisle, Tina's eyes were already overflowing. Surreptitiously, she dabbed at them with her hanky. They were all here and she loved them all, she wanted them all to be happy more than she had ever wanted anything else in the whole world! Val's marriage had been a disappointment, Maude's a disaster, but there were still chances of happiness ahead for all of them, if only they did as she advised! After all, no two people had ever been as happy as she and Ted, so her advice was worth taking. Look at William and Cara, like a couple of lovebirds when everyone had said their marriage was doomed. Tina, who had said it louder than anyone, conveniently forgot this unpalatable fact.

She looked across the church, to where Mabel and Frank stood, with Lenny fidgeting next to them and losing no opportunity of exchanging a word with Sebastian, who was beside him. They were happy and didn't they deserve it after all their trials and tribulations? And Simon and Jenny with their little family were a picture, though of course they were not together, since Simon was standing right at the front of the church, by Nick.

They looked lovely, the two cousins. Equally tall, equally broad-shouldered, one so dark and the other so fair. When Nick came back from his honeymoon they were going to start rebuilding the flats and garages in Granville Gardens; they would all move back up there and work on it together. Tina envied them. To be young, to be starting life again, after these harsh years, and to be working all together to build your future; that was a wonderful thing to look forward to.

She was worried about Otto and Val, though, and about Maude and Bill. She had not had much chance to talk to Val, but what conversation they had managed to snatch had not been reassuring. As she had feared, there was nothing for Otto in Germany, no chance of betterment. And they did not think it would be possible for them to remain in England long, because Otto's English was too poor for any work other than perhaps as a farmhand, and Val could quite see that this would never do for him. As for Maude and Bill, the girl had made a mistake and had done the sensible thing by parting from her husband. But the unhappiness in Bill's eyes! Tina could not bear to look at him when he thought himself unobserved. No matter how Maude might feel, Bill was still body and soul in love with the girl, and deeply though Tina disapproved of Bill she saw, now, that Maude had done him a wrong by marrying him if her love could not withstand the difficulties of readjustment.

'With this ring I thee wed; with my body I thee worship . . .'

Nick's voice rang with strength and confidence. Tina stopped worrying about the rest of the family and gave herself up to the blissful contemplation of the ceremony taking place before her. They would be happy, she knew they would!

'It's been a lovely day and a lovely wedding,' Val said, stretching and giving a huge yawn. 'My, but I'm tuckered out! I suppose we ought to be going indoors and getting some sleep in what's left of the night.'

Val and Otto, Jenny and Simon, and Maude and Bill were sitting on the terrace despite the fact that it was after midnight. It was a beautifully mild night though, the stars huge and milky white above them, the moon a creamy curve through the cedar tree. Enchantment held them where they were, as much as laziness, for it had been a wonderful day, the sort of day that stays in one's mind for years and years as an example of what a wedding should be. Val, thinking of her own wedding in Berlin with a couple of witnesses and a tearful Frau von Eckner, sighed happily. Trappings did not matter : . but she was glad she and Otto had managed to get home for Nick's wedding.

'You're right, we ought.' Simon stood up and heaved Jenny to her feet. 'Goodnight, one and all. See you at brekker!'

'And then there were four,' Bill remarked, when the conservatory door had closed behind Jenny and Simon. 'I wasn't invited to spend the night, but I'm too tired to drive back to Lowestoft right now. I'll kip down in the car.'

'You can't share my bed,' Maude said quickly. 'I'm sharing with Betty – well, not the bed but the room. And Coppy's with us, too.'

'Forget it. I said I'd sleep in the car.'

There was a short silence and then Maude sighed and cuddled closer to Bill. 'I suppose I could sleep in the car too, just so that we could chat. I'm wide awake, though I know I ought to be tired.'

'Why don't the pair of you sleep on this swing seat?' Val suggested, taking Otto's hand and biting the fingers lightly. 'We've actually been allotted a whole single bed between us, so we'll allow you to use our share of the seat, won't we, darling?

'Of course!' Otto tried to bow, but seated, and swinging, it was not a great success. He laughed when the others did. 'I cannot say the words I wish, English for me is hard. But . . .' he turned and spoke rapidly in German to Val.

'What was that?' Maude asked lazily. She snuggled closer to Bill, almost purring with pleasure.

'My husband, not the most tactful of men, asks why you two are living apart and talking about divorce, when it's obvious to him that you're wild about each other,' Val said bluntly. 'I've been wondering the same all day.'

'You can love someone but find them impossible to live with,' Maude said. 'Dammit, I want to be with Bill, but . . .'

'We'll have another try, give it another go,' Bill said. It was impossible to see his expression in the darkness, but Val could hear the straining anxiety in his voice. 'This time, it'll be different, Maudie, this time . . .'

'Bill, you know how hard I tried! I tried for two whole *years* and I made allowances and so on because of the war, but when the war ended it got worse, and then worse and then worse again. And then you brought that floosie home and . . .'

'I didn't bring her home, I brought her to the house. I wanted, if you must know, to make you jealous, to see if . . .'

'Well, that's no way . . .'

'We'll bow out and let you tear each other to bits in peace, I think,' Val said, getting up off the swing seat and pulling Otto towards the house. 'We have problems of our own but none, thank God, to compare with the problems you two seem to enjoy making for each other.'

Inside the house, they were crossing the hall on tiptoe when the baize door opened and Tina came out. She was looking rather pleased with herself and carried a tray laden with hot drinks.

'Ah, Val and Otto! I was going to bring this out to the terrace so we could all sit in the lovely starshine and have a nightcap together, but since you're indoors . . . Where are the others?'

'Simon and Jenny went up to bed and Bill and Maude are quarrelling,' Val said, taking the tray from her mother.

417

'Leave them, love; perhaps by now they'll have got some of the acid out of their systems. At any rate, Maude said she'd spend the night on the terrace with Bill, which can't be bad.'

'Oh! Look, come into the kitchen; I've wanted to get the pair of you alone all day because I've an idea.'

The three of them settled down, their hot drinks before them, and Val looked enquiringly at her mother.

'Well, Mama? What's this idea?'

Tina tried not to smirk. The idea had come to her in a flash during the wedding ceremony, when she had been wishing Ted was beside her to watch their youngest son take his marriage vows. It had brought to mind a letter she had received some days before from their solicitor.

'Bear with me if I start at the beginning. Have you ever told Otto how your father came to marry me?'

'Not in so many words. I told him about the rabbit skins of course, and the ship going down, because that's family history. Why?'

'Because it all starts from there. You see, Otto, my husband came from New Zealand, where he farmed with his brother Mark.'

'This I understand,' Otto assured her. 'Val explains that there are still Neyler cousins farming in New Zealand.'

'Good.' Tina turned to Val. 'Darling, do you remember Grandfather Karl Neyler's will?'

'No, I don't think I ever heard about it. Why?'

'The two boys, Ted and Mark, had worked terribly hard on the peninsular farm together, when they were young and after they had left the Waihola property, but Daddy left before it was in its prime, and never went back. So when Grandfather Karl died he left the Waihola place to Ted, on the understanding that Daddy gave up all claim to the peninsular farm. Which Daddy was glad to do being very fair-minded. I think he thought that one day Mark's

418

eldest son, Johnny, might be glad of the farm. But Johnny ran away, you know, and was never heard of again, and Mark's second wife only gave him daughters. So the Waihola place has been in the hands of a manager until recently, when the chap inherited a place of his own and left. The solicitor who wrote said the manager had been slack for years and the neglect is unbelievable. He wrote to ask me if I wanted to sell, since Ted left it to me in trust for you children, but . . . Well, it was Ted's birthplace, the family started there, and I wondered . . . Otto did say he enjoyed working on the land . . . You see it's there, waiting.'

Val's eyes were round, but no rounder than Otto's. They both looked unbelievingly at Tina, who now allowed the smirk to break out in its full self-satisfied splendour.

'Well? Isn't someone going to say something?'

Val gave a sort of war-cry and leaned across the table to squeeze Tina until her eyes started from her head, but it was Otto who spoke.

'Was not Grandfather Karl a German? And his wife, she was English, was she not? It seems meant, as though this place has waited through the years just for us.'

'That's how I felt when I thought of it. As though the story had come full circle, at last. You'll go, the two of you? It will be my wedding present to you.'

Val took Otto's hand and squeezed it convulsively. Then she spoke for them both.

'We'll go. And we'll make it the biggest success since . . . since the Normandy landings!'

419

Epilogue

As Jane Kittle's small car reached the ridge, the sun came up. She had visited the old Neyler homestead several times since Val Eckner became pregnant, but never at this time in the morning, and the view before her brought an involuntary gasp to her lips.

It was so beautiful that despite the need for haste she slowed, seeing as if for the first time the great mass of the forest, the clear colours of the pastures and hayfields painted by the early sunshine, the misty blueness of the distant hills.

The Neyler place nestled – there was no other word for it – in a fold of the hill, with forest on one side and cultivated fields on the other. It was L-shaped, where the family had built on, because another couple lived there with them, cousins, she thought they were, so when they had moved in the first thing Otto and Bill had done was to build another wing on to the original house. Both buildings were really little more than log cabins, but they were a mass of flowering creeper and had a look of solid permanence as if they had been there for ever. Smoke was issuing from the chimneys and the hens and ducks were close to the door, pecking up grain from between the cobbles. It was plain they had just been fed.

Jane put her foot on the accelerator once more; down there, she reminded herself, there is a woman in labour. No time to admire the beauty of the countryside nor the way the young people had brought the old Neyler place on

– teutonic efficiency had its merits especially when it was mixed with Val's particular brand of delightful vagueness.

She drew up in the yard, left the car and ran across the cobbles, to knock and then enter at once, without waiting for admittance.

It was a moment she would never forget. Otto knelt by the bed, the child in his arms; the baby was pink and wailing from its birth struggles, but plainly in the best of health and Val was beaming up at her husband as though he had been the one to produce that incredibly noisy bundle. Otto was grinning and Maude, in the doorway, was smiling too. Over her shoulder, Jane could see Bill, just a Cheshire cat smirk.

'Hell, I missed it!' Jane said, rustling across the room and taking the child from its proud father. 'A boy, too! There you are, Maudie, now you've only got to follow suit in a coupla months, and there'll be two fine lads to help their dads work the farm.'

'True.' Maude patted her own distended stomach. 'If I have a girl, though, it'd be a ready-made wife for this little 'un.' She turned to Val, still lying back and grinning. 'What will you call him, now that he's arrived at last?'

Otto answered for her.

'Edward, of course. After the first baby to be born in this house.' His English was almost perfect with only the slightest of accents.

Jane nodded approvingly. 'Very nice. Ted. They'll call him Ted, of course, same's they did his grandpa, from what my ma told me.' She poured hot water into the tin bath, tested it with her hand, and lowered the baby into it. His shrieks immediately subsided into sleepy mutters and the sleepy mutters stopped, too, as the warmth enfolded him. Jane washed him, dried him, and then handed him to Otto since Maude and Bill had disappeared back into their own part of the house. 'Now you take care of your son,

Otto, whilst I see to Val. And whilst I do, I'll tell you a funny story; did you ever hear what your grandpa said, Val, when your father was born?'

Val chuckled. 'Let her drink coffee, wasn't it?' She turned to Otto. 'Karl was the meanest man in the world, not a bit like you, you big softy, and after the baby was born Anna fancied a cup of coffee. I gather he said no, and then changed his mind and ran after Mrs Kittle and told her to buy some beans, because it wasn't every day he had a son. Is that right, Jane?'

'You've stole my story,' Jane grumbled, bending over the bed. 'Strange, isn't it, how the wheel turns? My ma never saw your pa born, Val; arrived too late, just like I did.' She laughed. 'But I'll bet *she* didn't miss it because she stopped at the top of the ridge to see the run rise!'

'One day, my Ted will stand on that ridge and watch the sun rise,' Val said softly. 'It's his inheritance. What we fought the war for. So that our sons and daughters could watch the sun rising in peace.'

Otto came over to her, bent down and placed the child in her arms, and then kissed her.

'It's all the inheritance mankind needs – peace and the sun rising over Waihola. And now go to sleep, my love, you've done your work for the day.'

Val was still smiling as she fell asleep.